T0029836

DANGEROUS CHOICES

SUSAN HUNTER

SEVERN RIVER
PUBLISHING

Copyright © 2023 by Susan Hunter.

All rights reserved.

No part of this book may be reproduced in any form or by any electronic or mechanical means, including information storage and retrieval systems, without written permission from the author, except for the use of brief quotations in a book review.

Severn River Publishing
www.SevernRiverBooks.com

This is a work of fiction. Names, characters, businesses, places, events and incidents are either the products of the author's imagination or used in a fictitious manner. Any resemblance to actual persons, living or dead, or actual events is purely coincidental.

ISBN: 978-1-64875-462-3 (Paperback)

ALSO BY SUSAN HUNTER

Leah Nash Mysteries

Dangerous Habits

Dangerous Mistakes

Dangerous Places

Dangerous Secrets

Dangerous Flaws

Dangerous Ground

Dangerous Pursuits

Dangerous Waters

Dangerous Deception

Dangerous Choices

Dangerous Games

To find out more about Susan Hunter and her books, visit

severnriverbooks.com/authors/susan-hunter

A good friend will help you move.
A great friend will help you move a dead body.

For Pat Casey,
who knows where the bodies are buried.

PROLOGUE

August 1982

Eddie Garcia is finally doing what he's longed to do all summer. He's hanging out with Mac and Chrissie. That's not their real names, it's just what their friends call them because they're both so good at tennis, like John McEnroe and Chrissie Evert. Eddie isn't their friend, but he'd really like to be. Eddie doesn't care much about tennis. Baseball is his favorite sport, but he cares a lot about Mac and Chrissie. They're both twelve—almost three years older than Eddie, and they're both really cool. Usually, they ignore him. Chrissie does, anyway. Mac teases him about being a baby sometimes. But today, the last Saturday before school starts, Mac invited him to ride bikes with them out to a secret place they know. Eddie is over the moon.

He has to pedal super-fast to keep up with them on the five-mile ride out of town. The No Trespassing sign on the fence at the end of the rutted gravel road worries him a little. But he's not about to say that out loud. He scrambles over the fence and follows them on a barely visible, overgrown path to their secret hideout. He's a little disappointed when he sees that it's just a burned-out old house and a sagging storage shed in the middle of the woods. But that's not enough to diminish the thrill he feels at being singled out by them and asked to come.

"Okay, Eddie. Now, if you really want to hang out with us, you gotta pass the friendship test. You gotta climb down to the bottom of that old well."

Mac points in the direction of what looks like a wishing well, without the little roof thing on top. Eddie's not excited anymore. He tries not to show it, but he's scared.

"What's the matter? You look like you're afraid. Are you, Eddie? What, you think there's a monster at the bottom of that or something?" Mac asks.

"No. I'm not afraid. It's just that I, um, I don't know how to swim." He pushes up the glasses that have slid down his nose and blinks rapidly.

"There's no water in the well, dummy. It's abandoned. That's why there's a cover over it. It's kinda damp down there, but that's all. You don't have to jump down, you know. We got a rope ladder in the shed you can use. Both me and Chrissie have done it."

Chrissie isn't as cool as Mac, but she's pretty, and sometimes she's a little nicer to Eddie than Mac is.

"Oh. Um, well, I don't know how to climb a rope ladder. And, uh, if I get my jacket dirty, my mom will get mad."

"Then take it off," Mac says. "Come on, you and Chrissie help me get the cover off the well."

The three of them tug and wriggle what looks like an outsized manhole cover off the top of the stone well. Mac goes to the shed and comes back with the rope ladder. He hooks it over the rim of the well and drops it down inside.

"I'll show you how to do it. Here goes," he says, after swinging his leg over the edge. His head and shoulders quickly disappear.

In seconds Eddie and Chrissie hear him shout, "Piece of cake, I'm—what the hell?"

Mac's voice breaks off. Eddie and Chrissie hear an eerie, growling sound echoing up from the bottom of the well. Mac shouts, "No! Get away from me! Get back!"

Eddie rushes forward.

"Chrissie, something's got Mac! We have to—"

He stops when he hears Chrissie's laughter behind him and sees Mac's head pop into view. Mac is laughing, too.

"I'm glad you guys think this is so funny," Eddie says. "I don't."

Mac is trying to stop laughing as he says, "Hey, don't be that way, man. We're just teasing you a little. That's what friends do, right? They joke around."

"You need to get over yourself, Eddie. If you can't take a joke, we can't be friends," Chrissie says.

"That's right, Eddie. Me and Chrissie don't hang out with just anybody. You have to show us you've got the right stuff if you really want us to be friends with you. That's what you want, isn't it?"

Eddie nods.

"So, what are you waiting for?"

Mac and Chrissie aren't afraid of anything. Almost everything scares Eddie. But he knows this is his only chance with them. He grits his teeth. He won't let himself blow it.

"Okay. Okay, I'll do it."

He takes off his jacket, carefully folding it and laying it on the ground. He pushes his glasses up on his nose again, then wipes his sweaty palms on his pants. His stomach is doing flip-flops.

"Geez, Eddie. Get a move on. We don't want to waste the whole day. If you're too scared to do it, say so and go home," Chrissie says.

Her taunting finally pushes him to make the climb down. It's dark and smelly inside the well, and he takes it slow. Then something crawly with lots of legs skitters across his hand. He flings his arm out. The ladder sways and his heart thumps wildly. He manages to steady himself, then continues down. It takes him a lot longer than it took Mac to reach the bottom. But he feels a rush of pride when he does. He looks up through the darkness at the circle of light above and sees the silhouettes of Mac and Chrissie looking down.

"I made it! I'm at the bottom!"

Mac leans over and yells back, "Good job, man!"

Then he quickly pulls up the ladder. Eddie can hear their laughter as they run away.

In the dank, dark bottom of the well, Eddie is very frightened. So frightened that he no longer cares if Mac thinks he's a baby. He shouts as loud as he can.

"Mac! Chrissie! Come back you guys, throw me the ladder!"

He waits, but there's no answer. He can't believe it. They really left him. How long before they come back? He wasn't even supposed to leave the house. He begged his dad to let him stay home alone when the babysitter canceled. He promised he wouldn't even go outside. But he had. He was only going to ride his bike to the park. But then he ran into Mac and Chrissie, and he'd gone with them instead. Why did he do that? He should have known they were just tricking him. They weren't ever going to be his friends. What if they left him here all night? He can't stay here. He has to get out. He hollers as loud as he can, "I want to go home! I want to go home!"

In the empty well his voice echoes around him until he starts to cry. His crying echoes, too, until he feels like the well itself is sobbing with him. Still, no one comes. He feels in the pocket of his jeans for the baseball card he always carries with him. It's his lucky charm. When he gets anxious, just holding the card makes him feel better. When his fingers fail to find it, he tries his other pocket. It's not there either. His lucky card is in his jacket, lying on the ground far, far above him. It can't help him now.

Eddie's chest begins to tighten. He coughs. Then the wheezing starts. He knows the signs. He's having an asthma attack. He has to calm down. He reaches for his inhaler. Then he remembers. It's in his jacket, too. Panic sweeps over him. His heart races. His breathing is fast and shallow. His coughing gets worse. He can't catch his breath. He gasps for air, but mucous clogs his throat. His lungs are desperate for oxygen. His small body writhes with his struggles. He tries to call for his mother, but he can't speak. He's choking now, horrible, harsh sounds. His hands claw at his throat. He's terrified. He can't breathe . . . he . . . can't . . . breathe. The gasps get fainter. Then they stop. Eddie isn't struggling anymore.

An hour later, Chrissie and Mac return.

"Hey, Eddie! We're home!" Mac calls out in the singsong voice of a sitcom actor.

There's no answer. Chrissie feels a flutter of alarm.

"What if he's hurt?"

"He's not," Mac says with certainty. "He's just trying to pay us back for messing with him."

When they reach the well, he calls down, "Eddie, watch out, here comes the ladder!"

He hooks it to the edge and tosses it down. Still nothing from below.

Mac shakes his head.

"Fine, man. You want to play it that way? I'm coming to get you."

He moves quickly down the ladder while Chrissie waits. She has a very bad feeling.

When Mac comes back up, Eddie isn't with him.

"Is he hurt?"

"No, he's not hurt. He's goddamn dead!"

"Oh my God! Are you sure? Mac, are you sure?" She grabs his arm and shakes it. He throws it off and shouts at her.

"He's not breathing! I shook him, hard. Yes, he's dead, Chrissie!"

"Oh, my God," she repeats, this time in a low moan. "He must've had an asthma attack."

"Eddie has asthma?"

"Yes! He showed us his inhaler last month, like it made him special or something. You just never listened to him at all, did you?"

"Like you did?"

"Oh, stop it, it doesn't matter! What are we going to do? We killed Eddie!" She begins to cry.

Mac puts his hands on either side of his head. He begins walking in a circle, rocking his upper body back and forth, saying, "Shit, shit, shit!"

Chrissie is sobbing now. He grabs her shoulders and shakes her.

"Shut up will you? Stop it! I can't think!"

She stops crying then and wipes her eyes and nose on the sleeve of her shirt.

"We killed Eddie! What's there to think about? We have to get the police!"

"No! We're not getting the police. And we didn't kill Eddie. His asthma did. We didn't do anything to him!"

"We made him go down there! Now he's dead. We have to tell the police. We—"

"No. That's not what happened. We didn't make him do anything. It was his choice to go down there. Listen to me, if we go to the police, they're going to blame us. We already got busted for shoplifting that candy from JT's Party Store. They know we were with the kids who spray-painted the water tower, too, they *just can't prove it. What do you think will happen if we tell the cops about Eddie?"*

"But we have to tell them. Eddie's dead," Chrissie wails.

"Stop saying that, okay? Yeah, Eddie's dead. And that's sad. But we didn't kill him. My dad is already talking about sending me to military school. If this comes out, I'll be going to juvie instead. You will, too. Get real."

"But—"

"Chrissie, Eddie's gone. Going to the cops won't bring him back. You should think about your mom." Mac's voice had changed from impatient to coaxing. "She tried to kill herself two weeks ago. If she couldn't handle the divorce, what's she going to do if you get arrested for killing Eddie? You don't want her to try it again, do you?"

In her mind, Chrissie sees her emotionally fragile mother, lying in her room for days on end with the shades drawn, unable to force herself to get out of bed. She hears her Aunt Louise saying, "This is your fault, Chrissie. All that trouble you've been in this summer on top of everything your father put her through! It's too much for her to deal with. If you keep this up, you're going into foster care, young lady. I mean it!"

Chrissie hesitates. Mac seizes the moment.

"Go get Eddie's jacket and toss it in the well. This never happened. Look, you're leaving tomorrow. All you have to do is keep quiet."

"What about you?"

"If the cops ask me, I'll say I saw him riding his bike toward Riverview Park, and a white van was driving kind of slow behind him. They'll think a kidnapper got Eddie."

Mac can see Chrissie is wavering. He pushes harder.

"Listen, it's terrible about Eddie. I feel bad, too. But we don't have to wreck our lives—and your mom's—because of what he did to himself. We don't say anything. Ever. You know I'm right."

After a minute she nods.

"You get his jacket and throw it down the well. I'll get his bike."

Chrissie obeys. She feels strange. As though it's someone else picking up the green jacket Eddie had so carefully folded, and then throwing it down into the well. She steps back, still with a sense that this isn't really happening.

"It was a bitch getting this through all the undergrowth. Here, give me a hand!" Mac says as he returns and pushes Eddie's bike to the edge of the well.

Again, Chrissie obeys, still feeling as though she is watching, not participating in the scene. Together they lift up the bicycle and turn it on one end so it will fit into the opening. Then they drop it down. It clatters against the stone sides of the old well. It hits the bottom with a soft thud. Its landing is cushioned by Eddie's body.

Chrissie's stomach heaves suddenly. She turns away and is violently ill at Mac's feet.

"Jesus, Chrissie. Ugh! That is so gross! Come on, help me get the cover back on, then let's get out of here."

As they leave, Mac in the lead, Chrissie notices something lying on the ground. It's Eddie's favorite baseball card. He talked about it all the time. Tears fill her eyes as the image of Eddie's round face fills her mind—his brown eyes shining, his glasses slipping down his nose, his words tumbling out as he tells her yet again how he got the real player to autograph the card for him. She had barely listened. Eddie was always trying to get her attention, always trying to belong. Now, he'll never tell that story again. He'll never do anything again. And that's their fault, hers and Mac's.

But she knows Mac is right. Telling the truth won't bring Eddie back, and for sure it will put her into so much trouble. If she doesn't go to juvie, her aunt is sure to send her to foster care. Eddie is dead and there's nothing she can do to fix it now. But as she slips the card into her pocket, she knows she'll never be able to forget it, either.

"Chrissie, come on! Let's go!"

Mac and Chrissie don't speak on the long ride home.

1

Two hours of my life had slipped away as I sat in an almost airless meeting room at the Grantland County courthouse on a muggy, rainy, eighty-eight-degree August afternoon, covering the Board of Supervisors meeting. I don't regularly work as a reporter anymore. But when the weekly paper I co-own is short-staffed, I sometimes volunteer to fill in. Right then I was wishing I hadn't.

The AC in the courthouse wasn't working, but that hadn't sped things up any as the seven-member board trudged its way through a lengthy, but largely inconsequential, agenda. Finally, freedom loomed. The board had reached the last item on its agenda, the slot allocated for public comment. I reached for my purse to put away my notebook. I was the only one in the room who wasn't on the board or a member of the county administration, and there was no way *I* was going to say or do anything to prolong this torture.

My name is Leah Nash. I bought the *Himmel Times* weekly with my business partner after the hedge fund that owned it had decided to shut it down. I can't argue that sinking all the money I'd earned from my first true crime book into purchasing the paper was a great business decision. The financial struggle is real and it's ongoing. But I believe in community journalism. My partner and I are committed to reporting that's local, factual, and relevant to the people who live here. Building community is important to us, and that's where local journalism shines. I haven't ever regretted my choice.

As I shoved my notebook into my bag, the sound of a chair crashing to the floor startled everyone in the room. I looked behind me and saw a tall, heavyset, older man, wearing a Carhart T-shirt and jeans. His weathered face was very red. As he weaved his way past me, I caught a whiff of alcohol.

When he reached the podium at the front of the room, his fumbling hands shook as he tried to adjust the microphone. Mary Beth Delaney, the board member closest to him, jumped up to help, but he pushed the mic away in frustration and began shouting before she reached him.

"You damn supervisors, you think you run the world, don't you? You don't care about the people who voted you in. You think the only ones you answer to is the rich!"

At last. Something interesting. I reopened my notebook.

"Boyd, you need to identify yourself, and you need to calm yourself down," said Dwight Hightower, the board chair.

"F you! We graduated high school together Dwight Hightower, and you sure as shit know my name is Boyd Hanson. You also know—and every one of you know—what you did!" he said with a sweeping hand gesture that encompassed the entire board.

"I don't know what you're talking about Boyd," said Mary Beth, looking at him in surprise. Though it's true that ever since the facelift she insists never happened, Mary Beth always looks slightly taken aback.

"I'm talking about your damn board putting the kibosh on the CAFO that wanted to buy my farm. I had a deal, a real good deal all set with them. But then Mr. Rich Guy, Miller Caldwell, he told you all to deny the CAFO permit request. You did just like he said, like the good little sheep you are!" He pounded on the podium for emphasis. "None of you had the balls to stand up to Caldwell. You're just a bunch of crooked ass-kissers!"

CAFO is the acronym for Concentrated Animal Feed Operations, and generally refers to industrial-size livestock farms usually raising cows, pigs, or chickens kept in confined spaces. The problem we're seeing in

Wisconsin is that the tremendous amount of animal waste generated by such big operations has to go somewhere, and in most cases its finding its way into our rivers and lakes. How to fix the situation, or even getting everyone to agree that the CAFOs are causing a problem, is causing heated debates across the state.

Out of the corner of my eye, I saw Mary Beth discreetly wipe some of the droplets of fury that Boyd's yelling had expelled into the room from her cheek. I also noticed that the chairman was rapidly texting someone.

"Boyd, we voted on that at our last meeting. You could've attended and made your case then. The matter is settled now," Jerry Frederickson, another board member, said.

"Well how was I supposed to go, when I didn't even know it was on the agenda?"

"Now, Boyd," Dwight said in a placating tone. "Our agenda is right there on the county website before every meeting. If you would've come, we'd have been happy to hear your comments. But it's a done deal now. We know the whole thing with concentrated animal feed operations is a touchy issue. Some of us are farmers ourselves. But we've already got eleven CAFOs in the county. We're seeing some real issues with manure getting into our streams and rivers. We got to figure out a better way to manage all those tons of poop those cows generate before we bring in any more CAFOs. It's as simple as that."

Boyd's face had become redder as Dwight spoke. He was either going to explode or have a stroke.

"This is the public comment time, and I'm the public. I'm the one that gets to talk. You didn't vote no because you care so much about water—which by the way, we got plenty of! You vetoed that CAFO because Miller Caldwell told you to. He wants to live in the country, he just don't want to see or smell anything to do with farming. I could've sold my farm and made a good profit—which I need. But Caldwell thinks it's his right to keep people like me from making a living. And you all wouldn't stand up to him!"

I had my head down taking notes when he turned his anger on me.

"I know you," he said pointing at me. "What are you writing down there? What really happened, or what Caldwell wants you to write down? You're not going to print the truth about your boy Miller—that he's a homosexual pervert trying to take over the county with his money. Him and his cash keep your paper going. You're just his little secretary. That's what you are!"

He left the podium and began walking toward the front row where I was sitting.

Everyone's eyes swiveled from Boyd to me. I considered bolting toward the nearest exit. At that point the Grantland County Sheriff, David Cooper, entered the room from the side door.

"Hey, Boyd, what's going on? I could hear you hollering from way down the hall. What's the problem?"

The sheriff moved toward the podium as he spoke.

"The problem? The problem is, I'm losing everything—my farm, my money, my promise to my dead wife, and it's all on them!"

As he shouted, Boyd flung out his arm again and pointed toward the supervisors. Unfortunately, he hit the sheriff's shoulder as he did.

A less experienced officer might have increased Boyd's rage and resistance by putting a hold on the unruly and obviously intoxicated man. Instead, Coop, as most people call him, spoke to him in a firm but sympathetic tone.

"I can see you're hurting pretty bad, Boyd. I'm sorry. It sounds like you're carrying a lot on your shoulders. You don't want to add disorderly conduct to it, do you? Let's step outside and you can tell me the whole story. If there's anything I can do to help, I will."

Boyd hesitated, his eyes darting back and forth between Coop and the board. Everyone in the room was silent, waiting. Finally, he nodded.

"Good man, Boyd. Let's go somewhere cooler and we can talk things through."

This is probably a good time to disclose that Coop and I are lifelong friends and recent romantic partners. That fact didn't affect my opinion that he had handled the situation exactly right. From the relieved looks on the faces of the board members, they agreed.

Coop put his hand lightly on Boyd's shoulder. It was a friendly gesture, but it allowed him to gently steer him out of the room. However, Boyd turned back for one last verbal shot as they reached the door.

"You're all greedy cowards, you know that? Caldwell says jump and you say how high. I know you're all bought and paid for, and I'm gonna make sure the rest of the county finds out! And you, too!" he said jabbing the air in my direction before turning and stumbling a little as he walked through the door with Coop.

2

"*Chica!* I can't believe I missed the Board of Supervisors meeting today when something so exciting happened!"

Miguel Santos is the senior reporter at the *Times*. He and I were sitting in McClain's Bar and Grill having a drink that evening following the board meeting. Wednesdays are kind of the end of the week for us, because that's when we put the print edition of the *Times* to bed. I say "kind of" because now, although we still publish on Thursdays, we update stories daily on our website. So, there isn't quite the same weekend feeling there used to be when I started at the paper in my first reporting job, more than a decade ago. But a post-production gab at McClain's is still a Wednesday night tradition. And McClain's will always be my favorite bar. I love the film noir atmosphere of the place, with its dark interior, scuffed tables, and duct-taped vinyl booths.

"Yeah, it was at least a seven on the excitement scale for county meetings. For a second there, I thought Boyd Hanson was going to ask me to step outside to settle things. But then Coop showed up."

"I love that your *novio* rushed in to save you. It's very romantic," Miguel said.

"What? Are you saying you don't think I could take down a drunk seventy-something guy? Maybe Coop rescued Boyd Hanson from me."

He laughed and clinked his bottle of Spotted Cow against mine.

"You're right. What was I thinking?"

At twenty-four, Miguel is ten years younger than me. He's smart, funny, kind, and extremely good-looking. He'd be my dream man if it weren't for the fact that he's gay. Instead, I've adopted him as the little brother I never had.

"Exactly. But go back to the word *novio*. That's like boyfriend, right? As you know, I'm on the hunt for a different word to describe Coop. Calling him my boyfriend sounds so junior high. It's really too bad that 'manfriend' isn't a thing. But it sounds too much like Manfred. That could get confusing. Maybe I could make *novio* a thing."

"If you let him put a ring on it, you could call him your fiancé."

"Okay, stop. Neither one of us is interested in that."

"Really?" He asked the question with a little uplift of his eyebrow to convey his skepticism.

"Really. Every romance doesn't have to end in marriage, Miguel. In fact, it seems to me that marriage is more likely to end the romance."

"You are such a cynic," he said.

"Okay, then why aren't *you* engaged to someone—or even in a steady relationship?"

"Because I'm just a boy who wants to have fun. I'm too young to settle down. But you? Well, early thirties, they turn to mid-thirties, and then late thirties, and then—"

"And what happens when late forties turn to early fifties, Miguel?"

We both looked up then at the smiling face of my friend, business partner, and the object of Boyd Hanson's rage, Miller Caldwell.

"Miller, hi! What's up?"

McClain's isn't exactly a regular hangout for him.

"Your mother said you were here. I have a couple of things I wanted to talk to you about. First, I read the story about Boyd and the CAFO online. You did a good job with it," he said as Miguel scooted over to make room for him, and he slid into the booth. "I didn't realize that Boyd was counting so much on the sale of his farm. That certainly makes his anger understandable."

"It does, but Boyd was still way out of line. Maybe that's why he wouldn't pick up the phone or return the voice mail I left. I had to track down his son Noah to get the backstory. Turns out he's a friend of our Troy. But that didn't make him feel any friendlier toward me."

Troy Patterson is the other full-time reporter at the *Times*.

"Noah's pretty mad, too, although it's at both you and his father. I didn't use everything he said because, well, everyone doesn't have to know every detail about their sad family story. But apparently, Boyd's wife ran the business side of things at the farm, and she died a few years ago. Boyd made a lot of bad choices after that, and then made worse ones trying to fix the mess. He kept Noah in the dark about it until today. Selling the farm to the CAFO was Boyd's last, best hope to stave off financial ruin."

"If I thought Boyd would talk to me, I'd reach out to see if there's anything I can do. I'm still against bringing another CAFO into the county, but I'm sorry the board decision impacted him so severely."

"You're kind of too good to be true, Miller. Boyd Hanson called you a perverted homosexual at a public meeting and you still feel sorry for the guy?"

"It's not that I'm 'too good,' Leah. It's that I understand how it feels to hit bottom, and to know your own bad choices got you there."

A few years ago, Miller had a beautiful wife, two lovely children, and was on the verge of becoming a force in state politics. Then, a story I was chasing inadvertently led to the complete upending of his life. After many years of hiding the fact, and torturing himself because of it, Miller had outed himself as gay. His wife was bitter and furious. His children were confused and angry. His elderly parents were devastated. He lost his budding political career and was dropped by many people he had considered friends.

"Even if Boyd would talk to you, I don't think it would matter," Miguel said. "Noah told me that the CAFO sale was the only way for his dad to fix things. He owes so much money."

"Well, if you discover from Noah that there's something I could do, perhaps without Boyd or his son realizing where the help came from, please let me know. Meanwhile, if Boyd needs to lash out at me to help him get through the moment, I don't begrudge him that."

"You're proving my too-good-to-be-true point. You are also clearly the moral compass of our partnership. Lord knows, I'm not up to the job."

"That is wholly untrue. But our partnership is the second reason I came looking for you. I asked your mother to schedule a meeting of the news staff for tomorrow morning. Charlotte has an idea she'd like to present, and I think everyone should be there to hear it."

"What kind of idea?" I asked, feeling a little wary.

Miller's daughter Charlotte had recently given up a lucrative position in Chicago to return to Himmel to work with her father. In addition to his law firm and the newspaper, Miller also owns a property development business. That's where Charlotte's focus was supposed to be. But a few months ago, she had decided she wanted to understand more about the newspaper business her dad and I were in together. She spent a few weeks earlier in the summer shadowing staff to learn about the business from the ground up. The faint sense of alarm that Miller's words had awakened came from my negative experiences with MBA types who have ideas.

"She didn't give me many details, and what she did say, she asked me not to share in advance," Miller said.

I did not feel reassured. Never once in our partnership had Miller tried to direct coverage, or objected to editorial decisions, or indicated in any way that he regretted his decision to invest in the paper. But maybe Charlotte didn't feel the same way. If her ideas involved staffing cuts and other changes—which are the kind of thing the MBAs I've been around seem to favor—would he support that?

"I'm just curious about the sort of idea we're talking about. Ways to get more advertisers? How to increase subscriber numbers? Or is it more on the cutting side of things—staff, hours, expenses? What?"

"Leah, don't sound so worried. Everyone will have a chance to weigh in. No decision is going to happen tomorrow. You and I are partners. We'll decide together if Charlotte's idea has merit. But I promised I wouldn't preempt her by giving anything away in advance. So, this time, I'm sorry, Leah. No scoop for you."

I like a play on words and the *Seinfeld* reference was on point, so Miller's remark made me laugh. But my laughter didn't mean that he'd eased my concern. He hadn't.

3

Although McClain's isn't far from my place, it was raining when we walked out so I accepted a ride home from Miguel. As we headed to the car, voices were raised behind us. Both of us turned and saw Miller talking with a man who was leaning in menacingly and pointing a finger at his chest. I walked back toward them, Miguel right beside me.

"I mean it, you stay away from my son!" The man's voice was tight with anger.

"I'm sorry, I don't know who you are. I'm Miller Caldwell. I think you might have the wrong person. I really don't know what you're talking about," Miller said in a reasonable tone.

"I got the right person, all right. I'm talking about I found your business card in my boy's room. He said you gave it to him at some school career day or something. I'm Dennis Warby and my son is DJ Warby. He's still in high school. I won't stand by and let you try to recruit him into your perverted lifestyle!"

"You don't want your son to be a lawyer?" Miguel asked.

I knew he was trying to deflect the guy's anger with a little light trolling. Miguel is more a lover than a fighter, but Dennis Warby—a stocky, muscular guy with a shaved head and a short beard—wasn't in the mood.

"I know who you are," he said, turning his angry eyes on Miguel. "You're a faggot, just like him. You think you're funny with your gay podcast and your homo lifestyle. You're not going to pull my son into it, either one of you!"

He turned back to Miller then.

"I'm giving you fair warning. You come near my son just one more time, and you won't be going near another boy ever again. You hear me?"

He poked Miller in the chest with a short, thick finger and walked away.

The three of us looked at each other without speaking for a second. Then Miller said, "Well, I seem to have made a second enemy today without even trying."

"Do you know what he meant? About his son, I mean."

"I'm afraid it's a case of good intentions creating a bad outcome."

"Yes. I think so, too," Miguel said, nodding in agreement.

"Would either of you care to let me in on the story?"

"A few weeks ago, a high school boy called into my podcast," Miguel said. "He didn't give his name, but now I think it was that man's son, DJ. He was very upset, very worried. He said he wanted to come out to his parents, but he was afraid to. I gave him the name of an LGBTQ support group for teenagers in Madison. I said he could find some help there."

I made a connection then.

"I get it. Miller, the guy's son DJ, he didn't meet you at a school career day like he told his dad. He met you last month when you were a guest speaker at that LGBTQ event in Madison, didn't he?"

Miller nodded.

"DJ came up to me after the meeting. It was obvious he was in a great deal of distress. I encouraged him to stay connected to the support group. But I was worried about him. LGBTQ teens are significantly more at risk of suicide than their peers. I gave him my card and told him to call if he needed to. I was trying to help him feel less alone. But now with his father so angry, he's going to be even more afraid to talk to his parents openly. I didn't handle that well."

"Yes, you did," I said. "It's his dad who can't cope."

"Many parents can't," Miller said. "Including my own father. I was a middle-aged man, and it was still crushing to feel the full weight of his disapproval, his anger. How much worse must it be for a teenage boy to go through that? We reached a kind of peace before he died, but our relationship was never the same."

"Dennis Warby is an asshat, and you and Miguel were right to reach out to that kid. I've told you before. People are stupid. Go with that premise and you'll never be surprised, or disappointed," I said.

Miller laughed then.

"Leah, if you were half as cynical as you pretend to be, I'd be worried. But I know that you're not. People can act stupidly sometimes, but when they do it's usually out of fear. I think that Mr. Warby is afraid of something he doesn't understand. Fear is what's making him so angry."

"Miller, I'm sorry this happened today, on top of the whole Boyd Hanson meltdown. You don't deserve either of those things."

"We don't always get what we deserve in life, Leah—and that goes for the good and the bad. I think it's time for the three of us to get out of the rain. I'll see you both tomorrow."

When we got into his car, I asked Miguel something that I never had before.

"How did your family react when you came out?"

"I didn't have to. I've always loved fashion and sparkly things and my favorite toy was my cousin Maria's Holiday Barbie. The green velvet, the sparkles! My mother, I think she just always knew."

"She didn't mind?"

"No. I remember once my cousin Reuben, he was teasing me. He called me a 'gay girly boy.' I ran to my mother crying. She said, 'Miguelito, I love you how you are. We are all different in our family, but we have one thing the same. We all love each other, and nothing will change that. We are lucky that way.' And then she talked to Reuben and that was all."

"Wow. That's a great thing to say to a kid. I hope when DJ finally tells his family, his mother says the same thing to him."

We were both quiet then, lost in our own thoughts on the short ride to my place. Mine centered on what was going to happen at the next morning's meeting. When Miguel pulled up to the back door of the *Himmel*

Times building, which also houses my apartment on the third floor, I brought it up to him.

"What do you think Charlotte's idea is? I hope she doesn't want to get more involved in the paper. She's smart, and I like her, but she's got zero experience in journalism. I don't want the reincarnation of Rebecca at the *Times*," I said.

Rebecca Hartfield had been named publisher at the *Times* back before Miller and I bought the paper. She had wreaked havoc with it, at the behest of her corporate overlords, A-H Media. She had also caused a serious rift in my long friendship with Coop. And oh, yeah, she had married him, too.

"That won't happen. Charlotte is nothing like Rebecca."

"That's true. But I don't know how good her judgment is, she's pretty young."

"She is two years older than me, and you think my judgment is fine . . . don't you?"

"Of course I do. But you're an old soul, Miguel."

"Think positive. Maybe Charlotte's idea is to do more things like my podcast."

"No, I think Miller was prepping us for a bigger idea. Besides, I don't see how more podcasts would help the *Times* unless we could clone you."

In addition to his reporting duties, Miguel also writes a column in the *Times* called "Ask Miguel." He's so in his element dispensing advice on fashion, shopping, makeovers, romance, life choices, and anything else he's asked, that he agreed to start a podcast based on his column. It's one of the most-clicked links on our website, and not just by locals, either.

"That reminds me. Will you please come on my podcast for an interview?"

"No."

"Why do you never say yes?"

"Because I never want to do it."

"But it would be so fun. We can talk about how you started being a reporter. And how you and Coop fell in love—only you are not very bright about romance, so you didn't know it. And then how you followed my advice and now you are living happily ever after. And—"

"Not that you were close to making the sale," I interrupted, "But you definitely lost it with that. I am not going on your podcast to talk about my personal life. Full stop."

"Okay, then come on my podcast and talk about your new book. You can talk about what it's like to write fiction instead of true crime. And . . . wait. Why am I talking to you, who always says no? I'm going to talk to your agent Clinton. I'm sure he will want the publicity for you."

Clinton Barnes is a very good, very driven agent who was the only one willing to take me on when I wrote my first true crime manuscript. He wasn't able to place that one with a publisher, but he didn't give up. He did very well for me with my second try and did his best for me on the ones that followed. There have been some bumps along the way, but he's never lost faith. He'd recently persuaded me to try my hand at fiction. Miguel was right, Clinton would be all about the podcast idea. And once Miguel talked to him, Clinton wouldn't let go until I agreed.

"Fine. I surrender. But I can't do it right away. I just turned in the first draft of my fiction book, and there will be edits and revisions, I'm sure. Plus, I don't even have an approved title yet. Once things are settled, I promise I'll come on your podcast to talk about the book."

"Oh, that makes me so happy!"

"But remember, I said talk about the book, not about anything else. Especially nothing about me and Coop. Understood?"

"Yes."

"Good."

4

Coop was sitting at the island that separates my kitchen from the living room when I walked in. He held a Leinenkugel beer in one hand as he read something on his phone.

"Hey you, we missed you at McClain's tonight," I said.

He looked up and smiled. "Sorry, I got caught up in some things at work and I didn't finish until about fifteen minutes ago. How was it?"

"Okay. It wound up being just me and Miguel. But we did have an unexpected guest. Miller showed up to drop a news bomb and then run away."

"What do you mean?"

"Well, he said he stopped to tell me I did a good job on the county board story and—"

"He's right, you did. I was just reading it."

"Thank you, but let me finish with the news bomb. I think what he really wanted to do was warn me about a news staff meeting in the morning. Charlotte is going to tell us about an idea she has," I said, putting air quotes around the word "idea."

Coop didn't respond.

"Well? What do you think?"

"About what? That Miller wants to meet with the staff of the business he co-owns? How is that a news bomb?"

"Come on. You know Miller doesn't mess with the news side. I think we've had maybe two all-staff meetings with him."

"And so?"

"And so? You really don't see the implications, Coop?"

"I really don't."

"Let me spell it out for you. Miller's daughter spent a month at the *Times* observing how things work. She learned how my mother manages the office, and what Troy and Miguel do when they cover stories, and why we have stringers, and how we manage them. She spent time with Maggie to understand what goes into editorial decisions. For her sins, she even spent time with Courtnee at the reception desk. And now she has an idea for the paper?"

"Why do you keep saying 'idea' that way?"

"What way?"

"Like Charlotte is Lex Luthor with a plan to destroy the planet."

"Well, if you think of the *Daily Planet* as a stand-in for the *Times*, you could be right," I said, then immediately self-corrected.

"All right, that's not true. I like Charlotte. I don't think she's evil, but she's not very experienced. And she has a master's degree in business. I've seen this before at other papers. Business people always want to cut staff, and overtime, and benefits, and how many pens you buy. Anything they can think of to increase profits."

"You're getting way ahead of yourself. Has Miller ever done anything to make you believe that all he cares about is the bottom line?"

"Well, no, but—"

"Leah, why not assume the best instead of the worst? Maybe Charlotte has an idea for expanding coverage, or increasing circulation?"

"Isn't the saying 'Hope for the best, but prepare for the worst?'"

"I'd say you've got the part about the worst nailed. Where's the hope come in? You're wasting the present worrying about the future. And if something bad does happen that means you go through it twice—worrying takes the pleasure out of the present and it doesn't change the future."

"I know, I know. It's just that getting the paper up and going again has been a hard slog. So far, it's taken all of my money, a big chunk of Miller's, and we're still just barely hanging on. If we make big changes, and they're the wrong ones, we could lose it. And I don't mean just me and Miller and the people who work there. I mean the community. Himmel needs a community news source. And that sure isn't *GO News*."

"*GO News* isn't even open right now. Spencer is in rehab, and I don't think there's much chance of him coming back to town."

GO News is an online-only "news" operation that specialized in shoddy reporting and sucking up to local officials. But a lot of people in the county had subscribed to it. It shut down when the publisher, Spencer Karr, got caught up in a drug bust and then went to rehab.

"Not now, no. But the building still has all the equipment in there. Why, if he's not coming back? Even if he doesn't, someone else could buy it and be just as bad as he was—or worse."

"Now you're just looking for things to torture yourself with. *GO News* shouldn't even be a part of this conversation. Listen, Miller isn't going to agree to Charlotte's idea just because she's his daughter. She'll have to prove her case not just to him, but to you, too. He hasn't let you down yet. Accept that for once there's no reason to worry."

"That sounds like something my mother would say."

"That's not a bad thing. I love your mother. After all, she brought you into the world, didn't she?"

He smiled then and leaned over to kiss me.

"I hate when you do that."

"Do what, kiss you?"

"No. Get all charming and sweet to win an argument."

"Are you saying I'm not charming and sweet all the time?"

"I won't say it because I don't want to ruin the moment. Right now, I'm thinking that I'm pretty lucky to have you for my *novio*."

"What's a *novio*?"

"It's a Spanish word for boyfriend. I'm thinking of calling you that when I talk about you to other people, because boyfriend sounds not quite right at our age."

"You talk about me?"

"Constantly. Especially on the days when you save me from having to engage in hand-to-hand combat with septuagenarians, like you did today. I was really proud of the way you handled the situation with Boyd Hanson."

"Just doing my job, ma'am," he said, like a cowboy in an old Western. Then he stood up and held out his arms.

"C'mere a minute."

When I did, he hugged me, and then put his hands on my shoulders. As he looked me in the eye he said, "I think we're both pretty lucky."

"I agree. But let's not jinx things by talking about it anymore. Tell me what happened after you got Boyd out of the room."

"Not much. I let him talk. I think deep down he knows Miller isn't to blame for the mess he's in. But that CAFO sale made him hope he could put things back together again. When Miller argued against it, and it fell through . . ." Coop shrugged and shook his head.

"You didn't charge Boyd with anything, I assume."

"No. I drove him home. His son Noah took over from there. I'm pretty sure Boyd won't be attending any more commission meetings. Noah might though. He's pretty mad, too."

"Yeah, I got that when I talked to him," I said, my words ending on a yawn.

"Looks like it's a good time to call it a night. You need a good night's sleep so you can be ready for all those expansion plans Charlotte is going to unveil tomorrow, right?"

"I remain hopeful but prepared for the worst," I said.

As I lay awake at three in the morning, Coop snoring gently beside me, I tried to convince myself that he was right. Still, I couldn't shake the nagging feeling that something bad was coming. Maybe it wouldn't turn out be Charlotte's proposal, but something was looming out there in the dark.

5

"Good, the meeting hasn't started. I thought I was going to be late," Troy Patterson said as he came dashing into the conference room where the rest of us—me; Maggie McConnell, our managing editor; my mother, our office manager; and Miguel—were seated around the table.

"That's okay, Troy. The starting pistol hasn't gone off yet for the Tour de Himmel," Maggie said, in reference to the cycling gear Troy wore. He's into fitness in a major way and usually starts his day with a ten-mile bike ride.

"Sorry. I didn't have time to go home and change. What's the meeting about?" he asked.

Troy is even younger than Miguel. We hired him fresh out of college. With his freckled face, shy manner, and guileless eyes behind round glasses, he's sometimes mistaken for a high school student. He's learned to use it to his advantage. People underestimate him, so he sometimes gets more out of them than a seasoned reporter would.

Everyone had turned their eyes toward me for the answer to Troy's question. I was saved from looking a clueless leader with no answers because Miller and Charlotte walked through the door just then. Charlotte strongly resembles her mother, Miller's ex-wife Georgia. She's tall and slim, with straight blond hair and large brown eyes. Just then, Miller said something to her, and she looked up at him with a smile. I just hoped I'd feel like smiling when the meeting was over.

Miller took a seat and Charlotte put the briefcase she was carrying next to his, then walked to the front of the room.

"Miller, since you gathered us all together this morning, would you lead things off?" I asked.

"I'll be brief. Charlotte came to me a few days ago with an interesting idea. I got only a sketchy outline of it myself, so I'm eager to hear more about it. Charlotte, do you want to take the floor?"

"Sure, thanks, Dad."

She began speaking with the self-assurance of someone who is used to commanding attention—an assurance conferred by her wealth, her education, and the bonus of being a young and attractive woman.

"I know that all of you believe in what my dad and Leah sometimes call 'the mission.' That is, to make sure that Himmel—and Grantland County as a whole—doesn't become a news desert without a local paper, like so many other rural areas have. When Dad first told me he was buying the paper with Leah, I told him that with all of the online sources of information available—Facebook, Twitter, Instagram, YouTube, etc., I wasn't sure a community newspaper was necessary anymore." She nodded in the direction of me and Miller and smiled. He smiled back. I did not.

"The month I spent here job shadowing everyone really opened my eyes about how the paper works, and how dedicated all of you are to serving the community. I think you do an amazing job with the crew you have. But—and this won't come as a surprise to any of you—looking at the spreadsheets, it's hard to justify keeping things as they are."

There it was. Charlotte was laying the groundwork for cuts—or maybe even worse. I glanced at Miller. His face revealed nothing.

"I know that you're all working for less money than you could get other places, and you put in very long hours. You've made the most of the resources you have—bringing on more stringers, stepping up the *Times* website. The podcast Miguel does is innovative for a paper as small as the *Himmel Times*. But it's been an uphill battle. Businesses have so many other online and social media options to reach their customers that we can't compete effectively for advertising dollars. And we can't raise the price of subscriptions enough to make up for that lack of ad revenue."

Maggie was sitting next to me. I'd been sensing the tension building in her as Charlotte spoke. Finally, she couldn't hold back.

"Charlotte, I get the feeling that you're about to drop the hammer. You don't need to butter us up with how great we are so you can let us down easy when you tell us we have to cut staff, or just shut down. I've got a finite amount of time left in this world, and none to spare for nonsense. Get to the point, can't you?"

I've never appreciated Maggie's I'm-seventy-two-and-I-don't-give-a-damn attitude more. I could see that Charlotte was taken aback, but she recovered quickly.

"Maggie, you're right. I'm spending too much time on the wind up. I need to get to the pitch."

Here it comes, I thought, she wants us to shut down, or start buying canned content, or quit producing a print edition and abandon the people in the community who don't have, don't want, can't afford, or won't use the internet.

"I'm recommending that we beef up spending on the full-time reporting staff, increase the budget for overtime and stringers, change the focus for our sales staff, and send management—that would be you Maggie, to a small newspaper in Ohio similar to the *Times*, to see how they've made the transition from a failing operation to a successful one. Anyone interested?"

We'd been bracing ourselves to argue the case yet again for community journalism. Now we all just stared at her. But the silence didn't last long. I was thrilled that Charlotte was advocating for expanding, not contracting, the paper's coverage and staff. But I needed more details before I did my happy dance.

"Charlotte, I love everything you said, but how are we going to afford to do all those badly needed things? You've looked at our bottom line. It's pretty wobbly. I'm willing to throw anything I can scrape together into the pot, but still . . ." I said, my voice trailing off as my brain ran through the enormity of the changes she was suggesting.

Miller stepped in, too.

"Yes, Charlotte. I don't want to throw cold water on an exciting idea, but before Leah and I can approve it, we'll need a lot more detail. Our original three-year plan for reestablishing the *Times* turns out to have been a bit optimistic. We're managing, but just barely. How do you see us funding your proposal? How long before further investment would turn to profit?"

"That's the beauty of it, Dad. We're not going to make a profit. We don't need to, because we're going to turn the *Himmel Times* into a nonprofit news organization."

"I'd have to say mission accomplished on that front," Maggie said. "I don't see how deliberately deciding not to make money is going to help us any."

She had moved her tortoiseshell glasses from the top of her thick gray hair to her nose, a sign she remained skeptical but was willing to listen.

"Basically, we reorganize and recreate the *Times* as a nonprofit entity. That allows us to seek funding from partners and sponsors, major donors, membership support, and foundations. Ideally each group will be about a quarter of our revenue. We still need to balance our income and our expenses, of course. And although it's called "nonprofit" we actually can make a profit, and I think we will. But the profit goes back into the work of the organization, not to shareholders or investors."

"So, it's like the *Times* becomes PBS?" Troy asked.

"In a way, yes."

"Will we do fundraisers? I would love to host a telethon," Miguel said. "And I could do something with the podcast, and . . ."

"We're not there yet, Miguel. But if the decision is made to convert the *Times* to a nonprofit, I can't think of anyone better to host a fundraiser," Charlotte said.

"I concur," Miller said. "I'm intrigued with your idea Charlotte. But Leah and I are going to need to see a formal proposal outlining the steps for moving to a nonprofit, the budgeting process, the possible funding sources, the—"

As he was speaking, Charlotte walked to the chair that held her briefcase. She opened it, and pulled out two thick file folders, handing one to her father, and then coming back to hand one to me.

"Of course you do. And it's all here. I'll send you both the electronic files as well. But I know you prefer to have paper in front of you, Dad. It's all detailed."

She turned back to look around the table at everyone.

"I know you all have meetings to cover and stories to write," she said. "I won't take up more of your time. But as you think about it—and I'm sure some of you will be researching the idea yourselves—please email or text me with your questions, and copy Dad and Leah in on them, too. If I don't know the answers, I'll find them. I should add that going nonprofit isn't a magic solution. Every one of us will have to be prepared to take on expanded or even very different roles. But I believe that changing the way we're doing things is the only way to ensure that the *Times* is here for a long time."

6

The others were talking excitedly among themselves as Charlotte, Miller, and I left the conference room.

"Charlotte, I know there are some nonprofit news outlets around the country, but I never really considered that organizational structure for the *Times*. Now that you've outlined it, though, I'm not sure why I didn't. Lack of a business perspective, I guess."

"It didn't occur to me at first either, Leah. But I came across a case study on a paper that had transitioned to nonprofit status. I started reviewing the research available and talked to some of the papers that are doing it successfully. The more I learned the more it seemed feasible for us."

"Leah, you and I have some homework to do," Miller said. "Let's each take a few days to read through and think about the proposal, and we can talk about it next week. I'll have Patty set up a meeting for us, how does that sound?"

"Great, Miller, thanks. And thank you, Charlotte for all the work you put in on this, and for believing the *Times* is worth keeping alive."

"My pleasure, Leah. I'm just glad for the chance to work on something that really matters. I learned a lot at the property development firm I worked at in Chicago. But they were more about knocking down old neighborhoods than building them back up. I came home because I want to be part of rebuilding things, not tearing them down. That includes the *Times*. I guess you could say that when I grow up, I want to be like my father." She smiled at Miller.

He looked back at her with a mixture of pride in her and embarrassment at her praise. I felt a twinge of envy for the relationship I'd never had with my own father.

"You picked a great role model," I said.

"I know I did. I just hope I can live up to it."

"All right, I think that's enough flattery for the morning," Miller said. "I've got a client meeting in fifteen minutes. If you're coming back to the office with me, we have to go."

"I don't need a ride, Dad. I've got a coffee date across the street. I'll see you later. Happy reading," she said with a nod at the folders we both held in our hands. "Call me if you have any questions."

Back upstairs I made a cup of tea, fluffed up a couple of pillows on my window seat, and sat down to read the file folder from Charlotte. First though, I spent a few minutes staring out the window, sipping my tea and feeling relieved that my premonitions of trouble ahead had come to naught.

I looked at the tree-lined street three floors below and saw Charlotte walking into the Wide Awake and Woke coffee shop across from the *Times* building. A man coming from the opposite direction reached the door just ahead of her and held it open for her. She smiled up at him and I wondered if he was her coffee date or just a polite stranger.

My phone rang before I could go full-on Miguel and spin a romantic tale for Charlotte and her possible beau. When I looked at the screen, I saw the call was from my agent Clinton. For once I answered without a trace of guilt. I had turned in my manuscript well before the due date.

"Hi, Clinton! I know you're not calling to nag, because I already turned in my manuscript. So, you must want to tell me what you think about it."

"Yes, that's why I'm calling. Is this a good time?"

That brought me up short. Clinton is a dynamo, always on the move.

When a thought enters his head, he immediately picks up the phone and calls with no qualms about disturbing me. The only time of the day that's safe from one of his rapid-fire phone calls is between one and six a.m. And he's even breached those hours on occasion.

"What's the matter?" I asked.

"Nothing. Why would anything be the matter? I just have a few things to go over with you. You're not in the middle of anything, are you?"

"Clinton, you never ask if I'm busy. And you always get right to the point. Why are you stalling now?"

"No, no, I'm not stalling. I just wanted to be sure you've got time to talk about some changes that I think will polish up your manuscript."

"What kind of changes?"

"Nothing major. Nothing you can't knock out in a few weeks."

"A few weeks? That sounds like a lot more than 'polishing.'"

I worked to keep my voice neutral, but my stomach had lurched the way it does when you start the descent from the top of a Ferris Wheel. The mystery novel I'd just turned in was my first try at writing fiction. Clinton had talked me into it, despite my reservations. I'm used to reporting stories, not imagining them. I gave it my best shot, and I'd felt pretty good about it when I finished. Obviously my satisfaction had been premature.

"No, no. That's not true," he said. "Your idea for the plot is strong, and the solution to the mystery is clever. The issue is with Jo Burke, your main character."

"What's wrong with her?"

"There's nothing 'wrong' with her. There's just not enough of her."

"She's the whole book, Clinton. It's written in first person. Everything the reader gets from the story is through Jo's perspective."

"It's not enough for Jo to talk about what she does, or where she goes, or who she suspects. You have to let readers see who she is, help them under-stand how her experiences shape the choices she makes. The story needs more heart."

My go-to when criticized is usually to fire back. It's not my best trait, but I'd rather play offense than defense. However, because I lacked confidence in my ability to write fiction, Clinton's words didn't inspire a quick come-back. They made my heart sink.

"I don't think I can do that."

"Of course you can. This was a first draft."

"No, it was my best draft. I wrote and revised it half a dozen times before I sent it off to you. You're telling me it's not good. So, now we know. I don't have the right stuff to be a fiction writer. I tried to tell you that. I shouldn't have let you talk me into it."

I knew I sounded petulant and childish, but I couldn't seem to help it. Clinton's criticism, while delivered kindly enough, had struck right at the very heart of my fears about writing fiction.

"Leah, that's not what I said. The plot is good, the setting is great, there are plenty of twists, and the solution is clever. All you need to do is revise Jo so that it doesn't feel like you're observing her from fifty thousand feet. There's a really good book here, it just needs some work. I'll email you the marked-up copy. You can look over the suggestions and then we can discuss them more."

"I don't think so, Clinton."

"What do you mean?"

"I mean I gave it all I had, and it wasn't enough. It was worth trying, but I'm done. I don't want to go back and do it all over again."

"Leah, you have a contract. You accepted an advance. You have to complete the book."

"I'll give the advance back. I can't do it, Clinton. You can't get blood out of a stone."

"You're not a stone, and I don't want your blood. I want a revised manuscript with heart. I'm hanging up now because I know you need some time to think. I'll talk to you soon."

7

Right after Clinton hung up, Coop called.

"Hey, I've been waiting to hear from you. How did the meeting go?"

"It went fine. Better than fine, really. Charlotte wants to turn the paper into a nonprofit organization. That would broaden our funding base so that the *Times* could draw on partners, sponsors, major donors, foundations, grants—in addition to membership support, which basically means subscribers."

"What would that mean for your business partnership with Miller?"

"I don't know yet. We have to read through the details and figure all that out, but it's the first new idea we've had—or rather Charlotte had—to turn things around. It's worth exploring."

"That sounds good. So, why do you sound so bad? What else happened?"

Apparently I hadn't done as well as I'd thought at disguising the sting left by Clinton's call. And because I hadn't had time to work through my feelings, Coop got them raw and unprocessed in answer to his question.

"Because every time something good happens, something bad follows. Clinton hates my book. I'm a terrible writer. I never should have tried fiction. That's what happened."

"That doesn't sound like Clinton. What did he really say?"

"That my writing has no heart. That readers won't relate to Jo or the other characters because I don't gush all over the page about them."

"What did he say about the book overall—the structure, the plot?"

"Oh, he said the plot was fine and the solution was clever."

"That sounds good. Leah, it's your first try at something new, and something pretty hard to do. It's not all or nothing, you know. Besides, you always have revisions to do after you turn in a manuscript. Why are you so down about it this time?"

"Because when I'm writing as a journalist I know what I'm doing. Writing fiction is a whole different thing. I did my best, but it wasn't good enough."

"You wouldn't let me read it before. How about letting me take a look at it now? If I think it's unfixable, I'll be honest with you."

"Fine. I'll email you a copy. Save it for bedtime so it can bore you to sleep. Which I'm sure it will."

"I think you're taking what Clinton said way too hard."

"I'm just trying to be realistic. Writing fiction was like taking a jump in the ocean without knowing how to swim. I flailed around, swallowed a lot of water, finally figured out how to dog paddle to shore, and just when I was within reach of the beach, a shark swam up and bit my leg off."

"The shark would be Clinton?"

"Yes! Well, no. To be fair, he's actually more of a lifeguard than a shark. See, I told you writing fiction is beyond my ken. I can't even write an extended metaphor."

"'Beyond my ken'? You know I love it when you talk fancy to me."

"Oh, stop it. I'm serious."

But he'd managed to break through my self-pity a little and he could hear the reluctant smile in my voice.

"I'm serious, too. Put it out of your mind for now. Let me read it, and I'll give you my honest reaction."

"I'll try. I need to focus on Charlotte's proposal anyway. And at least I know that will be well written. I'll see you tonight."

I forced myself to stop thinking about my failed manuscript and returned to a deep dive into Charlotte's proposal. She had delved into both the pros and cons and had detailed both thoroughly. It was true, we'd have to do some heavy lifting to realign ourselves as a nonprofit organization, and we'd have to rely a lot on Miller's contacts to bring in that initial donor and sponsor support—but Miller definitely had the connections. The constant knot between my shoulder blades that had fluctuated between barely noticeable and sharply painful for months, dependent on how the *Times* bottom line looked, eased up a bit.

Just as I finished lunch, Gabe called. Gabe Hoffman is Miller's law partner. Before Coop and I got together a few months ago, Gabe and I had been seeing each other. Our breakup was painful, but we were both on the other side of it now.

"Hey Gabe! How are you? I haven't talked to you in days."

"I'm good. I've been pretty busy getting things ready for Dominic to come home from his mom's. I'm flying to New York on Saturday to pick him up. I've really missed that kid of mine this summer. You sound pretty cheery. Did you get good news on your manuscript?"

"No, I did not."

"I'm sorry, what happened?"

"Oh, nothing that a grown-ass woman shouldn't be able to handle. But apparently I'm not one of those. But I don't want to talk about it right now. I'm still licking my wounds."

"Well, when you feel like it let me know."

"Thanks. It was nice of you to check in and see how my book project is going. Even though it's going terrible, and I don't want to talk about it."

"Okay, now you're making me feel bad. That's not why I called. I actually need a favor."

"Oh? What is it?"

"I'm stuck in Madison and Barnacle is at the vet's getting his teeth cleaned. When I dropped him off this morning, they said they're closing at four thirty today. It looks like I won't make it back by then. I don't want him to have to spend the night there. Could you possibly—"

"Yes, sure. I'll pick him up. Which vet do you go to?"

He gave me the name and address.

"Barnacle's supposed to be done around four. Thanks for doing this."

"Sure, no problem."

"I owe you one."

"No worries. I know where to collect."

It was ten after four when I parked my car. I had almost reached the entrance at the veterinary clinic when someone shouted my name. I turned and saw Davina Markham standing by her car and waving at me. I tried getting away with just a jaunty wave in return, but she was already moving toward me.

I walked to meet her, hoping to take control of the conversation and bring it to a close in a friendly but fast way. Davina can be quite a talker and I didn't want to have to pound on locked clinic doors to free Barnacle.

"Hey, Davina, I haven't seen you around much. Things must be jumping at the Purrrfect Kitty Boutique. How's Sabrina doing? Did you pick her up, or drop her off?" I asked.

Sabrina is Davina's much-loved Persian cat. I watched in surprise as she teared up in response.

"Sabrina passed away. Just yesterday," she said.

"Oh, I'm so sorry. What happened?"

"She had cancer. Dr. Tom tried everything, but it was just too advanced."

She snuffled loudly and nodded her head. Then she reached into her purse—for a tissue, I assumed. Instead, she brought out a small plastic bag —the kind you pack a sandwich in—and held it up toward me, her hand shaking a little.

"Here she is. They do on-site pet cremation at the clinic. I just picked up her ashes," she said. A sudden, loud crashing sound made us both jump. I looked at the street and saw that a car stopped at the corner had just been rear-ended. Hard.

"Whoa! That was—Davina, what's wrong?"

She was crying and pointing wordlessly at the ground, where her cat's ashes had spilled when we'd both been startled by the car accident. I dropped down and began pushing them into a little pile with my hands.

"Hey, it's okay. It's not windy. We can get them back in the bag. Don't cry, Davina."

But she couldn't seem to stop. I pulled my reporter's notebook out of my purse, ripped out a page, curled it into scoop shape and used it to funnel the ashes back into the bag.

"There," I said, standing up and handing the plastic sack to Davina. "I got most of them."

"Thank you, Leah! Thank you so much. I'm sorry I'm so emotional. I need Sabrina's ashes for a piece of cremation jewelry. So I can always have her close to me. When I dropped them and they spilled, it was like seeing Sabrina go, all over again."

Her tears started up once more. I snuck a peek at my watch. The office was going to close shortly, but I couldn't just walk away.

"Well, you've got them back now, Davina. You can still use them for cremation jewelry. Though I don't exactly know what that is. Is it like a locket or something that holds some of Sabrina's ashes?"

"No. I mean yes, that's one kind of cremation jewelry. But I'm going to have Sabrina's ashes made into a diamond I can wear on a necklace. I've got the brochure that tells about it right here," she said, searching in her capacious shoulder bag. "Now where is it?"

"No, that's okay, Davina." I glanced at my watch again. "I should get going. I—"

"Yes, they're closing early today. You know, some of my friends are telling me I should get a new cat to help me get over Sabrina. But I don't want to get over her. She was my best friend for fourteen years. That's seven years longer than I was married."

Her lower lip trembled as she finished her sentence. I patted her on the shoulder, mindful of the minutes slipping away and Barnacle waiting inside.

"I'm sure when the time is right—if the time is ever right—you'll know. But, speaking of time, I really have to run. Again, I'm so sorry about Sabrina, Davina. Take care."

She nodded sadly and I scurried guiltily away.

8

....

I had expected to breeze in, pick up Barnacle, and be on my way. But when I went up to the front desk and explained my mission, the receptionist said that Dr. Fuller wanted to see me before I left with Barnacle. That alarmed me a little. I wondered if there'd been a complication in what should have been a simple dental cleaning procedure.

I was ushered to an exam room in the back where I used the sink to wash Sabrina off my hands. Though they had looked like fireplace ashes, when I handled them they'd felt gritty, more like fine sand, and they'd left my fingers feeling sort of sticky. As I finished drying them, a vet assistant brought in a slightly loopy Barnacle, still feeling the effects of his sedation.

"Hey, how are you doing boy? You're looking good," I said as I bent down to pet him and rub behind his ears. He gave a small wag of his tail and then flopped down on the floor next to my chair.

I couldn't see anything obviously wrong with Barnacle. Maybe Dr. Fuller, the vet, liked the personal touch, and wanted to see me to go over the discharge instructions.

After a few minutes, I checked the time. It was four thirty. I wondered if we'd been forgotten. I had decided to give it five more minutes before I hunted someone down, when the door opened. George Clooney walked in. My heart skipped a beat, but my killjoy brain told me that the drop-dead

handsome man with salt and pepper hair and dark eyes was the veterinarian, not the movie star.

He lifted his eyebrows in surprise when he saw me.

"You're not Gabe," he said.

"I'm a friend of his. Leah Nash. I'm picking up Barnacle for him. I take it
you're Dr. Fuller. Is there something wrong with Barnacle?"

Barnacle had lifted his head at the sound of his name. Dr. Fuller leaned
down and rubbed under his chin as he said, "No, not at all. Barnacle's a
very good boy. The procedure was routine and went well. Why do you ask?"

"It's just that the receptionist was pretty insistent that you wanted to see
me before I left with Barnacle, so I wondered."

"Ahhh. I think I know what happened. I wanted to talk to Gabe about a
legal matter he's handling for me. Not to anyone who happened to pick up
his dog. The clinic is expanding. We've added a veterinarian and additional
help at the front desk. Charmaine is new and must have misunderstood
what I told her. I'm sorry you had to wait."

He smiled and his resemblance to George Clooney got even stronger.

"That's okay, Dr. Fuller. I was just a bit worried because Barnacle is
pretty important to a little boy I know."

"Dominic. Yes, I'm aware. The first time he and Gabe brought Barnacle
in, he made me show him my diploma to prove that I was really qualified to
take care of his dog. And please, it's Tom."

The door opened behind him then, nearly hitting Tom in the back. A
woman with lots of layered blond hair burst into the room. Her eyes were
the same color as the blue smock she wore, and they had the sparkle of
someone who thinks life is a pretty fun gift. She was pushing a vacuum
cleaner with one hand, and a pair of yellow gloves peeked out of her
pocket.

"Oops! Sorry, Doc!" she said in a cheery voice that didn't convey much
sorrow at all.

"Jan, please remember to knock before you come into an exam room.
I'm with a client."

It was clear to me that Tom wasn't pleased, but the woman seemed
oblivious.

"Right, absolutely. But I knew everybody was leaving early today, so I thought all the rooms were empty. Hi," she said turning to me. "I'm Jan Hudson. Sorry for barging in. That's a real cutie you've got there," she said, bending low to pat Barnacle. As she stood up, she said, "Wait a second," and peered closely at my face.

"You're Leah Nash, aren't you? My sister's reading one of your books right now. Your photo on the back looks just like you. Well, your hair is a little fancier in the photo. But I guess you had to get all dolled up when they took your picture, right?"

"Yes, I'm Leah Nash. And yes, they made me get 'all dolled up' for the photo. Most of the time, I look pretty much like this."

I waved my hand in the general direction of my reddish-brown hair, falling out of the clip intended to keep it off my neck, my face sans makeup, and the Badgers hoodie and jeans I was wearing.

"Hey, you know Miguel Santos, right? I listen to his podcast all the time. Do you think you could get me on it? I'm working on a book myself. It's about vampires. Did you see the Twilight movies? Well, my book is sort of like that, only—"

She had leaned a little on the handle of her vacuum cleaner, as though settling in for a chat.

At that point, Tom seized control of the conversation.

"Jan, would you excuse us, please?"

"What? Oh, sure, Doc. Sorry. I'll go across the hall, catch this one on my way back. No problem."

I was fighting hard not to laugh, because she was either unaware that her boss was unhappy with her at the moment, or she didn't care.

"Hey, do you have a business card or something, Leah? So I can follow up with you?"

"I'm sure Miss Nash—"

But I was already reaching in my purse as Tom spoke, and I handed it to her before he finished.

"Absolutely. Here you go, Jan. It was nice meeting you."

"Same here," she said with a grin. "Don't worry, Doc, I'll remember to knock next time."

She winked at him and then sashayed out of the room with the confidence of a woman very comfortable with herself.

"Jan is . . . you could say a big personality, I guess. I'm sorry for the interruption."

"It's fine. I liked her."

"I'm sorry your name didn't click at first. I know your partner at the paper, Miller, very well. His cat Sam is one of my patients. Tell him I shot a thirty-seven on the back nine at the club, and I'm going to smoke him the next time we play."

"I'll do that. So, are there any special instructions for Barnacle beyond what's in the discharge papers?"

"No. He's good to go."

"Okay, then. Thanks."

"My pleasure, and I'm sorry you had to wait."

"No worries. It was nice meeting you. I'll give Dominic a good report on you."

9

When Barnacle and I arrived at my place, I got out the cozy dog bed I keep for such occasions. He performed his ritual circling before lying down. After he did, he lifted his head slightly and smiled at me. Yes, I'm one of those people who believe dogs can smile.

"You're welcome, Barnacle. I'm just going to run downstairs and see what's going on. I'll be back shortly."

His eyes had closed before I left.

I found Miguel in the break room.

"Why's it so quiet? Is everyone gone for the day already?" I asked. Officially the office closes at five o'clock, but except for Courtnee, the receptionist, most of the staff work later.

"Maggie left early. Your mother is out front having a talk with Courtnee."

"What about?"

"You don't want to know."

"You're probably right."

As office manager, my mother does as good a job as anyone could supervising Courtnee. But trying to keep her focus on her job duties instead of her social calendar is a tough ride.

"Where's Troy?"

"He's using up some comp time taking some Scouts on a bird walk."

"Wait. Now Troy has a Scout troop? What about his seniors biking group, did he give that up?"

"No, no. It's Roger Delaney's troop, but Troy, he knows a lot about birds, so Roger asked him to lead the walk."

"Our Eagle Scout strikes again. Is Allie around? She said she wanted to talk to me about the clip portfolio she's putting together for her journalism class."

"She's doing a feature at the fairgrounds that Troy can't do because of his bird walk."

Allie Ross is a high school student who works part-time at the paper.

"She's really coming along, isn't she? Ross is afraid so much exposure to journalists is going to turn his daughter into one. I haven't had the heart to tell him it's too late. Allie already has the bug."

Allie's father, Charlie Ross, is a detective with the sheriff's office. He doesn't think much of reporters in general, and for a while he couldn't stand me, in particular. The feeling was mutual. But now we get along pretty well, most of the time.

"She does. But I know you didn't come down just to ask where everybody is. You came down to tell me yes about the 'One for the Books' fun run, didn't you?" Miguel asked.

"Actually, I did not."

"But you didn't come to tell me no, did you? You're still thinking about it, right?"

I sighed. I don't like turning Miguel down but running is not something I enjoy. In fact, I pretty much hate it.

"Miguel, I'm not still thinking about it. I already know my answer, but I didn't want to look in your puppy dog eyes when I say no. I've tried to get into running before. I just don't like it. I get hot. I get thirsty. I get sweaty, I mean really, really sweaty. And the last time I attempted it, I got shin splints. Why would I do that to myself?"

"Because the first ever "One for the Books" is a fundraiser for the Himmel Library. Because it's a fun run, not hard at all. Because you are a famous author and lots of people will make pledges for you, and we can raise more money. Because you love Miss Fillhart the librarian, and she's counting on you. Because it's only five K. Because—"

"All right, hold it right there. 'Only five K?' Miguel, that's over three miles."

"Just a tiny bit over. You can do it. It's not until the end of October. Troy already put together a training program for you."

"You asked Troy to do a training program for me before I've even said yes?"

"I'll do it with you. We go very easy at first, and then we build up. Before you know it, you'll be able to run ten miles if you want to."

He looked at my face and immediately amended his prediction.

"But why would you, when five K is the perfect amount for a morning run, or a charity run? Come on, it will be fun. It's for Miss Fillhart," he added in a wheedling voice that hit hard against my soft spot.

I love the Himmel Library. And Miss Fillhart. She helped me through one of the hardest times of my life, the year my sister Annie died, and my dad left. I'm not knocking counseling. But it was "reading therapy" that got me through.

"All right. Fine. I'll sign up to do the run. But I'm holding you to your promise on the training."

"Yes! We will start Monday!"

"Take it easy. I need to get running shoes. And I've got to spend some serious time on Charlotte's proposal. Plus, I have some other things on my plate. Let's start next Wednesday instead."

"I will pick you up Wednesday morning at six a.m."

"Six o'clock in the morning? What happened to the Miguel who hates to get up early?"

"If we want to stay on schedule then we should train early in the day before anything else can get in the way."

"Did I just overhear Leah commit to running in the library fundraiser?"

My mother asked the question as she walked through the doorway.

"You did, Carol. We are going to start training on Wednesday."

"I've been trying to persuade Leah to run with me for years. She always says no."

"She tried to tell me no, too, but—"

"But he's even better at guilting me than you are, Mom. He kept hammering that it was for the library and Miss Fillhart. I caved."

"I think that's great. I'm running in the fundraiser, too. We can have a little competition to see who has the best time. Winner buys the other two a drink at McClain's."

"You and Miguel can do as you like, but I'm opting out of any competition against *you*. You run every day! Don't you know that a mother is supposed to build up her child's confidence, not try to humiliate her?"

"Oh, stop it. You're not that bad—although it's true, I am that good. I probably would destroy you." She smiled to show she was joking, but I wasn't fooled.

My mother is very competitive and justifiably proud of her running prowess. She does three to five miles most days, and at sixty she's fit, trim, and looks a lot younger.

"Not probably, Mom. You would definitely destroy me. I'm in this for the fun part—if I can find any."

"But Carol, you have a good idea. Not about competing with our times, but we could do it with our pledges. We can see who will bring in the most."

"Another sucker bet," I said. "Only this time you'll be the clear winner, Miguel. In addition to the million people that you're close personal friends with, you've got all those strangers who listen to your podcast, and all you'll have to do is reach out to them."

"I think Leah's right. Let's just each do our thing, and all come together for the Himmel library," my mother said.

"Oh, sure, Mom. When you're not a shoo-in, all bets are off."

"You've got to know when to fold 'em, Leah. And I'm not about to go head-to-head with Miguel in the 'who has the most friends?' category. Hey, I thought Barnacle would be here with you. I saw you walking in with him a few minutes ago."

"He's upstairs resting. I picked him up from the vet's for Gabe. Oh, that reminds me, I ran into Davina Markham when I was going into the building. Did you know her cat Sabrina died? She's pretty upset."

"Oh, that's awful. She adored that cat. She brought her to work with her at the boutique every day. I wonder if they've ever even been apart before."

"Well, they won't be apart for long. Davina's going to be wearing Sabrina around her neck. She's having her cat's ashes made into a cremation diamond."

"What on earth is a cremation diamond?" my mother asked.

Courtnee unexpectedly supplied the answer as she came into the room.

"My grandma did that with my grandpa. See, you know like how diamonds are made of coal that gets squashed all together really, really hard? Well, ashes are made of the same thing coal is. So, if you want a diamond made from a dead person, you just take their ashes and squeeze them like super hard. I don't mean you, like a person, squeezes them. There's a machine that does it that can put like this whole lot of pressure on them."

"Courtnee, diamonds aren't made of coal. Coal and diamonds are both made of carbon, but coal has too much other junk in it to ever become a diamond."

"Well, that's what my grandma told me. And she has a cremation diamond of her own, so I think she probably knows, Leah."

Her pout indicated that she was ready to make a stand for her fact-free tutorial on cremation diamonds.

Miguel gave me a look that I knew meant: *She's not going to give up. Just let it go.*

"Courtnee, I think that's very nice for your grandma. With the grandpa diamond she can always be close to her *novio* who she loved so much," he said to placate her.

"She didn't like Grandpa that much, really. When he died, Grandma said, 'The cheap bastard never got me a diamond ring. Now he's going to *be* one!'"

As frequently happens when engaged in conversation with Courtnee, none of us knew what to say to that, so we all just stopped talking and walked away.

10

"Leah, thanks a million for picking up Barnacle," Gabe said.

"You're welcome. According to your vet, he came through like a trooper and just needs a little time to sleep away the aftereffects of the anesthesia."

"You saw Tom? I only ever get a vet assistant for checking out."

"There was kind of a mix-up at the front desk. He wanted to see you, to ask a question about some legal work you're doing for him, but his instructions got garbled by the receptionist. He was a little surprised to see my smiling face waiting for him in the exam room."

"I'll give him a call tomorrow. Listen, I have to run now. But seriously, call if you want to talk about your book."

"My non-book, you mean? Thanks. Right now, I'm still feeling too whiny to get into it."

We both turned at the sound of the door opening behind us. Coop walked in, carrying a Bonucci's Pizza box. I love him very much.

"Gabe, hey. How you doing? I hear my best deputy sheriff Dominic is due back in town this weekend."

"Hi, Coop. Yes, he is. He'll be ready to report for duty, I'm sure."

Coop smiled. He really likes kids.

"Good to know. Tell him I'll be in touch after he gets settled back into school. How are things going at the sheriff's office?" Gabe asked.

"Not bad. Hey, I've got hot pizza here, do you want to join us?"

"I would, but I've got a date with a realtor."

"A date-date, or a looking for a house date?" I asked.

"Looking for a house. The duplex feels like it's getting a little small for us, and I'd like Dominic to have a bigger yard to play in. She's showing me a couple of houses tonight, and we'll see. Come on boy," he said, bending down and attaching Barnacle's leash.

"Thanks again, Leah."

"No worries."

───────────────

"So, this is what you get up to when I'm hard at work. Clandestine meetings with your ex-boyfriend," Coop said as we moved around the kitchen getting plates and glasses.

"Yes, Barnacle is our cover story. Are you jealous?"

"Should I be?"

"You can ask me that when you came in carrying Bonucci's pizza for dinner? You can keep your Chris Hemsworths, and your George Clooneys, even your Idris Elbas. My allegiance is to the man with the Bonucci's pizza in hand."

"Oh, so you'd have the same feelings for the pizza delivery boy?"

"Umm, let me think a minute. If he looked like you, maybe."

I don't think about it often, probably because I've known him so long, but Coop is very good-looking. He's tall, with short dark hair, and dark gray eyes. He has a quiet demeanor, a wry sense of humor, and a great smile.

Coop's phone rang and while he answered it, I finished setting drinks and plates on the kitchen island. I could tell it was work from his end of the conversation and also that it wasn't great news.

"So, am I eating this alone?" I asked, pointing at the pizza. "It sounded like something serious is going on."

"It is, but Charlie's got it under control. He's out at Boyd Hanson's farm. Looks like Boyd killed himself this afternoon."

"Oh, no! His poor son Noah! Is Ross sure it's suicide?"

"There's no note at the scene. And it's not officially suicide until the medical examiner calls it, but Charlie says the signs are all there. Boyd was shot with his own gun, sitting at his kitchen table, with an empty bottle of Jim Beam beside him. No signs of a struggle or a break-in. Connie told Ross she'd be pretty surprised if the autopsy doesn't verify suicide."

Connie Crowley is a retired physician who works part-time as Grantland County's medical examiner.

"I can't imagine feeling so down and desperate that suicide seems the only way out."

"Me either, but I guess we've been lucky enough never to have been out of options. Boyd felt like he was. It's a damn shame."

He shook his head and rubbed the back of his neck with his hand, a sure sign that he's troubled.

"Who found him? I hope it wasn't Noah."

"Afraid it was. And it gets worse. Noah told Charlie that he and his dad had a bad argument. Noah stormed off and went to a friend's house. He got feeling bad about it this afternoon and drove back out to the farm to apologize. But when he got there, Boyd was dead."

"It couldn't get much worse than that. Suicide leaves such a load of guilt for the people left behind. And when you think how hopeless, how lost, the person who killed himself must have felt . . ." I said.

"Yeah."

We sat down to our pizza, but neither of us had much appetite, or much to say. It's not that either of us knew Boyd well—in my case, I didn't know him at all. Still, when you hear bad news, even about someone you're not close to, it hits you with the reminder of how tenuous your own hold on happiness is. Or maybe that's just me. I've lost enough people I love to never take just being alive for granted.

After dinner, Coop brought up my book.

"So, I had a chance to read some of your manuscript at lunch."

"And? Come on, just get it over with."

"I think it's good."

"You didn't think that the lead character doesn't come alive? You must not have read far enough."

"I read enough to know I like the plot, and the setting, and the pace. But I—"

"But you think there's 'no there, there' when it comes to Jo Burke right? You couldn't connect, she's not fleshed out, etc., etc. Go ahead, you can say it. It's not like I haven't heard it already."

"Leah, could I finish a sentence, please?"

"Fine. Finish."

"Now don't get mad at what I say, just listen for a minute."

"That's not the greatest way to start out."

"I thought you were going to let me finish."

I leaned back, my arms crossed in front of my chest. "So, finish."

"I agree with Clinton that Jo's character doesn't really come to life. But I think that's because you don't want her to. You don't want readers to see how she feels or understand why she reacts to a situation the way she does."

"Oh? And why would I want to write a lead character who has no inner life and no emotions?"

I had tried not to sound defensive but didn't succeed. Sometimes, even if you don't admit it, you really do want unconditional support from the people you love, not hard truths.

"Because Jo is so much like you, and you don't like people to see that beneath your tough exterior, there's a lot of vulnerability. You're not letting readers see the whole Jo, because you don't like people to know the whole you."

I felt an unexpected, and unwelcome, jolt of recognition, but I fought to deny it.

"Oh, really? When did you find time to pick up both a psychology degree and a literary criticism minor? I'm very impressed."

He shook his head.

"No, you're irritated because what I said is spot on and you know it. I imagine it's a risk all writers take—revealing themselves through their characters."

"You're wrong," I said flatly. "I'm not afraid of revealing myself through Jo. It's fiction, remember? Jo isn't anything like me. She's in law enforcement for one thing. She grew up in an intact family. She's older than me—she's in her forties. She's taller. And thinner. She—"

"I'm not talking about physical characteristics, or family situations, or careers. I'm saying she responds to situations like you do—she's intuitive, she's smart, she's funny—and she's prickly sometimes. But she doesn't feel real, because you don't let anyone know what motivates her, why she's the way she is, what hurts she's hiding."

"Oh, I see. So, you're saying the book would be better if I had her dissolving into a sticky pool of sentimentality on every third page."

"You know that's not what I said. And you gave me your manuscript to read for my response. Bottom line, here it is. The writing is good, the plot is engaging. But Clinton is right. It's hard to connect with your main character because you don't show the reader anything about why she says and does things. That's all."

"Noted. I don't want to get into a fight with you. Let's just drop it."

"If that's what you want."

"It is."

It wasn't, not really. What I wanted was for him to tell me that my book was great, Clinton was wrong, and I was right to want to just pack it in, return the advance and pretend it never happened. Since he wouldn't, or couldn't, I moved on.

"New subject. I really think that Charlotte's proposal could work for the *Times*. And if *GO News* stays in shutdown mode, that will take a lot of pressure off. Miller and I are going to meet Tuesday to talk about it."

"That's good to hear. Want to expand on the particulars?"

"No, I'll wait to drown you in details until after Miller and I go over things. How about your work stuff? I haven't heard anything about the Grangers lately. It's not like them to be so quiet. Anything new going on?"

The Grangers are a sprawling family whose members mostly make their livings by dealing drugs, illegal sports betting, small-time breaking and entering, and assorted miscellaneous crime-ing.

"Nope. It could be that Harley Granger getting sent back to prison put the fear of God into them, for now, anyway. It's actually been pretty quiet at the office. Had a disappointment today, though. The woman I offered Owen Fike's old job to turned it down. She got a better offer in Marathon County. It's a lot bigger office, more room for advancement."

"Hey, I've said it before, you should ask Marla to apply for the job."

Marla Jarvis has been a road patrol deputy her entire time with the sheriff's office. She tried for promotion under previous regimes, but she didn't get anywhere.

"She's smart. She's experienced. She's capable. And she finished her bachelor's degree last year. She's supervised and trained new recruits. She—"

"She also told me when I was still at the Himmel Police Department that she was counting the days until she could take early retirement."

"That's because she never caught a break from Dillingham or Lamey when they were the sheriff. It's different now with you there. She could do a great job for you, Coop. She already knows every nook and cranny in this county, and who frequents them. She's only forty-five. That's too young to retire."

"You don't have to hard sell Marla to me. She's a good cop. She's got initiative, too. She just came to me with a tip on someone selling weed to high school kids at the park. She developed the source, so I'm letting her run with it. But she's never said anything to me about wanting to move up. I have to figure it's because she's not interested."

"It could also be because the door's been shut in her face once too often. And she's not eager for it to happen again."

"That's possible. But she needs to put herself out there if she wants it."

"She could probably use a little encouragement. I'm telling you she wants to do more than write speeding tickets and settle bar fights. Doesn't the fact that she came up with the weed-in-the-park lead and is running with it prove that? I really think she could do a good job for you. You should give her a chance."

"If she wants to be considered for promotion, she needs to make her own case. If she does, we'll see."

11

I spent most of the weekend reading Charlotte's proposal, making notes, and researching nonprofit news organizations online. By late Sunday afternoon, I was ready for a break. I stood up from the window seat, stretched my arms up high, gave a yawn so large and loud it would have made a waking lion proud, and then called Coop.

"Hey, how do you feel about meeting at McClain's for a burger basket? I just finished my final run-through of Charlotte's proposal and I could use some sustenance—and a Jameson."

"Sounds good. But make mine a cheeseburger and a beer. Give me half an hour. I've been working on the bookcase I'm building for my sister, and I need to clean up."

"Great. I'll order for you. See you shortly."

It was pretty empty when I walked in, which is typical for a Sunday night at McClain's. I had no problem snagging a booth in the back.

"All alone, Leah? What's the matter? Did you and Coop have a fight?"

"Sorry to disappoint you, Sherry, but no, we didn't."

She shrugged. "Doesn't hurt to ask, right?"

Sherry is a very pretty waitress with big brown eyes and curly hair. We were in high school together. She's dialed back the obvious crush she has on Coop since we "came out" as a couple. Her question told me she hadn't given up all hope, but it's not a crime to hope.

"Nope, it doesn't hurt to ask. Coop should be along in a minute. How about bringing me a burger basket, a glass of water, and a Jameson. And make it a cheeseburger basket and a Leinenkugel for Coop."

The door opened just then, letting a stream of light into the gloomy bar as Coop walked in and over to the booth.

"Hi, Leah. Hey, Sherry, how are you?"

She smiled and batted her eyelashes at him. "Just fine, Sheriff. Leah gave me your order and I'm just off to the kitchen to put it in. You let me know if there's anything else you need."

"Thanks, I will."

She walked away slowly to give Coop ample time to admire her trim but curvy figure. Which, I am happy to say he did not—or if he did, he was too subtle for me to see it.

"She still has a crush on you, you know. One of these days she's going to hit me over the head with a beer bottle and take off with you."

"I'd have to be willing for that to happen. You play your cards right, I won't be," he said with a grin.

I rolled my eyes in response. As I did, I caught a glimpse of Charlotte Caldwell approaching our booth.

"It's so dark in here coming in from the outside I wasn't sure it was you," she said with a smile.

"Hi, do you want to join us?"

"Thanks, but I'm just here to pick up a to-go order at the bar. I'm having dinner with a friend."

I wondered if the "friend" was the man I'd seen her with outside of Woke coffee shop a few days ago.

"Order up for Caldwell!"

Charlotte looked over her shoulder and waved to indicate she'd be right there.

"It looks like I'd better get going if I don't want to deliver cold burgers."

"Just a sec, Charlotte. I have to tell you how impressed I am with your proposal. I have a meeting with your dad about it on Tuesday morning. You did some great work on it."

To my surprise she flushed with pleasure. I never think that people like Charlotte—poised, perfect, professional—need praise. But I guess when it comes down to it, we all do.

"Thank you. That means a lot. I—"

She was interrupted by a commotion coming from the pool room in the back of the bar. As we all looked in that direction, we saw Miguel and Troy walking toward the front door of McClain's with a friend who didn't look too steady on his feet. Miguel saw us and waved, but he didn't come over like he normally would. He and Troy seemed to be trying to prop up their friend or hold him back. We soon saw which it was.

"That's Noah Hanson," Coop said. He looked up as though he'd heard Coop and squinted in our direction, trying to bring us into focus. Then he shook off Miguel and Troy and stumbled toward our booth.

"I know who you are!" he said, when he came within a few feet of Charlotte.

"I'm sorry. Have we met?" she asked.

"I'm sorry. Have we met?" he repeated her words in a high-pitched mockery of Charlotte's pleasant voice. "No, we haven't met. I'm Noah Hanson. Boyd Hanson's son. But I know who you are. I saw your picture in the paper. A happy little story about you and your dad, so happy to work together." The slight slurring of his words confirmed that he'd had too much to drink.

"I see. Well, yes we are. But if you'll excuse me, I—"

"Excuse you for what your dad did to mine? I don't think so. Thanks to *your* asshole father, I don't have one anymore."

"Noah, come on, let's go," Miguel said, putting his hand on Noah's shoulder. He ignored it.

"Did you know my father killed himself?"

"I don't—"

"You don't what? Don't know? Don't care? Don't know what to say? My dad shot himself because your rich old man took away the only chance he had. And I, he was, I—"

He swayed on his feet a little and tripped over his words, whether because of the alcohol or the emotion I couldn't tell. He took a breath and went on.

"My dad was good man, a good father, and he died thinking he wasn't. What do you care, though? You've got your rich daddy, your perfect life. You Caldwells, you have everything. Why did you have to take away the one thing that my father needed? My dad wouldn't be dead if it wasn't for your father. I hate Miller Caldwell. I hate you, too. I hate your whole effing family."

Noah started to cry then, covering his face with his hands as harsh, ugly sobs wracked his body.

Charlotte's face had drained of color.

"Noah, let's go back to my place. Come on, it's been a hard day," Troy said.

He succeeded in getting his arm around Noah's shoulder. In a swift aside Troy said, "I've got this, Miguel. We'll catch you later."

The fight seemed to have left Noah, and he allowed himself to be led out of the bar.

"Charlotte, I am so sorry," Miguel said. "Noah didn't mean it. Today was just a very, very bad day for him. He's been drinking too much and thinking about his *papi*. If we knew you were here, we would have taken him out the side door."

"No, it's all right, Miguel. Don't worry about it. It's fine. I understand," Charlotte said. But it was obvious she was shaken by the verbal attack—who wouldn't be? She excused herself and left.

"Miguel, sit down a minute," I said. "What was that all about? I mean, I know it was about Boyd's suicide. But what triggered Noah to make such a scene—just the sight of Charlotte?"

"You said it was a very bad day for Noah. What happened?" Coop asked.

Miguel had slid into the booth next to me, but before he could answer, Sherry delivered our orders.

"Wow, what was up with that guy? I couldn't tell what he was saying, but I could hear him yelling all the way in the back," she said.

"He just had too much to drink, and he didn't want to leave," Coop said. I knew that he was trying to keep Noah's meltdown from entering the Himmel gossip pipeline.

Miguel did his best to distract Sherry by complimenting her new haircut. She preened in response, but I had no doubt the story of Noah's attack on the Caldwell family would soon be circulating. Sherry would get everything out of the bartender later. When she left, Miguel answered Coop's question.

"Today, we went with Noah to pick up his father's ashes and take them to his farm. Noah wanted to scatter them where his mother's ashes are. He's all alone now. He has no family. No brothers or sisters. Not even any cousins. I cannot imagine," Miguel said. He grew up without a dad or siblings, but with a lot of family in the form of his mom, his aunts, uncles, cousins, and a grandmother.

"That must have been a tough thing to do. I'm glad he had you guys with him," I said.

"It was very sad, but then it got even sadder."

"How?"

"Noah is staying with Troy for a while. He needed to get some things from his house. He went upstairs to get them while we waited, and when he came back, he was crying so hard we couldn't understand him."

"You mean because it was so emotional, being back in the house where his dad died?"

"No, it was because he found a letter from his father. His dad put it under a family picture in Noah's bedroom."

"What did it say?"

"That he was so sorry for losing the farm, and so ashamed he used the money they saved for Noah's medical school to try and save it. And that he was so tired, and so lonely. Then he said he loved Noah so much, but he would be better off without him now. It was time for him to go to Dottie—that was Noah's mother."

Miguel's words took me back to when I had read a similar letter my dad left behind—and the gut punch it had been.

"Yeah, that would knock the wind out of anybody," Coop said. "But maybe later on, he'll be glad that his father didn't leave without saying goodbye."

"I don't think so. In the letter, his father also told him there is a life insurance policy he took out when Noah was born. He said now Noah can use it to pay for medical school. Noah kept saying 'My dad killed himself for me. What am I supposed to do with that?'"

"That's a hell of a burden for him to carry," I said.

Miguel nodded.

"We got him away from the farm and we thought we would come to McClain's for something to eat. He has hardly eaten anything since his father died. But when we got here, he just started drinking. And he kept saying over and over how he never had a chance to say sorry to his father for the big fight they had. We finally got him to leave but when we came out, there was Charlotte and . . ." His voice trailed off.

"What was his dad thinking? Noah will never get over this," I said.

My father hadn't committed suicide, but he'd made a terrible mess of his life, and ours, like Boyd had for himself and his son. And like Boyd, he'd made things so much worse by deciding we would be better off without him. My heart ached for Noah.

"I doubt Boyd was thinking," Coop said. "He was feeling, and what he felt was loneliness, and guilt, and failure. He just wanted it to be over. The bad thing is, it's over for Boyd, but it's going to be with Noah for a good long time."

12

"Well, Miller, I've had my say, now tell me where you land on Charlotte's proposal."

We were sitting in Miller's office on Tuesday morning, and I'd come out strongly in favor of moving the *Times* to a nonprofit organization.

"I think the proposal is well thought out, and we need to do something to ensure the viability of the *Times*. There is another way we could go, though. Before Charlotte's proposal, I'd been thinking we might invite some additional investors in. How does that idea strike you?"

I concentrated on keeping a neutral expression at the suggestion of investors as I formulated a reasoned response. But my instant reaction was a hard no. The *Times* didn't need a gaggle of investors all expecting to make a profit and all filled with ideas about how to water down the news to do it. That would be only slightly better than having A-H Media, the hedge fund that had killed the original *Himmel Times*, own us.

"Leah, if anyone invites you to play poker, I'd suggest you decline. I can see exactly what you think of the idea of investors by the expression on your face."

He smiled then, and it was easy to see why a lot of women in town had wept into their brandy old fashioneds when he had come out as gay.

"I said I'd been *thinking* about investors, not that I had started preparing an IPO. But I believe Charlotte's idea is a much better fit for what we want to do."

"Whew," I said as I mimicked wiping my brow. "I'm glad we're in agreement. But we're going to have to rethink some of the positions at the *Times*. Like the sales staff. Randy and Lori are going to need training to shift from selling ads to cultivating sponsors and members. I think Lori will be good, but Randy? I'm not sure."

"I agree, but I'd like to make that Charlotte's challenge, not ours. What do you think about naming her head of this transition project? I know she's young. But—and I'm not saying this as a doting father, even though I am one—she's very bright, and she works hard, too. She came up with the idea, I'd like to let her run with it."

"Hey, you don't have to convince me. Restructuring an organization is way out of my skill set, and you certainly don't have the time. I'm good with Charlotte in charge of it. We'll both be there to consent or put the brakes on if we need to."

"Thank you, Leah."

"For what?"

"For trusting that I'm not making the recommendation based on nepotism. And thank you for inviting me to join forces with you. Turning things around for the *Himmel Times* is one of the more meaningful projects I've been involved with."

"'Inviting you,' Miller? As I recall, I begged you. And there wouldn't be a *Times* today without you—or much happening in downtown Himmel, either. I owe you the thanks. I feel really lucky to have you for a business partner, and for a friend."

"I appreciate you saying that, Leah. Since Boyd's suicide I've been questioning myself. Wondering if I've been too focused on the vision I want to pursue, and not enough on the impact my choices have on others."

"Put that out of your head. Boyd's suicide is not your fault. It was the tragic end of a long line of bad choices that Boyd made, not you. I really believe that, and you should, too. Now let's finish up this meeting before Patty kicks me out."

We talked more about a possible timeline and the logistics of things, but soon realized we didn't have enough information to come up with the answers.

"Let's do this. You tell Charlotte what we've decided. Then let's meet again with Charlotte, you, me, and the staff so they know what the plan is, and that Charlotte will be getting very involved in our daily lives as she pulls things together. I don't see much pushback. Well, maybe from Maggie, a little. We just need to emphasize that Charlotte's in charge of the transition, and we need everyone to be on board with it," I said.

"Agreed."

"The sooner the better for the meeting. How about this afternoon?" I asked.

"I can't do it today. How about tomorrow morning?"

"How early? I'm supposed to start training for the October library fun run with Miguel tomorrow. He'll think I just set up the meeting to get out of running. We're supposed to run at six, and I'll need time to take a shower and possibly oxygen after we get done."

"I'm doing the 'One for the Books' run as well. We can't let Claudia down, can we? How about eight thirty?"

"Yeah, that sounds good. Oh, I forgot to tell you. I met Tom Fuller the other day when I picked Barnacle up for Gabe. He said to tell you he shot a thirty-seven on the back nine, whatever that means, and he's coming for you. He was pretty cocky about beating you next time you play."

"He'll have to do better than that. The day I can't beat a Sunday golfer like Tom is the day I hang up my golf shoes."

"Miller! That's some pretty great trash-talking. If only the world knew that beneath your calm and pleasant exterior lies a cutthroat competitor."

"It's how I keep my edge, Leah. Don't put the word out."

"Your secret is safe with me."

"Thank you. Now, let me double-check my calendar for tomorrow to be sure it's clear for our meeting."

As he opened his computer and pulled up his calendar, Patty knocked and walked in.

"Are you self-scheduling again, Miller? I'm here, right outside your office. I'm your secretary. We've talked about this before. When we both schedule business meetings, that's when you get into scheduling conflicts, and that's when I have to sort them out."

"Guilty as charged, Patty. Do you have some kind of radar that goes off when I touch my calendar?"

"No, but that's something I'll look into. I just wanted to remind you that you need to leave in the next ten minutes, or you won't make it to your meeting in Madison on time."

She gave me a stern look to indicate it was past time for me to go. Many people are deceived by Patty's soft white curls and twinkly blue eyes. But I know that underneath her Mrs. Santa Claus facade, she can be as tough as a drill sergeant—especially when it comes to protecting Miller's schedule.

"Okay, okay, Patty. I'm leaving, but not without a toast to the future of the *Times*, which, thanks to Miller and his brilliant daughter Charlotte, is looking much rosier. Come on, join me," I said, picking up a bottle of water and raising it high. Patty was not in the mood.

"I'm very happy for you, but Gabe is leaving for court, and I have to find a file that he's misplaced. I don't have time for nonsense this morning."

"Way to kill my buzz, Patty. Miller, I'm out of here. I'll ask Mom to get the meeting together on our end. Have a great rest of your day. And despite your scolding, I wish you the same, Patty."

I lifted the water bottle in a mock salute.

She shook her head, but as I moved past her I saw the small smile on her face. She won't admit it, but I know she likes a little nonsense now and then. I would have savored my happy feeling more, if I had known then that it would be a long time before I felt that lighthearted again.

I called Coop on my walk back to the *Times*.

"Hey, I had a great meeting already today, and it's not even nine o'clock. What are you doing tonight?"

"I've got a poker game with the guys at eight. Why?"

"I want you to come over for dinner tonight to celebrate. I promise you won't miss your game, and I'll make my signature dish."

"You're in a good mood! By signature dish, are you referring to Honey Nut Cheerios with blueberries added?"

"No, not that signature dish. My Grandma Neeka's meatloaf. I'll also throw in some mashed potatoes and a veg. Dessert might even be on the menu, too."

"That must have been some meeting. What happened?"

"The takeaway is that Miller and I are going full steam ahead on Charlotte's idea, and I am feeling uncharacteristically optimistic about it. If you want to share my joy, I'll see you around six and give you all the details. Plus feed you."

"Sounds great. I've got some news you're going to like, too."

"What?"

"Nope. I want to deliver this in person. I'll see you later."

13

"So, that's the story, Mom, in brief. Could you get everyone together for an eight thirty meeting here, tomorrow with Miller, me, and Charlotte? And please don't forget to check in with Patty. You know how she guards his calendar."

"Well, it isn't easy being a secretary to a busy man like Miller."

"It's not easy being a receptionist either," Courtnee chimed in as she entered the break room where Mom and I were talking. She paused as she caught her reflection in the toaster and fluffed out her blond bangs before she continued.

"My mom says you guys take advantage of me and I should go back to the job I had at Himmel Tech."

"If that's still an option—which I somehow doubt—feel free to exercise it if you're not happy here, Courtnee," I said.

"I didn't say I wasn't happy. But like if everything's going to be so great like I heard you telling Carol, then I think I should get more money. And an assistant."

"I think you missed eavesdropping on the part where I said this was going to be a lot of hard work for everyone, and people will need to adapt and be patient while we figure things out. There are no plans for anyone to get an immediate raise. So, maybe you should listen to your mom and look for another job. Mother knows best, right?"

"I'm glad, though startled, to hear you admit that, Leah," my mother said. "But I think Courtnee needs to get back to the front desk. She and I can discuss her job goals later, right Courtnee?"

Courtnee stopped just short of rolling her eyes—she's a little scared of my mother. But her expression clearly said, "Okay, boomer." Still, she left without comment.

"I've got to return a few phone calls," my mother said, pushing back her chair and standing. Then she added, "That reminds me, did you get feedback from Clinton on your book yet? I still can't believe you didn't let your own mother read your draft."

I'd been putting off telling her the bad news about my book. She'd made such a big deal of telling me how she knew I could do it, what a good writer I was, how confident she was in me. I didn't want to disappoint her. But now that I had the opening, I knew I should get it over with.

"There isn't going to be a book, Mom. I got the word from Clinton that my draft is bad, and I need to do major revisions. I don't want to do them. I tried, Mom, but I'm just not a fiction writer."

"Oh, hon, I'm so sorry. But that doesn't sound like Clinton. He's always been in your corner. Did he really say your book was bad?"

"Not exactly, but that was the gist of it. He said my lead character was flat and readers wouldn't relate to her unless I let them see more of her feelings, and motivations, and things. I don't know how to do that."

"Don't know how, or don't want to?"

A suspicion began to form in my mind. Her next words made it take shape.

"I've read that fiction writers can't help infusing their characters with at least some of their own personality. Maybe it's not that you can't write the character, it's that you're holding back from doing it. Is that possible?"

"Wait just a minute. You've been talking to Coop, haven't you?"

"I talk to Coop all the time. We're very good friends. In fact, I talked to him just this morning when I ran into Woke for a latte. I want him to refinish my end tables. They've got a lot of scratches, and Paul is not good about using coasters, no matter how often I remind him. And then we got talking about you and Coop driving to Madison with us next weekend for lunch at Monty's Diner, and—"

"Mom. Much as I'm fascinated by your furniture problems, and excited by the prospect of lunch at Monty's, I think what you and Coop have talked about recently is his theory."

"What theory would that be?"

"Give it up. Your casual comments about my writing difficulties are almost exactly the same thing that Coop said. You already knew that Clinton wants a rewrite, and I don't want to do it, didn't you?"

"Fine. Yes, I did. I just thought if you heard the same encouragement from two different people you might give it a little more consideration. Leah, don't be so stubborn. From what I understand, Clinton said some very nice things about your manuscript. I know it had to hurt to hear him say you missed the mark on your lead character, but I don't understand why you want to just quit. That's not like you."

"Writing fiction isn't like me, Mom. I'm not quitting. I'm just facing facts. Anyway, I don't want to talk about it anymore, okay?"

"Okay. Then just *think* about it longer, before you make up your mind. And one of the things to ponder is if it's possible that you're not 'facing facts.' Instead, you're not facing your fear of failure. Writing fiction is new to you. So you didn't nail it the first time, so what? You'll get it—if you want it bad enough. Fear of failure will hurt you more in the long run than the actual fail. And if you put aside your self-doubt, you won't fail. I know you can do this."

"Mom, thanks. I appreciate your faith in me, I really do. I'll think about it some more, but—"

"Stop right there. 'I'll think about it' is enough for the moment. Would you like some comfort food while you're thinking? I've got some brownies in the freezer at home."

"Those will be perfect for dessert. I'm making Grandma Neeka's meatloaf for dinner with Coop tonight. Thanks for the offer, and for the support, and I guess, all right, thanks for the advice. I'll see you later."

After lunch I checked my cupboards and realized I'd have to run to the store to pick up the ingredients for my promised mealtime extravaganza. It's not that the menu called for anything unusual. It's that I rarely have the building blocks of a substantive dinner in my kitchen. If you're looking for snack foods, ice cream, or a PB&J sandwich, I'm your girl. If you're in the mood for a meal, some shopping needs to happen. I dashed out to the grocery store, picked up what I needed, made a stop at my mother's freezer for the brownies, zipped home, and got to work.

When all was in readiness—meatloaf in the oven, potatoes peeled, and kitchen returned to its normal state of pretty clean instead of the chaos I'd created, I sat down for a minute to relax and check something in Charlotte's proposal. I went to get it, but it wasn't on my desk where it should have been. I realized I'd left it at Miller's office when Patty hustled me out. It was only four thirty. I had time to make it there before the office closed.

Patty wasn't sitting at her desk when I walked in. Her computer was turned off, so I knew she had left for the day. Miller's door was closed, but I just needed to grab my folder, so I tapped on the door and opened it.

"Hi Miller, I hate to bother you, but—Oh! I'm so sorry!" I added as I noticed the woman seated in the visitor's chair in front of Miller's desk.

"I didn't realize you were with someone, or I wouldn't have barged in. I'm sorry," I repeated, this time directing it toward the woman who I assumed was a client.

"That's all right, we're finished," she said, standing to leave. She was fine-boned and very thin—the kind of woman who makes me, with my sturdy Midwestern build, feel like Paul Bunyan's long-lost daughter.

"I'll just be a minute, Leah," Miller said as he rose to walk his client to the door.

"Thank you for everything. I'll let you know how it goes," the woman said.

When he came back to his desk, I apologized again.

"I wouldn't have come in, but I saw Patty was gone. I know she never deserts her post unless you don't have any appointments."

"Patty had to leave early today to pick up her grandson. I assume this is what you came for? I was going to drop it off on my way home," he said as he picked the folder up from his desk and handed it to me.

"That's out of your way, so I'm glad you didn't. But speaking of home, I have to scoot. I'm making dinner. A real one with meat, and potatoes, and a vegetable. Shocking, right? Don't try to deny it. I see that look of surprise you're trying to hide. I *can* cook—a few things, anyway."

I took the folder and smiled at him, then turned to go.

"I'm never surprised by the things you can do, Leah. You even turned me into a newspaper man, when that was the last thing on my mind."

It was a casual remark, delivered with a smile. But I felt a warm rush of pleasure at his words. I surprised both of us by giving him a quick hug.

"Thanks, Miller. You're the best. And you know what else? I'm just putting this out there, but if you ever decide to reconsider the whole gay thing, you'd go right to the top of my back-up list in case things don't work out with Coop."

"I'm honored," he said. "But I'm afraid 'the whole gay thing' isn't going to change. No matter how tempting the prospect of being on your back-up list is."

"That's fair. Like I said, just putting it out there. I'll see you tomorrow."

"I'm looking forward to it."

14

"That was really good," Coop said as he finished the last bite of his brownie.

"Thank you. I can't take credit for the brownies. Those were from Mom's freezer. But the rest I did."

"Well, it was great. And so was the news about the paper. I'm happy for all of you and I hope it works out the way you want it to."

"It will," I said. "I just have a really good feeling about this. But I spent the whole dinner talking about my stuff. Your turn. What's going on at the sheriff's office? On the phone you said you had some news I'd like."

"Marla is taking the sergeant's exam."

"Really? She's decided not to take early retirement?"

"Yes. After you and I talked, I called her in—"

"You talked to her about rethinking retirement? Coop! That's great. I can't believe you actually listened to me."

"Just because I don't always do what you want me to do, it doesn't mean I don't listen to you. Yes, we had a good talk. She told me pretty much what you'd said about being tired of hitting a wall every time she tried for a promotion. I told her it didn't have to be that way, but if she wanted to move up, she'd have to put herself out there—take the sergeant's exam and apply for the position. She's going to do it."

"But Owen's position was lieutenant."

"I can't justify jumping Marla up from deputy to lieutenant. She needs more experience as a supervisor and more time leading investigations, too. But I can change the position we're looking to fill. I think Marla will do really well."

"Then why did you give me such a hard time when I brought the idea up?"

"I don't think I did. I just like some time to think things through. When I have, then I decide."

My phone rang and I saw the call was from Miguel.

"Hey, Miguel. Did you get the word from Mom about the meeting tomorrow?"

"Yes, I'm very excited. But I'm calling to be sure you remember about our date tomorrow."

"Our date? Sorry, I'm drawing a blank."

"I don't think you are. You just don't want to remember that you promised to start training with me tomorrow morning. But you did, *chica*, you did."

"Well, but it's raining pretty hard. Thunder and lightning, too. It's not safe to run in a lightning storm. I think we should start training next week."

"It's storming now, yes. But I checked the weather. It will be over by midnight and then we will have a perfect morning to run tomorrow. I will pick you up at six a.m. We have to start the training and stay with it. You don't want to finish last, do you?"

"I'll just be happy to finish at all."

"No, no. By the time you are trained, you will be ready to run a very good race. And you will love it. See you tomorrow."

"Six a.m. I'll meet you out back in the parking lot."

"Where are you going at six a.m.?" Coop asked when I hung up.

"Didn't I tell you that Miguel pressured me to enter the 'One for The Books' run for the library?"

"You hate running."

"I know, but Miguel knows how to get to me. He used Miss Fillhart. You know how I feel about the library. So now we're training for it, starting tomorrow. Want to come along?"

"No thanks. But tell Miguel I'll want pictures."

"No way. But let's get back to Marla. I'm proud of you."

"Because I did what you told me to do?"

"No, because you recognized her potential and you're giving her a chance. Also, I didn't tell you what to do."

"Really? 'You need to give her a chance, Coop.' Sounds like an order to me."

"I forgot to say the first part. *Do you think* you need to give her a chance. But it was implied."

"Uh-huh. Okay, I've got to get going or I'll be late for my poker game. Dinner was really good, thank you. Good luck on your first day of training. Call me when you get back."

"If I survive, I will."

***

"Okay, how much farther do we have to run?"

I huffed out the words the next morning as Miguel and I neared a curve in the trail at the county park.

"Not far," said Miguel, who was breathing much more easily than I was.

I also had rivulets of sweat running off my neck and down my back, while he had not yet begun to glow.

"We'll stop at the water fountain around the curve, outside the tunnel and then run back the way we came. You're doing great!"

"If by great you mean breathing so heavy I sound like an obscene phone caller then yes, I'm doing great."

"It's the first day. I'm telling you, you will love it. I—" he slowed as we rounded the curve where the promised water fountain waited.

"Hey, why are you slowing down? I've got to get to that water or I'm going to pass out," I said.

"No, look!"

He had come to a full stop, and I followed the direction his arm was pointing. An ambulance was parked near the entrance to the old railroad tunnel that had been incorporated into the main running trail through the county park. We didn't see anyone lying on the ground, so whoever needed medical attention must be in the tunnel.

"Probably someone who was training for the race passed out, like I'm about to."

Then I noticed a sheriff's car parked off to the side, and we both heard the sound of sirens approaching.

We looked at each other for a second. Even if what had occurred inside the tunnel was a medical emergency, it wouldn't bring out so many cop cars. Something bad had happened.

We moved closer to the scene, taking care not to get in the way as we tried to see what was happening. Miguel called Maggie. We can't pick up police calls on the scanner anymore, because all the departments in the county use encrypted channels now. But Maggie is still plugged in to more sources than anyone I've ever worked with. While Miguel spoke with her I walked up to the small group of onlookers who had begun to gather.

"Hey, what's going on? Anyone know what happened?"

"No," said a short, bald guy. "Me and Bobby, here," he said, pointing to the chubby, middle-aged man next to him, "This is our first day running. We were headed this way to take the tunnel trail. But the ambulance come in like gangbusters ahead of us. We been waiting to see what's happening."

"I told Doug this is a sign we shouldn't be doing this," his friend said. "I'll bet that guy had a heart attack. We only been a quarter mile and I about feel like I'm gonna have one."

I had found my people.

There was movement at the entrance to the tunnel. I looked up and saw two EMTs pushing a gurney toward the ambulance.

"Out of the way! Get back!"

More cops had arrived and began herding us all back where we belonged, well away from the scene. As we moved, all of us had our eyes fixed on the gurney. As it got a little closer, I could see this was no heart attack victim. The person being wheeled to the ambulance had the handle of a knife sticking out of his body.

I turned to point it out to Miguel, who had come up behind me. His eyes widened as he looked over my shoulder. I whirled back around. I caught a glimpse of the man lying on the gurney just before they loaded him into the vehicle.

It was Miller Caldwell.

15

I started toward the ambulance, but a beefy hand clamped down on my arm and held me back.

"Leah, no. Stay back."

It was Charlie Ross.

"Charlie! What happened?"

He guided me away from the crowd as the ambulance left.

"How bad is Miller hurt? Is he going to be all right? Who would do that to him?"

"Slow down. I don't know much yet. Dispatch got a call that someone just got stabbed in the tunnel on the running trail. I was at the diner havin' coffee, so I was first on the scene. I found Miller layin' on his side with a hunting knife sticking out of his belly. He wasn't conscious. The EMTs got here right after I did and—"

"When was that? Who called it in?"

"Call came in at 6:10. Anonymous. Dispatcher couldn't tell if the caller was male or female. One of those in-between voices, plus he—or she—was pretty emotional."

"What did the caller say?"

"Just that someone was stabbed at the county park in the tunnel. When the operator tried to get more information, the caller hung up and turned off their phone."

"They obviously don't want to be questioned. Do you think the person who called it in saw anything? Maybe they hung up because they're scared."

"Could be. We'll be checking the cell tower records to see if we can find the number that called 911, and then find the guy. Or girl."

"Well, even if they didn't stick around and don't want to talk, at least they called it in. Miller could have died!"

Ross pressed his lips together as though he were trying to keep the words inside.

"What? Miller isn't going to die, is he? He's going to be all right, isn't he? What did the EMTs say?"

"You know those guys. They don't tell you anything. They just checked him over and then loaded him on the ambulance. I've seen guys hurt worse come out fine. But there's no sense tryin' to guess. We have to wait and see."

"I've got to get to the hospital."

"Yeah? Are you gonna jog there?"

I'd forgotten I was in running shorts, a headband, and a T-shirt.

"No, I came with Miguel. He'll want to be there, too. You?"

"I'll be along. I need to talk to the guys taping off the scene. I'll see you there."

"I don't understand it, Miguel. Why would anyone stab Miller? And in a public place like the county park?"

We were both in Miguel's car, driving significantly over the speed limit to the hospital.

"I don't know. But if somebody knew that Miller runs every morning here, it would be easy to hide in the tunnel and wait for him. Do you think it was the attacker who called it in? Sometimes they do."

"That's what I wonder, too. I don't know. I can't think straight. I just want him to be okay. Stab wounds can be really bad. Miguel, what if Miller, what if he—"

I couldn't bring myself to say the word we were both thinking.

"I know. But he won't. Don't think that. It's bad juju. Miller is strong, he's an athlete, he will be okay. Just keep thinking that."

———————

When we got to the hospital, Charlotte was pacing back and forth in the waiting room. I hurried over to her.

"Have you heard anything?"

As I spoke she turned, and I saw the tears streaming down her cheeks. She looked, and probably felt, like a frightened five-year-old. I hugged her hard.

"I'm so sorry, Charlotte. But your dad is a strong guy. The emergency room staff here are great, too."

I felt her nod against my shoulder, but I knew it hadn't helped any. Nothing really does when someone you love is seriously ill or hurt.

When she stepped away, she wiped at her face with her hand, until Miguel appeared with a box of tissues. She grabbed a handful and blew her nose and dried her cheeks.

"*Ay dios mío!* Charlotte, I am so sorry."

"I can't understand how this happened. How could anyone want to attack my father?"

Her voice broke off then. The door at the far end of the room had swung open and a man in scrubs stood there. He nodded toward Charlotte, and she ran to meet him.

Miguel and I waited silently as Charlotte unleashed a frenzied round of questions before the doctor could even speak. He put a hand gently on her arm and talked to her in a voice too soft for us to hear. I grabbed Miguel's hand and began squeezing it to stem the tide of fear that was rising in my chest. Charlotte's shoulders slumped and her head dropped into her hands. The doctor looked up and saw us. He nodded and we moved quickly toward her as Charlotte's body began to shake with heart-wrenching sobs.

I took the weeping Charlotte in my arms and held her.

I didn't need to hear the doctor say the words to know that Miller was dead.

16

I didn't go home from the hospital. I didn't want to talk with anyone just yet. I needed to be alone to mourn my friend. So I went to Riverview Park, where there's an ancient maple tree, way at the back.

Over the years, its roots have grown above ground and entwined themselves until they now form a comfortable lap to sit in. No one can see you there, unless they make the trek to the far end of the park, and even then, they'd have to walk around the tree. Hidden by the large trunk I let the tears fall as I tried to make sense of Miller's death. How could this have happened? I had a hard time imagining a world without Miller.

He was more than my friend. He was both my backstop and my forward thinker. He was the steady hand that had guided me away from the edge of some of my worst impulses—impatience, quick judgment, stubbornness. At the same time, he was quick to support my ideas and applaud my successes. I couldn't count the number of times in the last few years when I'd turned to him for help or advice. He'd always been there. He'd always treated me as a full partner—even though he'd put far more money into the paper than I had. There was nobody like Miller. The personal loss for me was huge. The loss for the town was equally large. And if I felt this awful, how much worse it had to be for Charlotte and her brother Sebastian.

After a while, I couldn't stand to be alone with my thoughts any longer. But I wasn't ready to face all the questions, and the shock, and the need to get a story out that would be taking place at the paper. But there was somewhere I could go and find a listening ear for my roiling emotions.

Father Gregory Lindstrom, the priest at St. Stephen's, was in his office at the parish hall. I'm not Catholic—well, I was raised Catholic, but I stopped going to church a long time ago. After my sister Annie died, and my dad took off, people told me to trust that God was there for me. That even if it didn't seem like it at the time, I should have faith that He was working things out for the best. I tried to believe, but by the time I hit twelve, I decided to take "working things out" into my own hands. Because it sure seemed to me like either God wasn't as good as advertised, or His heart wasn't really in it.

If ever I were lured back to organized religion, it would be due to the little white-haired priest across from me. Not because of any theological argument he might make in defense of faith, but because he lives what churches talk about—mercy, compassion, justice, love.

"Father, I saw Miller yesterday afternoon. We were making plans for the paper. We were supposed to meet this morning. I can't make myself believe that I'll never see him again."

"Leah, I'm so sorry. I know Miller was very dear to you. It's not easy to find answers to a loss as painful as this."

"Well, points to you, Father, for not telling me that Miller's death is some kind of strategic move on God's chessboard that we aren't meant to understand. Miller should not be dead. He's a survivor. He fights back. And Father, you know how much he's given of himself—his time, his talent, his money. Why did this happen? He was happy. His kids were back in his life, his plans for Himmel were really taking off, he was doing so much good. How can it be that people like Spencer Karr and Harley Granger run through life like human wrecking balls, ruining lives without a second thought, and they're still here, but Miller is gone? Make it make sense, Father."

"I'm afraid that's something each of us has to do for ourselves, Leah. For me, the fact that Miller was so happy at this point in his life gives me some consolation. I can't think of a better time to move from this world to the next than when a man has found and is fulfilling his purpose."

"That's because you believe in a next world. I'm not sure I do. And if this is all there is, then Miller was robbed. We all were—his kids, his colleagues, his friends—all of us. He should have had more time. We should have had more time with him. Miller was more than my friend, more than my partner. He was like, like . . ." I searched for the word to describe what Miller had come to mean to me over the past few years.

"Like your father, Leah?"

His words startled me.

"No. Not at all. Miller wasn't anything like my father."

"Perhaps I should have said like you wished your father to be? A constant and supportive presence in your life?"

He was looking at me with such empathy in his eyes that I almost started crying again.

"I don't know, Father. Maybe. I've got all these feelings tumbling around inside me—grief, anger, guilt, regret. Part of me just wants to curl up in a ball and cry, but the other part of me is so keyed up I feel like I might explode if I don't do something!"

As if on cue, my phone rang.

"Charlotte, hi. How are you doing?"

I cursed myself as soon as the words were out. How was she doing? Her father was just murdered, of course she was doing terrible.

"I'm all right, Leah. I've been thinking things over, and I have a favor to ask. A big one."

"Sure, anything I can do, I will."

"I'd like you to investigate Dad's murder. I know, the sheriff's office is handling it. I've talked with Detective Ross already. He seems all right, but I don't know him. I know you, Leah. I remember what you did to find the truth after your sister Lacey died. To Detective Ross, my father's death is just another case. To you, it's personal."

"I'll do it." The words were out almost before she finished asking.

"You will? Oh, thank you so much! I know that it could be awkward for you, because of your relationship with Coop, I mean."

"I'll take care of that. I'm more concerned about how your family is going to handle my involvement. Your mother, in particular. She's not my biggest fan. What does Sebastian think about this? And your uncle and your grandmother?"

"They don't know. I haven't said anything to them. I didn't want to until I knew if you would agree or not. As for my mother, she's got nothing to say about it. The same with Uncle Fourey, Dad's brother. He wasn't in touch with Dad much in the past. I don't think he should have a say over things now. Sebastian will agree with me, I'm sure. As for Gran, as you know, she's not been well for the past year. The news about Dad was very hard on her. I'm not sure how much longer she can last—or wants to. I'm not going to involve her in this at all. I'll handle the family if anyone objects. Leah, I have to know why this happened. I have to know who did this. If I can just understand it, maybe I'll be able to accept it."

"I feel the same. I'm all in, Charlotte."

After I hung up, Father Lindstrom said, "From what I heard, you won't need to explode anytime in the near future. You can put your grief and your energy to work in finding out why Miller died. But be careful, Leah, not to bury your pain too deep. It's in feeling our sorrow that we learn how to move through it."

"I can't spend much time on feeling my sadness just yet, Father. I won't be able to do that until I know why Miller was killed, and who did it. Thanks for listening to me. I have to get to work now, and I'm glad of that. I'll see you soon."

I left Father Lindstrom's and went straight to Coop's office.

Jennifer Pilarski, my friend since kindergarten, is also Coop's administrative aide. She was sitting at her desk and her warm brown eyes were full of sympathy when she greeted me.

"Leah, I can't believe the news about Miller. It's such a shock! He was such a nice man. How are you holding up?"

"Okay, at the moment. Still reeling, like everyone else, Jen."

"You're going to investigate, aren't you? Of course you are," she said without waiting for me to answer.

"Charlotte asked me to. I couldn't say no. Truthfully, I didn't want to say no. I need something to do. I can't just sit around and talk about what a great guy he was and how sad I am. I've kind of lost my bearings here. Maybe I can get them back if I take some action."

"Charlie's leading the investigation."

"Yes, I know. And before you say it, I know he won't like it, but I can't help that. I have to investigate, too."

Coop was sitting at his desk when I came in, paperwork spread out in front of him, but he was just staring into space. I knew he was having a hard time processing what had happened, too. He stood immediately and came over to me and hugged me before he said anything.

"Leah, I called you a couple of times."

"I know, I'm sorry. I just wasn't ready to talk."

"That's what I figured. I feel pretty bad, but I know you've got to feel even worse."

I nodded and took the water he handed me from the small fridge in his office. Then we both sat down on his sofa. I talked through everything that had happened, ending up with Charlotte's request.

"I have to do it, Coop. It's Miller. I can't just sit on the sidelines."

"I know."

"It's not like I'll be working against your investigation. I'm just supplementing it. If I find anything, I'll share."

"Leah, it's okay. I understand why you need to do this. I think Charlie will, too."

There was a knock on the door and Ross walked in.

"I saw your car in the parking lot. Let me guess. You want to be part of the investigation."

"Ross, Charlotte asked me to help. I know you'd probably rather I didn't, but I have to. I really do."

He sighed heavily and shook his head, but his voice was surprisingly gentle when he spoke.

"Leah, it's not a good idea—now, now, let me finish," he said as I started to interrupt. "I'm not sayin' you don't have skills. You do. And I get Miller's important to you. But that's why it's not a great idea. You're too close."

"No. Being close is why I have to do it. I need to be part of this. Look, I'm not trying to be a jerk, but I don't need your permission. Though I'd like it better if you weren't fighting me on it. We've collaborated before and it didn't turn out so bad, did it?"

"Charlie, Leah's right. She doesn't need permission to ask questions. As long as she doesn't do anything that jeopardizes your investigation, it's probably better to have her cooperating than running wild."

I considered defending myself against the casual assumption that I'd be "running wild" if I went totally on my own but decided against it. Ross usually comes around, but he likes it to be his choice, not my push.

"All right, all right. But no feedin' leads to your paper. We want to solve Miller's murder, not make headlines," Ross said.

"I won't. But what Miguel or Troy find on their own, they find."

"Fine. I gotta go. I'll check in with you later, Coop. And I suppose I'll be talking to you, too, Nash."

17

Early Thursday morning Charlotte called.

"Leah, hi. I hope I didn't wake you."

"No, I just finished breakfast. What do you need?"

"Well, it's a pretty big favor. I hate to ask but—"

"Charlotte, I told you, whatever you need. What is it?"

"It's Sam. Dad's cat. I took him home with me yesterday, but I can't keep him. My lease doesn't allow pets. Besides, Sebastian is going to be staying with me, and he's allergic to cats. It's why Dad never had one when we were still at home. I asked Patty, but her husband doesn't like cats. I could board him at the vet's I know, but poor Sam is already confused and upset without Dad. I know it's a lot, but I wondered if . . ."

"Yes, sure, I can take him for a little while," I said, slipping in the caveat so she knew I wasn't offering to adopt Sam. I don't have anything against cats, or pets in general, but I hadn't had one since I left home. I like the freedom of not having another living creature to take care of on a regular basis.

"Oh, thanks so much. It won't be forever, I promise. I'll start looking for a permanent home for him right away. Would it be all right if I brought him over in an hour or so?"

"Sure, I'll see you soon."

"Thank you so much for doing this, Leah. And I mean it, it's not forever. As soon as I can find a good home for him, I will. It's just that right now with everything . . ." Charlotte said.

"Hey, don't worry about it. I'm sure we'll get along fine."

Actually, I wasn't all that sure. I'd helped her transfer Sam and all his accoutrements—his bed, a favorite blanket, a small bag of toys, his litter box, kitty litter, and his favorite food to my apartment. But when Charlotte opened his carrier, Sam, a brownish-gray tabby cat, cast a long suspicious look at me with his green-gold eyes. Then he dashed away in the direction of my bedroom.

"He's very affectionate usually, but right now he's confused and frightened. He'll come around. You just have to let him make the first move."

"Yeah, of course. Hey, would you like something to drink—coffee, tea, water, Diet Coke?"

"Water would be great, thanks. I've been crying so much I feel like I'm dehydrated. But I guess I can't be. There are always plenty of tears when I think about Dad—which is almost all the time."

"Give yourself a break, Charlotte. It just happened. You need some time to adjust to a world without your dad in it. We all do."

"I'm not sure I can. Dad was always there. If I had a question, if I screwed up, if I wanted to share good news, or bad news, or anything at all, I knew I could turn to him. He didn't tell me what to do, but somehow he always knew the right questions to ask to help me figure out the answers on my own. It's starting to sink in now that I really am on my own. And it's terrifying."

I didn't bother to suggest she had her mother Georgia to comfort her. Comforting and Georgia don't belong in the same sentence.

"It's really hard, I know. But try to keep in mind that Miller had total faith in you. And there are lots of people who will support you and help you in any way they can."

"I know that. I really do. But right now, everything seems so overwhelming. Mother is no help. In fact, I'd say she's a hindrance. She's acting like this is all about her. Although she always acts like everything is about her, so I shouldn't be surprised. Uncle Fourey is trying to help, I think, but he doesn't do well in a crisis—though he's spending a lot of time with Grandmother, so that's something. Sebastian feels as terrible as I do. In fact, it's probably even worse for him. He was really angry at Dad for a long time. Now in addition to grief, he's dealing with guilt and regret."

She sighed and took a drink of the water I handed her.

"I'm sorry. I don't mean to complain about it. The ironic thing is that this is just the sort of time when Dad would step in and organize things, and give us all tasks to do, and make everyone feel like it was going to be all right. And he's not here, and I'm not him. I don't know how to do it. There's the funeral to plan, and so many business decisions to be made, and I want to be there for Gran, and it's just . . ."

Tears had welled up in her eyes and spilled over. She swiped impatiently at her cheeks when I handed her a Kleenex.

"Thank you," she said. "I can't be falling apart every other minute. I just can't."

"No, you can't. But you don't have to be a stoic either. As for the things that need to happen—well, Patty is a great resource. And Gabe is there to make sure the law practice keeps ticking while you figure out what needs to happen. I'm sure what's his name—Bryson? I mean the one who's the head guy in your dad's property development firm. He'll step up, too, won't he?"

"It's Brayden. Brayden Townsend. And yes, I'm sure he will. I don't mean to sound all 'poor me,' Leah. Lots of people have offered to help and I know they mean it. It's just I feel so disorganized, and that's not like me."

"The thing is you don't have to figure out everything all at once. Everyone will carry on. Your dad didn't get where he was by hiring incompetent people. Things will bump along with Gabe at the law firm and Brayden at the property development business for a while."

"And there's the paper, too."

"That should not be your worry right now. Miller didn't do daily decision-making or oversight. Neither do I, for that matter. Between Maggie and my mother things will go along fine for a while. Nothing has to be decided immediately."

"Well, but one thing does. The partnership agreement that you and Dad had. I'm sure you know that the insurance component of the agreement provides the cash so that you as the surviving partner can buy out Dad's share."

I felt a flash of panic. I hadn't factored in what Miller's death would mean to the partnership we set up when we bought the paper. Yes, I could use the insurance money to buy his half of the partnership from his estate. But I didn't want to. The nonprofit idea we'd agreed on had seemed like a lifeline. But I didn't have the skills, the smarts, or the time to acquire them. I couldn't bring it off without Miller. And if we didn't go that route, I didn't have the money to keep the paper afloat without Miller being our financial backstop. I pushed those thoughts down. I couldn't let my worries add to Charlotte's burden. If she wanted to get out from under the newspaper now that she had so much else on her plate, she should.

We both spoke at the same time.

"Yes, of course, Charlotte. I'll get with Gabe and find out what I—"

"I hope you won't exercise that option I'd really like—"

"Wait a minute. Are you saying you don't want out of the newspaper business? That you want to take over Miller's partnership role?"

"I do, if it's all right with you, Leah. I'd like to work with you on what will be a big project—transforming the paper into a nonprofit news operation. It's something Dad was really excited about. I'd like to see it through, for him."

"Charlotte, you have no idea how happy that makes me. I'm here a hundred percent to do whatever needs doing on that front. But I won't lie, I'm relieved that I won't be doing it alone. We can get with Gabe on how we have to move ahead, but again, it doesn't have to be done right away."

"I'm relieved, too. I wasn't sure how you'd feel without Dad in the picture."

"I've gotten used to having a Caldwell to count on."

She smiled and looked so much like Miller for a second that it made my heart hurt.

"Leah, you can count on me, absolutely. And I'll count on you, the way Dad always did. But there is one other thing I wanted to talk to you about."

"Sure. What is it?"

"Detective Ross told me that Dad—that is Dad's body," she stumbled a little over the phrase, but soldiered on, "Dad's body will be released by the medical examiner today. He wanted to be cremated, so that's what we'll do. The memorial service will be Saturday. I'd really like it if you'd be one of the speakers. Would you?"

I didn't answer right away, and she mistook my silence for reluctance.

"I don't want to pressure you. I know it will be hard. Sebastian's already said he just can't do it. And I understand if you feel the same. I just think Dad would like it."

"No, no, I'd be honored."

"Really? All right then, that's good. I'll let you know more when we've got things planned out. I should go. Thank you, Leah. For everything."

18

"Damn it to hell, Gabe."

I had just flopped down on the sofa in his office at Caldwell & Hoffman, LLC.

"I know. I can't believe it. I canceled my appointments for today. I sent Patty home. She's a basket case. Hell, I'm a basket case. Do you know anything more than you did yesterday when I called you?"

"No, not really. I told you Charlotte had asked me to dig into things, right?"

He nodded.

"The trouble is, I haven't been able to focus enough to get started. Every time I try, I stop because I can't believe that he's really gone."

"I'm having a hard time focusing, too."

"You'll keep the practice going, won't you?"

"Yes, definitely. We'd been talking about bringing someone else in as an associate. Miller needed to free up more time for his property development business. He had some big plans for the county. We talked to someone last week that we both liked. I need to reach out to her and see if the interest is genuine. I won't be able to keep my head above water if I don't get some help in fairly quickly. Have you thought about what you're going to do about the paper?"

"Charlotte wants to take over Miller's share of the business, and I'm glad of that. Did Miller mention that he and I had decided to move the paper into a nonprofit set-up? Charlotte and I will keep heading in that direction."

"No, he didn't say anything. But I was just reading an article about papers going nonprofit. It sounds like a solid idea for the *Times*."

"I think it is. Miller was so proud of Charlotte—she's the one who came up with it. We were going to meet with the staff about it yesterday morning."

"Yeah, he and I were supposed to have dinner together last night. Instead . . ."

We both fell silent. I assumed that Gabe, like me, was thinking about all of the everyday things—quick check-ins, casual conversations, business meetings, fun lunches, light teasing, minor disagreements, serious conversations—that would never happen again. And we'd had no warning. Miller was there, and then he wasn't. And there was not one thing either of us could do to change that. But I could help find out why—or go down trying. Gabe's next remark made me think he'd been reading my thoughts.

"So. Where are you going to start investigating? And how do Charlie and Coop feel about that?"

"Surprisingly okay—with the usual caveats. Stay out of their way, don't feed information to the paper. I'm not sure where I'm going to start yet. It's hard to think that Miller could have brought out the kind of anger that would lead to such a violent death. He was such a good man."

"Not everyone thought so."

"You mean Boyd Hanson? Yes, sure. He blamed Miller for losing his farm. But he's dead, now, too."

"No, I meant his son, Noah. Sherry told me about his run-in with Charlotte at McClain's. According to her, he had to be restrained from taking a swing at Charlotte. Then Miguel and Troy literally carried him out the door."

"She's embellishing. You know Sherry. Noah was really upset, yes, but he didn't physically threaten Charlotte. And Miguel and Troy didn't carry him out the door. Though Noah was pretty drunk. People say a lot of things they don't really mean when they've been drinking."

"True. But sometimes drinking frees them up to say things that they do mean, but wouldn't say sober. If Noah thinks Miller's actions led to his dad's suicide—well, revenge is a strong motive."

"You're not wrong. And I'm sure Noah is at the top of Ross's list of suspects. But I don't know that shouting at Charlotte in a bout of drunken grief equates to committing a brutal murder two days later."

"Fair point. What about Miller's family? There's a lot of money involved."

"Are you seriously suggesting that Charlotte or Sebastian knifed their own father to get money?"

"No, but they're not the only people in the family. I don't know about his brother Fourey, but Georgia's got money problems of some kind."

"Wait a minute. Georgia has plenty of money. Miller felt so guilty over what his coming out did to her that he was extremely generous. Miguel got all the details from her when it happened."

"Miguel and Georgia are confidants?"

"They forged a bond when he worked at his aunt's hair salon. According to him, and I've never known him to be wrong about his local intel, Georgia got a huge cash settlement from Miller, plus the family 'cottage' on Lake Michigan. It was enough for her to leave town and set herself up in Chicago in the style she's been accustomed to. She's got all that she needs, and more."

"I don't want to destroy your faith in Miguel's intelligence gathering—"

"Impossible."

"But I've got some first-hand information of my own."

"How? You don't even know Georgia. She was gone before you came to town."

"Well, I know *of* her. And last week I met her in person, though she wasn't at her best."

"Okay, quit stringing me along. What are you talking about?"

"She was here to see Miller last week. I was in here, and she was in Miller's office with the door closed. I could hear voices, mostly hers, but I couldn't tell what she was saying. Not that I was trying. In fact, I was just short of putting my hands over my hears and humming to drown out the noise. I got up to shut my door, just as she came out of Miller's office. I stepped back in because I didn't want to walk into the middle of something.

Georgia wasn't speaking very loudly by then, but she was intense, and I could hear every word she said."

"Well, come on, out with it, what did she say?"

"Something like, 'I need that money. If I don't get it, the truth is coming out.' Then she left."

"Did Miller say anything to you later?"

"No. He left right after she did, and my door was closed. Patty was at lunch. I don't think he realized that I'd been here. I didn't say anything to him because it was obviously something private between him and Georgia."

"'The truth is coming out.' What truth? It almost sounds like Georgia was blackmailing him. But everyone already knows that Miller was gay."

"Maybe being gay wasn't Miller's only secret."

When I got back home, I stopped in the newsroom. My mother was on the phone, so she just waved through her office window at me. Troy was out on an assignment. Miguel had left the night before for a long-planned family birthday for his mother and wouldn't be back until Friday. He had offered to stay, but at this point there wasn't anything urgent happening. And life does keep moving on, no matter what tragedy befalls us.

Maggie was at her desk, so I sat down on the visitor chair in her office.

"Anything new on Miller?"

"Shouldn't I be asking you that? I hear you're going to be looking into his murder for Charlotte."

"I am. But the usual rules apply, Maggie. No leads, well, maybe the very subtlest of nudges, from me about anything I might discover. This isn't about a story for the paper. It's about Miller. Of course, if the paper comes up with something on its own, that's different. But you know how touchy Ross can be."

"I see."

Maggie frowned. She had pulled her tortoiseshell glasses off the top of her head and jammed them purposefully on her nose. I knew what she was thinking.

"Come on, Maggie. It's not access journalism. I didn't promise we'd clear our reporting with them first, in exchange for crumbs of insider info. All I mean is that I'll consider what's said between me and Ross—if I can get him to tell me anything that is—off-the-record. There are no constraints on Troy and Miguel working whatever sources they have. I just won't be one of them."

"I get it. But I don't like it. We're walking a fine line."

"We live in a small town, and I'm romantically involved with the sheriff. As long as those two things hold true, we're always going to be walking a fine line, right? I'll keep doing my best to make sure we don't cross over on either side. If I do I'm sure you'll let me know. And you should, okay? Now, anything new on Miller's murder?"

"The autopsy's done. We've got the basics, no surprises. Manner of death is homicide, cause of death organ failure caused by stab wound to the liver and internal bleeding. There's a press conference at four o'clock today."

"Is it Coop or Ross doing the presser? Or both?"

"Neither. It's still 'No comment on the investigation at this time' from the sheriff's office. The district attorney called the press conference. You know how Cliff Timmins enjoys his time in the spotlight. I don't expect much to come from it. How about on your end? Have you started working on things yet?"

"I've tried but to be honest, I haven't done much. The memorial service is Saturday. I need some family background from Charlotte and Sebastian but I'm going to wait until that's over. I'll try to talk to Noah Hanson tomorrow. I'm sure Ross has already done that. Noah's been pretty public with his feelings about Miller."

"You could say that."

"Could say what?" Troy asked as he entered the newsroom.

"That Noah had some pretty negative feelings about Miller. Leah's going to be looking into the murder for Charlotte."

"You think Noah could have killed Miller?" Troy asked. He sounded shocked.

"I think that Noah might have felt he had reason to," I said.

"He was really angry, sure. But Noah isn't a killer. He could never stab someone!"

"Not even someone he thought was responsible for his father's suicide?"

"No," he said firmly. "Noah texted me a little while ago. He said Detective Ross had come by to talk to him this morning."

"Then we should be asking *you* what Detective Ross thinks. What did Noah say?"

"We didn't get into it. I was on my way to an interview. He's still staying with me. I'll see him tonight. Do you think Noah should be worried?" he asked.

"It might be a good idea for him to talk to an attorney if he hasn't already."

At his look of dismay I added, "It's just good sense, Troy. It's not only guilty people who need a lawyer. When people get questioned by the cops, they get nervous. A lawyer can make sure he doesn't say something that makes him look guilty if he isn't."

19

Back upstairs, I saw that Miller's cat Sam hadn't touched the food I'd put out for him, though it looked like he'd had some water. He wasn't in the bed Charlotte had brought with him, which I'd left in the living room near the end of the couch, either. I searched for him in the bedroom and in my office, but there was no sign of him. Puzzled, I walked back and scanned the living room. I spotted him then, curled up in the corner of the window seat, half-tucked behind the curtain as though trying to escape notice.

"Hey, Sam, how are you doing?" I asked. I moved to sit next to him, but he hissed, swiped a paw at me, and ran off to my bedroom.

"Hey," I called after him, "I'm sorry. How about a truce? I don't touch you, and you don't maim me, okay?"

He didn't answer, which I hoped meant that he was considering my offer.

I got my supplies ready for my favorite thinking spot, the corner of the window seat opposite the one Sam had claimed. I poured a glass of Diet Coke with lots of ice, dug out my yellow legal pad, and grabbed a mechanical pencil. I prefer pencils over pens. They feel like less of a commitment. Then I piled up some pillows and sat on the window seat.

I wrote down the first names that came to mind. Noah. Fourey, Miller's brother. Georgia, his ex-wife, Charlotte, and Sebastian. I tapped my pencil on the pad for a minute, then added Dennis Warby, the guy who had accosted Miller outside of McClain's and accused Miller of grooming his son. I was pretty sure that Noah would be Ross's initial focus because of his strong motive and his habit of shouting out his feelings about Miller in public.

Despite what I'd said to Gabe, I knew I couldn't ignore Charlotte and Sebastian as potential suspects. They would inherit a sizable estate from Miller. And greedy (or needy) family are responsible for an awful lot of murders. However, it was hard to take either of them seriously as possibilities at this point.

Miller's brother Fourey was an unknown quantity. I knew that Fourey's given name was Raymond William Caldwell IV. Miller had mentioned once that the family had called him Fourey when he was a kid to distinguish him from his father, and the nickname had stuck.

He was only a year or two older than Miller. He lived in Florida and returned only occasionally to Himmel. He wasn't involved in any of the local Caldwell enterprises except, I assumed, to collect his share of the money from them. My family and the Caldwells didn't move in the same social circles, so our paths had never crossed. I was curious to meet him.

As for Miller's ex-wife, Georgia, I knew exactly what to expect from her, hostility. She grew up in Himmel in a working-class family from which she had been anxious to escape. And, because she was fairly bright, focused, and exceptionally pretty, she had made it out. Marriage to Miller had given her entrée to the life she wanted to live, and she had lived it to the hilt. She was a very big fish in the very small pond of what passes for "society" in Himmel, and she had enjoyed her position and her power greatly.

I never could understand why Miller had married her—except perhaps to escape family pressure and to hide the truth of his secret self. But surely there were nicer women he could have found. Talking with her would be a challenge—if she agreed to see me.

Usually, I go into an initial interview with an attitude somewhere between neutral and friendly. My hope is that whoever I'm talking to is lulled into a sense of comfort and pours out more information than they realize they're giving me. However, if I offered a sympathetic ear to Georgia, she was more likely to pour poison into it than unguarded confidences.

I began tapping my pencil again as I tried to decide where to start. My mind kept returning to what Gabe had said just before I left his office. *Maybe being gay wasn't Miller's only secret.*

It had surprised me when he said it. Miller was circumspect about his private life, but I assumed it was because he was a naturally reserved person. As far as I knew, his one big secret, and it was a doozy when it came out, was his gayness. But that was the kicker, wasn't it? *As far as I knew.* And how far was that, really? When it comes right down to it, usually we only know what people want us to know. Miller had hidden the fact that he was gay for years. Could he have been hiding something else as well? Did he have some other secret, maybe something from his past that had caught up with him?

I turned the thought over in my mind, but then rejected it. There was no evidence, or even any hint of Miller's involvement in evil deeds of any kind, despite the ominous warning Gabe had overheard Georgia deliver.

Then it hit me. Not that *Miller* had a dark secret, but that he might have known one that belonged to someone else. And that someone might have killed him to make sure it stayed hidden. But who? Someone in his family? A secret that belonged to Sebastian or Charlotte? Or his brother Fourey? But what secret that belonged to someone else would both Georgia and Miller know? And why would Miller pay up to keep her quiet, as her threat had implied? Also, why the heck would she need money after everything she got in the divorce?

My thinking was interrupted by a plaintive meow. Sam had emerged from the bedroom and was standing in the doorway.

"Well, hello there. How about a little treat?"

I got up and found the bag of cat treats Charlotte had left. I held a couple out in my hand for Sam, thinking that it might help him warm up to me. He approached warily, sniffed a little at the fish-flavored snack in my palm, but when I tried to pet him with the other one, he swatted at me again. This time he made contact and left a scratch on the back of my hand. Then he ran back to the bedroom. A special treat would have worked great on me. Apparently Sam's affections weren't as easily won.

"Okay, fine. I refuse to grovel. Come to me when you're ready," I called as he retreated.

As I washed my hands I saw that the scratch was a little deeper than I'd thought. It wasn't bleeding profusely, but it kept welling up. I gave it a little extra scrubbing, then put a Band-Aid on it. As I finished Coop called.

"Hey, I thought you said you were coming over for barbecued chicken tonight and that you'd make dessert. Are we still on?"

"Yes! I'm sorry. I got busy and I didn't notice the time. I'll be right over. But I can't stay tonight. Sam's here and I don't want to leave him alone all night."

"Who is Sam?"

"Miller's cat. I'll fill you in when I get there. But I have to make a stop at Woodman's first."

"I thought you said you were *making* dessert, not buying it."

"I am. Wait and see."

20

"I think this qualifies more as assembling, than making dessert," Coop said as he licked the remains of his third s'more off his fingers.

"Did I not purchase the ingredients? Did I not lovingly combine them into a delectable assembly of graham cracker, toasted marshmallow, and Hershey bar? You don't have to bake a dessert to make a dessert."

"I stand corrected. And satisfied."

"Good. So, now we're at the part of the evening where I ask you about how your day at the office was, and I listen with rapt attention to your answer."

"Did you stream the press conference Cliff Timmins did?"

"No, but I read Troy's write-up online."

"Well, that's it in a nutshell. Now you know what I know. Your turn. How is your investigation going?"

"Coop, do you seriously expect me to believe that the self-promoting nothing burger Cliff Timmins offered up is where the sheriff's office investigation stands right now?"

"Actually, Cliff dropped a few facts into his nothing burger. We do have Miller's official manner and cause of death, we are pursuing all leads, and we have no prime suspect. I wish, though, that he hadn't said we were closing in on the identity of the anonymous 911 caller. We're not really. Not yet. We're getting the cell tower records so we can identify phones in the area at the time Miller was killed, but that doesn't mean we'll be able to find the owner. Especially not if he was using a burner phone."

"You mean because whoever it was could ditch their phone? But if they really don't want to be found, they probably already did. Unless they never watched a cop show and don't know how burner phones work. Do you really not have a prime suspect yet? I've got one and I haven't really even started investigating. I'll show you mine if you show me yours."

"You first."

"Georgia Caldwell. She's been furious at Miller since the divorce. And she had a fresh argument with him pretty recently. Also I really don't like her."

I explained what Gabe had told me about Georgia and her threat. Then I added my own thoughts on Miller and dark secrets.

"So, if Miller was keeping a secret for a friend or a client, or even a family member, and that person thought he was going to reveal it, that would be a motive for murder. It expands the field of possible suspects anyway. What secret did Miller know, and who wanted it to stay buried?"

"It does, but in a murder investigation, you want to narrow the field, not expand it."

"True, but that's as you progress. At the beginning you don't want to narrow your vision so much that you don't see all the possibilities."

"So how are you going to find this person with a secret?"

"I'm not sure yet. How's Ross doing? I'll bet he's zeroing in on Noah, isn't he?"

"He's questioned a few people, just building his case out slow and steady. That's Charlie."

"Come on, are you saying that you don't know what he's doing? Because that I don't believe."

"I'm saying it's Charlie's case and I trust him to develop and support his theory of the murder. I already told you I wasn't going to be your middleman on this. It's up to you two to figure out what you're sharing and when—unless you hold back something that slows down the official investigation. You're not doing that, are you?"

"No. I'll share if I find something useful. But I need room to develop and support my own theory of the case—just like Ross. My methods may be more fast and furious than his slow and steady pace, but we both want to see Miller's killer caught. We just go at it different ways."

"I agree that you each bring different things to the table. That's why sharing is a good thing. Keeping progress hidden in order to be the one to solve the case is more likely to slow it down."

"I hear you. And I never try to hide things from Ross."

Coop lifted one eyebrow.

"All right. Almost never. But thank you, for acknowledging that I have skills."

"I'll never say you don't, and in a lot of different areas," he said with a smile, shifting the tone of the conversation.

"Are you flirting with me ?" I asked.

"If it's working, then yes," he said.

"It would be, but I have to get going. Charlotte asked me to speak at Miller's funeral. It's been at the back of my mind all day, trying to figure out how to say meaningful and true things about Miller without getting all schmaltzy about it. He'd hate that. I've got a lot of work to do before Saturday. Also, there's Sam. It's his first night in a new place and I really need to get back to him."

"Eulogizing Miller will be a tough one. But I'm glad you said yes. Nobody will do it better."

"Thank you. I hope I don't let you—or Miller down." I leaned in for a goodbye kiss. "Once Sam settles in a little more, I'll invite you over for a slumber party with us."

21

I'd forgotten to leave a light on, so my apartment was in darkness when I opened the door—which I closed quickly in case Sam was wandering about. But he didn't come out to greet me and he wasn't on his cat bed or the window seat. I found him sleeping in the middle of my bed. His eyes opened and he gave a disconsolate mew, as though he'd been hoping Miller would be the one he woke up to see.

"It's just me. I'm sorry. He's not coming back, Sam. I miss him, too. I know it's weird for you here, but I'll do my best until Charlotte finds the perfect home for you, okay?"

I walked toward the bed, but he jumped off and scurried under it.

"All right, all right. I'll just get my pjs and get out of your way. I'll be in the living room if you need me."

I worked on my eulogy for Miller for a couple of hours and wound up with nothing to show for it. Everything I wrote sounded trite and stupid, and I spent more time deleting than I did writing. Finally, around midnight I closed up my laptop, brushed my teeth, and headed for bed. When I saw that Sam was once again asleep on my bed, I backed quietly out of the room. I didn't have the heart to disturb him, and I knew he wouldn't welcome me as a sleeping partner.

I went back to the living room, lay down on the sofa, pulled the afghan off the back of it, and settled in for the night.

In the morning, Sam was no longer on my bed when I checked. He wasn't anywhere else visible, either, but I noticed that some of the food was gone from his dish. Good. At least he'd eaten something. I changed his water, took a shower, and pulled on a pair of jeans and a T-shirt.

"Okay, Sam, I'm going out for a while. If you're hungry the coast will be clear for a couple of hours. See you later."

On my way to Troy's, I picked up coffee and muffins for myself and Noah. My night on the couch hadn't been very restful. My morning brain fog was dense enough that I forgot Troy had moved to a duplex on Dalton Street. I was two miles out of town before my unconscious mind finally spoke up and reminded me.

Dalton Street is in an older part of town that could definitely use a facelift. It's a mix of bungalows, two-story houses of no discernible architectural style, and a few duplexes like Troy's. On the plus side, it's a wide street with lots of leafy shade trees, and there's a retention pond behind it that gives the illusion of being a small lake.

Troy's modest duplex has a nice front porch. A double garage sits between both units, giving the residents of each side a bit of privacy. Somewhere in its distant past, there might have been a landscape plan for the front lawn, but things had gotten seriously out of hand.

I mounted the steps to the porch and knocked on the front door. When no one came, I knocked again harder. There was still no answer, but the blue pickup on Troy's side of the driveway said someone was there. I walked around the house to find a window to tap on, but the bushes were too thick to give me easy access. I went back to the porch and put my all into pounding on the door.

After a few seconds, Noah Hanson opened the door. His eyes were red-veined and bleary as though he'd spent the night either drinking or crying —or maybe both. His wet hair explained why my knock hadn't been answered. He'd obviously been in the shower and was now shaved and dressed.

"Hi, Noah, how are you?"

I had my hand on the doorknob and was gently pushing it further open as I spoke, causing Noah to reflexively step back and open the door wide enough for me to slip inside. It's my go-to move when I know the person at the door isn't thrilled to talk to me, but I really want to talk to them.

"Troy's not here. He left for work about half an hour ago."

"Oh, that's all right. You're the one I want to see. It won't take long. I brought you some coffee and a muffin from Woke coffeeshop. Cranberry pecan. They're really good."

"I don't think I—"

"No, seriously this will only take a few minutes. I just need to clarify a few things with you. We can sit at the kitchen table, no need to mess up Troy's living room."

I knew the way to the kitchen because I'd gone to a housewarming party for Troy a month earlier. I moved confidently forward as though I was the host and Noah was the guest.

"Here you go," I said, putting his coffee and muffin down on the table. I dropped into the chair across from them.

"I don't understand why you're here," he said, still standing. "What is it you think I can 'clarify'?"

"Sit down and I'll tell you."

I pulled back the tab on my coffee lid and took a sip. Noah hovered for a minute, then sat down.

"I just a have a few questions about the morning Miller died."

"I don't know anything about it. I already told that to the police. Anyway, what's it got to do with you?"

"Miller was my friend and my partner. I want to find out why he was killed."

"Isn't that the cops' job? "

"It is. And Detective Ross is very good at his job. But I'm good at mine, too. Miller meant a lot to me. If I can help solve his murder, I'm going to do it."

"Yeah, well, okay, good for you. But you're talking to the wrong person. I wasn't anywhere near the park on Wednesday morning. I don't know anything. I already told that to Detective Ross. I've got a lot going on right now. So, excuse me, but I don't see why I have to add answering your questions to everything else."

His tone was aggressive, but from the way he was jiggling his leg under the table, I knew he was nervous.

"You don't, actually. But it might help you as well as me if you do. I'm very sorry about your dad, truly, and about everything else you're dealing with now. But you're a smart guy. You have to know that after you verbally attacked Miller's daughter at McClain's and shouted out to all the world how much you hated Miller, of course you're going to be questioned about his murder."

"I told you, I wasn't at the park. I didn't even know Miller Caldwell was dead until Troy told me. Ask him."

"I will. But I'm asking you, now." I didn't bother to keep the impatient note out of my voice.

"And I told you I don't know anything. Yes, I got drunk, and I mouthed off to his daughter, and I'm sorry I did that. But that's all it was. Just talking. And since then, I've kind of had a lot to handle trying to get my sucky life together."

"I know it's been rough—"

"Do you know? Do you really? I don't think you do. Not unless you've ever had your whole world collapse in on you. Everything was fine just a couple of weeks ago—my dad was alive, I was headed to medical school, I had no money worries. Now, I don't have a home—or I won't in a few weeks. The bank is going to foreclose on the farm. I'm not starting med school this fall. I've got a huge financial mess to untangle. My dad committed suicide, and oh, yeah, he killed himself so I could collect his life insurance. If I hadn't acted like such a selfish asshole, maybe he'd still be alive!"

He dropped his face in his hands, shaking his head. I moderated my tone.

"Noah, I know you've got a lot to contend with. But if you don't want being prime suspect in a murder to be one of those things, then talk to me. First off, I don't think you were a selfish asshole."

"You're wrong there. We had a huge fight when he finally told me everything that night after the Board of Supervisors meeting. I called him a failure. I told him Mom would be ashamed of him for stealing the money I needed for medical school. I accused him of being a coward for not telling me what he'd done. I said because of him I'd lose my place in the fall class —there wasn't enough time to line up the loan money I need for tuition. It was the last thing he needed to hear."

"Don't be so hard on yourself. You had a major gut punch. It's natural to lash out."

"Not as hard as I did. My dad had his flaws, but he was a good father. And when he needed just a little understanding from me, I treated him like crap. I knew the farm was struggling, but I never asked about it. He was crying when he told me, and all I could think about was me, and medical school, and how my plans were upended. After I finished yelling at him, I went to Troy's for the night. The next day, I felt pretty terrible about how I'd acted toward my dad. I wanted to apologize, but at the same time I was still mad about what he'd done, you know?"

"I do. Just because you've done something wrong, it doesn't mean the other person is blameless. You felt bad about treating your father the way you had, but were still reeling from what he'd done," I said.

"Yeah. I wanted to get that out of my system before we talked. I didn't want to wind up yelling at him all over again. So, I spent the morning on the phone and online, figuring out what I needed to do about school and financial aid and stuff. I felt better after I started getting my arms around it. I called Dad at two o'clock. He didn't pick up, but I left a voice mail to say how sorry I was, and that we could figure things out together. I told him I'd be out around five with a pizza. When I got there that afternoon, I found him. After the autopsy I learned that he never even heard my message. He didn't know I didn't mean the things I said. He was already dead when I called."

He stopped talking and stared down at his hands. I waited silently. There really weren't any words that would comfort him.

"I thought he left me without even saying goodbye. I didn't find the letter he wrote me until after we scattered his ashes in the meadow."

He looked at me then, his eyes so sad it was hard to look into them.

"My Dad killed himself so that I'd have the money to go to medical school. He died thinking I hated him. In the letter he said he hoped that I'd have a son someday who I loved as much, and was as proud of, as he was of me!"

The anguish in Noah's voice was hard to hear.

"I'm so sorry, Noah. But your dad was trying to comfort you. He was telling you that no matter what you said or did, it didn't matter. He loved you."

Noah's situation was different, yet in a way similar to how I'd felt when I learned how and why my own father had died. I had no trouble imagining how he was feeling.

"Troy and Miguel. They tried to help, but nothing they said made any difference. I mean, I had to face the fact that my dad had killed himself so that I'd have the money to go to medical school! How was I supposed to handle that? I got pretty drunk and—well, you know what happened. I saw Miller's daughter Charlotte at McClain's, and I lost it. I don't even remember what I said. Detective Ross refreshed my memory. So yes, I get why I'm a suspect. But I didn't kill Miller Caldwell. I lashed out and blamed him, but deep down, I knew it was my fault, not his."

"All right. So tell me then, Noah, what did you do the morning Miller was murdered?"

"Nothing. I was asleep. I'm not being a smartass. I don't sleep very well right now. The night before, Troy got called out around eleven to cover an accident or something. I finished the movie we were watching and went to bed. I was tired, but I couldn't fall asleep. I got up, messed around on my laptop for a while. Troy got in around one and we talked for a minute, but he was tired, and he went to bed. I did, too, and I finally fell asleep. Hard. I woke up about seven thirty. Troy was already gone. I didn't find out Miller Caldwell had been killed until Troy texted me around ten. That's it. That's all I know."

"I have to tell you that's not a great alibi."

"I didn't know I'd need one. You can believe me or not, but it's the truth."

He looked me straight in the eye as he spoke, his face earnest and his voice firm. I had a husband once who used to look at me exactly like that. It took me a while to figure out that was his "tell." He always looked me straight in the eye whenever he was lying his head off.

"I hope it is, Noah. I really do."

22

"I saw your car turn into the parking lot. I thought you would come to the news room!"

My phone had rung moments after I got back to my apartment.

"Hi Miguel. I—"

"You have to tell me everything about your investigation. I can't believe I had to find out about it from Carol. Why didn't you text me?"

"Because I thought you deserved a couple of happy days with your family, without thinking about the sad craziness here. How did your mom like her surprise party?"

"She loved it! My cousin closed his restaurant for the night, and we filled it up with family. So many uncles, aunts, cousins, my grandma's little sister—she's eighty-five—flew in from Texas for it. We danced, we laughed, we sang, it was a total Santos *celebracion*. But even though it was fabulous, I still had Miller on my mind. I'm coming right up so you can tell me everything."

"I think I should come down there. Sam is sleeping, and he seems to be pretty nervous around strangers."

"There are no strangers when I'm there, you know that. Who is Sam? And why is he asleep in your apartment?"

I explained the cat situation.

"Don't worry. I'm the cat whisperer. Sam will be purring on my lap before you can even believe it. I'll be there in a minute."

"Miguel—"

Too late, he was gone. Moments later, he tapped lightly on my door and walked in. Sam, who had been curled up on the window seat, lifted his head, saw Miguel, and fled to the safety of my bedroom.

"Don't take it personally. He's been like that since Charlotte dropped him off. C'mon, have a seat," I said, leading the way to the couch.

"Poor Sam. Cats are very sensitive. He misses Miller," Miguel said.

"He's not the only one. I can't even tell you how many times in the last few days I've thought 'Oh, I need to tell Miller that,' and then I remember. I can't. I saw someone in Woke this morning when I was picking up coffee and a muffin to take to Noah, and for half a second, I thought it was Miller. Weird how your mind tricks you like that."

"I know," he said, patting my hand. "I know. But tell me, you saw Noah? Who else? What is happening? How can I help?"

"Noah is the only one I've spoken to so far. I've got Charlotte and Sebastian on my list so I can get some family background before I talk to Miller's brother Fourey. And I'm putting off Georgia for obvious reasons, which do not include respect for her feelings of loss. I'm pretty sure that's nonexistent."

"I don't know for sure, but I think things were not good between Miller and his brother."

"What have you got?"

"This is from Georgia. You know I was always her favorite when I used to be shampoo boy on the weekends at Making Waves. I'm telling you, when I start to massage the conditioner in with nice, slow circles, my ladies the eyes close, and the talking starts. I have heard many things."

"I'm sure that's true. So, spill what you know about Fourey."

"He was his *mamá's* favorite. He was everyone's favorite except his *papá's*. But then he did something that made his father so angry, he cut Fourey off from all the money except for a little tiny trust fund," Miguel said, bringing his forefinger and thumb close together to illustrate just how tiny the amount was. "Miller's mother has a life interest in the estate, but everything went to Miller when his father died."

"Wow, that's harsh! What did Fourey do to make his dad so mad?"

"That, I don't know. But if you are the oldest and you get nothing, you could be very angry at your brother, who got everything."

"But it wasn't Miller who cut him off, it was their father."

"Yes, but maybe Fourey thinks Miller turned their father against him, and he wanted revenge. Revenge is good for a motive."

"It is. But I'll have to check out what you know, especially given your source of information. I don't doubt that Georgia revealed her truths under the gentle ministration of your magic fingers. But Georgia is incapable of seeing things from anyone's perspective but her own. She may have shaded the truth to suit her personal narrative."

"I could help."

"How? You don't work at the salon anymore."

"No, but Georgia is still a big donor to the Art Center, even though she doesn't live here anymore. I could tell her that I want to have her on my podcast to talk about all that she has done for its success. I think she would like that. Then I could do a preinterview with her over a glass of wine and see if she will talk more about Fourey."

"I'm not doubting your charm, Miguel, but I think Georgia will be more wary of you now because of your connection to me—even if you showed up with a bottle of hair conditioner. Let me have a run at her first, and you can be my backup if I don't get anywhere."

"Okay, but I'm ready whenever. How was Noah when you talked to him?"

"Angry, sad, worried. About how you'd expect a person to be if their father committed suicide, and a week later the man you blamed for his death was murdered. And Noah should be worried. He's got no alibi, a hell of a motive, and plenty of people who can testify that they heard him say he hated Miller."

"But he said that when he was so, so, upset. Also, he was drinking that night at McClain's. He doesn't think that now."

"That's his story, but what else would he say?"

"You think that he did it?"

"I don't know. But I'm not sure he's telling the truth about where he was on Wednesday morning."

"Why? What did he say?"

I ran through Noah's story, which didn't take long, because there wasn't much there.

"And then at the end, he looked me right in the eye and swore he was telling the truth. That's what really made me wonder."

"Why?"

"Because it's exactly how Nick used to look at me when he was trying to convince me of some major lie. I fell for it often enough back then, but I'm bulletproof now. That kind of big-eyed stare tends to make me feel suspicious, not sympathetic."

"Oh, but that is not fair. Noah isn't Nick."

"I know that. And I'm not saying Noah is guilty. It's way too early for that. But it's also way too early to say that he isn't."

"I think he isn't guilty. But I think he was very scared you wouldn't believe him, and he is very alone."

23

The family held a private service for Miller on Friday. Saturday was the day for the community to mourn. The anticipated crowd was so large that the memorial service had been scheduled in the auditorium at Himmel Technical College, with room in the foyer for the overflow to watch the service on a big screen.

Several people spoke before it was my turn and they each talked eloquently about Miller as a man, a father, and a community leader. When it was my turn, I shared how much our partnership had meant to me, not just because we'd managed to keep the paper alive, but because of what I had learned from him about acceptance, resilience, and faith in people.

My voice had started to quaver. By the time I finished, I could barely get the last words out. An overwhelming sense of loss rose, and I couldn't fight it off. I began to cry. Not quiet cry. Ugly cry. I was sobbing so hard I couldn't catch my breath. I felt an arm around my shoulders and turned to see Allie Ross standing beside me. She handed me fresh Kleenex, and then to my surprise, she gently moved me aside and stepped in front of the microphone. Someone, I'm not even sure who, led me off the stage and I stood at the side to listen as Allie spoke.

"I'm Allie Ross. I wasn't on the list of speakers because I didn't really know Mr. Caldwell very well, and I don't know that much about all the things he did for our town. But I know what he did for me, so I asked Charlotte if I could just take a short minute to tell you about it," she said, looking at the front row where Charlotte and the rest of Miller's family were sitting. I saw Charlotte nod her head.

"Uh, now that I got myself up here, I'm a little nervous," Allie continued.

I knew it was true by the way she kept tucking a strand of her curly dark hair behind her ear. She took a deep breath, let it out, and began again.

"Here goes. Some of you know that I did something really stupid last year. Actually, probably all of you know since it was all over the internet. It was embarrassing enough to live through it; I'm not going to talk about the details again here.

"When everything was happening and I was so ashamed and humiliated that I didn't even want to leave the house, Miller Caldwell came to see me. I was shocked. I was just this dumb high-school kid who worked part-time at his newspaper. I'd never said anything more to him than hello. But he went to the trouble to find out where I live, and he came over to my house to tell me something I'll never forget."

I stared at Allie. I'd never heard the story before. Ross was sitting toward the back of the room. I looked to see if he knew what his daughter was talking about, but his face was as surprised and curious as everyone else's.

"He told me that he knew what it was to hide a secret you were ashamed of. How scared and worried you feel all the time. How afraid you are about what people will think if they find out. But the funny thing is that once your secret comes out, you're free. That thing you dreaded has happened, and you're still here. You might feel bruised and battered, but one thing you don't feel is scared. He said the reason we hide things is because we're afraid if people know they'll judge us and decide that we're not good enough.

"But nobody gets to decide who we are, or if we're good enough, unless we let them. He said if I put my sense of self in someone else's hands, I'd always be afraid—to take a chance, to tell the truth, to make a mistake. And that's no way to live. He said that he hoped it didn't take me as long to figure that out as it had taken him.

"Lots of people were pretty mean to me after my big mistake went public, and some were very nice. But no one said anything to me that meant more, or that I'll remember longer than what Mr. Caldwell said. I know I'm not saying this very well and I'm taking way too long, but I'm almost through," she said with a nervous half-smile.

"He wasn't just good and kind to important people or people that were his friends. He was the same way to a high school kid he barely knew. I know there are plans for ways to honor him, scholarships in his name, and plaques going up, and buildings named after him, and that's great. But I think the best way to remember him is to try and be more like him. That's what I'm going to do."

As she stepped away, I wondered if others were remembering their own encounters with Miller's quiet kindness, as I was. From the silence that followed, I had to believe many of them were.

The reception following the memorial was held outside, and there were so many people milling about it was hard to find anyone.

"Coop, do you see Charlotte?" I asked after I had scanned the crowd unsuccessfully.

"I think that's her over there," he said, pointing to a table across the lawn that had been set up with photos and other Miller memorabilia. "There's no one with her. Let's go over now, before she gets swamped," he added.

"Sheriff Cooper, hi, you don't know me, but my name is Margie Grossman. I'd just like to ask you a question."

Margie, a short woman with gray hair in a close-cropped pixie cut, had planted herself in front of Coop. Her face wore the determined expression of someone who is not going to be put off easily—though Coop tried.

"Nice to meet you, Margie. But could I get you to give me a call at the office? Miller was a good friend of mine and I'd like to pay my respects to the family."

"Oh, I'll only be a minute. I just want to know if it's true what your deputy told me last week. See, my neighbor, his name is Henry Dearing, well, he got a dog just to upset my cat, Greg."

Coop gave me a look over Margie's head. I nodded my acknowledgment that he'd be awhile, and I slipped away.

As I approached Charlotte, she came forward to meet me.

"Leah! Thank you for that wonderful tribute to Dad. I appreciate it so much."

"You're welcome, Charlotte. I wish I hadn't lost it at the end. But I thought Allie's was amazing. I didn't know Miller had talked with her after that awful sexting thing she went through. But it's just like your dad, isn't it?"

She nodded.

"She asked me not to put her on the program in case she got too nervous to get up there in front of everyone. But she did a beautiful job."

"So, how are you holding up? Is there anything at all I can do?"

"You're already doing two important things—taking care of Sam and finding out who killed Dad."

"I'd like to talk to you and Sebastian tomorrow about that, to get some family background information."

"Yes, of course. How about my place, say ten o'clock?"

I hesitated for a second. I'd been hoping to meet them on more neutral ground because I didn't want to risk their mother, Georgia, interrupting the interview and derailing it.

"Sure, that's fine, if you don't think we'll disturb your mother."

She gave me a wry smile.

"Mother isn't staying with me. I have a third bedroom that I use as an office, and it has a nice pull-out sofa. But as you can imagine, Mother isn't a pull-out sofa kind of woman."

"Okay, then, tomorrow at ten at your place will be fine."

While we were speaking, I noticed Marilyn Karr out of the corner of my eye. She's the ex-wife of Paul Karr, the man my mother's been seeing for years. She's also the mother of Spencer Karr, owner of the now-shuttered *GO News*. Marilyn blames my mother for stealing her husband—though they'd been divorced for years before he and Mom started a relationship. Now she blames me for Spencer's problems. It doesn't matter to her that he'd probably be dead if it weren't for me. I'm not bragging about it. I had to think pretty hard about whether or not to rescue him. I'm still not sure I made the right decision.

When I saw the man with her, I did a double take. He was tall, with an athletic build, thick brown hair, and a handsome face. At first glance, he looked just like Miller.

24

It was, of course, his brother Fourey. When he and Marilyn reached Charlotte and me, Marilyn elbowed me out of the way and zoomed in to envelop Charlotte in a hug and a cloud of Chanel No. 5.

While she was gushing platitudes, I stepped aside and introduced myself to her companion.

"Hi. I'm Leah Nash, and you must be Miller's brother, Fourey. I'm so sorry for your loss," I said, holding out my hand to shake his.

He sandwiched it in a two-handed grip as he said, "Thank you. I know who you are. Miller talked about you a lot. He really enjoyed that little newspaper business you got him involved in."

"Well, there wouldn't be a newspaper if it weren't for him. But, I have to say this, when I first saw you for a second I thought—"

"You thought you were seeing things, right? The resemblance between us was even stronger when we were kids. My father used to ask me how we could look so much alike but be so different. I was the wild one who drove him crazy. Miller was the straight arrow."

Now that I was able to observe him up close, I realized the resemblance was mostly quick impression stuff. Same height, same build, same hair. With him standing directly in front of me, I could see that his eyes were a lighter shade of blue than Miller's had been. His mouth was fuller though, and his nose was thinner and sharper than Miller's.

"You live in Florida, is that right?"

"Yes. I left the family business years ago and ventured out on my own. My ideas were a little too bold, shall we say, for my father. Things turned out quite well for me."

He said it the way people do when they don't want to brag, but they want you to know they have something to brag about if they *did* want to. Now wasn't the time, but I was very interested in hearing more about him venturing out on his own. That was a nice way of putting that he'd been kicked out of the family by his father, as Georgia had told Miguel.

"What's your line of work, Fourey?"

"I'm in property development."

"Oh, like Miller!"

"Well, not exactly like Miller. I've been more involved in resort and high-end property. I admire what Miller managed to do here in Himmel, but it's not for me. I like the thrill of making money. It appeals to the gambler in me."

"I used to work in Florida. What part of the state are you in?"

"I'm all over the state. It's a big market and I've got a lot of connections."

"But you have a home base, don't you?"

"Wherever I drop anchor. I mean that literally. I live on my boat. When I find someplace I like, I stay until I get tired of it."

"I can see the appeal in that," I said. "How long will you be in Himmel?"

"I'm staying indefinitely. Mother's health is failing so rapidly. I've moved into the guest cottage so I can be close to her, but not underfoot in the house. Mother is on a lot of medication now, and we have home health care in round the clock. There's not a lot for me to do, but I want to be there."

"I'm glad you're able to do that, especially now with Miller gone."

"Yes, she relied on him a lot. He was always the good son. I was more the fun son. I could always make her laugh."

"Well, that's important, too," I said to be nice. He was in mourning, after all. But was he really? He didn't seem very sad about losing his brother, or the prospect of losing his mother.

"Thank you. Not everyone thinks that. My father certainly didn't."

He'd given me an opening to ask more about his relationship with his father, but I didn't want to get started and have the conversation interrupted, as was likely to happen. Marilyn had to be winding up with Charlotte soon. That thought caused me to shift a little abruptly to another topic that interested me.

"I noticed Marilyn Karr is with you. Is she a close friend of your family's?"

I was curious about the depth as well as the nature of their friendship. Marilyn is on the far side of sixty-five, making her close to fifteen years older than Fourey. Most men like Fourey would consider Marilyn past her sell-by date. And by "men like Fourey," I mean attractive charmers who usually prefer a younger woman on their arm.

"No, I met her last spring. Mother was feeling well enough to go to the Art Center show in March. Marilyn was there and we hit it off. I've been helping her with some investment advice. And she's been kind enough to invite me to some local events."

Anyone who says they "hit it off" with Marilyn gives me pause. I wondered if Marilyn's investment questions had anything to do with selling the GO News building and business.

"I've been doing most of the talking, Leah. Now I want to ask you a question. Charlotte said that she's asked you to investigate Miller's death. No offense intended, but I don't really understand why. It looks to me like the police are pursuing things vigorously. What's your role?"

"No offense taken. You're right. The sheriff's office is very competent, but as a journalist I do a lot of investigating, too. Miller was very important to me. I can't just sit on the sidelines. Sometimes people are more willing to talk to me than to a police officer. I just want to help if I can."

"Well, I'm all for putting every resource possible into finding out who killed my brother. Anything I can do to help, don't hesitate to ask."

"Fourey."

Marilyn Karr's voice cut sharply into our conversation.

"I see Father Lindstrom. You said you wanted to speak to him."

She linked her arm in his and began drawing him away without acknowledging me.

I should have just let her go. But I did not.

"Marilyn, it's lovely to see you, even under these circumstances. I'll call you soon for coffee. I'm dying to hear all about how rehab is going for Spencer."

She glared at me, which I may have deserved for trying to bait her.

"Fourey," she repeated.

He smiled down at Marilyn, who by now was practically tugging him away from me, and then turned to me. "Leah, it was good to meet you. Since I'll be around for a while, I hope we'll see each other again."

"Yes, I'm sure we will," I said. I turned to say a formal goodbye to Charlotte, but there were several people waiting to talk to her. Coop was at the end of the line, so I walked over to talk to him instead.

"Well, did you answer Margie Grossman's question about the dog and cat situation?"

"I answered, but not to her satisfaction. I think she's planning to liven up the next Board of Supervisors meeting."

"I'll make sure I'm not subbing for Miguel at that one. Oh, I see Tom Fuller over there. I want to ask him if there's anything I should be doing for Sam to help him adjust better. He's not eating all that well, and he's still hiding under my bed or behind the curtains most of the day. After that, I'm ready to go. This whole thing has been a lot."

"Okay, sounds good."

Tom was watching the video remembrance of Miller's life, which was playing on a loop on a table set up beneath a small canopy. I waited off to the side, not wanting to disturb him. I'd helped Miguel put it together, and it had been a hard assignment. Looking at images and video of Miller as a young father—holding Charlotte on his shoulders, teaching Sebastian how to play tennis, swimming in Lake Michigan with both kids, all three of them splashing and laughing—it wasn't bittersweet to me. It was crushingly sad.

When Tom turned away from the video, I said, "Hi, Tom. How are you doing?"

"Hello, Leah. About like everyone else, I guess. Stunned. Sad. Not quite able to believe Miller is gone. I've known him almost all my life. Admired him, too. But I never told him that. I keep thinking, why didn't I call him for a golf game instead of just thinking about doing it? I've been really busy, but I shouldn't have been too busy to get together with a friend."

"I know what you mean. That old Joni Mitchell song is right. You really don't know what you've got until it's gone."

He nodded and we stood there for a few seconds.

Finally, I said, "I saw you talking to Charlotte before the service. Did she happen to mention that I'm taking care of Miller's cat while she looks for a permanent home for him?"

"Yes, she did. In fact, I'm trying to help her find one. Is there a problem with Sam?"

"Well, not a problem, really. I didn't say anything to Charlotte about it because she's got enough on her mind. But Sam isn't eating very well. And yesterday when I tried to pet him, he sort of hissed, and then he scratched me. I don't think he likes me."

"Don't take it personally. I've been handling cats for years and I still get nailed occasionally."

He smiled and pushed up his sleeve to reveal a rather large Band-Aid on his forearm. "Happened this week. Unhappy Maine Coon Cat. Sam is probably just anxious and confused. Did you wash the scratch well and are you up to date on your tetanus vaccination?"

"Yes, and yes. I'm not worried about that. I want to know how to make Sam not hate me."

"He doesn't hate you. He's missing Miller. You said he's not eating well. Is he drinking water, using his litter box?"

"Yes."

"Well, give him a little more time to adjust. If you're still concerned in a few days, bring him in and I'll check him over."

"Thanks, Tom. I will."

I saw Coop waiting for me as I left Tom. He put his arm around me, squeezed my shoulder, leaned his head down, and said, "You look done in. How about we change our clothes and then go for a walk in the woods? It's a nice afternoon."

"Sheriff Cooper, that is the best idea I've heard in a long time."

25

The trees were already changing colors and a sprinkling of dried leaves crunched under our feet. Coop and I were walking the woods on a piece of property outside town that he was planning to buy.

"Mmm. Take a deep breath. Can't you smell fall in the air? I love this time of year. Thanks for thinking of this, Coop. It's been a tough few days. That memorial service just about ended me."

"I know it did," he said, squeezing my hand. "People say you need the ritual of a service because it helps you grieve and makes death real, and maybe that's true. But every one I go to feels harder to get through than the last."

"I think it's because they're cumulative."

"Meaning?"

"I mean that going to a funeral brings up a lot of past sadness that you've packed away. You don't only mourn the person who just died, your heart is grieving for everyone you've ever lost. You know, I practiced over and over again what I was going to say, because I wanted to do right by Miller. I wanted people to think about him and what a wonderful person he was, and not about me bawling my head off. I feel really bad that I messed up and lost it."

He stopped on the path and turned me to face him.

"Leah, stop. Your feelings about Miller are so strong, they broke through, and that's all right. You up there crying wasn't messing up. It showed what you were trying to say about Miller—that he was a great person, and his death leaves a hole in your life. You did Miller proud."

I reached up and pulled his face close to mine and kissed him.

"Thank you. That was a really nice thing to say. Also, if I'd realized you were such a good kisser, we might have gotten together a lot sooner."

"Well, if we had I wouldn't have had so much time to perfect my technique. It takes a lot of practice to get this good."

"Oh, really? Just how much practicing did you do before you finally woke up to the fabulous woman right in front of you?"

"I was always woke when it came to you. You're the one who was asleep at the switch. But I had to fill the time waiting for you somehow, didn't I? And now, you're the beneficiary. And if we're going to compare romantic pasts, I've got a list of names I'd like to go over with you, and they go way back before Nick."

"Okay. I'm sorry I brought it up. Let's go back to talking about how nice it is out here, so peaceful and soothing."

As if in direct counterpoint to my remark, a roaring, grinding, and at the same time whining noise rent the air and sent a flock of birds calling and squawking out of a nearby tree.

"What the heck is that?"

"I'd say it's a chainsaw."

Immediately after, another loud noise—this time it sounded like a backhoe starting up—shattered our quiet walk.

"Whoa! You're going to have some noisy neighbors out here. What's next, dynamiting?"

"The noise won't be my problem. I'm not buying the place."

"What? I thought you'd made an offer."

"I did, but the owners didn't accept it. They're selling to someone with cash who pushed the price too high for me to match. This is our farewell walk out here."

"Coop, I'm sorry. I know you really like this property."

"I do, yeah. But I don't feel so bad after what my realtor told me."

"What's that?"

"Part of what I liked about this place is the peace and quiet out here. But the place next door was sold to a couple of brothers, name of Dietrich. They own a construction firm in Omico. They're going to build a snowmobile racetrack there. From the sound of things, they've started work."

"A snowmobile racetrack? Holy cow! Can you imagine the *Vroom! Vroom! Vroom!* Of snowmobiles every weekend, all winter long?"

"Exactly. So, I'll keep looking. Let's take a last walk down by the creek and then head back to town, okay?"

We resumed walking hand in hand along the path.

"You know, my realtor called me about a house she thought I might like. It's in town, but it's on a double lot with a high hedge all around it, so there's privacy. The pictures online look good, but she warned me it needs a lot of work. And it's pretty big for one person. It has three floors. But the top floor might be a nice office space. A writer's suite even. A private space to get away from it all."

"Coop, come on. I thought we talked this through already. I don't want to move in with you. Not now, anyway. When you bring it up, my chest tightens up, and a little voice in my head says, 'no, no, no, don't do it.' I feel like I should listen to that voice."

"Leah, I'm happy being with you. I think you feel the same about me, don't you?"

"Yes, I do."

"Then isn't living together the next step? We could spend more time together. We're both so busy it's hard to see each other sometimes. If we lived together, things would be easier, not harder."

"It doesn't always work out that way. We've both experienced that. Moving in together could make things worse, not better. I've had one marriage fall apart and a couple of live-in arrangements that didn't work out. And do I need to bring up your marriage to Rebecca?"

"No, you don't. Look, I know that living together is the beginning of the end for some relationships. I don't think it would be for ours. But you feel how you feel. So, okay. I won't push you, if that's what it seems like I'm doing."

"It kind of does. I'm sorry that I'm not explaining it very well. But I just don't want to do it."

"Ever? Or now?"

"Now for sure. Ever? I don't know."

"All right. No more discussion. But I'll be checking in for status updates periodically. It doesn't hurt to check in now and then, does it?"

"No," I agreed. "It doesn't."

Then, in keeping with Nash family rules, which hold that a problem ignored is a problem solved, I moved away from a fraught emotional topic and changed the subject.

"What's Ross been up to? I looked for him today after the service, but I couldn't find him."

"He's turned up some things. But you should get that from him."

"Things about Noah Hanson? Things about the Caldwell family? What kind of things?"

He shook his head.

"Call Charlie and ask him. I thought you guys were going to cooperate with each other."

"We are, but I don't have much of anything to share. I didn't get anywhere with Noah Hanson. Did Ross? Come on, he did, didn't he?"

He held up his hand in a stop gesture.

"That's all you're getting from me."

"I don't know whether to thank you for dropping a hint or punch you in the arm for not telling me what Ross is on to."

"Why don't we do this instead?"

He stopped and turned me around to face him, then bent down and kissed me.

"Maybe we should go home now," I said when we moved apart.

And we did.

26

Charlotte Caldwell answered the door of her two-story brick townhouse on Sunday morning wearing gray yoga pants and a long-sleeved T-shirt. Her hair was pulled back in a loose ponytail and her brown eyes were tired and red-veined. The blotchiness of her pale skin told me that she'd been crying recently. I felt guilty for intruding and said so. But she waved my apology off.

"No, no, please don't. I asked you to help, and I'm fine, really. Just tired. Come in. Baz and I are in the living room. What would you like to drink? I have coffee, bottled water, or tea."

"Baz?"

"Sorry, it's Sebastian's family nickname. He prefers Sebastian now. Sometimes I still call him Bazzie, which he really hates," she said with a smile.

Sebastian stood up from the sofa as I came into the room. He had Miller's blue eyes and athletic build, and when he spoke, his voice was pleasant and low like his father's.

"Leah, I didn't get a chance to tell you yesterday, but thank you for speaking at the service," he said. "The story you told about when the two of you decided to buy the paper was great. It was so Dad, and you told it so well. Now that it's over, I kind of feel like I let him down by not speaking at the service myself. I just knew I wouldn't be able to get past the first words."

"Well as you saw, I barely managed to finish. But don't think for a second that you let your dad down. I doubt you ever could. Miller was so proud of you and so glad that you decided to go to law school. He must have told me that a dozen times."

"Thank you for saying that. I was so angry at Dad after he came out that I wasted a lot of time barely speaking to him. I'd give anything to see him one more time to tell him again how sorry I am that I acted like such a selfish brat."

Funny. That was almost the same thing Noah had said to me about *his* dad.

"Don't, Sebastian. Your dad understood how hard it was on you and Charlotte. He wouldn't want you to feel guilty."

"I know he wouldn't. But I still do. Anyway, please, sit down."

The chair he pointed me to was so luxuriously padded it almost swallowed me up. When Charlotte came back with my water, she sat next to Sebastian on the sofa, and they both looked at me expectantly.

"I'm here because before I talk to anyone else in the family, it would help if I had some background. I apologize in advance if things get a little awkward, but I need to understand some of the family history."

"It's all right, Leah. I asked for your help. We can't very well refuse to answer questions you have because they might be awkward," Charlotte said

"Good. So, let's talk first about money and get that out of the way. How did Miller leave his estate?"

"Everything goes to me and Sebastian, an even split."

"What does everything include?"

"The property development business, his share of the law partnership with Gabe, his house, his bank accounts, his stock portfolio, some real estate investments he had separate from the property development business."

"Is it true that when your grandfather died, his entire estate went to Miller—your uncle didn't get anything?" I asked, verifying the intel Miguel had picked up from their mother, Georgia.

They exchanged glances. It was Charlotte who spoke.

"Yes, that's true. Except that our grandparents had a prenuptial agreement that provided a trust fund for Grandmother in the event of divorce or my grandfather's death. So, Grandmother has that, but it reverts to the estate when she dies. Dad was the sole trustee who oversaw how the trust money was distributed. Baz and I are both successor trustees."

"Just so I've got this straight, you're saying that your grandfather did cut Fourey out of his will?"

"Yes," Sebastian said.

"So, how much money are we talking?"

"Grandfather's estate was fairly large. Combined with what we inherit from Dad, it's in the neighborhood of about fifteen million dollars," Charlotte said.

"That's a nice neighborhood. Tell me, did Fourey do one, big, terrible thing that got him cut out of the will, or was it cumulative?"

"We don't know," Charlotte said. "Grandfather never discussed it. Dad wouldn't either. He said it was between our grandfather and Fourey."

"What about Fourey? Did you ever ask him?"

"No. It was just one of those family things that you know you're not supposed to talk about. And we didn't see much of Fourey. He left Himmel before either of us were born. He came back to visit now and then. I loved it when he did. He was funny, and he played games with us, watched movies with us, took us to fun places like the Dells. I asked Dad once why Uncle Fourey didn't live in Himmel, and why he always stayed with us instead of at Grandfather's."

"What was his answer?"

"That Uncle Fourey and Grandfather had disagreed about something and were still unhappy with each other. That it was between them, and we should respect that."

"How about you, Sebastian, did you ever ask your father about Fourey's exile status in the family?"

"No, I just accepted that he was this kind of fairy godfather who breezed in and out of our lives, and always came with an armful of presents."

"Did your father and Fourey get along well?"

"As far as I know. I never heard them argue or anything," he said.

"Did your family ever visit Fourey in Florida?"

"No. But he used to tell me that one day he'd take me scuba diving with him off his boat. It never happened. It won't for sure now. He told me that he sold his boat in Naples and when he leaves here, he's not going back there."

"Where's he going?" I asked. This was an interesting twist. When I talked to Fourey just the day before, he'd made it sound like he was committed to the vagabond lifestyle on his sailboat. He'd also been vague about where it was docked at the moment. I filed those two thoughts away for the moment.

"He said he didn't know yet. He just knows it's time for a change."

"Does Fourey have any children? Has he ever been married?"

"He had a wife once, but we never met her. He doesn't have any children. At least none we know of. I guess it sounds strange to you—how little we know about our own uncle, I mean," Charlotte said. "But you need to understand something about the Caldwells. In our family, we don't talk about unpleasant things. The Fourey and Grandfather situation was unpleasant, so none of us discussed it."

"If your grandfather kicked him out of the family, how did it work when Fourey came to visit? Didn't your grandfather get angry that Miller was hosting him, when he'd made it clear that Fourey wasn't welcome in the family?"

"My dad and Grandfather were pretty close before Dad came out. But Dad wouldn't have let Grandfather dictate what he should do. Grandfather could choose not to see Fourey, but Dad didn't want to lose contact with his brother, I guess," Sebastian said.

"Your grandfather sounds like a harsh man."

"He could be very stern," Charlotte said. "But that's why it was always a thrill to have him tell us we'd done well. He had high standards. If he praised you, it meant a lot because you knew that you had really earned it."

"I don't think Uncle Fourey earned it very often," Sebastian added. "Grandfather took life very seriously. Uncle Fourey doesn't. I don't think they got along well even when Uncle Fourey was young. He used to tell us stories about some of the things he did that drove his father crazy," Sebastian said.

"What kind of things?"

"Skipping school, sneaking out when he was grounded, getting caught drinking the wine when he was an altar boy, stuff like that. Things a lot of kids do, but not Caldwells."

"Finally, Grandfather sent him to military school to get some discipline," Charlotte said. "He settled down enough to make it through college, and then Grandfather gave him a job at the bank. He told me once that he hated it. It was somewhere around that time that whatever happened between them happened."

"But you really don't have any idea what it was?"

"No. We really don't."

27

"You haven't talked about your grandmother. It must have been really hard for her, having to cut off contact with her oldest son."

"It would have been, but she didn't," Charlotte said. "Grandmother always deferred to Grandfather, but they were devoted to each other. Grandfather never forbade her to see Fourey. I think he loved her too much to hurt her that way. But he just kept himself away from things when Fourey was around. Which wasn't all that often."

"Okay, let's circle back to being indelicate about money. How did your uncle react to your grandfather cutting him off with nothing?"

"Sorry to keep saying this, but we don't know," Sebastian said. "I mean, it wasn't as though we all met in the lawyer's office for a reading of the will, like in the movies. Grandfather's attorney met with Dad and Grandmother. Then afterward, we—and I guess Fourey—were told. He could've been upset, but he didn't say anything to us. Dad didn't either."

"Charlotte, as the administrators of your grandmother's trust, now it's you and Sebastian who approve what she does with the money?"

"Yes."

"So, she couldn't start just funneling money to your uncle?"

"No, we'd have to agree."

"Does your uncle know about the trustee arrangement—I mean that you two will be filling Miller's role with regard to your grandmother's trust?"

"He hasn't asked me anything about it, but I assume he knows. Has he said anything to you, Baz?"

"No. But why are you even asking that, Leah? Do you think that Uncle Fourey killed Dad so he could start getting money from Grandmother? That's crazy."

"I don't think anything yet. I'm just trying to get enough information to start seeing the whole picture."

"Well, I hope that picture includes Noah Hanson. To me, it seems like he's the most logical suspect."

"Okay, let's talk about Noah a minute. You're roughly his age, Sebastian. Did you know him in school? Is there some reason you think he'd be capable of the kind of violence that killed your father?"

"I knew who he was, but we didn't hang with the same people. He told Charlotte that he blames Dad for his father's suicide. That seems like a pretty obvious motive for him to come after ours."

"Is that what you think, Charlotte?" I asked.

"I don't know what I think yet. It's hard to accept that anyone would want to kill Dad. I'm hoping you come up with the answer, Leah."

"I'll do my best. For now, I just have one more question for each of you. Charlotte, could you tell me what you were doing on the Wednesday morning when Miller was killed?"

"I was here in my apartment."

"Alone?"

"Yes. Dad had called me the night before to say that you both were all in on the nonprofit idea for the *Times*. I was so excited I had trouble sleeping. I got up early to start writing up my to-do list to get things rolling. I got the call from Detective Ross about six thirty and raced to the hospital. You know the rest."

"Sebastian, how about you?"

"I was in Chicago, in my apartment, alone. I was sound asleep when Charlotte called to tell me about Dad. I threw some things in a duffel bag and drove to Himmel. I had to stop for gas outside Janesville, but that's the only stop I made. You know, it's hard to believe that you're asking either of us for an alibi."

His tone wasn't exactly angry, but it wasn't as friendly as he'd been either.

"Bazzie, come on. I thought you agreed we should do any and everything to try to find out who killed Dad."

"I do agree. I just don't think that wasting time questioning people in our own family is going to find the answer. Leah's not the police, and if all she can come up with is asking us questions as though we're suspects, then maybe we should just rely on the real cops."

"I'd probably feel the same way if I were you, Sebastian. I'm sorry I upset you. Like I said, I'm just gathering as much information as I can. And if Detective Ross hasn't already asked you, he'll want to know where you were the morning of the murder, too."

"So if you're just going over the same territory, why do we even need you?"

"I don't think you 'need' me. Detective Ross is very competent and very thorough. But I have one motivation that he doesn't have. It's the same one that you and Charlotte have."

"What's that?"

"I loved Miller, too. That's why, whether or not it makes you angry, I have to keep asking questions. You don't have to answer them, but I won't stop until we know who killed Miller and why."

28

After I left Charlotte's, I followed up on Coop's hint that Ross might be making more progress than I was and called him.

"Hey, Ross. Are you home?"

"No. I'm at Jennifer's. Takin' care of her kids.'

"I didn't realize you had a side hustle as a babysitter. Do you have a card? I think Gabe might be interested in hiring you."

"Hey, I kinda got my hands full here. Allie was supposed to babysit, but she came down with some kinda stomach bug. I don't have a lotta time for kiddin' around. Whaddya want?"

From the shouting of Jennifer Pilarski's twin boys in the background, I knew that he was speaking the truth.

"I've got some information for you, and I need to ask you a couple of things."

"Yeah? Well—hang on a minute."

He broke off the conversation to break up a fight between Ethan and Nathan, Jen's six-year-olds. From what I could hear, an argument between the boys over whose toy dinosaur was the best had erupted into a physical fight.

"I gotta call you back," Ross said.

"No, I'll come over to Jen's. I'll give you a hand with the boys in exchange for some shared intel about Miller's murder."

I hung up before he could decline.

I tapped on the front door at Jen's house, then shouted hello as I walked into the living room.

"Leah!"

Both little boys came rushing out of the kitchen and ran up to me, waving their dinosaurs in the air. Both began talking excitedly at once.

"We're making a dinosaur army! My dinosaur, Spiney—I call him that because he's a Spinosaurus—he's the general of the ocean because Spin-osauruses can swim. And Nate's is—" Ethan began.

"My T-Rex is general of the jungle," Nate cut in, not willing to have his brother speak for him.

"Yeah, and—"

"Okay, guys. Tomato soup and grilled cheese is on the table. Now quit bouncin' off the walls and go sit down and eat. You think you can be alone for a few minutes without killin' each other while I talk to Leah?"

"Yes, Uncle Charlie!" They both shouted as they ran back to the kitchen.

"Geez!" Ross said. "Those kids had me runnin' all afternoon. I need a beer."

"When's Jen getting home?"

"She said around four thirty, so—" he looked at his watch. "Another hour and I'm free. Sit down. I'm going to," he said as he collapsed on the sofa. "All afternoon, always jabberin', always runnin' around, always hungry. Now that I say it out loud, it's kinda like spendin' time with you. No wonder I'm so tired."

"You're hilarious, Ross. Or should I say, 'Uncle Charlie'?"

"No. You shouldn't. Now what's this information you got for me?"

I told him about my conversation with Charlotte and Sebastian and that there was some mystery about Fourey's relationship to the family. He wasn't impressed.

"That's all you got? I had that the first day."

"Oh, really? Sorry. I guess I'm not as good at investigating as you. But we did agree we'd share, so I'm just honoring my commitment. Your turn."

He shook his head.

"I didn't say I'd share anything with you."

"Oh come on. You're looking so smug, you must have something good. What is it?"

"You're right, it is good. Nothin's wrapped up yet, but I guess I can give you a little heads up, to keep you from runnin' in circles. It's not gonna be too long before we make an arrest."

"What? You're ready to make an arrest? Would you have told me anything if I hadn't called you today?"

"I would, but maybe not on your schedule. I didn't call you because you're not on my investigation team, and you're not my boss. Also, I was waitin' until we had it nailed down. But we're so close now, I don't see any way out for the killer. When the lab results come in, that's gonna seal the deal."

"It's Noah Hanson, isn't it? I was hoping it wouldn't be him."

"Hope isn't how you solve a murder, Nash. It's keepin' your shoulder to the wheel, not tryin' to come up with fancy theories. Just good, solid evidence. And we got plenty of that."

He had leaned back on the sofa, and he looked pleased with himself. It was the best time to press him for some details.

"I thought Noah was hiding something when I talked to him Friday," I said. "He doesn't have much of an alibi, and he seemed really nervous."

"Same when I talked to him Thursday. But now we got the results on a fingerprint we found on the water fountain outside the tunnel. When I told him yesterday, I thought he was gonna cry."

"I didn't know you had a fingerprint from the crime scene."

"Thumbprint, yeah. There was some other smudged prints, but that thumb was nice and clear. When we ran it through the database, there he was. Noah Hanson, from when he had to get printed to work at some camp this summer."

"But how can you be sure that he left the print the day Miller was killed?"

"You sure like pokin' holes in the evidence when it's not yours, don't you? I know Noah's the one who left it there, Jessica Fletcher, because that water fountain was torn up and outta commission the whole month before. Some bozos vandalized it beyond repair. A county crew put in a brand spankin' new one on the Tuesday afternoon before Miller was killed. They didn't finish up until after six p.m. The only time Noah coulda left his print there was Wednesday morning, when Miller was killed."

"Well, but—"

"If you're goin' to say Noah mighta gone for a midnight run and left it there then, don't. You're just embarrassin' yourself. We had a storm front that blew in around seven that night, remember that?"

"Yes. It was a big one."

"Right. So nobody was out runnin' in the dark in the county park in the middle of that. And it kept up until after midnight."

"Okay, I see your point."

"You do? Great. Now I got somethin' to put in my diary."

I hadn't picked at his fingerprint evidence because I doubted Ross. I did it because I knew he'd get annoyed, and when that happens, he sometimes says more than he means to. Like he proceeded to do.

"That print isn't all. We also got a nice blood sample from the base of the water fountain outside the tunnel. I figure there's no way a fit guy like Miller doesn't fight when someone comes at him with a knife. I'm willin' to bet the killer got cut and that blood on the fountain is his. And when we get the DNA results back, that sample from the fountain is gonna belong to Noah Hanson."

"How long before you get the results?"

He shook his head and when he answered, the triumph in his voice had been replaced by irritation.

"There's a big backlog at the crime lab. We got a rush on our sample 'cause it's a homicide. It's still gonna be at least ten days, they say. But we got just about the whole package on Noah already."

"What's 'the whole package'?"

He began ticking off the particulars of his case against Noah.

"Like I said, there's the thumbprint, that puts him at the scene. Then there's his motive, revenge, and it's a two-fer in Noah's case. He blames Miller for his dad losing the farm and for his dad's suicide. And he hasn't been shy about sayin' that. Another thing, he's a medical student. He knows where to poke in a knife to do the most damage, fast. Then, when I gave Noah enough rope to hang himself yesterday, he basically said how high."

"What are you saying?"

"I'm saying that what he told me first is that he was home asleep in his bed when Miller was killed. Then, when I hit him with the fingerprint and asked how it got there, he panicked. Best he could come up with is to say that he lied the first time, because he was scared, but now he was ready to tell the whole truth. Then he came out with his new alibi."

"Which is?"

Ross hesitated, suddenly realizing he'd given me basically his whole case.

"Come on, Ross. You might as well tell me. I'm sure if he told you, he's also told Miguel and Troy. I can get it from them, or from Noah himself."

"Hey, hey, hey. Don't you go tellin' Noah we're about to make an arrest."

"I'm not going to do that. Are you going to tell me and save me some time, or do I just go ask Miguel what Noah's said to him?"

"All right. But this goes nowhere, including to your newspaper buddies. In Noah's new version of his alibi, he says he couldn't sleep. So, he decides to get up, go for a run at the county park and clear his head. It's about five thirty when he gets there. He starts his run, goes hard for a couple of minutes, but it's pretty dark still. He slips on some gravel, takes a fall, and cuts his arm on a sharp stone. He says his thumbprint is on the fountain because he went there to wash it off. When it won't stop bleeding, he gives up on his run and goes home. He gets there around ten after six, puts a bandage on his arm, and he goes back to bed and falls asleep. He doesn't hear Troy when he leaves, and the first thing he knows about Miller's murder is when Troy calls him later that morning."

"Well, that does explain how Noah's thumb print got there, and also where the blood you found on the fountain came from," I said. "And it could also explain why he seems so nervous. He wasn't telling the truth because he knew that it would look suspicious if he admitted being at the park."

"Come on, that story was a Hail Mary play. He just made up something to account for the thumbprint. He doesn't know about the blood sample yet. And when we match up his blood with the blood on the fountain, it's all over. That's the whole thing wrapped up with a little bow."

"If you're that sure, why haven't you arrested him already, or at least taken him in for formal questioning?"

"I don't want him to lawyer up yet. If we take him in, he's sure to. Right now, he's stewin', but he's hopin' his story is good enough. And the longer he stews, the more likely he'll be to crack wide open when we do bring him in. Also, Timmins agrees—but that's probably because he's in Las Vegas. He took off right after Miller's service and he's not gonna be back until Tuesday night. He doesn't want us to make an arrest until after he's back to get his mug in front of the cameras. We got a solid theory of the crime—motive, means, and opportunity. You got something better?"

"No," I admitted. "I'm just getting started. I've only interviewed Noah, Charlotte, and Sebastian so far. I don't have anything yet."

"So, you're mad because I beat you to it?"

"No, of course not. I guess I just really don't want it to be Noah. I feel sorry for him."

"Hey, I'm not happy with who it is, either. I think the kid's had some real tough breaks. But murder ain't the answer."

"I know, Ross. But if you're right and it's Noah, I'm not going to get what I was looking for."

"Yeah? What's that?"

"A sense of satisfaction, I guess, that justice has been served. I know that if Noah did it, he has to be held accountable. But if it's Noah, then I'll just feel like two people died and another one ruined his life, and all for what?"

There was a loud clatter in the kitchen. Ross said, "I gotta go check that out."

He clapped me on the shoulder and said, "Nash, don't waste your sympathy on Noah. He did what he did. And he has to pay for it. That's how it works."

29

Once home, I poured myself a small Jameson over ice and headed to my window seat. Sam was sitting in the opposite corner, which he seemed to have claimed as his spot. He looked up and flicked his tail once, then his head sank back down on his paws and his eyes closed. At least he hadn't run away.

I took a sip of my drink and enjoyed the slight burn that followed as I stared out the window. Not much traffic on a holiday weekend, but Wide Awake and Woke was open until five, so there were a few people going in and out, laughing and talking. Farther up the block was Davina's Purrrfect Kitty Boutique, and I wondered how she was doing without Sabrina. It occurred to me then that she might be a match for Sam, but it was probably too soon. I took another small sip and my mind wandered, as it had since he died, to thoughts of Miller.

Looking down the street, I could count four buildings that wouldn't be there if not for Miller's vision and hard work. And I wouldn't be sitting where I was in a space that I love if it weren't for him. He'd taken an old department store and turned it into offices on the ground floor that the *Himmel Times* had rented even before he and I bought the paper. He'd intended the second floor as office space but hadn't found a tenant. He'd been thinking about turning it into more apartment space like mine. He'd had a lot of plans—for his properties, for the paper, for the town. Was everything gone now because a grief-stricken Noah had allowed his own guilt and his rage to overwhelm him? It was so senseless, and so sad.

"You know, Sam, I didn't want to admit it to Ross, but I do feel bad that I'm not going to be the one who solves Miller's murder. I've lost the chance to do something to pay him back, at least a little, for everything he's done for me and for Himmel."

Sam had raised his head at the sound of my voice. As I finished, he meowed at me, gave me a stern look, and went back to ignoring me.

"You're right. Self-pity is a useless emotion," I said.

I realized then that there was something I could do in remembrance of Miller. Allie had told us all what it was. Try to be the kind of person that he had been. Miller was the embodiment of one of his favorite sayings. "Keep calm and carry on."

What exactly did that mean? Well, it sure didn't mean pouting and feeling sorry for myself when Clinton broke the news that despite my best efforts, I hadn't produced a manuscript ready for publication. It didn't mean being a jerk to Clinton, and Coop, and my mother when they tried to talk to me about it. When Miller lost his dream of a political career, he didn't whine and feel sorry for himself. He found another way to serve. Surely I could find another way to write.

"Sam, I'm going to call Clinton, apologize for acting like a ten-year-old, and tell him I'm ready to start revising the manuscript. Are you listening, Sam? I'm going to channel Miller and act like a grown-up for a change."

I made the call, prepared to deliver the apology Clinton deserved and the promise to start work again on the manuscript. It felt a little anticlimactic when he didn't pick up and I had to leave a voice mail. No sooner had I hung up than my phone rang.

"Clinton, hi! I just—"

"It's not Clinton. It's me, Miguel. I have to see you now! I have proof!"

"Proof of what?"

"Proof that Noah did not kill Miller."

I didn't say anything for a minute, trying to figure out how to let him down easy, without telling him all that Ross already had on Noah. Miguel shouted into the silence.

"*Chica*, did you hear me?"

"Miguel, I know he's your friend, and I know that you think Noah is—"

"No, no! Listen to me, please. I don't *think* Noah is innocent. I know he is. I have the proof!"

"What kind of proof?"

"Come to Troy's, right now. It's here, you'll see!"

"Miguel, I've been out most of the day. I should stay with Sam for a while, I think. He's having a hard time adjusting. Maybe tomorrow I can hear what Noah has to say. Right now, I'm just—"

"Noah isn't here now. Neither is Troy. It's just me and Sadie. You are not understanding me. I have proof. Real evidence."

"Who is Sadie? And what kind of evidence?"

"Just come."

When I knocked on the door at Troy's, Miguel hollered for me to come into the kitchen. Sitting at the table were two little girls about ten and six, I guessed. Miguel was sitting across from them, and next to him was a pretty woman with curly red hair and lots of freckles. She looked about my age.

"Leah, these are my friends, Miranda and her two girls, Sadie and Delia. Miranda, Sadie, Delia, this is my friend Leah who I told you about."

I had no idea what was going on, but I shook Miranda's hand, and when Sadie, the older one, confidently reached out with hers, I shook it, too. She had hair the color of her mother's, but it was straight and pulled back in a long ponytail. She had her mother's freckles, too. Delia, her little sister, had her mother's curls, but hers were light brown, and she had no freckles. She smiled shyly at me when I said hello to her.

"It's nice to meet all of you, but Miguel, I'm not sure why I'm here," I said.

"He wants me to tell you what I told him. And my mom is here because Miguel invited her, and she wants to know, too. My sister Delia is here because she always has to be where I am," Sadie said before Miguel could answer.

"I see. . . . But not really, Sadie. Miguel, didn't you want to tell me something about Noah?"

"Yes! This is all about Noah, and Sadie is the one who has the story."

"I'm a little confused."

"You won't be. Sadie, can you tell Leah what you told me about how you saved your dog from Mr. Crabby? Tell the whole story just how you told it to me."

30

Sadie, who clearly enjoyed playing to an audience, sat up very straight in her seat and began in a whispery voice, as though she were telling a ghost story around a campfire.

"Well, Mr. Crab—sorry, we're not supposed to call him that. Mr. Crabtree is really his name. Me and Delia call him Mr. Crabby because he's so mean. My story is that one morning last week, Wednesday morning I—"

She hesitated and looked at her mother. "Mom, you won't get mad, will you?"

"Sadie, I'm already mad, but I'll be madder if you don't tell the truth, all right?"

"But she already fibbed to you, Mama. And she was mean to me. She said she would take my Peppa Pig and hide her if I told. So, I didn't."

"Well, we'll sort that out later at home, Delia. Let's let Sadie tell her story. I'm curious to hear it, too."

"Yes, Squealia—I mean Delia," Sadie said.

"Sadie," her mother said in a tone that took me right back to my own childhood.

"Yes, Mom. Sorry, Delia. But now can I tell my story?"

Hearing no objections, she began again.

"Mr. Crabtree is this really mean man who lives down the street. And he hates dogs. And sometimes our dog Thor, he's a very, very nice dog and wouldn't hurt anyone, but sometimes Thor digs under the fence and gets out. When he goes by Mr. Crabtree's house, he shoots at him with a BB gun! And one time he hit Thor! And he cried and cried. Thor I mean, not Mr. Crabtree.

"Mom talked to him, but he doesn't care. And I told him that I would watch Thor really, really well, but that he's a good digger and sometimes he might still get out. Then he told me if he does, he's going to shoot Thor with a real gun! And he took it right out of his shed and he showed it to me! That made me really worried because it *could* happen again. Because like I said, Thor is a very good digger."

Sadie looked at me as if to make sure that I was following the story. I was, but I had yet to understand the relevance. I nodded. That seemed sufficient. Sadie continued.

"I couldn't let him shoot my dog!"

"No, of course not, *chiquita*," Miguel said.

"So last week, on Wednesday morning, I got up really early and I—"

"And she sneaked out of the window, and she told me not to tell, because Mama would get very mad."

"But here you are, Delia, telling," Sadie said.

"Delia, we'll discuss this later. Right now, let Sadie tell her story," her mother said.

"I got up very early, like, I set the alarm on my phone for five thirty, because I didn't know how long it would take. I knew I had to be back before Mom came to wake us up at six thirty or I'd be in big trouble. Everybody on the whole street was still sleeping. It wasn't totally light yet, but I could see all right.

"I went really quiet and careful, behind the houses so nobody would see me. When I got to Mr. Crabtree's house, I went into his garden, and I unlocked his shed. I knew where the key was because I saw him hide it after he told me he was going to shoot Thor if he came back. It was under a fake rock."

"That man! Keeping a gun in his garden shed! I'll have a talk with him all right," Miranda said. She added, "But don't think that Mr. Crabtree's bad behavior is going to get you out of trouble for yours, Sadie. We have a lot to talk about later."

"Well, you're probably not going to like the rest of the story very much either," Sadie said. "When I opened his shed, I took his gun."

"Sadie! That was very dangerous! It was also stealing," her mother said.

"I know, Mom. But I had to protect Thor. Besides, it was the lesser of two evils. That's when you do a bad thing because the other thing is way worse."

"I'm aware of what it means, Sadie. Go on with your story."

"Well, I took his gun, and I went down to the retention pond, and I dropped it over the fence. Then I climbed over it myself, and I took the gun and threw it as far as I could into the water. Then I climbed back over and came home. But when I got to Troy's side of the duplex, I heard a car coming down the street. I dived down behind the big bush beside the porch so they wouldn't see me."

She got off her chair and crouched beside it, peering carefully around the edge as she acted out her narrative.

"Then the car drove into our driveway! And a man got out and he came right toward the porch, right where I was. I quick took his picture with my phone, in case he was a robber so I could show the police if he robbed Troy."

"Yeah, like you robbed Mr. Crabtree," Delia said, finding her voice yet again. "You're a robber. The police should come and get you!" Sadie's threat to Peppa Pig must have cut deep.

Sadie ignored her sister.

"But then he got closer, and it was Noah, Troy's friend. I waited until he went inside so he wouldn't see me. Then I ran over to our side of the duplex and climbed through the window and got back in bed. It was 6:16 on my phone, and my mom didn't even know I was gone! Until now."

Sadie's story fit with the timing of the revised alibi Noah had given to Ross.

"Miguel! You're right! It wasn't Noah," I said.

Sadie took offense at that.

"Yes it was Noah. See, here's the picture I took," she said, pulling out her phone and scrolling through a number of photos before she found what she was looking for, and handing it to me.

"I take a lot of pictures," she said. "I'm thinking of being a detective, so I'm practicing watching people."

"Well, this is a great one," I said as I looked at the image of Noah. I clicked the info button and there it was, the date and time stamp. Wednesday, September 3, 6:11 a.m.

"Sadie Louise Tomlin, you are in so much trouble. Give me your phone, right now," Miranda said.

"But Mom. Dad wants me to have it. In case of an emergency."

"I didn't like it when your father gave it to you. You're too young. Maybe when I tell him what you've been doing, he'll agree. But for now, hand it over."

"Mommm, no!"

"Sadie."

Miranda held out her hand.

Sadie gave the phone to her.

"Girls, I want you to go home now. I'll be right there. I'm going to talk with Leah and Miguel for a minute. And then, Sadie, I'll want to talk to you."

Sadie looked aggrieved but knew enough not to push back.

"Yes, Mom. It was nice meeting you, Miguel. You, too, Leah," she said.

"I am so happy I met you, Sadie. You don't even know," Miguel said.

"It was great meeting you, Sadie. You, too, Delia," I said. "I'll see you around."

"Probably not for a long time," Sadie said sadly. "Come on, Delia."

She nudged her sister, who had been listening with the keen interest of someone who knows she's not the one in big trouble.

"I'm coming. Bye!" Delia said as the two of them left by the kitchen door.

"Miranda, your girls are really cute. Sadie is scarily precocious. I know you have to make sure she understands the danger of what she did. But I hope you keep in mind that she just might have saved Noah's life. I'll let Miguel explain. I've got a call I need to make."

A few hours after I had updated Ross, he called me back.

"Yeah, okay, you win. The kid's story holds. We found the gun in the retention pond where she said. We got the photo with the date and time stamp from her phone. Unless he did some time traveling, I can't see any way Noah Hanson killed Miller. I'm not lookin' forward to meeting with the DA about this. I was just so sure. I mean, how could that lame-ass alibi be true?"

Ross's voice was weary, deflated, and chagrined. Pleased though I was that Noah Hanson wasn't the killer, I understood Ross's feelings.

"Hey, look at it this way. Timmins will be mad, yeah. But it's better to find out your theory doesn't hold up before you make an arrest than it is after."

"Yeah, I know. I'm still pretty pissed at myself, though. I shoulda known it was comin' together too easy. Things never go that smooth. I feel like a real dumbass."

"What did Coop say?"

"He wasn't happy that I got too far over my skis, but he didn't beat me up too bad."

"I'm sure he knows you're doing a fine job of that yourself, Ross. But it's not like you just came up with an idea out of nowhere. You had good reasons to suspect Noah. Heck, you pretty much convinced me."

"Nash, why are you bein' nice to me? I thought you'd be jumpin' up and down because I was wrong about Noah. Now you got another chance to beat me to the punch."

"Hey, I'm always nice to you. I keep telling you, we both want the same thing, to find out who killed Miller. Can we just move ahead, maybe help each other out a little, and not worry about who's beating who to the punch?"

"Yeah, well, we'll see. Right now, I'm gonna have a beer, watch the Brewers game, and go to bed. I'll start over again tomorrow."

"Where are you going to start?"

"Well, that missing watch might be more important than I thought."

"What missing watch?"

"I didn't tell you about that?"

"No, you did not."

"Huh. I thought I did. Well, might be nothing, might be something. Miller's ex, Georgia, she took me up one side and down the other when I interviewed her. Wanted to know when Miller's personal property would be returned. I told her there wasn't much. The clothes would stay as evidence, the only other thing he had on him was an ID holder with his driver's license in it. She went ballistic. Said Miller had a fancy runner's watch that his kids gave him for his birthday last year, worth a few thousand bucks, and a cop or the EMTs musta taken it."

"That's ridiculous."

"It is. I checked with Miller's kids to confirm that he had a watch like Georgia said. I got the make and a serial number from them. I notified pawn shops in the area. Got nothin' back on that yet. I was thinkin' maybe Noah took it. He was hard up for money, and a watch like Miller's coulda brought him a thousand bucks or more. I was waitin' to hear back from the pawnshops before pushin' him on that. I had enough other stuff on him—I thought. Now, I gotta look at it different."

"Different how?"

"Someone's been sellin' weed to high school kids at the county park— early mornings and late evenings before the park closes. I'm thinkin' maybe that's who made the anonymous 911 call."

"And you think whoever it is witnessed something, but won't come forward because it would come out that he's selling?"

"That's one angle. Or, maybe, he went after Miller himself, to get the watch. He could get decent money for it. He coulda threatened Miller with the knife, things got outta hand, and he stabbed him. I'm not gonna land too hard on anything just yet. I gotta take another look at the family, too. I don't trust that Fourey guy. Way too smooth. What about you?"

"I press on. I need to talk to Fourey and Georgia. Then maybe to Dennis Warby, that guy who accused Miller of trying to turn his son gay."

"Who's Dennis Warby? Are you sayin' that you got a suspect I never even heard of? How long were you gonna sit on that?"

"I guess about as long as you sat on the missing watch."

"Touchy," Ross said. Which I knew was Ross-speak for touché. "But I wasn't hidin' the watch from you, it just didn't seem that important."

"Same here with the Warby guy. I wasn't keeping him from you on purpose. He's just not that high on my list. I haven't spent any time on him yet. But since we're doing a little teamwork here, did you know that Georgia and Miller had an argument in the office a week or so before he was killed?"

"Go on."

"Gabe overheard them. Georgia was pretty upset. It sounded like she asked Miller for money, he refused, and she threatened him."

"Threatened him how?"

"She implied that she knew a secret that she was going to share if Miller didn't come through with the money. You should talk to Gabe. I'm just giving it to you secondhand."

"Thanks for that investigating tip, but I already know how to get witness testimony."

"Don't be like that. You told me about the watch and the drugs in the park. I told you about what Gabe heard and Dennis Warby. See how well we do together?"

He made a guttural sound that could have passed for either agreement or disagreement. I decided it was agreement.

"I gotta go. The game's already in the third inning. I'll catch you later. And uh, thanks, Nash."

"You're welcome, Ross."

After hanging up with Ross, I made a quick call to Charlotte to let her know that it looked like Noah was in the clear. I didn't know how soon the story would be in the *Times* and I didn't want her to learn about it online.

I called Coop to check in with him, but I had to leave a message when he didn't pick up. Then I made myself a tomato sandwich with a really juicy, red, ripe tomato on toasted sourdough bread with just the right amount of mayonnaise and cracked pepper. Delicious.

Sam came into the kitchen as I was standing at the counter. He ignored me, but at least he didn't run to the bedroom. When I finished, I grabbed my legal pad to start rethinking things. I sat in my corner of the window seat while Sam took up "his" spot on the other.

With Noah out of the picture, the focus had to be on the family. Yes, there was the wrong place/wrong time possibility Ross had suggested. Namely that Miller's death was the result of a random theft gone wrong. It didn't feel right to me. Besides, Ross had better resources than I did to check into that. First up for me would be Georgia, and then on to Fourey. Depending on what I learned, I might continue down that road, or take a detour to Dennis Warby.

When my phone rang, it was Coop.

"Hi! I've been dying to talk to you! What about Noah Hanson? Wait, what's all that noise in the background? Where are you?"

"I'm at the Dietrich property—next to the place I tried to buy."

"The snowmobile racetrack place? What are you doing there?"

"The guys working on the construction found a skeleton. A human one."

31

"A skeleton! Is it a man? A woman? Can they tell how long it's been there?"

"It's a child's skeleton," Coop said, his voice serious and sad. "I think it's Eddie Garcia."

The name stopped my questions for a minute.

Eddie Garcia was ten years old when he had disappeared from Himmel in 1982. That was before my friends and I were even born. But we all knew his name, because our parents evoked it when warning us about "stranger danger." The cardinal rules that underpinned our ability to roam freely around town were: don't talk to strangers, don't take food or candy from strangers, and never, ever, get into a stranger's vehicle, not even if the stranger says that your mother sent him to pick you up. The closing admonition was always, "You don't want what happened to Eddie Garcia to happen to you, do you?"

And, no, we did not want to be kidnapped and driven away in a white van, never to be seen again. That was the police theory on what had happened to Eddie, based on reports from several kids who had seen Eddie the afternoon of the day he went missing.

A massive hunt with hundreds of volunteers had ensued for Eddie. The police investigated every actual and suspected pedophile in the county, talked to Eddie's neighbors, interviewed all the kids who had been at

Riverview Park that day, and nothing had come of any of it. The Caldwell family had even put up a reward for any information leading to the solution of the case. It was never claimed because Eddie was never found.

"Oh, my God, Coop! All these years he's been missing, and he was less than five miles from home? How was he found?"

"The crew working for the Dietrich brothers were tearing down what was left on the property—a burned-out house, a shed, and an abandoned stone well. Eddie's skeleton was at the bottom of the well, along with a kid's bike. It matches the description of the one Eddie was riding the last time he was seen."

"If the bike was down in the well that means Eddie couldn't have fallen in by accident."

"Exactly. Somebody must have tossed his body in there like a sack of trash and his bicycle after him to get rid of it."

"The kidnapper in the white van?"

"That's getting too far ahead of things. We need to confirm that the skeleton is actually Eddie's. I don't have any doubt, but we have to get a positive ID. Connie's out here now. She already put in a call to Paul Karr to find out if Eddie was a patient of his. He was, and Paul has the dental records."

"I'm surprised he has them back that far."

"Me, too. But Paul said Eddie was one of his first patients when he went into practice. Like everyone else, he felt terrible when Eddie disappeared. He decided the one thing he could do was keep his records in case Eddie was ever found."

"So, are you going to wait to tell Eddie's dad until the identification is finalized with Paul's records?"

"No, not with the way word travels around here. I don't want him to hear some half-true story from a well-meaning neighbor. I'll tell him we're still waiting on confirmation, but there's not much doubt. The bike matches the description of Eddie's, and there was an inhaler down there, too. Eddie had asthma. So . . ."

"Sounds like it would be a miracle if it's not Eddie. How much of this are you releasing to the public?"

"Miguel just got here. I'll give him pretty much the same information, so if you're wondering what to share, you don't need to. But I'm going to tell him that he needs to wait to publish until I have time to talk to Eddie's father, Benny. I'm heading to see him as soon as I hang up with you."

"Coop, I'm sorry. That's going to be a tough conversation to have."

"Yeah."

"All right, well, I'll let you get to it. Are you coming by later?"

"No, I don't know how long I'll be with Eddie's dad. Then I'm coming back out here, and I want to check in with Connie, too. I don't know when I'll finish up tonight. I'll call you tomorrow."

"Oh, hey, wait a sec. We didn't even talk about Noah Hanson. I'm glad he's in the clear, but Ross is feeling like he really screwed up."

"Yeah, well, the only real mistake he made was getting ready to take a victory lap before all the evidence was in. I understand why. But if we'd arrested him and then the blood sample from the fountain didn't match Noah's DNA, it would've been a mess. That didn't happen, so I'm counting it as a win. Listen, I need to get over to see Benny Garcia before he hears about Eddie from somewhere else."

"Sure. I'll talk to you in the morning."

I couldn't settle down after Coop called. I kept thinking about Benny Garcia, and how after all the years of hope, and despair, and grief, and longing, he was finally going to get an answer. But that answer would tear open whatever he'd covered the hole in his heart with. Maybe there would be some small measure of peace that came from knowing what had happened to his son. But would you really want to know if it doused the small flicker of hope that you'd kept alive all this time? Facing the reality that your darkest imaginings and your deepest fears were true seemed like cold comfort at best.

Finally, I sat down on the window seat and stared outside. Sam jumped up and joined me. For once, he didn't retreat to the far corner. He chose a spot somewhat closer to me, though not close enough for me to pet him. He let out a plaintive meow. I knew it wasn't a request for food or water. He had plenty in his bowls. It was almost as though he was offering me a little sympathy. As long as I didn't get too familiar.

"I got some bad news from Coop. Not personally bad, but it's pretty awful."

I told Sam the story of Eddie, as much as I knew. As I did, my mind quieted down enough to wonder who was going to handle the case. Ross was tied up with Miller's murder. Coop had decided to have Marla fill Owen Fike's spot, but she didn't have the experience to lead a murder investigation yet—especially not one that was forty years old. There wasn't anyone in the sheriff's office to step up except the sheriff. Coop would have to take on the Eddie Garcia case.

32

The next morning, I read our online story about the skeleton found at the snowmobile race track construction site. It didn't definitively identify the remains. However, the context of the article made it pretty clear who the victim likely was to anyone who knew the Eddie Garcia story. And in Himmel, almost everyone did. By seven in the morning when Coop called, Miguel's piece already had hundreds of hits.

"Coop, hi! How are you doing? Have you got time to stop by for breakfast? I've got a brand-new box of Cheerios."

"I'd like to, but I can't. I've got a call with the district attorney in half an hour. We already had a chat last night about both Miller's murder and Eddie's case, but I guess he's got more to say. He's not scheduled to get back until tomorrow night, but he wants to be 'more hands-on' because he thinks the sheriff's office isn't 'hitting the mark.'"

"Cliff Timmins is such an asshat. Did you tell him he's not the boss of you?"

"More or less, but I still need to work with the guy, at least until he wins that judgeship he's chasing."

"You're going to take the lead on Eddie Garcia's case, aren't you?"

"Have to. There's no one else to do it right now. I'm going to work with Marla on it, see how she does. It's going to take a lot of patience. A case this old, the leads aren't just cold, they're frozen. I'm kind of concerned, too, that the records from forty years ago might not be all that complete. The sheriff's office had different standards back then."

"Yeah. Somehow I doubt that Art Lamey's dad was any better at being sheriff than Art was."

"That's probably true. I just hope he wasn't any worse."

Art Lamey had been the sheriff before Coop, and his short time in the job had been rife with corruption.

"Cosign that. How did it go with Benny Garcia last night?"

"It was pretty tough. I told him what we'd found, then I showed him a photo of the bicycle and he confirmed it was Eddie's. He said he knew for sure, because Eddie got the Batman bike horn on the handlebars as a birthday present. When Benny recognized that horn, he just broke down and couldn't stop crying."

"That must have been awful. For him feeling that pain, and for you witnessing it."

"It was. He lives alone—his wife died a few years ago. I called his sister for him—she lives in Omico. And I stuck around until she got there. I couldn't leave him alone like that. While we waited for her, I thought it might help him to tell me stories about Eddie. It seemed to at first. He talked about how smart Eddie was, and the things he liked to do, the trips they went on as a family. He showed me an album Eddie had put together of his favorite baseball cards. That summer when Eddie disappeared, his dad had taken him to see a Brewers game, and Robin Yount signed Eddie's baseball card for him."

"Who's Robin Yount?"

"Only one of the greatest players the Brewers ever had. He played shortstop and center fielder for them for twenty years. He was Eddie's favorite. Benny said after Eddie got the card signed, he carried it with him everywhere so he could show it to people."

I could tell from his voice that Coop was having a hard time with the story. He stopped for a few seconds before he went on.

"The thing is, Benny asked me if the card was with him when we found Eddie. He said he hoped so, because it meant that Eddie had something he loved with him when he was so scared and alone like he must've been. I had to tell him no. He cried so hard then, I thought he'd never stop. He blames himself because he agreed to let Eddie stay alone for a couple of hours that Saturday when the babysitter canceled at the last minute. He just couldn't get past that. I was really glad when his sister walked in."

I felt my own eyes prick with tears.

"Oh, Coop, that's heartbreaking. But I'm sure you did help him. He needs to talk about Eddie, and you let him."

"I've had to do death notifications before, but this one . . . that sad, lonely, old man has spent the last forty years of his life hoping his son would come home. Now he knows he never will. It was brutal. It really got to me."

"That's because you really care about people, and about your job. It's why you're so good at it. What's going to happen next?"

"They're going over the dental records this morning. So, we'll probably issue a press release with formal identification later today. I'm sure Cliff will want to hold a full press conference as soon as he gets back. At least he'll be distracted from giving us hell for not having Miller's case solved already. What have you got going today?"

"I want to talk to Georgia this morning, and then I'll move on to Fourey and go from there. How about dinner and a slumber party with me and Sam tonight?"

"You still have a roommate? I thought it was just temporary until Charlotte could find a home for him."

"It is. But she's got a lot to think about right now, so I'm not going to bug her about finding a home for Miller's cat. We're doing all right. So, what about tonight?"

"I'd like to, but I'll have to let you know for sure later. It depends on how the day goes."

33

"Thanks for seeing me, Georgia. I appreciate it."

Miller's ex-wife and I were in the living room of the Airbnb rental where she was staying. It was, like Georgia, upscale and well decorated. Much as I'd like to say otherwise, Georgia is a good-looking woman in her early fifties. As she settled herself across from me, the scent of an expensive perfume wafted my way.

I had declined her grudging offer of coffee. Usually, I accept such gestures. That's because when people cast themselves in the role of host, it makes an interview feel less like an interrogation than a visit. However, I knew there wasn't enough hosting instinct in the world to diminish Georgia's hostility toward me.

"Charlotte informed me that she had asked you to investigate Miller's death over my objections. I don't think you have any business getting involved in a family tragedy, but apparently what I think doesn't matter. So, please, get on with it."

"Okay, let's jump right into the deep end. Where were you the morning Miller was killed?"

"You can't be serious. You're asking me for an alibi?"

"What's the matter, don't you have one?"

"I don't need one because it's absolutely ridiculous to think that I had anything to do with Miller's death."

"Not really. It's pretty common for a family member to be the killer, especially if there's a lot of money or a lot of anger involved. So, where were you when Miller was killed?"

She glared at me, but then seemed to decide that answering was the best way to get the interview, and me, out of the way.

"I was here. Sleeping. Like most people would be at six in the morning."

"Any witnesses?"

Again, she gave me a withering stare. Luckily, I'm immune to it. I looked back at her with my head tilted to convey innocent inquiry and didn't speak. Georgia, like most of us, couldn't tolerate the silence that dragged on, so she answered.

"No. I was alone. And even if I weren't, it would be none of your business. I have nothing to prove to you. And since Miller and I were divorced, and I inherit nothing, I have no possible motive for his murder. Now, if that's all—" she started to rise, but I stopped her with another question.

"What about anger, or revenge? It's no secret that you were furious with Miller when he came out. He humiliated you. He made you a laughing-stock. He forced you to move out of town to escape the whispering behind your back. It must have been hard for you to fall so far from the top of the social ladder. You did all that work and all that scheming to turn yourself from Crystal Bailey who lived in a trailer park to Georgia Caldwell who was the wife of the wealthiest man in town. And then Miller ruined everything. If I were you, I'd be pretty mad."

I laid it on thick, trying to goad her into a level of anger that would force an honest response out of her.

"Well, you're not me, and you never could be. First of all, you don't have the looks. Second, you don't have the guts. Third, you don't have the brains. Everything I have, I earned. My mother parked me with my drunk grandfather and came in and out of my life when she felt like it. I had to raise myself. And I had to figure out how to dress, and how to talk, and how to act so that a rich man like Miller wanted to marry me."

I was surprised at her level of honesty, and my face must have shown it.

"Don't look so shocked. Miller got fair value from me. I had his kids, I hosted his parties, I charmed his clients, I organized our family life. I put

up with his smug, condescending parents. I supported his political ambitions. And just when we had a chance to really become a power couple not
just in Himmel, but in the whole state, he threw it all back in my face
because he was tired of being 'dishonest'!"

Her voice was low, but with an undercurrent of pure fury.

"Georgia, I—"

"I'm not finished. I worked my ass off to get to the position I had in
Himmel. Miller was born into his. He wasn't brave, he was weak. Too weak
to admit he was gay. Too weak to stand up to his parents. At least Fourey
has always been his own man. Miller pretended to be the good son, but he
was lying to his parents and to everyone else his whole life. Then one day
he decides he wants to be 'honest.' He chose to upend his children's lives,
my life, his parents' standing in the community, without once thinking
about anyone but himself. And I'm supposed to be okay with that?"

"It wasn't an easy choice for Miller to make, Georgia. And given what
attitudes were for most of his life, and still are in some quarters, it's understandable why he hid who he was. And yes, it was brave of him to do. He
lost a lot, too."

"Of course, you'd defend him. It's your fault he did it. If you hadn't gone
poking around into your druggie sister's death, he wouldn't have outed
himself. Don't expect me to pity him. He's St. Miller now, so brave, so
honorable, so good. But me, I'm the villain because I didn't just lie down
and take it. Because I fought to protect my children and my rights. And now
Miller gets himself murdered and you're trying to make me out to be his
killer?"

"I never said that you killed Miller. I just asked where you were the
morning he died. But some people might think that you had reason."

"I did have a reason! But I didn't kill him. He was the father of my children, after all. And I'm not done in this town. With Miller gone and his
mother not far behind, I'm coming back. At least for long enough to make
everyone who laughed at me or turned their back on me regret it. Marilyn
Karr may think she runs things now. We'll see how that plays out."

"Georgia, you just outlined a pretty good revenge motive for murder.
With Miller dead, you can come back, settle some old scores, and put your-

self back on top. You'll also have access to plenty of money through your kids."

"I don't need it. I have my own money. I was smart enough to get a good settlement out of Miller. I didn't kill him, but I'm not sorry that he's dead. Now, if you don't have more questions," she said, beginning to stand.

"I do, though. If you have all the money you need, why did you threaten Miller a few weeks ago? Why did you say, 'I need that money. If I don't get it, the truth is coming out.'?"

Though I'd expected her to be surprised by what I knew, she didn't miss a beat.

"I suppose Gabe Hoffman told you that. I didn't realize that he was in the office until it was too late. Obviously he eavesdropped just enough to cause trouble. I wasn't threatening Miller. Someone took advantage of me on a business deal. I asked Miller for advice on how to get my money back. He recommended that I just accept the loss. I want to take legal action— that's what I meant by the truth coming out. It's got nothing to do with Miller. And it's definitely got nothing to do with you. Obviously you're just floundering around trying to insert yourself into our private family business. I don't know what Charlotte was thinking asking you to get involved. It's ridiculous. It's also time for you to leave."

"Were you trying to extort Miller? Because that's what it sounds like."

"I was not trying to extort Miller. My private business concerns are just that, private. Stop trying to make something out of nothing."

She had walked to the door while talking, and now held it wide for me. "Goodbye, Leah. It's been very unpleasant seeing you, and I hope not to see you again."

34

"That was quite a shock to look at the *Times* website and see the story about Eddie Garcia this morning," my mother said as she poured tea for the two of us at her kitchen table. I had to drive by her house on my way to see Fourey, and I had stopped by on impulse. The fact that I knew she had made apple bread the day before had nothing to do with that impulse.

We talked for a few minutes about Eddie, and his dad, and the difficulty of solving a forty-year-old case. Then she asked about what was happening with Miller's case and was it true that Noah Hanson was no longer a suspect.

"Mom, how did you hear that already? It only happened last night."

"I ran into Miranda Tomlin at the gas station this morning. She volunteers at the soup kitchen with me. She told me about meeting you and then she told me Sadie's story. Sounds like Noah lucked out—if you can call what he's had to go through lucking out."

"He did. But if you want more on how and why, you'll have to get it from Ross."

"No, I don't need anymore. I'm glad for him, that's all. So, where are you on your investigation?"

"I talked to Georgia just before I came here."

"How did that go?"

"About like you'd expect a conversation between me and Georgia to go. You know, it's easy to see why she married Miller, but I will never understand why he chose someone as horrible as her."

"Probably because she wasn't horrible to him. And she's attractive and can be quite charming when she wants to be."

"Yeah? I've yet to experience that side of her."

"That's because you don't have anything she wants or needs. I've seen her in action a few times. She's good at making people feel happy to do things for her. It's her gift. I imagine that she put everything she had into landing Miller. And that changed her life. Still, I don't think it changed how she felt inside."

"Okay, Dr. Freud, I'll bite. How did she feel inside?"

"Unworthy. Like an imposter who could have everything taken away from her once she was unmasked. And that's what happened when Miller came out. She lost her social position in town. And it gave people the chance to look down on her again, the way they did when she was Crystal Bailey who lived in the trailer park. The way they hadn't dared to do when she was Mrs. Miller Caldwell."

"Are you trying to make me feel sorry for her? Because it's not working."

"No, I'm not trying to do that, I'm just sharing my insights. And this time they aren't about you. Be happy. I think there's good reason to feel sorry for Georgia. But there's also good reason to be wary of her. Sometimes, deep childhood wounds make people more compassionate. Other times, they make the people who experience them want to hurt others—as if wounding someone else will take their own pain away. I suspect that's the case with Georgia."

"She kind of went on about her trailer park life when I saw her today, but was her childhood really that bad?"

"We weren't living here then, so I didn't observe it firsthand. But what I've heard from people who were is that it was pretty awful. It's remarkable that she managed to get herself away from that life. And you know how she reveled in being Mrs. Miller Caldwell. Then, without warning, she lost it. It's not surprising that it turned her bitter and angry."

"Mmm, I'm going to have to disagree with you on that one. I think she's always been like that. Only now she doesn't bother to hide it."

"Georgia is not a nice person. I agree with you. I'm just pointing out that there are reasons why she's the way she is. And, in her favor, despite the way Sheila treated her as a child, she's taken very good care of her mother the last few years."

"How's that?"

"Sheila had a stroke and couldn't live alone anymore. This was maybe a year or so before Georgia and Miller divorced. Georgia brought her back to Himmel and got her into Highview Assisted Living. It's an excellent facility and it's very expensive. She's still living there, and she wouldn't be if Georgia wasn't paying for it."

"Oh, come on. Making sure your mother has good care in her old age seems like a bottom-line basic thing you do, not something you get good person points for."

"I'll file that away for future reference. But you've never met Sheila."

"You have?"

"When she first moved in at Highview, she was on the list of people for the St. Stephen's Visitation Committee to see. She swore at us, complained about everything there, told us that her daughter was—and I quote—'an ungrateful bitch,' and her grandkids were spoiled brats who didn't visit her. I was relieved when she said she didn't want us there either."

"She sounds like Georgia unchained to me."

"I'd say that Sheila is what Georgia might have become if she hadn't had so much ambition."

"Well, sad backstory notwithstanding, my opinion of Georgia stands. And speaking of standing, I've got to go see Fourey," I said as I pushed away from the table.

"Wait a sec. Let me wrap up some apple bread for you."

As she cut several slices and put them in a plastic bag she said, "So, what's going on with your book? I hope you've been thinking about what Coop and I said to you."

"Oh, I see. You're plying me with apple bread hoping to get me to submit to your will. Well, in another win for moms everywhere, yes, I thought about what you said, and what Coop said, and also about Miller and how he handled setbacks. Then I called Clinton to tell him I'm ready to start revising."

"Leah! That's such a good decision. What did he say?"

"Nothing. He didn't pick up. I had to leave a message. But now I'm wishing I hadn't sounded so committed to getting right on it. I called him when I thought Ross was right about Noah and that Miller's murder was solved. Now that isn't the case, and I don't have the time I thought I'd have. Which is why I have to get going now. Thanks for the apple bread. I'll talk to you later."

35

On the drive to Maple Hill Farm (the Caldwells are the kind of family who have a name for their house), I went over what I knew about Fourey. He had been kind of a wild kid, and he'd never gotten along well with his father. As an adult, he'd done something so bad he got thrown out of the family. He'd moved to Florida and done well there on his own. Or at any rate, he claimed that he had. He had maintained a relationship with Miller and his family, but they weren't close. Georgia seemed to like him, which in my book was not a point in his favor. He had some kind of friendship with Marilyn Karr, also not a point in his favor.

But did Fourey have a good motive to kill his brother? Well, unless he was operating on some Zen level of nonattachment, he had to be angry or at least resentful that Miller got everything, and he got nothing. But that had been the situation for a long time. Why would he suddenly decide it was time to kill Miller?

Money wasn't a motive. Fourey didn't get anything when Miller died.

But, maybe Fourey wasn't as successful as he claimed. Sebastian said that he'd sold his boat. Maybe he needed money, asked Miller for it, and Miller had refused. That had infuriated Fourey, and he'd killed the brother who had everything but wouldn't give him anything. That didn't seem right either. Especially the part about Miller refusing to help his brother if he needed it.

By the time I reached that point in my speculating, I'd also reached the Caldwell home. Maple Hill Farm is about a mile outside of the city of Himmel. A long driveway leads to the main house on top of the hill. It also branches off in the direction of the guest cottage where Fourey had said that he was staying.

When I knocked on the door, he appeared almost instantly with a welcoming smile on his face. Although I hadn't scheduled my visit, he didn't seem surprised.

"Leah, hello. How nice to see you. Please, come in. I assume you're here to talk about Miller."

The guest cottage was small, but well furnished. The floor plan was open, the kitchen was well equipped, and the living room was cozy. A short hallway presumably led to a bedroom or two and a bathroom.

"Can I get you something to drink? Water? Coffee? Something stronger? It's a holiday today, plus it's five o'clock somewhere."

"Water would be great, thanks."

He handed me a bottle of water before pouring himself a glass of red wine and sitting down next to me on the couch. I scooched into the corner so I could turn to look at him while we talked.

"I want to say at the start if my questions offend you, I'm sorry. I'm just gathering information. I'm not accusing you of anything. But I like to get right to the point when possible."

"Not very much offends me. Let's get to it," he said with a smile.

"I know that you were estranged from your father for a long time, and that he cut you out of his will, leaving everything to Miller. Did that make you angry?"

"At who? My father for being immovable up to the end? No, I expected that. And how could I be mad at Miller? It wasn't his decision. It was our father's."

"Why was your father so 'immovable'? What had you done that was so heinous he threw you out of the family?"

"Let me explain a little about my father. He was what most people would call a good man. He was active in his church, careful in his businesses, and diligent in his duty to help what he called 'the deserving poor.' By that, he meant people who didn't drink to excess, didn't swear, didn't divorce, and didn't complain about their wages, their lot in life, or their betters. And by betters, he meant people like us, the Caldwells."

"He sounds like kind of an asshat."

Fourey laughed.

"I'd like to have seen you interacting with Miller. I imagine that he didn't know quite what to make of you sometimes."

"Actually, we got along very well."

"Oh, I'm sure you did. I just meant that I'd have enjoyed seeing Miller a little looser than he usually let himself be. You probably taught him a thing or two."

"It was Miller who taught me. But let's get back to you and your father."

"Yes, ma'am," he said, giving me a small salute.

"When I was born, my father was looking for a carbon copy of himself. I definitely wasn't that. I never set out to disappoint him or anger him, but I managed to do both most of the time."

"What kind of things did you do?"

"I wasn't a very good student. I didn't always do as I was told. I questioned him—he'd say that I 'defied' him. I had friends he didn't like. We got up to some mischief now and then. My father didn't approve of mischief."

"What kind of mischief?"

"Just kid stuff. One night we let the air out of the tires of all the cars parked at the country club for the Winter Sno-Ball. Then we hid and watched all the drunk parents come out and try to figure out what happened. Unfortunately, someone did figure it out and we got caught. It was worth it though. Another time we climbed the water tower and spray-painted it. We made prank calls, played a few practical jokes, just regular kid things. Then a couple of us went too far on a dare and we got caught shoplifting. That's when my father made good on his threat to send me to military school."

I had not been on the leaderboard for good citizenship awards when I was a kid, but what Fourey described as "kid stuff" was nothing me or my friends would ever have done. I could see why his behavior had driven his staid and upright father to take drastic action.

"How did that go?"

"I was pretty mad at first, but I settled down once I realized I was out from under my father. The school was strict, but there were ways around things. Plus just getting sent there had taught me a lesson about taking things too far. I did all right. My father was relieved not to have me around, and I was glad not to be under his thumb. It was kind of a peaceful period for us. But then came college."

"What happened?"

"I was on my own. I had a car. I had money. But I wasn't gifted with Miller's sense of responsibility or caution. I drank too much, skipped too many classes, dated the wrong girls, my grades were bad, and to cap it off at the end of the first semester, I got arrested for dealing weed."

"How did your father respond to that?"

"The dealing charge was bogus. He straightened things out with the cops and the college, but he was furious with me. I think he only went to bat for me to protect the family 'honor.' He made it clear that unless my grades were stellar the second semester, and there was no hint of trouble, he was done paying for college, or anything else. That sobered me up. I made it through the rest of my college years without any serious incidents."

"So where does the big rift between you and your dad come in?"

"I took a job at the bank after I graduated, like all good Caldwell sons have done for multiple generations. My father wanted me to learn the business from the ground up. He started me out as a teller. I didn't mind. I'm a social guy and I liked interacting with the customers. But that's why things went south, in a big way."

"How?"

Fourey got up and poured himself another glass of wine before continuing.

36

"As I said, I like people. They seem to like me, too. I developed a good rapport with the customers. In fact, I had something of a following— people would wait in my line so I could help them, even if another window was open. One of the other tellers used to call them my groupies."

He said it with a self-deprecating smile, but I recognize a humble brag when I hear one.

"There was one old lady in particular who would never let anyone else help her. I'd chat and flirt with her a little, make her laugh. But she was beginning to have memory problems. Sometimes I'd have to remind her to take the cash she withdrew with her. Other times she'd take it with her, but then forget she'd withdrawn it. When she asked me to fill out her deposit slips because it confused her too much, I thought I should alert my supervisor about the situation. I waited too long."

"What happened?"

"Her son from Minnesota showed up at my window one day and accused me of stealing money from his mother's account. I explained the situation. He wouldn't listen. He started demanding to see the bank president—my father."

Fourey then waited to go on for so long that I had to prod him.

"Then what?"

He took a big drink of his wine before he answered. His tone of voice was no longer jaunty.

"We both met with my father in his office. My father told the woman's son that he would start an internal investigation to find out what had happened and ensure it wouldn't happen again."

"And that satisfied him?"

"No. But my father also said that he didn't want any customer to feel their money wasn't safe in the bank. He told the guy that he'd reimburse him on the spot for any shortage in his mother's account, just to name the amount. Well, that made the woman's son calm down immediately. He named a ridiculously high amount. My father didn't blink an eye. It was clear to the man, and to me, that my father didn't believe me, and he was willing to pay the price to make this go away. And it did. For the man and his mother. But not for me."

"What did you do?"

"I had it out with my father. He called me a liar, and a thief, and a disgrace to the family. He said I would always be a failure because I always took the easy way. He was through trying to make me into a man worthy of the Caldwell name. He ordered me to leave his bank, his house, and never to come back to either again. He was done with me. I told him I couldn't be happier to leave, and that he'd never hear from me again. I went home, packed a bag, said goodbye to my mother. And I left."

"Is that when you went to Florida?"

"Yes. A buddy of mine lived there and I stayed with him while I tried to figure out what to do. Then a chance to get in on the ground floor of a real estate project came up. I had no money, of course, but my mother had a little cash of her own. She kept it from my father, but she sent me what I needed to get started. Things took off from there and I never looked back."

"But did you really never even talk to your father after he threw you out?"

"I really never did. We were alike in one way. Once we make up our minds, we don't back down. I wasn't about to make the first move, and neither was he. The only time I was ever even in the same room with him again was when Miller got married. He and my mother both wanted me there, and my father finally agreed, but I wasn't to approach him or try to talk to him. I accepted, even though it was awkward and humiliating, to say the least, because I wanted to be there for my brother."

"And you stayed in touch with Miller over the years, right?"

"I did. And my mother, too, though we kept it low-key. She's very old-fashioned and believes the husband should make the decisions. But she's also a mother and I was her favorite. She took a stand. I'll give my father this much credit, he loved her enough to give in, with restrictions. It's the only time I can remember that he ever relented about anything. Still, Mother could only see me when I was staying at Miller's, never at the family home, and never where there was any chance my father would also be there."

"Wow. That's hard-core. It's difficult to imagine that your father wouldn't have softened at least a little over the years. You were his son."

"When my father was dying, my mother begged him to reconcile with me. She'd already talked to me, and I was willing, for her sake. I thought maybe he'd be willing, too. He'd managed to reconcile with Miller, after all. But he wasn't interested. He refused on his deathbed, with my mother weeping beside him. That's how hard-core he was."

I heard the bitterness in Fourey's voice, despite his insistence that he wasn't at all bothered by the way his father had treated him.

"It must have hurt when your father patched things up with Miller, but not with you."

"The two of them were always tight. Miller being gay was a big hill for my father to climb. It took a while, but he eventually did it, for Miller."

"But not for you."

He shrugged. "That's life."

Fourey was a good storyteller. I wondered how much of it was true, especially because I knew he'd lied to me (but why?) about loving life on his boat, when it had already been sold.

"So, I was intrigued when you told me about living on a boat and moving on when the mood strikes you. I think a lot of people would like to have that opportunity."

"Yes, I realize how fortunate I am."

"Then why did you sell your boat? Sebastian told me today that you had and that you weren't going back to Naples when you leave here."

I watched his face carefully to see how he responded to being caught in what might not technically be a lie but was definitely a misleading statement. At the memorial service, he'd implied he still owned the boat and was very happy with his easy breezy lifestyle.

Instead of looking embarrassed or taken aback, he smiled.

"Seller's remorse? I made the decision to sell on impulse, but the deal hadn't been finalized when I mentioned it to Sebastian. I had second thoughts and tried to get out of it. It looked like I'd be able to when I talked to you. That's why I spoke to you in the present tense. But the buyer got nasty and threatened legal action. I really don't have energy for that right now. So, we finalized the deal."

"I see." What I saw was that Fourey was quick on his feet, and a fairly convincing liar.

"But you can buy another boat, right? That sail away life sounds pretty idyllic."

"It is. But I'm a firm believer in reading the signs. It's why I've been successful. Not being able to get out of the deal is a sign that I need to move on and try something new."

"But not in Naples?"

"No. There's a big world out there. I don't have a wife or children to hold me back. I've got the means to do it, so I'm going to do some traveling after Mother passes. I've always wanted to attend Wimbledon. I'd like to visit the wine country in France. I spent a great summer in the Canadian Rockies when I was in college. Maybe I'll go back for another visit."

"Your options sound endless," I said.

"They're open. But I worked hard to get to this point. Maybe I owe my father something after all. Everything I have, I got myself, no help from him. And there are no strings attached. I'm not weighed down by family business obligations, like Miller was. And now Sebastian and Charlotte are. They've inherited all the money, but they're saddled with all the responsibility, too. I'm happy that's not me."

"It really does sound like you're at peace with what your father did. Most people would be angry, I think. Not just at their father, but they'd resent, if not outright hate, the sibling who inherited everything. You don't seem to feel that way at all."

"Maybe I would if my life was a failure, and I had no money. That's not the case. Also, I'm not most people."

"I guess not. So, one last question to wrap up. Just for the record, where were you the morning Miller was killed?"

"Ah, the alibi question. I don't have one. I'm not an early riser. The morning Miller was killed, I was right here, sleeping. Luckily for me, I have no motive. I didn't resent Miller at all, and I get nothing from his death."

His phone, which was sitting on the end table closest to me, rang just then. I turned and picked it up to hand to him at the same time that he reached across me to grab it himself. Our arms collided and the half-full glass of red wine he was holding spilled onto me. While he apologized profusely, I jumped up and poured some water from my bottle and began dabbing at my white shirt.

"I'm so sorry. I'm not usually that clumsy," he said, ignoring the phone, which finally stopped ringing.

"It's okay. I am. I'm kind of used to it. Can I use your bathroom and try to salvage this?"

"Of course. It's down the hall to the right."

As I left, he was checking his phone to see who had called.

⁕ ·········

The bathroom was quite swank. I grabbed a washcloth off the towel bar (which was heated!). I managed to lighten the stain with plain water. If I used some peroxide and dishwashing liquid at home, I might get it to all come out. When I tossed my washcloth in the hamper, I caught the scent of expensive perfume. I spotted a robe on a hook next to the shower and leaned closer, thinking I might breathe in Marilyn Karr's Chanel No. 5. Instead, the same perfume that Georgia had been wearing that morning filled my nostrils. Now that was very interesting.

As I walked back to the living room, I heard Fourey on the phone. I stopped for a minute to listen. When opportunity knocks, it's rude not to answer.

"Georgia, I can't talk. She's still here. No, don't do that. Miller's dead.

There's no leverage anymore. In fact, if it comes out now, it could bite us in the ass. I'll talk to you later."

I retreated a few steps and closed the bathroom door loudly, then coughed slightly so he wouldn't worry that I had overheard him.

"Looks like I did some damage with that wine. I'd be happy to pay for a professional cleaning," he said, noting the large wet spot, with undertones of brownish red on my shirt as I entered the living room.

"Don't worry about it. Besides, I'm not sure who collided with whom."

"Well, the offer stands if you change your mind. I just had a phone call from a friend, reminding me that I promised today. I'm afraid I have to leave. Did you get all your questions asked?"

"Yes. Thanks for your time. I'll be in touch if I think of anything I forgot to ask."

"Feel free to call me anytime."

37

As I walked to my car, I saw a woman carrying a large woven basket over her arm coming briskly down the path from the main house.

"Mrs. Obuchowski! How are you?" I waved and shouted as I recognized her.

Glenda Obuchowski is a wiry woman with frizzy gray hair and a ready laugh. She'd been the Caldwells' housekeeper since long before I was born. But she'd also volunteered at the Himmel Library circulation desk when I was a kid, and that's how I knew her.

"Leah! So nice to see you. I'm fine. I don't need to ask what you're doing here. I heard that you're investigating Miller's murder. I'm not surprised."

"You know me well, Mrs. Obuchowski."

"I guess I do. I'm glad you're on it because I know you won't give up. Remember when I told you that you couldn't check out more than five books at a time? So you tried it with another volunteer at the circulation desk, and she told you no, too. And then you appealed to Claudia Fillhart, and she told you no. And then you wrote a letter and brought in the U.S. Constitution to make your case?"

"I do remember. I argued that the library's five-book limit was abridging my privileges as a U.S. citizen under the fourteenth amendment. I won, too."

"I don't know that it was on legal grounds, but Claudia said that any patron who wanted to read that bad shouldn't be denied."

She shook her head and laughed. And then she sobered up and said, "I hope you haven't changed. Fourey's a charmer, don't let yourself be fooled."

I pointed at the basket she had put down on the ground as we talked.

"Is that wine for Fourey?"

She nodded. "He called the house this morning with his list. I swear, he's going to go through his father's entire wine cellar before he leaves."

"He told me that he's staying until after his mother passes away. But you sound like you wouldn't mind if he left today."

"I won't say he doesn't make his mother happy. She lights up when he walks in. But mark my words, once he gets what he wants, he'll be gone, whether she is or not. Like always."

"What does he want?"

"He says to spend time with his mother. But he's spending a lot more time with Marilyn Karr than with Mrs. Caldwell."

"He told me he's advising her on some investments."

"Depends on what you mean by advising. But Marilyn Karr wouldn't be the first woman to make a fool of herself for a younger man out to get what he can."

"You make him sound like a gigolo," I said.

She shrugged. "If the shoe fits."

"Okay, Mrs. Obuchowski, quit teasing me. What do you know about Fourey? You were here when his dad kicked him out of the family. What's the real story on that?"

"All I know is it had something to do with the bank. The Caldwells have always treated me right. But they're not ones to confide in the help."

"Maybe not, but you've been around them for forty years. You must know something."

"I really don't, Leah. I'll tell you who probably does—Martha Newman. She was the head teller at the bank, and she worked there for almost fifty years. Started right out of high school and didn't retire until the arthritis in her hands got so bad she couldn't count out the money. She's not one to gossip, and she was very loyal to Mr. Caldwell. But with him gone now, and Mrs. Caldwell not long for this world either, she might tell you a thing or two about Fourey. I know she had no use for him."

"Thanks for the tip. Is she still in town?"

"Yes. She lives on Washington Avenue in the senior apartments there. You'll probably find her home. She doesn't get out much anymore. Now I've got to get this wine to Fourey and get back to the house to get lunch on for Mrs. Caldwell. Not that she'll eat more than a bite."

"How long are you going to keep working, Mrs. Obuchowski? You told me once that when you retired, you were going to Greece."

"Imagine you remembering that after all these years! Yes, that's still on my bucket list, but I can't leave Mrs. Caldwell now. That last heart attack nearly did her in, and I can see she's losing strength every day. Miller's death really took a toll on her. Fourey might be her favorite, but deep down she knows Miller is the one she could rely on. I'll stay until the end. Greece has been there a long time. It'll wait a little longer for me."

38

The talk about lunch from Fourey and Mrs. Obuchowski had made me realize I was hungry. Also, I wanted to check in on Sam, so I went home to grab something. Once there, I realized the better choice would have been a drive-through hamburger. My cupboards were Mother Hubbard bare. I needed to do more than a quick run through the aisles for the fixings for one meal. Time to replenish my larder. I managed to scrape enough peanut butter off the side of the jar to make a sandwich. I wrote a grocery list while I ate it and Sam sat on a kitchen stool watching me.

"You're judging me, aren't you? Well, you're not the one who should be talking. Or actually, maybe you should be. I think I'd enjoy a talking cat. But that aside, you're not eating well either. I'll pick up something special for you when I go to the store."

Sam's ears pricked up and I thought that meant I'd whetted his flagging appetite with my suggestion. Then he jumped from the stool and ran to hide behind the curtains. That's when I heard someone tapping on the front stairway door that opens into my office. Allie Ross was standing there when I opened it.

"Allie, hi! You're not working on a holiday, are you? You're going to get us in trouble for violating child labor laws."

"No, I just finished pulling together the clip portfolio of the stories I wrote this summer to turn in for my journalism class."

"Did you still want me to take a look?"

"Um, yeah, but, um, that's not why I'm here. Can I talk to you for a minute?"

"Yes, sure. Come on in."

She followed me to the kitchen.

"Would you like some water? It's the only beverage I have on hand. I don't have any snacks to offer either. I ate the last of the Oreos for breakfast."

"No, thanks. I just came for some advice."

"You're in luck. I may run out of cookies, but I never run out of advice."

I smiled but she didn't return it.

"Allie, are you okay?"

"I'm fine. Sort of. This isn't about me. Well, it is kind of, but I'm not the one who's in trouble. It's a friend of mine from school."

She began twisting a strand of her hair around her fingers. Her straight eyebrows had come together in a worried frown.

"Allie, what is it?"

"The thing is, he's going to feel like I betrayed him if I tell. But I'm really afraid that he, that he, oh, this is all kind of a mess. But I think he might—" she stopped, and wiped impatiently with her sleeve at the tears that had begun running down her cheeks.

"You think he might what, Allie?"

She gave a shuddery sigh before she answered.

"I think he might kill himself. I'm not being hysterical. I really think he might. He's so freaked out about Miller, and he thinks—"

"Miller? What does Miller have to do with this?"

"It's because of Miller. Because he was murdered. DJ thought if he turned off his phone they couldn't find him. But he read what the district attorney said about the investigation. Now he knows they can. He's really worried, and depressed, and so scared that nothing I say is making any difference."

When she said "DJ," a little bell had gone off in my brain and began to call home several bits of information mixed in with the jumble of thoughts I call my mind.

While she wiped her eyes again and blew her nose on the tissue I handed her, I marshaled my ragtag band of half-formed ideas into a coherent sequence.

DJ was the gay son of Dennis Warby, the man who had threatened Miller outside of McClain's. The caller who had found Miller and phoned 911 had hung up without giving a name. Cliff Timmins, the district attorney, had said at a presser that police were using information from cell towers to find phones that had been in the park when the 911 call had been made.

"Allie, does DJ know who killed Miller? Is he the one who called 911?"

"No. Maybe. I'm not sure. I mean yes, he called 911, but he didn't see who killed him. Not for sure."

"What does 'not for sure' mean?"

She hesitated.

"Allie, you've come this far, don't hold back now. Tell me what you know, please."

"I promised I wouldn't. If he finds out I did—"

"He won't."

"But he hasn't told anyone else. If you ask him about it, he'll know it's me who told you!"

"It's pretty rare that a secret is only known by the person it belongs to and just one other. There are almost always more people who have parts of it, even if they don't realize that what they know belongs to a bigger picture. In this case, one of them is me."

"You? What do you know about DJ?"

"I know who DJ's dad is. I was there when he accused Miller of grooming DJ. So, I also already know that DJ is gay if that's his secret."

"It's part of it."

"Okay, now tell me the rest."

"You can't tell my dad, okay?"

"He already knows about DJ's father, because I told him yesterday. He could already be following up on that. But he needs to know about DJ being in the park. It would be good if DJ came forward and identified himself as the caller. It will be way better than having the cops find out first that he's the owner of a cell phone that was in the park when Miller was killed. Your dad is the lead investigator on Miller's case. I have to tell him. But it would be nice if you told him first."

"I'm already breaking my promise to DJ by talking to you. It would be way worse if I told my dad. He's the police!"

"Allie, come on—"

"No, you don't understand, DJ is seriously messed up right now. See, I don't even know him that well. But he came to *me*. That says he doesn't have anyone in his life to turn to, doesn't it? If he knows I told when I said I wouldn't, he'll think he doesn't have anyone to trust. If I tell Dad, he'll just go right to DJ and freak him out so much that DJ will run away—or worse. I'm serious. It won't take much to push him over the edge. And that will be my fault."

"Okay, hold on. You're not giving your dad enough credit—don't tell him I said that. Yes, he can charge like a bull, but he understands how to interview someone. And if you talk to him first, he'll know that DJ needs careful handling. Let me ask you something. Why did DJ choose you if you don't know each other well?"

"I think because ever since last spring, I'm like this magnet for kids who make bad choices. I guess they figure if I was dumb enough to sext with a boy who put my photos on the internet, I don't have any room to judge whatever stupid situation they've got themselves into."

"Those kids aren't coming to you because you're dumb. It's because you did something that went way wrong, but you handled the humiliation and lived to tell the tale. They trust you to understand when other people won't. Like DJ did. Whether he knows it consciously or not, by talking to you, he was asking for help. You're not betraying him. You're giving him what he needs—a way out of the hole he's in. Allie, we've been through some things together. Haven't I earned your trust?"

I waited, knowing that if I pressed any harder, I risked losing her altogether. After a few seconds, she nodded and began to talk.

"DJ feels like his life is a lie, but he's afraid of what will happen when he tells his parents. His dad is super homophobic."

She stopped again.

"Let me fill in the blanks. DJ has two things he's worried about—telling his parents he's gay and getting arrested for selling weed at the county park."

Her eyes widened, and she looked at me as though I had revealed psychic superpowers.

"I'm not Miss Cleo, Allie. But I know the cops are interested in finding out who's selling weed to high school kids at the park. It's not a big leap to figure out that it's DJ. He was at the park to meet a buyer and found Miller, right?"

She nodded, and I continued.

"DJ found Miller, and called it in, but he couldn't say who he was or stick around, because he had weed on him. I also already knew from Miguel that DJ called into his podcast but wouldn't give his name. He told Miguel he wanted to come out to his parents, but said he was too afraid of the consequences."

"That's not all."

"I'm listening."

"The way DJ found Miller is that he was at the park waiting to sell to a kid who never showed up. He heard noises coming from the tunnel on the trail—he was up on the hill above it. He looked and saw someone running away. Then he ran to see if anyone was in the tunnel."

"Allie, if DJ knows who killed Miller, he has to come forward."

"He doesn't know, though. Not for sure. He only saw him from the back, and he was wearing a black hoodie. But he's worried it might have been his dad. Because his dad thought Miller was trying to turn DJ gay. If he was sure, he'd go to the police. But he didn't see the man's face. He can't describe him, not even if he was tall or short or fat or thin. He was too far away, and the guy was all in black. He doesn't want to make trouble for his dad if it wasn't even him."

"Allie, even if DJ can't describe the man who ran away, it was probably Miller's murderer. Every piece of information is critical to the investigation."

"I know, but DJ thinks if he goes to the police, they'll figure out that he's been selling weed at the park. You did. And then he'll get arrested. And then it will come out that Miller was helping him because he's gay. And even if it wasn't his dad that he saw at the park, his dad will know for sure that DJ is gay. And if DJ doesn't go to jail, his dad will send him to a conversion camp. You know, one of those places where they say they can change who people are. Today he said to me that maybe it would be better to just let the world go on without him. Then when he saw how freaked out I was, he said he was kidding. But I'm really scared, Leah. I don't know the right thing to do."

"Yes, you do, Allie. It's why you're here. You know that this situation is too big to handle, and you need help. Let me give it to you."

"How?"

"I'll talk to DJ—"

"But then he'll know that—"

"No, he will not know you told me anything. I'm investigating Miller's death. I witnessed his father confront Miller, and I want to talk to DJ about what his dad said. That's my entry point. You won't come into it all."

"What about my dad? Are you still going to tell him?"

"I am. But not until after I talk to DJ. Maybe I can get him to see that going to your dad on his own is the best choice. And if he doesn't, he'll assume that I'm the one who put your dad on to him. Which I will be, unless you decide to go to your father yourself. All of this has to come out. How it does depends on DJ, and on you."

She looked at me, an uncertain expression on her face. I knew she was weighing the merits of what I'd said. I'd made my case. She'd have to decide for herself what to do.

"I don't know, Leah. I just . . ."

"I have faith in you, Allie. You'll make the right choice."

39

It was after two o'clock when Allie left. I needed to write down some thoughts about my morning rounds of the Caldwell family, plus plan out what to do about Dennis and DJ Warby. I sat down at the kitchen island and jotted down the gist of my talks with Georgia, Fourey, and Mrs. Obuchowski. I added in Allie's revelations about DJ as well. Then I considered what I'd learned.

Georgia and Fourey shared a secret that they believed gave them a hold over Miller. But now that he was dead, Fourey was afraid it would backfire on them if they pursued it. What was it? I stared into space for several minutes but was not visited by an epiphany. I had no idea what they were hiding, but the knowledge that they were hiding something was significant in itself.

Fourey had taken pains to come across as candid and charming. But I didn't buy his version of what had happened during his brief tenure at the bank. Adding to my skepticism was Mrs. Obuchowski's dim view of him. I definitely needed to talk to Martha Newman.

And then there was Allie's surprise visit and the possibility that DJ Warby had seen Miller's killer—and that it might have been his father Dennis. I had to get with Ross on that, but before I did, I wanted to talk to DJ. I Googled and found an address for the Warbys. They lived right in town. I'd like to catch him without his dad around. I made a quick call to Allie.

"Do you know if both DJ's parents work outside the home?"

"He said his dad works third shift in some factory, and his mom works days at Woodman's. Why?"

"I think I'll have a better chance with him if they're not around."

"Then you should try today. They went to visit his dad's brother in the VA hospital in Tomah. They won't be back until late."

"That's perfect. Thanks, Allie. I'll talk to you later."

"Leah, you really won't tell him I talked to you, will you?"

"I really won't, Allie."

I mentally rearranged my afternoon. DJ first, then Margaret Newman, the teller who knew Fourey way back when. My grocery shopping trip whenever I could fit it in. I was getting ready to leave when I got a text from Coop.

"I'm at the Elite. Late lunch?"

I really shouldn't, but that skinny peanut butter sandwich hadn't really done the job. Plus, I wanted to see Coop.

"Not much time but order me a *döner kebab*. I'll be there in ten minutes."

The Elite Café and Bakery is a Himmel institution. I've been going there since I was a kid and I love everything about it. The smell of fresh roasted coffee and wonderful baked goods that hits you when you open the door. The clattering sounds coming from the kitchen where sandwiches and soups are being served up. The slanting wooden floor that squeaks when you walk on it. I took it all in with my usual pleasure as I walked through the door. I spotted Coop at a table in the back, talking to the owner Clara Schimelman.

"Leah, I don't see you since Miller died. I'm so sorry. He was a good man."

"Yes, he was, Mrs. Schimelman."

"Coop said you want *döner kebab*, but I make cranberry turkey sandwich for you today on sourdough bread. It's here for fall. You will like. It's the bomb," she said.

I caught Coop's eye and we smiled, both at Mrs. Schimelman's enduring love affair with slang—outdated or current—and at her belief that when it comes to long-time customers, she has not just the right, but the duty, to determine what they should be eating.

"It looks great, and you've never steered me wrong."

"Is true. So, I'm just steering Coop before you come in. You should be getting married soon, yes?"

I looked at Coop. He shrugged slightly and said, "I told Mrs. Schimelman that we just started dating."

"Dating schmating. You two been together since middle school. You're not kids now. Time to settle down. I tell your mother that, too," she said looking at me.

"Oh look, someone's at the bakery counter. I can see you're short-staffed today, Mrs. Schimelman. We'll let you go wait on that lady who looks like she really needs some suggestions on what to order. It was great to see you though," I said, then took a large bite of what was indeed a really good sandwich.

Mrs. Schimelman laughed heartily and swatted at me lightly with the tea towel that is perpetually slung over one shoulder.

"Okay, you get away for now. But you're not getting any younger, not neither of you. And such nice babies you will have."

"Just for the record, she started it. I didn't encourage her," Coop said as she moved away from our table.

"Oh, I know. She doesn't need any encouragement. Maybe I should get her focused on finding a match for Gabe to take her mind off us. What do you think about Jennifer?"

"As a person, or as Gabe's romantic interest?"

"I already know what you think of her as a person. But don't you think Gabe and Jennifer would be a good match for each other?"

"Listen, I'm happy that I'm with the right person for me. But I'm not qualified to judge who the right person for Jennifer or Gabe is. And I'm surprised that you're playing matchmaker. That's more Miguel's area, isn't it?"

"That's what he said when I suggested it. I'm not playing matchmaker, but when you're happy, you want other people to be happy, too. I know Jen's lonely, and I think Gabe is, too. They're both smart, funny, nice. They're both single parents . . ."

"All true. But it's none of our business. They'll find the right person for each of them, without our help. We did, right?"

He reached across the table and gave my hand a squeeze.

"Yes, we did. But it would probably be nicer for them if one of the two of them didn't have to almost die before they figure it out."

"Agreed."

"So, what's happening with the Eddie Garcia case? Were Paul's dental records a match?"

He nodded.

"Yeah, like we expected. Now Marla and I are going through the old files. We're not going to get any help from the original lead investigators. They're both dead, so we have to rely on the reports and their case notes. And those don't look too promising. I'm being generous when I say they're not as complete as the ones we do today."

"What about witness interviews?" I asked.

"We've got a list going. Keep your fingers crossed that at least some of them are still local."

"I will, but even if you find them, how reliable are their recollections of something that happened so long ago going to be?"

"They'll probably range from not very to not at all reliable."

"Oy! It couldn't get much harder, could it?"

"Well, I love a challenge. Why else would I love you?"

"I choose to take that as a compliment. Thank you. I love you, too. Now, do you want to hear about my day so far?"

"Absolutely."

I gave him the short version of my conversations with Georgia, Fourey, and Mrs. Obuchowski. I didn't get into what Allie had told me yet. I wasn't hiding it. I just wanted a chance to talk to DJ first.

"Have you talked to Ross? Is he still feeling so upset with himself? I'm glad about Noah, but I feel bad that Ross is so down about the way his theory tanked. And I don't think the random robbery idea he said he's going to pursue is very strong."

"You feel bad for Charlie? Really? Because I think I hear a touch of gloating there."

"You don't. My main concern is that Miller's murder gets solved, whether it's by me, Ross, or someone else. But I won't be unhappy if Georgia or Fourey, but especially Georgia, turns out to be the one who did it and goes to prison for life. Right now, they're running neck and neck on my suspect scorecard."

"Are you factoring in the way Miller was murdered? Stabbing a person is a very up close and personal way to kill. It wouldn't only take strength, it could take some serious anger, too. Fourey would have the strength, but would he have the anger? Georgia might have the anger, but does she have the strength?"

"Trust me, Georgia nurtures a grudge like my mother nurtures her prize rose bush. As far as strength, fury can get an adrenalin surge going. And don't forget the opportunity part. Neither she nor Fourey has an alibi and both of them would know Miller's running habits. Not many others would."

"Fair point, but there's this to think about, too," Coop said. "The park is a pretty public place. It's not exactly crowded early in the morning, but there are always a few runners, birdwatchers, and bikers around. Miller's killer must have been either desperate or reckless to choose that time and place. If Fourey has long-time anger and resentment against Miller, he could've picked a safer time and place. Same for Georgia."

"But maybe they didn't have a choice, Coop. Maybe it had to happen then, for some reason. Fourey says he didn't resent Miller—that he's made so much money on his own he doesn't care about being disinherited. But Mrs. Obuchowski stopped just short of calling him a male escort. If he's desperate for money, and Miller wouldn't give him any, it might have made him so angry that all this Cain and Abel jealousy festering in his heart erupted and he had to kill him. That could be the case with Georgia, too. Not the Cain and Abel thing, but just her fury at the way her marriage ended."

"But killing Miller wouldn't get either of them any money. And Fourey doesn't strike me as someone ruled by his emotions. I'm not sure he'd take that kind of risk just to pay Miller back for not giving him money—if he even needs it. If you're going that route, Georgia might be a better candidate," Coop said.

"Geez, I hope you spend as much time taking down Ross's theories as you do mine."

"I do," he answered. "And Charlie doesn't enjoy the critique any more than you do. Come on, if your hypothesis folds under a few questions, it's not a good hypothesis."

"I know, I know. But I don't really have a hypothesis yet. I'm just noodling around with possibilities. How about this, Georgia and Fourey did it together!"

"Why would they?"

"Well, maybe Georgia was mad enough to kill Miller, but knew she couldn't do it alone and get away with it. And Fourey had his own issues with his brother. So, Georgia plays on Fourey's resentment and convinces him killing Miller will be justice for both of them. And don't forget, with Miller dead, her kids have all the money, and they'd be softer touches for her than Miller was. She could have offered Fourey some of the money she hopes she can get from her kids, once their inheritance comes through. Do you disagree that the call she and Fourey had today means something is afoot between them?" I asked.

My phone rang before Coop could point out the holes in that scenario.

"You're saved by the bell," I said. Then, looking at caller ID, I picked up my phone. "Hi, Maggie. What's up?"

"Leah, I hate to ask, but Miguel was supposed to do a feature story this afternoon at Highview Assisted Living. A woman there, Birdie Mae Dawson, is celebrating her hundredth birthday. I told Mona Crandall, the activities director, that we'd be there. They're having a big shindig for it. But there was an accident on the highway, Miguel's stuck in traffic, and Troy is covering the Labor Day Games at the fairgrounds. I can't get hold of any of the stringers either. I'd go myself, but I've got dinner in the oven and my cousin is on her way over from Janesville. Could you?"

I wanted to say no because I had a full afternoon planned. But Maggie wouldn't have asked if she didn't really need the help. And Birdie Mae

Dawson, who was expecting the *Times* to show, certainly deserved coverage of her centenarian soiree.

"Sure, I can do it. When?"

"We're supposed to be there now. Mona will meet you in the foyer."

"I'm on my way. Bye."

"I take it you've got a better offer and you're leaving?" Coop asked.

"No, definitely not better than lunch with you. But Maggie needs me to do a feature on a lady having her one hundredth birthday today, and it's happening now. What do you say to dinner and a sleepover tonight with me and Sam?"

"Don't count me in for dinner. Cliff changed his flight and now he's going to get in tonight around six. He wants a debriefing on everything, but I can probably get there by eight thirty."

"I'll take it."

40

Highview Assisted Living sits on top of a hill, as you might expect, and overlooks woods and open fields, with a peek at the Himmel River in the distance. The grounds are well landscaped, with walking paths and strategically placed seating under lovely shade trees. The main building is red brick with lots of windows and a wide front porch that practically begs you to sit down and enjoy the view.

Mona, the activities director, greeted me at the entrance and led me to a large reception room where birthday festivities for Birdie Mae Dawson were in full swing. Birdie was a lovely woman with bright brown eyes and a wide smile. She was happy to pose for a photo and to share her longevity secrets. Among Birdie Mae's tips were to eat a bowl of oatmeal every morning, to have a shot of Scotch every night, and to never get married. It was a fun interview, and I didn't mind the brief detour from working on Miller's murder. Or at least it seemed like a detour, until I was on my way out.

Highview is quite a large facility. I assured the staff member who had offered to walk me out that I'd have no trouble finding the front door. However, after several wrong turns, I found myself not at the front entrance, but in a pleasant sunroom. Daunted but not defeated, I turned to retrace my steps when someone shouted from behind me.

"Hey, you, girl! I want to go back to my room. That stupid other girl left me here. I'm tired!"

I turned and saw that a woman in a wheelchair sat in one corner, half obscured by a large plant.

"Oh, hi! I didn't see you there. Can I help?" I asked as I approached her.

"I want to go back to my room. That's how you can help."

The old woman's face had none of the cheeriness of Birdie Mae's, and her voice was high and querulous.

"Okay, I can do that, but you'll have to give me directions. I don't work here. I was just at Birdie Mae Dawson's birthday party. I got a little turned around on the way out."

"Birdie Mae! So, she lived to be a hundred. Who cares? I'm eighty-five and no one gives a crap. And I had to go through a lot more to get here than that twit ever dreamed of. Go straight down that hall," she said, pointing in the direction from which I'd just come.

I got behind her and began pushing her chair forward.

"I'm Leah Nash," I said. "What's your name?"

"What's it to you?"

I considered leaving her at that point, but my better self kept me there.

"I'm just trying to be friendly, that's all," I said.

"Yeah? Everybody's too damn friendly and chirpy around here if you ask me. Pretending like this isn't the end of the road, the junkyard, the last stop before we all take the dirt nap. I'm Sheila. Sheila Bailey," she said grudgingly.

Well, well, well. Georgia Caldwell's dear old mother. This could be interesting.

I quickly considered my options. Tell her I was investigating her son-in-law's murder? Pretend I was a friend or relative of Birdie Mae's? I went with halfway honesty as the least complicated option.

"Nice to meet you, Sheila. In a way, we're connected. I was in business with your son-in-law Miller Caldwell. We owned the *Himmel Times* together. I know your daughter, Georgia, and your grandkids, too."

"Turn left here," she said. I tried again.

"I'm sorry for your loss. Miller was a very good man."

"Girlie, there's no such thing as a good man, much less a *very* good one.

But I guess Miller did all right by me. Set up a fund for my rent here. Guess he knew Crystal—that's 'Georgia's' real name if you don't know—couldn't be trusted not to toss me out on my ass if anything happened to him. I hear my grandkids got all the family dough. That must've frosted Crystal. This is my suite here. Door's not locked."

I reached around to open it and rolled her into a bright and cheerful living room with a bay window and a corner fireplace. Just off the living room in a small alcove was a kitchenette with a sink, a refrigerator, and a microwave.

"This is really nice," I said. "Can I get you something to drink? Water? Tea?"

"You can get me a beer. It's in the vegetable drawer, behind the bag of apples. The Nazis here only let me have one a week. I pay one of the janitors to bring me a six-pack now and then. I don't have enough to share. But you can have some water if you want," she added. And I realized that despite her angry attitude—or because of it—she was lonely.

I got her the beer, and myself some water, and pulled up a chair next to her. I turned the talk to her life in Himmel, which would naturally include some discussion of Georgia without making her suspicious.

"Have you always lived in Himmel?" I asked, though I knew the answer.

"No, thank God. I was born here. I hated this shitty little town when I was a kid. Got married to my first husband when I was seventeen and got out as fast as I could. That didn't last long. When we split up, I stayed in Milwaukee, got a job bartending. Those were some wild days, I can tell you that."

She paused to take a long drink of her beer, then wiped her mouth on the back of her hand.

"We knew how to have fun back then. I had this one boyfriend, he was a biker, and oh, he was a good-lookin' man. Good in the sack, too. We was gonna go out West, where it's sunny every day, I hear. But he got in a bar fight with a guy who was comin' on to me. I coulda handled it myself, but Roger, he was a real man. He cut that guy so bad he almost bled out on the barroom floor."

She stopped for another swig of her beer and smiled at the memory.

"Was he Georgia's father?"

"Hell, no. Roger went to prison. I wasn't one to wait around. Good thing because he never came out. Got stabbed while he was in there. What goes round comes round, I guess. I hooked up with Crystal's dad later. He was a no-good son of a bitch. Told me he was fixed, then said I musta got pregnant by somebody else. There wasn't nobody else. I never stayed with one man, but I never cheated on the one I was with. He left when Crystal was a baby. I tried to do the mother thing, but it just didn't suit me. I shoulda just give her away, like I did my first one. I took her to my dad's, let him collect the welfare for her. It was a good deal for both him and me."

I noted she didn't seem to care that it had been a very bad 'deal' for her daughter.

"You can't live your own life when you got a kid, you know? You got kids?"

I shook my head.

"Good for you. They're not worth the trouble."

"So, do you see your grandchildren much?"

"Hell no. I don't see anybody much. Crystal ain't been out here for months. You'd think she'd come by now and then to make sure I got a six-pack of beer in the fridge at least. After what I did for her."

Given Sheila's take on mothering, it seemed more likely that Georgia would bring her a six-pack of arsenic than of beer.

"What did you do for her?"

"I got her the best deal of her life, didn't I?"

"How's that?"

"She took my advice and hooked up with Miller, Mr. Moneybags."

"You set her up with Miller?" I asked, doubt heavy in my voice.

"Hell, no. How would I know a Caldwell like that? They was in school together, but I wasn't here much then. But I come back to sell my dad's trailer after he died. Had to stick around for a while 'cause he left everything a mess. Crystal had got herself through college by then. She was a real looker, like I was at her age. But she fancied herself up, learned how to talk like rich people do, and act all nicey-nice. She had it bad for Fourey Caldwell."

"Fourey? I thought you said Miller."

"It was Fourey first. He was a smooth customer all right, but I could see right through him. Underneath he was the same kinda man as my third husband—good-lookin,' smooth line, but a scammer through and through."

"So how did she wind up with Miller instead of Fourey?"

"She took my advice for once in her life, and it paid off."

"What advice was that?"

"Fourey had a real girlfriend. Crystal was just his piece on the side. But she kept believin' his line. Then Fourey got in some kinda fight with his old man, and he quit at the bank and left town. Left Crystal high and dry, too. I told her to go after Miller, reel him in, and do it fast, before his old man found out and put the kibosh on it. When they started seein' each other, I told her to get herself pregnant, or pretend she was, so he couldn't get away —or if he did, it would cost him a pretty penny."

Although my mother had told me that Sheila wasn't mother of the year material, I was a little shocked about her advice.

"And did she?"

"Hell, no. That's when she told me her and Miller wasn't even doing it. I asked her what was she waiting for? She says to me, 'Miller is gay. The closest we been is a goodnight kiss.' You coulda knocked me over with a feather. I never seen that coming."

Neither had I. Her words hit me like the proverbial ton of bricks. Georgia had known before they were married that Miller was gay. But she'd played the victim to the hilt when Miller came out, claiming to be shocked, devastated, destroyed by Miller's deception.

"How did she find out he was gay?"

"She said Fourey told her."

Whoa. Georgia was full of interesting tidbits.

"I can see why Miller would want to marry Georgia. He was struggling not to be who he was, and he thought marriage to Georgia would make him 'normal.' But why did Georgia marry him, knowing that he was gay?"

"Because I sat her down and told her what's what. I said looks only last so long. Money's the thing. Use what you got to get you some money while you can. You don't want to wind up like me, nothin' to show for myself but two kids I never wanted, no money, and no man worth a damn. She listened for once in her life."

Sheila stopped for another pull on her beer. I felt an unexpected twinge of sympathy for Georgia. In the space of ten minutes or so, Sheila had told me several times that she didn't want Georgia and regretted having her. What kind of things had she said to Georgia over the course of a lifetime?

Having finished her beer, Sheila went back to her story.

"You get that ring, I said to her. You do whatever you got to do to get knocked up by him as quick as you can. Give his uppity parents a grandkid and that'll shut them up. So what if he's got no interest in you in the bedroom? Don't give out that you know about how he is. He's goin' with you 'cause he wants to hide it. You just marry him and take your fun where you find it. Just don't get caught. It's the money that counts in the end."

"Words to live by," I said.

"Don't you even try talkin' down to me. People like us, me and Crystal, we do what we got to do to survive. I don't need to apologize to anybody for that. And it worked out fine for Crystal. Miller got what he wanted, too. She give him two kids and a beautiful woman to help him hide that he was a homo. And Crystal, she got to be queen bee around here. She had a good run until Miller come out. She's still got plenty of money, so I say she won that game. Get me another beer, will ya?"

41

Miguel called as I was leaving Highview.

"Where are you? How did your interview with Georgia go? Maggie said she sent you. I'm very sad I didn't get to do it."

"You wanted to go to an assisted living center?"

"Yes. I love to talk to older ladies. Maggie said Birdie Mae is a hundred! I would love to visit with her."

"Yes, she was fun. But she wasn't the only old lady I saw. Though I have to say the second one was more interesting than she was fun. I'll be home in about ten minutes. Why don't you come over? I'll fill you in. Also, I have a favor to ask."

"Yes."

"Yes, you'll come over? Or yes to the favor?"

"Yes to both."

"You don't even know what the favor is."

"*Chica*, you know it's always yes to you."

"But it's really true that Georgia, she doesn't even go to see her mother?"

I had just finished telling Miguel about my day, winding up with my serendipitous encounter with Sheila Bailey.

"Are you serious, Miguel? I just told you that Georgia knew all along that Miller was gay, Fourey may be a gigolo, DJ Warby may have seen the killer (and it might be his dad), Georgia and Fourey are quite probably having an affair, and your takeaway is that Georgia isn't good to her mother?"

"No, no, I heard everything else and it's very bad that Georgia pretended to Miller that she didn't know he was gay so she could get more money. But also, Miller pretended to her that he wasn't gay, and that was not good either. And yes, I can imagine DJ's father attacking Miller with a knife, and Fourey, he's not a good man. But still, to not go to see your own mother? That is not right."

"Wow, you're one of the few people that Georgia actually seems to like. And now you're turning on her? Welcome to the dark side, my child."

"I am not turning on Georgia, but I don't like that she ignores her *mamá*."

"Well, I can't believe I'm saying this, but I'm pretty much with Georgia on this one. Her mother is awful. She doesn't show any signs of remorse for acting like she didn't even have a daughter for most of her life. I don't blame Georgia for steering clear of her."

"I understand, too. But I think that sometimes we have to be better than other people deserve, or how will the world get better?"

"You are a very nice person, Miguel. But trust me, Sheila Bailey, if you ever meet her, will test your faith in the healing power of kindness. Anyway, on to the favor I need. Are you still willing to try to get some information out of Georgia?"

"Yes, of course. I will call her as soon as we finish. I will ask her to come for a glass of wine and talk about being on my podcast because she has done so much for the arts in Himmel. We'll have some wine, I will be sympathetic, she will have more wine, I will not. And then you know how that goes."

"Yes, I've experienced the *in vino veritas* effect a few times myself. If you can get her tipsy enough to tell you about her finances, and whether she has a man in her life, that would be great. If you can get her to say that it's Fourey, I'll give you my *Harriet the Spy* award. Which reminds me, did Sadie get in big trouble for her early morning gun theft? Her mom seemed pretty unhappy."

"She is grounded for two weeks, and she cannot have her phone. But she told me it's worth it, because she got to meet a real detective, Charlie. And he gave her one of those badges they have at the sheriff's office for when schools bring little kids for tours."

"He did? That was thoughtful of him. I'm seeing signs that Ross is mellowing in his old age. He babysat for Jennifer's twins on Sunday. That shocked the heck out of me."

"Charlie has always had a good heart. He just doesn't want people to think he's soft. But look how he is with Allie. He loves her to pieces. And you, too."

"Oh, come on. I'll go so far as to say that Ross likes me, despite himself. And I like him, too. But he hardly loves me to pieces."

Miguel shrugged. "I think you are wrong."

"Well, it's true, I am pretty lovable. And Ross's life would be a sad and lonely wasteland without me in it. Maybe you're right."

"You can tease how you like, but you love him, too."

"Let's not get carried away. And let's move on."

He grinned. "Okay. What are you going to work on next?"

"Finding out about Fourey. I've got a friend in Florida who works at a paper in the Naples area, which is Fourey's most recent neighborhood. I'm going to ask him to do some checking for me."

"*Him*? Is it Connor?"

"It is. Why are you saying it like that?"

"How did I say it?"

"Like Connor is a plot twist in a Hallmark movie. I'm calling him because he lives in Fourey's stomping grounds, he's a good reporter when he's sober, and he owes me more than one favor. Also, remind me never to have late night drinks with you again. Obviously I talk too much."

"But you hardly told me anything except that you lived with Connor for a while, and you left him because he couldn't stop drinking. He called you last spring to tell you he's been sober for six months. I was just joking a little. I know Coop is your bae."

"Except for the fact that I hate that word, yes he is. And Connor is a good person. Aside from that, I know if there's anything to find out about Fourey, he'll have it for me within a couple of days. And I'm counting on you to work your magic on Georgia."

⸻

Despite my protestations to Miguel that it was all good with Connor, I found myself feeling a little hesitant to make the call.

We were together for almost a year. I broke things off because I finally realized I wasn't helping Connor deal with his alcoholism. I was helping him make excuses. I cut off all communication when I left because I knew it would be easy for the rescuer in me to get drawn back into the chaos that had become his life.

I hadn't spoken to him in years until he'd called to let me know he was "working the program" in AA and wanted to apologize, even though he couldn't think of a way to make amends for being an asshat. That made me laugh. We caught up on our lives. I told him I was proud of what he'd done. He said the same to me and that was that. It had been over a year and neither of us had reached out to the other again.

But, as I'd told Miguel, Connor was a good reporter when sober, and he was working in the Naples area that Fourey had said he'd recently left. So, he was my best option.

"Connor? Hi, it's—"

"Leah! Great to hear from you. How are you?"

"I'm good, thanks. You?"

"All good here, too."

"Good. That's good. Remember when you called me a while back?"

"Of course I do. It was one of the toughest calls I had to make on my apology tour."

"Hey, it shouldn't have been. I don't feel anything but happy and proud of you for getting yourself straightened out."

"Thanks. I didn't do it alone, but I'm glad to be fully functional again."

"You know when you called, you said you wanted to make amends, and I said that you didn't need to. We both had things to be sorry for."

"Yes. I remember. You were very gracious."

"Well, the thing is, if the offer is still open, I could use a favor that you could put in your amends-making list."

I shook my head, glad that I wasn't talking to him face-to-face. Could I be any more awkward?

"Sure. What do you need?"

"Anything you can find on a guy, Raymond Edward Caldwell IV, who also goes by Fourey Caldwell. He's from here, originally, the black sheep of a wealthy family. He moved to Florida close to thirty years ago. He's back now and the story he's telling is that he made his fortune down there in real estate."

"And you don't think that's true?"

"I have my doubts. He says he came back because his mother is seriously ill and not expected to live much longer. The illness part is true, but I'm wondering if he's also here because something went wrong in your neck of the woods, and he needed to get away. He gives off some con man vibes and I know that real estate development in Florida is a wild and wooly place. He's good-looking, fit, early fifties, dresses well, speaks well. Can you find out for me what his financial situation really is, and if he's left a trail of broken hearts and empty purses behind him?"

"I'll do my best."

"Thanks, Connor, I appreciate it."

We reminisced for a bit about old stories we'd covered and mutual friends until Connor said, "Well, I should go. I've got a dinner date and she gets hostile when she's hungry."

"Sounds like me."

"There's no one like you, Leah," he said with a laugh. "I'll be in touch as soon as I have something."

"Thanks, Connor."

It was six o'clock when I hung up with Connor. It had been a pretty busy day, and I hadn't made it to the grocery store yet. But there was one more person I had to see.

42

A red-haired boy in sweatpants and a long-sleeved T-shirt was shooting hoops in the Warby driveway. He turned as he heard my car door slam.

"Hi! Are you DJ Warby?"

"Yeah," he said with a wary note in his voice.

"I'm Leah Nash. Could I talk to you for a minute?"

"What about?"

He held the basketball in front of him like a shield and everything about him—his eyes, his expression, his stance—said go away.

"I'm investigating Miller Caldwell's death."

"Are you with the police?"

"No. I'm a journalist. Miller and I owned the *Himmel Times* together."

"I don't know anything about it. I mean, I know he died, but I don't know him or anything."

"That's not really true, is it DJ? You met Miller when he spoke at an LGBTQ event in Madison. You were struggling with coming out. He gave you his business card and told you to call him if you ever needed to. I know that because I was with him a few weeks ago, when your dad accused him of grooming you."

His knuckles showed white as he tightened his grip on the basketball, and he didn't look at me as he mumbled, "I have to go." He turned and began walking quickly toward the house. I followed and put my hand lightly on his arm.

"DJ, wait, please! I just want to talk to you for a minute."

"I can't talk to you. Please, just go. My dad'll be really mad if he gets back and you're here. I can't help you."

"But maybe I can help you. I promise I'll only take a few minutes. Miller was there for you. I'm just asking you to give me five minutes for him."

I could almost see the thoughts running through his mind. *What if my parents come and she's still here? How much does she know about me? What do I owe to Miller? Why is my life so f'd up?*

"All right. But just five minutes. Come on."

———

"DJ, did you know that your dad had confronted Miller a week or so before he was killed?"

We sat at the kitchen table. DJ perched on the edge of his chair, poised for flight if I asked the wrong question. His green eyes were downcast, and he refused to look at me when he answered.

"Yeah. I wanted to call Miller after Dad told me that he 'sorted him out,' to tell him I was sorry. But I didn't. I was afraid my dad might find out and go after him again."

"What did you think your father might do?"

He shrugged. "I don't know. He just acts so crazy sometimes."

"How do you mean crazy?"

"He's got this friend at work, Craig. He told my dad all this stuff about how there's all these 'groomers' around with a 'gay agenda.' He said a teacher at school turned his daughter gay. He got Dad on all these websites that talk about some gay pedophile conspiracy to take over the government or something. I don't know. My mom tries to calm him down sometimes, but he won't listen."

"Does your mother know that you're gay?"

"I haven't told her. I don't think she wants to know. She knows how my dad feels. Everybody knows how my dad feels."

"How do *you* feel?"

"Scared, guilty, miserable. How would you feel if your dad thought being gay was worse than being dead? Maybe it is. It feels that way to me sometimes."

"Do you feel guilty because of Miller's death?"

He looked at me then.

"Why would I? I told you. I don't know anything about it. He was nice to me. He tried to help me. But I don't know anything about how he died."

"I didn't ask you about how he died. Why would you say that? What do you know about Miller's murder, DJ?"

"Nothing! I don't know anything. You have to go now. Please, just get out!"

His voice was both angry and afraid.

I had fumbled badly by pressing him too quickly.

I tried again.

"Did you know that the person who found Miller and called it in didn't give his name to the 911 operator? In fact, he just reported it and hung up. But that doesn't mean the police won't be able to find him. And they won't give up looking. Miller was stabbed so close to the time the 911 call came in that it's possible the caller actually saw the killer."

"I don't know anything about that. I'm sorry about Miller. He was a really nice man. But it's got nothing to do with me. Now, please, go !"

His voice rose and the tremor in it told me he was about to lose it. Was he so upset because he'd lied to Allie, and he really had recognized the figure he'd seen running away from the tunnel? If that was true, the chances were high that it had been Dennis Warby. But I'd been too heavy-handed. DJ wasn't going to talk to me.

"All right, all right. I'll leave. But DJ, think about what I said. The police are going to find the caller. If it *was* you, it would be a lot better if you came forward first."

"I don't know anything about it. How many times do I have to tell you?"

I grabbed a business card from my wallet and scribbled Father Lindstrom's name and number on the back and thrust it into his hand. "I think you've got an awful lot on your mind. This is someone who can help you sort things out."

He read the name and said, "I'm not Catholic. And I don't want to talk to any priest—or anyone else because there's nothing to talk about."

"He's not 'any priest.' He's like no one else I know. He won't judge you or tell you what to do. He's a really good person to talk to when you feel like you're backed into a corner that you can't get out of."

He went to the door and opened it wide. "You have to go now. Please."

I didn't push him any more. But as I left, I saw him put the card in his pocket.

I called Allie on my way back home.

"I just talked to DJ. I didn't get far. You're right, he's really scared."

"Did you—"

"No, I didn't mention you at all. But I pushed him too hard, and he shut down. Allie, I need to call your dad. It would be a good thing if you told him what you told me."

"I know, and I've been thinking about what you said. But it still feels like I'm letting DJ down if I go back on my promise. I don't want him to think he doesn't have anybody to trust."

"You're right to worry about DJ. He's wound pretty tight. But remember what you said at Miller's memorial, about secrets not having any power over you once they're out? You're not letting DJ down by going to your dad, you're helping him. I'm going to call your father in an hour. I won't bring you into it, but I hope he'll already know by the time I talk to him."

I did not feel great about how I'd handled things with DJ or with Allie. I'd pushed DJ too hard. And I'd sunk to guilting Allie—the last resort of a frustrated parent—to persuade her to talk to Ross. And I wasn't even a parent, which was no doubt a good thing.

I filled the time waiting for an hour to pass by going grocery shopping. When I got back, I tried to entice Sam to eat the new brand of cat food I'd bought. It promised that cats couldn't resist it. He proved the slogan false by drinking some water and tipping over his food dish, his irresistible dinner untouched.

As it turned out, I didn't need to call Ross. He called me.

"So, there's more to Dennis Warby and his kid than we thought," he said without preamble.

"Did you find out something new?" I asked.

"You don't need to pretend you don't know. Allie told me she already talked to you."

"Phew! I don't like being in the middle."

"Yeah, well, I don't like that she went to you instead of me. I told her I gotta work on bein' more calm and she's gotta work on trustin' me to come around even if my first response isn't that great."

"You did?"

"Don't sound so surprised."

"I'm not surprised." Though I was. "I'm just happy that you lived up to the advance PR I gave you. Did she tell you everything?"

"She told me DJ made the call, he was sellin' weed, and he's afraid he'll get arrested for dealin' if we find him. The big news is he saw someone runnin' away from the tunnel. Is there more?"

"I think there is. I talked to him a little while ago."

"Of course you did."

"I didn't know if Allie was going to tell you, and I wanted to get a feel for where DJ's head was. I thought he might talk to me because it would be less intimidating than talking to the police. But I didn't handle the interview very well. I didn't reassure him. I think I scared him more. And he got so upset that I think he might be more convinced that it was his father that he saw than he admitted to Allie."

"That's a tough position for a scared kid to be in."

"Well, I botched the interview with him. You're up to bat now. I'm focusing on Georgia and Fourey. I think there's a lot more to learn about them. Oh, did you get anything on Miller's missing watch yet?"

"Nah. I widened the alert to pawnshops outside the area, we'll see what turns up. There's a chance that maybe Miller wasn't wearing the watch for some reason. Maybe it's in a drawer in his house somewhere, or out gettin' repaired. I'm keepin' all the doors open from here on in as far as theories of the crime go."

I was about to give him the highlights of my interviews with Georgia and Fourey, but as I started, he cut me off.

"Oh, hey, the pizza delivery guy is at the door. I gotta go. Talk to you later."

43

It was eight o'clock when I hung up with Ross. His mention of pizza prompted me to choose one of the fine dining options I'd picked up in the frozen food department. While the microwave did its thing, I called Margaret Newman and set up an appointment with her for eight thirty the next morning. By the time I finished eating and cleaning up, Coop arrived.

"Well, you don't look like Timmins beat you up too bad at your meeting. How did it go? Did you get dinner? If not, I can offer you a choice of frozen entrees, cereal, canned soup, a cheese sandwich? I went grocery shopping," I said.

"No, we had a pizza, I'm good. I wouldn't turn down a beer if you've got one, though."

"Here you go," I said as I handed it to him. "Now, tell me all."

"It went about like I expected. Cliff is pretty pissed. He left town on Saturday expecting Noah Hanson to be arrested any minute. Then he could claim that on his watch, Miller's murder was solved in less than a week. Instead, we're back at the beginning. To someone like Cliff, who cares more about optics than justice, that's a big blow."

"He wasn't grateful that you guys saved him from having to backtrack out of a bad arrest? Now, that would've been embarrassing."

"The only thing Cliff is ever grateful for is a giant campaign donation or a front-page story all about him. I let him rant for a while, but finally I had to remind him that I don't report to him, and neither does Charlie. He settled down eventually. What've you been doing since lunch? And where's your cat?"

"Sam isn't my cat. He's hiding in the closet, probably making a nest of my favorite sweats. I'm a little concerned about him. He's still not eating that well. I think tomorrow I'll take him to the vet to make sure there isn't anything physically wrong with him. As far as my post-lunch activity, it was fairly noteworthy."

I gave him the overview and then focused on what I'd found most interesting.

"Georgia is such a terrible human being. Marrying Miller was a calculated decision to get what she wanted. But when he came out, a really hard thing for him to do, she added layers of guilt by pretending to be shocked and deceived. It makes me want to punch her."

"It's not the first time I've heard you say that."

"Yeah? Well, this time I have specifics on my side, not just general loathing of her. Also, Sheila told me that Fourey and Georgia had a thing when they were younger, and given the woman's robe, heavily scented with Georgia's perfume, hanging in Fourey's bathroom, I think they're having one now. I've got an interview in the morning with Margaret Newman, the woman who was head teller at the bank. I'm very interested in what she has to say about Fourey.

Oh, I almost forgot. I called Connor to ask him to check Fourey out. He's working at a paper in Fourey's old neighborhood in Florida. Do you mind?"

Coop knew the basics of my relationship with Connor, and he's not the jealous type, but I thought it best to get it out there.

"Should I mind?"

"No."

"Then I don't."

"So, what do you think about DJ Warby?"

"I think it's good Allie came to you, and even better that she talked to her dad about it. I know why you went to see DJ before you told Ross about him, but at least you told Ross, so that's progress."

I gave him some side eye but let the jab slide. "Ross is going to take it from here with DJ. I'm going hard after Fourey, with maybe a side of Georgia thrown in. How about you? Are you making any headway yet on Eddie's case?

"We've been reading through the reports, and it's been pretty discouraging."

"Why's that?"

"It looks to me like the white van story might not hold up."

"You mean the kids who said they saw it lied?"

"I wouldn't call it lying—at least not deliberate lying. Kids, or people in general, can be pretty susceptible to influence when it comes to recalling details in a highly charged situation, like Eddie's disappearance. Everyone was excited, speculating, ideas about what happened were flying around. It's possible that they convinced themselves they saw something they really didn't."

"What makes you think that?"

"None of their stories vary on the details."

"And so?"

"Eye witness reports usually aren't exactly the same. Say there's a hit-and-run car accident. Everyone agrees a vehicle hit a person and drove away. But one witness says the vehicle was a green car, another says it was blue, and the third person says it wasn't a car at all, it was a van. But all the kids' accounts read pretty much the same. White van following Eddie, male driver wearing a baseball cap, and that's it. No other details that one kid saw, and another didn't."

"You think they got together and made up the story? Why would they do that?"

"Not on purpose. But word that Eddie was missing spread fast when he didn't come home. There was plenty of time for people to freak out and start speculating about kidnapped kids. And for the kids to get together and talk. You know how stories get started."

"I do, but this is pretty bad if that's what happened. The whole investigation back then was all about the stranger in the van. So, what are you going to do now?"

"Some of the kids still live local. We'll try cognitive interviewing with them."

"What's cognitive interviewing?"

"You can use it any time, but it's really useful when you're working a cold case. Basically, you take your witness through four different ways of looking at a scene. It uses a set of specific steps to help them retrieve memories from a long time ago. With luck we might be able to tease out some new details or untangle their memories a little."

"I hope you can, because otherwise how will you get anywhere?"

"Well, we do have something new. The crime scene guys were able to pull two different sets of fingerprints from Eddie's bike and from his inhaler. Neither of them belongs to Eddie."

"Way to bury your lede, that's huge! But how do you know they're not Eddie's? Not to be crass, but how did you get fingerprints from a skeleton to compare against the other two sets?"

"We didn't. Eddie's prints were taken not long before he went missing. There was a program HPD offered to take kids' fingerprints because of the big 'stranger danger' scare back then. The program's still around in quite a few places. The prints aren't kept on file, they're given to the parents. Benny Garcia still has Eddie's. That's how we got them. Now, wait a second here. This is seriously—"

"Please don't say this is off-the-record. I know that this isn't for sharing, publicly or otherwise."

"All right, just trusting and verifying, that's all. So now that we know the prints aren't Eddie's, we'll run them through AFIS, the national database. Though we have to get in line for our turn. But if whoever killed Eddie didn't commit any other crimes, nothing will show up to compare the prints to."

"But even if you don't find a match, now you know that two people were involved in taking him, right? That's more than the original investigators had. Still, you didn't pick an easy case to get back into the thick of things again, did you?"

"No. But I'm glad I've got the chance to roll up my sleeves and investigate, instead of just oversee. I miss that part of police work more than I expected to."

"Well, you're the boss, Sheriff. You can investigate whenever you decide you want to, can't you?"

"In theory, yes. And I expected to have more opportunities to do that when I ran for office. However, I've found out in practice that there's an awful lot of other daily sheriff-ing to do, that doesn't leave much time for hands-on investigating. But with a case this old, there isn't the same time pressure as a current case, so I should be able to do it."

"You will. If the answers are out there, you'll find them."

44

At eight thirty on Tuesday morning, I knocked on Margaret Newman's apartment door.

"Hold on, hold on! It takes me a minute," a voice called from inside.

The woman who opened the door leaned heavily on a walker. She had white hair, cut short, hands that were gnarled with arthritis, and a fierce gaze that said she had no time for nonsense.

"I'm Leah Nash, Miss Newman. May I come in?"

"I wouldn't have told you that you could come over if I wasn't going to let you in. Come along, don't let the cold air in."

I followed her into a small, overheated, sparsely furnished living room. She chose a recliner chair—the kind with a motorized lift that helps you get in and out of it—and nodded for me to sit on the only other place available, a pale blue loveseat.

Not sure how long her patience would last, I jumped right in.

"As I said when I called, I'm gathering information from people who knew Miller and his family. I know that Fourey Coldwell was more or less exiled from the family by his father. Fourey said the rift came because despite his efforts, he'd never been able to live up to his father's expectations."

"He said that did he? It sounds about right."

"You mean it's true that Raymond Caldwell was overly harsh with Fourey?"

"Is that what I said?"

"No." I had a brief flashback to my no-nonsense seventh grade teacher, Mrs. Butler.

"I worked at the bank for many years—first for Mr. Raymond Caldwell and then for his son, Miller. But I wouldn't presume to comment on how Mr. Caldwell interacted with his family. I do know that after what Fourey did at the bank, he's lucky he didn't go to prison."

"That's not quite the story Fourey told. When I spoke with him, he mentioned a 'misunderstanding' involving a client with dementia. He said the woman's son accused him of stealing from his mother's account, and his father refused to believe him when he explained what had happened. Instead, he fired Fourey and threw him out of the family."

"There was no 'misunderstanding' at the bank. What Fourey did was a crime, plain and simple. He took advantage of an older client's confusion and stole a considerable sum of money from her. Then he tried to blame it on her failing memory, when it was plain to anyone who looked at her account what he'd been doing."

"Which was what?"

"He was filling out the withdrawal slips—he didn't even bother to disguise his handwriting—and pocketing the money."

"But why would Fourey need to steal money? The Caldwells are very wealthy."

"They are. But Mr. Caldwell believed it would be character building for Fourey to live on the salary that matched his position. But there was no way Fourey was going to be content on a teller's salary. I could see right away that wasn't going to work."

"Did you say anything to his father?"

"It wasn't my place to take issue with his father's judgment. And I didn't want to be the one to tell Mr. Caldwell his son was a thief. When I began to suspect what Fourey was doing, I did try to get Mrs. Conway—that was the client he was stealing from—to come to my window. But she loved Fourey. So, I sent a letter to her son, asked him to keep my name out of it, but suggested there might be a problem. He came here to find out. And find out he did. As did Mr. Caldwell."

"So, Fourey's dad replaced the money and banished Fourey. And kept it quiet to avoid a scandal that would tarnish the family name?"

"Mr. Caldwell was a very proud man. It would have killed him to have people know what his son had done."

"But wasn't he just making his son's criminal tendencies a problem for someone else? Maybe a stint in jail would have straightened Fourey out."

"There are some people who will never straighten out. They're born as morally bent as my spine is after years of arthritis. It's not how I would have handled it, but I've never had children. I have never told anyone this story. It was bank business. But with Mr. Caldwell gone, and Mrs. Caldwell to follow him soon, I don't see that it can hurt anybody to speak now. Except Fourey, and I have no qualms about that. But I won't speak a bad word about Mr. Caldwell. He was a hard man, but a good man. He treated his employees fairly. And that's really all I have to say."

I didn't have time to think much about what Margaret Newman had told me, because I had to zip home and get Sam for the vet appointment I'd made. I arrived late, which I hate to do, because I had underestimated how much time it takes to get an unhappy cat into his carrier.

"Good morning, Leah. How are you holding up? I heard you're investigating Miller's murder. That must be tough, given how close you were to him."

Tom Fuller, with his dark eyes gazing sympathetically at me and his salt and pepper hair sporting a fresh, close-cropped cut, looked even more George Clooney-ish than the first time I'd met him.

"Hi, Tom. I'm okay. You're right, it's hard, but at the same time it gives me something to do besides feeling sad and angry."

"At tennis last night everyone was shocked that Noah Hanson isn't a suspect anymore. What happened there?"

"He had an alibi that checked out. I'm glad it did, before he got completely ground up in the Himmel rumor mill. Small towns are great for a lot of things, but one of the not-so-great things is that it's easy for gossip and speculation that can really hurt people to spread. But I thought you were a golfer, not a tennis player," I added to change the subject. I understood why he was curious. Everyone was, but I didn't want to get into what Ross, or I, was doing. He took the hint.

"I like golf, but I love tennis. I've played since I was a kid. I was on the tennis team in college, even considered going pro. Those days are long gone. Now I play for the enjoyment, and to keep fit. Speaking of fit, tell me what's going on with Sam, here. He looks pretty healthy," he said. He had been petting the cat as he spoke, and Sam now looked blissfully relaxed.

"He's still not eating well, and he keeps to himself most of the time. I try to pet him sometimes, but he's pretty standoffish, not like he's being right now with you."

"You forget that Sam and I are old friends. Let me check a few things."

Although Sam no longer looked blissful as he was poked and prodded, he remained docile under Tom's probing.

"You're like Dr. Doolittle. What's the verdict?"

"He's a healthy feline, who is suffering from the loss of his human. I'll give you a short-term prescription to take his anxiety level down. In fact, I'll get him started with one right now. You should see a change for the better within a day or two."

"Thank you, Tom. I'd like to return him in good condition when Charlotte finds a home for him."

"You're doing fine. Just relax, don't crowd him, and let Sam decide when he's ready to warm up to you."

⸺

As I drove Sam home, my phone rang, and I saw the call was from Charlotte. Sam chose that moment to begin loudly meowing from the back seat.

"Hi, Charlotte. That sound you hear in the background is Sam singing the song of his people. We're on our way back from the vet."

"Is he sick?"

"No, I took him in because I was a little worried that he hasn't been eating well. But Tom Fuller said he's in good health, just depressed because he misses Miller. Don't worry. He prescribed a short-term round of medication to get him back on track, that's all."

"Oh, I'm so sorry he's being a bother. I haven't found anyone to take him in permanently yet, but I'll get on it."

"Don't stress about it. We're doing fine together."

A seriously prolonged wail from the back seat seemed to give the lie to that, so I talked a little faster and louder to distract Charlotte.

"How are you doing? Anything you need from me? Is Sebastian still with you?"

"No, he went back to Chicago this morning. His classes start on Wednesday, he needs something to keep him occupied. Baz tends to brood about things, and he's been beating himself up over lost time with Dad— you know, from when Baz was so angry at him when he first came out. We've talked and talked about it, until I told him the best thing he could do, the thing that would make Dad happy, was to go back to school, work hard, and get his law degree. So, that's what he's doing."

"I think you called it exactly right."

"I don't know if I did or not. I hope so. I don't want Baz to think I don't need him or want him around. But I know so much more about the businesses and the things Dad was working on, there isn't that much that Baz can help with. And going back to school might give him something to focus on besides feeling guilty. Still, I feel like I barely know what I'm saying half the time. There are just so many decisions that have to be made, about Dad's business affairs, about his house, about well, everything. I had no idea so much needs to be taken care of when someone dies."

"You sound so tired, Charlotte. Is there anything I can do?"

"No. I'm sorry, I don't mean to complain. I really called to see if you could come over tomorrow night for dinner and a glass or two of wine, around six or so. I'd like to catch up on how you're doing with the investigation. Detective Ross isn't telling me anything."

"That's pretty much how police investigations go. The cops aren't going to tell you much. They don't want to compromise their work. But I'm happy to come over tomorrow and share what I've been doing. I've picked up some useful information. I don't have a theory yet though, so don't get too excited."

"Mother said she spoke with you. It didn't sound like it went very well. Her fault, I'm sure. I don't know why she acts the way she does. But when she's unhappy, she wants everyone around her to be unhappy, too."

"Is there anything in particular that's making her upset?"

"Not that I know of. She's never been an easy person to live with, but after the divorce things got a lot worse. She doesn't like Chicago. In Himmel she was important. In Chicago, she's not, despite the way she tries to make it sound. I think she's lonely. And she's still bitter about the way Dad hid his secret life from her—from all of us. That's not to excuse her behavior, but it's an explanation. I think somewhere inside maybe she'd like to be a good mother, a better person, but she doesn't know how. I'm sorry she was so rude to you."

I doubted that Georgia harbored such aspirations in her cramped little soul. And now I knew for a fact that all her outrage and hurt at the time of the divorce—and still—was fake. But I didn't want to tell Charlotte that over the phone.

"Don't worry about it. I didn't take anything she said to heart. My focus is on finding why Miller was killed, and who did it. I don't care if it's the police or me or someone else who gets the answer. I just want to make sure it gets done."

"You know, when I heard that Eddie Garcia had been found, it hit me hard. The idea that we might not know for years, or ever, why Dad died, I mean. It's been forty years for Mr. Garcia, and still, he may never know. How are the police ever going to find out the truth so long after it happened? I don't want it to be that way for us."

"It won't be Charlotte."

After we said our goodbyes and hung up, I hoped I'd be able to come through with my confident words.

45

When Sam and I got home, I opened the cat carrier cautiously, and he took off for the bedroom. I called Ross.

"Hey, I just wanted to let you know I'm hard on Fourey's trail. I talked to a woman who worked at the bank at the same time he did. Fourey's story is that he was unfairly accused of stealing money from an old lady's account. He says the woman had dementia and was making withdrawals and then forgetting that she had."

"That doesn't sound fishy at all," he said sarcastically.

I gave him Margaret Newman's story.

"Okay, so the guy's a liar and a cheat. That doesn't mean he's a killer. Did you get anything more to link him to Miller's death? And what's his motive? He doesn't get any cash."

"There's a little more to the story."

"Okay, what else?"

I filled him in on my visits with Georgia and Fourey, including the Georgia-scented robe in Fourey's bathroom, and the phone conversation I over-heard. I gave him what I'd learned about Fourey and Georgia's past relationship, and what I suspected about their current one, plus my suspicion that Fourey wasn't the wealthy businessman he claimed to be.

"Same question. What do Fourey and Georgia get out of killing Miller?"

"I don't know yet. But it's the line I'm going to keep following."

"All right. You do you. I'm gonna stay with Dennis Warby for a while."

"Stay? Did you already talk to him? Did you talk to DJ first?"

"I haven't got to DJ yet. I talked to Dennis this morning. He works nights and I wanted to catch him when the kid wasn't there. He's a hostile guy with a lousy temper. And he's still plenty mad at Miller. He's got an alibi but not a great one. Said he wasn't at the park that morning. Claims he was out on Washburn Road bein' a Good Samaritan, changin' some guy's tire. But he didn't get the guy's name. Can't remember the make of the car. We'll be checking into the details on that, believe me."

"Who's we?"

"Steve Northam is back from medical leave. I'm grabbin' him to help me with things."

Steve is a laid-back road patrol officer who's been with the sheriff's office for years. He's a nice guy with no big ambitions, but he's good at his job.

"I hope you and Steve turn up something. I meant it when I said I don't care who gets there first, you or me, but one of us has to figure this out. For Miller."

"Agreed."

"Although, Ross, you should prepare yourself. Working with Steve won't be the same as working with me."

The previous spring, I'd spent about a week doing a ride along with Ross as research for my fiction book.

"I'm always thankful for small favors."

"Just admit it for once. I was your best partner ever. You're not going to build those kinds of memories with Steve."

"Goodbye, Nash."

"Goodbye, Ross."

Miguel stopped to see me later that afternoon.

"So, I had drinks with Georgia last night. I called her right after I talked to you. I think she is lonely. She was very happy to hear from me."

"If she's lonely, it's her own fault. How did it go?"

"Fine, of course. I am very good at getting confidences from the ladies. And the tapas bar was fun. Nice booths, a little dark, and they have someone who plays jazz piano. You should take Coop there. It would be romantic."

"I don't think Coop would like that kind of place."

"I think it is you who wouldn't like 'that kind of place.' Coop, he has the romantic soul. You? Not so much."

"Hey, I like romance. I just prefer a bar with some character, like McClain's. Anyway, enough about the bar's ambiance. What about the conversation? What did you find out?"

"That Georgia lost a lot of money because she made a bad investment in Bitcoin."

"Bitcoin? What does she know about Bitcoin?"

"She knows nothing about Bitcoin. That's why she lost so much money. But she had a new boyfriend and he told her that he could help her double her investment. And the more she invested the more she'd make. Only Bitcoin it has a lot of ups and downs. Georgia bought on the ups and had to sell on the downs. She blames Miller."

"How did she twist logical thought to reach that conclusion?"

"She said she never managed money, and Miller knew that. He gave it to her because he knew she wouldn't know how to invest it. He should have done it for her."

"Oh, come on. Like she would have let him. Did she say exactly how much she lost? It must be a bundle."

"No, she was too embarrassed to say how much, I think. But she said she thought she would have to sell the cottage on Lake Michigan to make up for it."

"Wow. That 'cottage' sits on a bluff that fronts right on Lake Michigan. It's got to be worth a whole lot of money. Do you think she was serious about selling it?"

"Maybe. She thinks she can get top dollar from Charlotte and Sebastian to buy it from her to keep it in the family."

"Nice. She's going to get the money she needs, or thinks she needs, by charging her own children an exorbitant price for the cottage. Then she'll continue to use it as though it's still hers, no doubt. She's really a piece of work. Much like her own sweet mother. Well, now we know why she wanted money. Next up is finding out what she and Fourey are hiding."

"You will, *chica*. You will. But you cannot work all the time. Courtnee and I are going to McClain's for dinner. Do you want to come?"

"With you and Courtnee? Oh, gosh, I'd like to. But I just bought a new toothbrush to clean the grout on my shower tiles. I'm very excited to use it. You two have fun without me."

That evening I did not clean the grout in my shower. Although it could have used it. Instead, I reread all the notes I'd taken to date, and tried to decide where to go next. Back to Fourey, for some direct questions about him and Georgia? Take another run at Georgia herself?

I was deep in thought, tapping my legal pad with my pencil when Sam jumped up beside me and began batting at it as though we were playing a game. It was the first time he'd initiated any playful contact with me.

"Hey, are you trying to distract me? Or do you have something you think I should write down? Please, I'm all ears to any new ideas."

We played with the pencil for a little while, but he lost interest as abruptly as he'd found it. Instead, he began kneading at the blanket that covered my feet. Then, he stopped and curled up beside them.

I was a little wary after Tom's advice not to push Sam too fast, but he was the one who started it, right? I reached out slowly and stroked his head between his ears. After a minute, he began to purr.

"Sam! Are you trying to say you like me?"

He turned and gave me a look that clearly said, "Get a grip, girl."

"Okay, so maybe it's your meds kicking in. I'll tamp down my excitement. But Coop is doing something with his dad tonight, and I could use a warm and comforting presence beside me. Thanks for stepping up."

46

When my phone rang the next morning, I was just finishing breakfast. Sam was, too, which was another good sign that the antidepression meds were working.

"Hi, Leah. Did I wake you?"

"No, Connor. I'm surprised though. Isn't seven thirty a little early for you to sound so chipper?"

"Not anymore. In my clean and sober life it's early to bed, early to rise. I've got something for you on Fourey Caldwell."

"Great! Tell me everything."

He proceeded to lay out a story of Fourey's life in Florida that was very much at odds with Fourey's version. He did not have a successful property business. Nor did he live on a boat he owned because he enjoyed the free and easy life of a water-based nomad. In fact, he didn't own a boat at all.

"Fourey specializes in charming wealthy older women—and there are plenty of them here on the Paradise Coast. By all accounts, he's a good dancer, a witty storyteller, an ace tennis player, and a decent golfer. Plus, he's got a good line and he knows how to use it."

"I bow to Mrs. Obuchowski for knowing a gigolo when she sees one."

"Who's Mrs. Obuchowski?"

"She's the Caldwells' housekeeper and has no use for Fourey. So, preying on rich ladies of a certain age is his specialty?"

"It is. But he hit a rough patch with his most recent lady friend."

"What happened?"

"He lost the $50,000 he'd persuaded her to invest in some real estate scam he was pushing. It wasn't so much the money—she's got plenty of that. It was the realization that she was nothing to him but a piggy bank."

"Did she turn him in? Did he go to jail?"

"Nope. You know as well as I do that white-collar criminals get away with it more often than not. Especially when the victims don't want to prosecute."

"Why didn't she?"

"She's about fifteen years older than Fourey. She was embarrassed and humiliated that her 'true love' was just in it for the money. She didn't want everyone at her country club to know what a fool she'd been. But she didn't want Fourey to get away with fleecing her, either. They struck a deal. If Fourey returned the money and left the area never to return, she wouldn't go to the cops. He did, and she didn't."

"How did you find out if she's trying to keep it quiet?"

"Turns out when I'm not drunk, I'm a pretty good reporter. Fourey's victim didn't go to the police, but she did confide in a 'dear' friend, who swore secrecy. Then the dear friend confided in a trusted close friend, who pledged not to tell. Then that friend confided in another friend, who in turn confided in *moi*. I then verified the story with other sources, and there you have it. How does this jibe with what you already know?"

"Perfectly. He's courting a couple of wealthy women up here right now, probably in search of his next score. When did this happen? And how did Fourey get the money to pay back the woman he scammed?"

"Late spring is the general timeline. I don't know where he got the money to clear up his problem, though."

Could Miller have loaned it to him? Maybe, if Fourey had presented a convincing sob story. But what would have happened if Miller found out the truth and told Fourey he was going to expose him? That might be a motive for killing him.

"I don't suppose you turned up any evidence that Fourey has a predilection for murder as well as theft, did you?"

"Sorry, no trail of dead bodies in his wake. Not even a hint. Are you hunting a serial killer now? How is that even possible? I thought Wisconsin was God's country. You know, 'where all the women are strong, all the men are good-looking, and all the children are above average'?"

"That's Lake Wobegone, not Himmel. And you'd be surprised what happens around here."

"Actually, if it involves you, I don't think I would," he said, laughing.

Connor always had a great laugh. It made me happy to hear it again.

"This is very helpful, Connor. Thanks, I owe you one."

"No, you don't. I'm still behind in the IOU department. But listen, before you hang up, I need to say this. I was angry and bitter at the time, but now I understand why you kicked me to the curb. You had to. I was dragging you down and look what you've been able to do once you got free of me."

"Stop it. We were dragging each other down. It was a codependent relationship, and we were both playing unhealthy roles."

"Sounds like somebody's been going to therapy. I recognize the lingo."

"Yeah, I went for a while about something else. I hated it, but I learned a few things. Anyway, regardless of the past, you're doing great now. I'm proud of you."

"If you call doing well starting over at a local weekly that pays half what I used to make, for twice the amount of work I used to do, then okay, I guess I am."

"Don't knock weekly papers—or starting over. I landed back here at the *Himmel Times* after I made some mistakes. It's worked out pretty well. You never know where the next step on the path will lead you. I think you're on your way to all good things."

"Thanks, Leah. I hope so. I do enjoy waking up in the morning and not wondering where I am. I also like knowing for sure that I don't owe anyone an apology for something I did the night before that I don't even remember. If you're ever down this way again, give me a call. I'll buy you a Jameson, and myself a Diet Coke, and we can reminisce an afternoon away—just the good parts."

"Same if you're ever in Wisconsin, Connor. Thanks again, and you take care of yourself."

So, my feeling about Fourey was right. He was a con man. No wonder his father had cut him off without the proverbial penny. But who was he conning now, Georgia or Marilyn? Maybe he'd come for Georgia, found out she had money problems of her own, and glommed onto Marilyn instead. But then what had he been referring to when I heard him talking to Georgia? What exactly had he said?

I grabbed my notes and flipped through them. There it was.

"There's no leverage anymore. In fact, if it comes out now, it could bite us in the ass."

What was the leverage?

Time for another visit with Raymond Edward Caldwell IV.

47

"Leah! I'm surprised to see you back so soon. I'd invite you in, but I'm just on my way out for a meeting," Fourey said when he opened the door and saw me.

"Really?" I let the skepticism I felt have full rein. "Interesting choice of outfit for a business meeting," I said, looking pointedly at the tennis shoes, gray sweatpants, and light blue sweatshirt he wore. It was exactly the color of his eyes. I wondered how long he'd had to search for the perfect match.

"I didn't say it was a business meeting. I'm having coffee with a friend."

"I won't take up much of your time, but I'd like to get your take on some new information I've got."

As I'd hoped, he was more curious to know what I'd learned than he was irritated to find me on his doorstep. He stepped aside and waved me in.

"Would you like something to drink? Water or coffee?"

"Water would be nice, thanks."

"So, tell me," he said as he handed me the glass and sat down across from me, "Are you and the sheriff's office running a good cop/bad cop act on me today?"

He took pains to put a teasing cadence into his voice, but his eyes revealed how annoyed he really was. Ross hadn't mentioned that he was going to talk to Fourey. In fact, he had barely seemed interested in the Fourey angle. Had he picked up something he hadn't shared yet?

"Sorry. I don't know anything about what the sheriff's office is doing. I'm here because I've learned some intriguing details about the reason you left the bank all those years ago."

"Really? From whom?"

"I spoke with Margaret Newman."

"Am I supposed to recognize that name?"

"Funny. She remembers you very well. She was a teller when you were there. She's the one who spotted what you were doing to the elderly woman with dementia. How you filled out the withdrawal slips for her, and then took the money yourself. Margaret didn't want to go to your father and tell him you were a thief. Instead, she wrote an anonymous letter to the woman's son. And we both know what happened after that."

"Exactly what I told you. I was unfairly accused. I never stole anything, let alone money from an old woman. I do vaguely remember a teller named Margaret, now that you give it some context. She developed a crush on me that was so obvious it was embarrassing. She was considerably older than me. When I told her, as kindly as I could, that I wasn't interested, she got quite angry. Obviously, she sent a letter full of lies to the woman's son to get some sort of revenge for me rejecting her. It's sad that all these years later, she's still clinging to her made-up story."

"I think you're the one who's clinging to a made-up story," I said.

"I am telling the absolute truth. Her story is entirely fabricated. But it's not my job to convince you of that. Now, if that's all, I—"

"Oh, but it isn't. Fourey, I know about Florida."

"It's a beautiful place, lots of sunshine, and I'd be there now, if it weren't for my mother's health."

"Would you though? I mean, you got away with real estate fraud once— well, maybe more than once, I don't have a full dossier on you. Yet. Would you risk going back? Though Florida is a big state. I suppose there are places left that you haven't grifted your way through."

I had to give him credit. He didn't flinch. His answer was smooth and unruffled.

"The real estate game takes smarts and a certain amount of courage.

You have to be able to roll with the punches. It's possible to make a tremendous profit, or to lose it all. I've never defrauded anyone. If I had, I'd be in prison, wouldn't I?"

"One would think. Unless your victim didn't want anyone to know she'd fallen for your line. Which has to be a pretty good one, I'd say, to keep you in the style you've been accustomed to all these years. But you conned the wrong woman last spring. You got out of it by paying back the money. But where did that money come from? Not from selling your boat, which you never owned. Not from your lady friend at the time—she's the one you scammed. Did you get it from Miller, Fourey? Did he bail you out because you made up a convincing story? And then did he find out and want you to face the consequences?"

"Are you suggesting that I killed my own brother? You are very far off the mark. I have never defrauded anyone. And I was nowhere near the county park the morning Miller died. I can prove it."

"How?"

"I have an alibi. I was with someone that night. I didn't leave the cottage until the next morning, after I got the call from Charlotte that Miller was dead."

"Then you lied to the police and to me. You said you were home alone when Miller was killed."

He shrugged and gave what I'm pretty sure Miguel's favorite show, *Bridgerton*, would describe as a rakish grin. I'm not a fan of the show, or rakishness in general.

"A gentleman never tells—unless he's in danger of being railroaded into a murder charge. I was with Georgia. Neither of us wanted to upset my niece and nephew. Their father's death is enough for them to contend with."

"You're saying that you and Georgia are having an affair."

"I think affair is too strong a word for what Georgia and I have together. Let's call it 'in-laws with benefits.'"

"So was it going on when she was still married to Miller?"

"Is that surprising to you? We all know that my brother wasn't prepared to give Georgia the passion she needs in her life. Who could blame her?"

"And what about you? Could you be blamed for sleeping with your brother's wife?"

"You're really quite judgmental, aren't you, Leah? Miller made a calculated decision to marry someone he was not ever going to be a real husband to. Where's the judgment against him?"

"Miller was desperate, not calculating. It cost him dearly for a very long time to deny who he was. And it cost him again when he acknowledged it. I reserve my judgment for the woman he married, knowing that he was gay but pretending not to because it suited her own goals. And I reserve it for you, too, Fourey. His own brother, who also knew."

I hadn't meant to let on how much of the backstory I had, but I was so incensed at his criticism of Miller that it just came out.

"Well. You seem surprisingly well informed," he said.

"I talked to Georgia's mother."

"Ah. The lovely Sheila. You no doubt discovered there is no love lost between Georgia and Sheila. But nothing that her mother may have told you alters the fact that both Georgia and I have an alibi. Each other."

"Neither of you is exactly credible. Can you prove it?"

"There's no recording of our tryst, if that's what you mean. However, there is a security camera here at the gate. It records everyone coming in and going out. The tapes are retained for thirty days, so you—or the police —will be able to see Georgia's car arriving at eight the night before Miller was killed, and not leaving until eight a.m."

That shut me up. I hadn't noticed a camera, but Fourey wouldn't have trotted out its existence so confidently if it weren't true. I switched back to the topic of timing.

"You said you didn't want to upset Charlotte and Sebastian with the knowledge that you were playing some kind of Uncle Daddy game. But now you don't care about their feelings?"

"Certainly I do. But do they really need to know? I'm hoping you can keep this confidential. It has no bearing on Miller's death, other than to remove us from suspicion. Keeping it under wraps would be a kindness."

"Why would I do you a kindness?"

"Oh, not me. My niece and nephew. If you reveal the unconventional friendship Georgia and I have, it could devastate them further than they already have been. Especially Sebastian. You know how sensitive he is. And Charlotte is stretched to the breaking point. Why give them more to handle when they really don't need to know?"

He smiled then and he looked exactly like Miller. I felt sick to my stomach at the contrast between the fine man who was gone, and the asshat who was there in front of me. If there really was someone in charge of the universe, I wanted to speak to the management.

"I'm investigating at Charlotte's request. I'm not about to hide what I find from her. She's an adult, not a child. And I think she's proven she can handle quite a lot."

"It will be on your head then, if there is a permanent rift in the family," he said.

His audacity was boundless. It had no doubt contributed to his success as a con man.

"Any rift that happens will be because of you and their equally morally bankrupt mother. Also, I'll not only share this conversation with Charlotte, but I'll also be informing Detective Ross. You can expect a return visit from him, I'm sure."

48

I called Ross as soon as I got back on the road.

"I've got something for you. About Fourey Caldwell. And Georgia."

"Yeah? I'm heading to the school to talk to DJ Warby. You got about five minutes before I get there."

I filled him in on Fourey's Florida background, his newly discovered alibi, and gave him what I'd learned from Georgia's mother.

"I already got the Florida stuff."

"When you saw Fourey this morning? Seems like he would have mentioned that when I told him I was going to give his story to you."

"I wasn't out there this morning."

I thought for a second. Fourey hadn't actually said that Ross was there. He'd asked me if the sheriff's office and I were running a good cop/bad cop play on him today. I'd made the assumption he was talking about Ross.

"Did you have Steve Northam interview him again?"

"Nope."

"Then why would Fourey tell me the sheriff's office had already been to see him?"

"I got no idea."

"How did you get the Florida piece on Fourey so fast?"

"I don't actually sit around waitin' for you to spoon-feed me information, Nash. I got a cop friend who retired down there. He works as a PI. He got me pretty much what your friend handed you."

"I thought you hated PIs."

"I do. Except when they're my friends. I hate reporters, too. Except when they're my friends."

"Thanks, Ross. I guess."

"Don't let it go to your head. But thanks for the Georgia/Fourey romance tip. I wouldna thought to interview Georgia's mother."

"Well, I didn't either, really. That one fell into my lap. But were you ever planning on telling me what you found out about Fourey?"

"In due time, Nash. In due time. But it doesn't matter, right? You got it yourself. You keep forgettin' I don't work for you."

"No worries. I never forget that. But I thought we were going to do better at sharing after the Noah thing. I've been keeping up my end."

I expected him to respond with a snort of derision. Instead, he was quiet for so long that I thought I'd lost the phone connection.

"Ross? Hello? Ross, are you still there?"

"You're right, Nash. And you been good. But I just got the word this morning from my PI friend. I woulda told ya. But I should've done it up front. Like you did."

Now I was the one who went silent. Ross had never admitted anything remotely like that before. I knew it had taken a lot for him to say it. And I knew he wouldn't want me to make a big deal out of it, or thank him, or really allude to it at all. So, I just went on. But I felt happy that he'd said it.

"So, what do you think? For now, all we have are Georgia, or Fourey, or both of them together, or long shot Dennis Warby, or even longer shot, random robber."

"I been thinkin' a little about another idea."

"Do tell."

"Miller was a lawyer, right? Plus he was a rich guy businessman, right? Both those jobs can make you a lotta enemies you don't even know about. There could be someone else like Boyd Hanson out there who was like, uh, you know. . . . Whaddya call it when you hurt somebody you didn't mean to while you're goin' after somebody else?"

"Collateral damage?"

"Yeah, that's it. Collateral damage from some case Miller had or something."

"Gabe said something like that, but so far I haven't seen anything that leads in that direction. Have you?"

"No. I just threw it out there because I'm stumped. Usually you're a big fan of out there ideas."

"Let's go back to Georgia for a second. I mean, Gabe heard her say that she knew something Miller wouldn't want to come out. And when I heard Fourey talking to her on the phone, he told her that with Miller dead their leverage was gone. It's not likely Georgia knew any secrets associated with Miller's legal practice. And for sure Miller wouldn't have confided in her, or even let her know anything at all about his life since their divorce. And if it was a pre-divorce secret, I can't believe she wouldn't have used it during her burn it to the ground campaign against Miller after he came out."

"How about if the thing Georgia was threatin' to tell was a secret that her and Miller both had together? It coulda hurt Georgia to have it come out, but maybe it would be way worse for Miller than for her, so she was willing to go there. He wasn't and that was her leverage."

"I don't know, Ross. I can't see Georgia doing anything that would hurt her in the slightest."

"My grandma used to say, 'Don't cut off your nose to spite your face.' The way I see it, Georgia is one spiteful woman. She'd hurt herself, as long as it hurt Miller more."

"Ross, you're a more astute judge of character than I realized. That's Georgia exactly. But if she was willing to have the secret come out even if it damaged her in the process, then the secret can't be her motive for killing Miller. It would be Miller's for killing her—which I would fully endorse—in order to keep the secret hidden."

"Listen, I gotta go. I'm at the school. Maybe we should grab a beer so we can kick things around more."

"Yeah, that would be good. Let me know how your interview with DJ goes. Talk to you later."

After we hung up, I wondered again why Fourey would have said that Ross had been out to see him, when neither he nor Steve Northam had been. Then it hit me. Duh. It must have been Coop. But why was he jumping into the investigation of Miller's murder, especially when he had the Eddie Garcia cold case on his hands?

49

As I drove up the street to Charlotte's condo, a man was walking down her front steps. From the back I didn't recognize him. I wondered again if she was seeing someone—maybe the man she'd met for a coffee date at Woke that morning back when things were normal, and Miller was still alive.

When she led me into the kitchen I was a little dismayed not to see any sign of food or the preparation thereof. My stomach had begun growling half an hour earlier.

Instead, a large cardboard box was open on the breakfast bar. She shoved it precariously close to the edge to make room for us to sit down.

"Sorry. Patty sent it over today from Dad's office. She's been cleaning out his desk and these are some of his personal letters and things. I've been going through it, but it's just so hard."

"You know, you don't have to push yourself on something like that right now."

I noticed then that her eye makeup was slightly smudged and surmised that she'd been crying earlier. I started to chat about non–murder-related things to give her a chance to get her bearings as she handed me a glass of wine and refilled her own. She did not offer me anything to eat. I wondered if she'd forgotten about the dinner part of our get-together.

"Hey, I'm not trying to be nosy—well I guess I am, since I'm asking—

but are you seeing someone, Charlotte? I noticed a guy leaving when I turned the corner onto your street. I think it's nice, if you are," I added.

Her eyes filled with tears.

"I was. I just broke up with him."

Ah, that was the reason for the messy mascara, not Miller. Also, maybe for the absence of any dinner happening.

"Oh, I'm sorry. Do you want to talk about it?"

"No. Yes. I mean I want to, but I'm ashamed to."

"Why are you ashamed?

"It was Tom you saw. Tom Fuller."

I was shocked on two counts, and though I tried, I didn't succeed in minding my own business.

"But he's old enough to be your father! And he's married!"

"I know," she said, her voice clogged with the tears she was fighting off. "And I know what you're thinking. I'm a terrible person. But I didn't intend for it to happen."

"How did it?" I asked, this time achieving a more neutral tone. It was her life, not mine, and she clearly needed to talk. I tried to channel Father Lindstrom and listen without judging.

"It's been going on for a few months. I took Sam in for Dad one day, and Tom was just so kind, and so funny, and he's so good-looking, too."

"Yes, we can agree on that."

"I didn't think, 'Oh, I'm going after that guy' or anything like that. But then I ran into him at the Elite one day, and we had coffee. It just developed from there. We found out we like a lot of the same things—hiking at Devil's Lake, going to Olbrich Gardens in Madison, poking through bookstores on a Saturday afternoon. His wife doesn't like doing any of that. They've been unhappy for a long time. I'm not trying to excuse myself. He's married and I knew that from the beginning. But we were just so drawn to each other.

"Tom was honest with me. They've got a son in college and a daughter in high school. He said that he couldn't hurt them by breaking up the family. I didn't want that either. I told myself that it was all right as long as we kept it quiet. I thought I was fine with things as they were. Until the night before Dad died."

"What happened?"

The tears began to spill from her eyes then. I yanked a paper towel off a roll on the counter and handed it to her. She wiped her cheeks and swallowed hard before she answered.

"Dad called me. He asked if I'd like to go to dinner. I said I was working on something, and I really wanted to finish it. I asked him if we could make it the next night. He said sure. Only the next night never came for him. The last thing he asked me to do, I said, 'No, sorry. I can't.'"

She started sobbing in earnest then, and I got off my stool and put an arm around her.

"Hey, hey, it's okay. You couldn't know it was going to be his last night," I said.

"But I lied to him. The real reason I couldn't go was because I was seeing Tom. He was supposed to come over at eight thirty, after the clinic closed. But he didn't. He called and said that just as he was locking up, a woman came to the door with her dog. He'd been injured in a hit-and-run. He couldn't turn her away. I know that's part of his job. But after we hung up, I started thinking. He'd canceled on me a couple of times before for other emergencies. He was cheating on his wife with me. Did he give her the same excuse that he'd given me? Was he cheating on me with someone else? Once the thought came into my head, I couldn't get it out."

I had returned to my own seat at the bar. I took a sip of wine to keep myself from saying something judge-y as she continued.

"I couldn't settle down. I didn't want to call him and come off as jealous and insecure. But I had to know if he was lying to me. Finally, I got in my car and drove to the clinic to see if he was really there. I saw the lights on, and when I pulled into the parking lot, his SUV was there. So was a car with an out-of-state license plate. Tom had said the dog owner was from out of state. I was so relieved when I saw that car. Tom wasn't lying to me. There really was an emergency. Only . . ."

She stopped again and took a huge gulp of her wine.

"It hit me then. The way I'd been feeling, wondering if Tom was lying to me, wondering if he was with someone else . . . was that how his wife felt when he lied to her to be with me? The guilty feelings I'd tried to ignore just came rushing in. I took a hard look at myself, and I was ashamed. I was the 'other woman.' That's when I decided to break it off."

"But Tom was here tonight, so you didn't?"

"Not then—the next day Dad died. But I haven't seen Tom except at the memorial service. When he calls I say I just can't with Sebastian here, or Mother is so demanding, or I'm just too busy settling Dad's estate. Those are all true, but they were also excuses because I didn't feel like I had the emotional reserves for the conversation Tom and I needed to have. He's been very patient and kind. But today he showed up at my door, about an hour before you got here."

"And?"

"I just went for it. I told him we had to stop seeing each other. It was wrong. He was really upset. He said he loved me, and he'd prove it by getting a divorce as soon as his daughter graduated next year. I told him not to do that on my account, because it was over. I didn't like who I'd become. I almost told him that I'd spied on him that night because I wasn't sure I could trust him. But I didn't want him to know how low I'd sunk."

"What did he say then?"

"It was awful. He kept saying he'd make it work if I just gave him time. I told him it was too late. It was over. He left just a few minutes before you knocked. Leah, I know it was the right thing to do. But part of me wishes I hadn't ended it. I never thought I was the kind of person who would sneak around and lie and all because of 'love' or whatever it is I feel for him. I'm just so ashamed and mixed up right now."

"Charlotte, don't be so hard on yourself. Yes, it was wrong, but you put an end to it. Tom is the one who's married. He's the one who's breaking his marriage vows. He could have told his wife he was unhappy and got a divorce before he started a relationship with you. He didn't. You're the one who took the hard step to make it right."

"It doesn't feel right. It feels like everything is broken!"

As she spoke, she flung out her arm. The box on the edge of the bar tipped and some of the papers fell out. She grabbed for it, but not before a small, blue ceramic bowl tumbled out and smashed on the tile floor.

"I made that for Dad when I was in fourth grade. He kept it on his desk all these years and now I ruined it. Damn it!"

"I'll get it. You get yourself together."

I emptied her wine in the sink and filled her glass with water.

"Drink this, then just breathe for a minute. It's going to be all right."

As she followed my instructions, I got down on the floor to retrieve the blue-glazed pieces of the bowl. It had broken into too many pieces to salvage. I crawled under the table to gather them. Then I grabbed the papers that had fallen, too.

One was the start of a gift list, probably for Christmas. Miller was an organized shopper. Under it was a baseball card—the collectible kind with a player and his stats on it. It was pretty worn. Miller must have kept it as a souvenir from his childhood all these years. I could understand that. I'm not embarrassed to say I still have a concert ticket stub signed by Nick Carter in my desk drawer. Well, okay, I'm a little embarrassed, but I do still have it.

As I backed my way out from under the table, Charlotte gasped.

"Oh my God! I can't believe this."

50

"Charlotte, what is it?"

She held a letter in her hand. Her eyes were wide with shock.

"Charlotte! What?"

"This! This was in the box. It's a letter to Dad from a jewelry appraiser."

All thoughts of Tom Fuller seemed to have left for the moment, so that was a good thing, I guessed, but I couldn't imagine what was freaking her out.

"Can I look at it?"

She nodded and handed it to me.

I scanned it quickly. The letter, dated a few days before Miller died, was a follow-up to a phone call Miller had with the sender. Miller had asked for an appraisal of his mother's jewelry for insurance purposes. The appraiser regretted to inform him that the ruby and diamond necklace was in fact not ruby and diamond at all. It was a well-made replica worth at most $1,000, not the $45,000 it had been appraised at some years earlier.

"There has to be a mistake. That piece has been in the family for generations. It was a gift from my great-great-grandfather to his wife, on their wedding day," Charlotte said. "Every Caldwell bride has worn it on her wedding day ever since."

It crossed my mind that Fourey's con man ways might be hereditary. Perhaps great-great-grandpa had given his bride a fake necklace.

"Do you think it was phony all along?"

"It can't be. The jewelry is reappraised every few years. If it wasn't real, it would have been discovered long before this."

"Well then, the real necklace must have been stolen."

"I don't know how. Gran keeps it in a safe in her room. The only people who are in there nowadays are Mrs. Obuchowski—who adores Gran and is as honest as they come—and the aides from hospice. They'd have no way of knowing the combination. Or even that there was a wall safe there at all."

"That narrows the field of possibilities to the family, then. You, Miller, Fourey, Sebastian. Obviously it wasn't Miller. If he'd replaced the real thing with a fake, he wouldn't have submitted it for appraisal. And I'm pretty sure it's not you or Sebastian."

"You think Fourey stole his own mother's necklace? Why would he do that?"

"Because he needs money, Charlotte. Fourey hasn't been living the life you think he has. That's part of the update I was going to give you tonight."

I proceeded to fill her in on Fourey's real life in Florida. Including his recent narrow escape from prison—made possible only by repaying his embarrassed former lover—and how that might tie in with the fake necklace.

"He could have taken the real one when he was home last spring, had a replica made, and then turned the genuine article into cash. I imagine with the kind of life he's led, Fourey would know that Miami is a major hub for fencing stolen jewelry—right up there with New York. He may even have pulled a similar trick on someone else in the past. He had easy access to your grandmother's necklace. And if he was lucky the theft might go unnoticed for years. He couldn't know that Miller was going to have your grandmother's jewelry reappraised this fall."

Then after hesitating for a minute, I went ahead and told her about the "in-laws with benefits" arrangement Fourey had with her mother. She wasn't as shocked as I'd expected. But then she knew her mother pretty well.

"Do you think Dad knew?"

"About Georgia and Fourey's relationship?"

"About all of it."

"He might have known about Georgia and Fourey but accepted it because he felt so guilty about his own deception. I don't think he realized they both knew he was gay all along. Otherwise, he wouldn't have let Georgia play the hapless victim during the divorce. And Charlotte, there's something else."

I decided that she might as well get the full run-down on her mother and her uncle. I told her about Georgia's threat to reveal a secret that Miller wanted kept quiet, and what I'd overheard Fourey tell her on the phone about lost leverage.

"Do you have any idea what the 'truth' Georgia was talking about could be?"

"I don't. I can't think of anything that Dad would have kept hidden. We talked a lot about the damage secrets do after he came out. I don't believe he would go there again. Maybe mother was just being a drama queen. She can be, at times. Anyway, how many dark secrets can one family have?"

I treated the question as rhetorical, because I didn't think it would be helpful to say, "Quite a few."

"But can we go back to the secret we know about, Leah? If Fourey really is the one who told Mother that Dad was gay, why didn't he tell my grandparents? It seems like he would have enjoyed throwing that in Grandfather's face, after Grandfather threw him out of the family."

"Fourey weighs the odds, I think. Sure, it would have hurt and angered your grandfather, and caused problems for Miller, but it wouldn't have really changed things for the better for Fourey. He held on to the knowledge about your dad because it didn't help him at the moment. But he had it in his back pocket in case the day came when it would."

"Mother hammered at Dad over and over about how he should pay for ruining her life. She tried to turn me and Sebastian against him. She said we could never trust him because he'd lied to all of us. But her lie is much worse in my mind. She pretended she didn't know so she could make Dad feel even more guilty. She didn't care how it affected us. Sebastian's always been really sensitive, and he felt so bad for Mother and so angry at Dad, too. Mother encouraged that anger, even though she could see it was tearing him up, because he loved Dad, too. It was such a hard, confusing time, and she made it worse. I've known who Mother is for a long time. But even I'm shocked at what she did. Baz always thinks people are better than they are. When he finds out what Mother did, I'm afraid he's going to feel like he's lost both his parents."

She went quiet. When she spoke again, she returned to Fourey and the necklace.

"Fourey stealing from Gran would have made Dad very angry. Not just about the theft itself, but it was a betrayal of Gran's love. Do you think Fourey could have killed him because Dad confronted him?"

"It's possible. Stealing a necklace that valuable would be felony theft. That's a ten-year prison sentence. If Fourey couldn't convince your dad to let it go—and I doubt at that point Miller would have been willing—killing his own brother might have seemed to be Fourey's only option. It was risky. But Fourey has been taking risks and getting away with them his whole life."

"This is a lot, Leah. I really don't want to believe it."

"I understand. And remember, it might not be true. We're just hypothesizing. But right now, the pieces sure seem to fit together. I'll talk to Ross tomorrow, see if he can put some legs under it."

"How?"

"He can interview the appraiser, try to get a line on a jeweler capable of making a replica of the necklace, get someone on the ground in Florida to check out possible fences for the real necklace there, that kind of thing. That's when being official law enforcement will be a big advantage."

"I'd really like to have it out with Mother and Fourey right now."

"I'm sure you would. Please don't. If Fourey realizes we know about the necklace, he might take off. And if he's the one who killed Miller, the last thing we want is for him to get away."

"I understand. But if you or the police don't find the answer soon, I don't know how long I can wait."

51

It was just past seven thirty when I walked through the kitchen door at Coop's.

"Oh my gosh, it smells so good in here. I'm so hungry!"

"Hungry? I thought you were having dinner with Charlotte."

"So did I. If you give me a plate of whatever you made, I will tell you a very interesting story."

Following completion of my second helping of beef stew, I did.

"So, to wrap up here is where we are: Fourey is a liar, quite probably a thief, and my odds-on murder favorite. Also, Georgia is just as awful as she has always seemed. Oh, and what I told you about Charlotte and Tom Fuller is confidential. I got a little carried away with my narrative. I should have left that part out. I'm sure she doesn't want anyone to know. I don't count you as 'anyone,' but she probably would."

"Not sure that I like not counting as anyone—but I won't say anything about their relationship."

"I should have said that you don't count as *just* anyone. You're my most trusted confidant. I know that I can tell you anything, unless there is a very good reason for me not to share a piece of information with you."

"Like when you don't want me to know because you think I'll try to stop you from doing something?"

"Yes. Like that. But also in this case, it's Charlotte's secret and it's really not mine to tell."

"Have you told Ross all your news?"

"I just found out about the necklace, so no. But I will. He has more sources and resources than I do as far as tracking down who made the copy and where the necklace was sold."

"It sounds like the two of you have hit pause on butting heads."

"Well, he's not going to replace Steve Northam with me, but we're working all right together for now. It's hard, though."

"You mean because you're both stubborn and want your own way, and you each want to prove that you're right?"

"No. It's because we each have our own methods and sometimes that causes conflict. Ross likes things to go more in a straight line. I like to learn all of the backstories because that's where the motives usually are."

"So you're saying there's method in your madness?"

"Do you doubt that?"

"If you're asking do I think you're crazy, no. Or only in the best possible way. I've told you before I think you have good instincts. Also, you're smart, and determined, and sometimes you're very right. But—"

"No, stop. It's good right there. No need to add anything."

"But," he continued, ignoring me, "you do get your mind set on an idea, every bit as much and as hard as Charlie does. I'm not criticizing you."

"It kind of sounds like you are."

"I'm not. All I'm doing is suggesting that you could take a page from Charlie's book and maybe try to follow a straighter line in your investigating—now hold on, a second and let me finish," he said as he saw me opening my mouth to reply.

"And Charlie could take a page from yours and be a little more creative in his thinking."

"This seems like a good place to move on to your day."

"First, I have a specific question. When I talked to Fourey today, he said the sheriff's office had already been to see him. I assumed he meant Ross, but

Ross told me he didn't know anything about it and neither did Steve. So it must have been you. But why? And why didn't you tell Ross? That seems a little Leah-like, doesn't it? Not that there's anything wrong with that."

"I didn't mention it to Charlie because it didn't have anything to do with his case. I went because of Eddie Garcia."

"Eddie? What's Fourey got to do with that?"

"Fourey was one of the kids who was interviewed after Eddie disappeared. Remember, I told you that Marla and I were going to try cognitive interviewing to see if the witnesses could retrieve memories from back then? Two of them did, Mary Beth Delany and Carl Weaver. They each realized that they didn't personally see Eddie or the van that day. They got carried away by the story of a kid who said he had. That kid was Fourey."

"I've been thinking of Fourey as a con artist. Maybe Pied Piper is more appropriate. Did you do a cognitive interview with Fourey?"

"It's why I went out there, but he didn't want anything to do with that. I couldn't force him to cooperate. He said he knows what he saw, which was Eddie, being followed by a white van. And it's not his fault if the other kids wanted to feel important and repeated his account as their own."

"Do you think he's telling the truth?"

"I'm not sure yet."

"Well, he lies as easily as he breathes. But so far, his lies seem to be to get something he wants or to get some advantage. What would be the point of lying about Eddie and the van?"

"He was a kid. He loved attention. Maybe he didn't think through the impact the lie would have. Maybe he convinced himself it was true. But now that Eddie's finally been found, he doesn't want to admit that his lie sent the investigation off in the wrong direction."

"I don't think you'll be able to shake him. He's always got an answer. Hey, did you get anything back yet from the AFIS database? Do the prints you found match any on file?"

He shook his head.

"We got them this afternoon, but no match. Still, if we're able to zero in on a suspect or suspects, we'll be able to use the prints to determine if there's a link with Eddie."

"So what's next?"

"We still have some interviews to do with other kids who talked to the police at the time. But they're not local anymore. Or maybe even alive. We're tracking them down. Could be they'll remember things differently than Mary Beth and Carl do now. Marla's taking point on that. I've got that conference in Milwaukee for the rest of the week."

"I thought that was next week."

"We talked about this not that long ago. I felt like we were having a two-way conversation about it, but maybe not?"

"Do you believe that I'm so traumatized by the thought of not seeing you for three days that I put your conference totally out of my mind? I mean so that I could make it through the day without collapsing in tears?"

"No. But I do believe that you're so focused on Miller's murder that it's crowding everything else out."

"Never you. Well, almost never. Coop, I'm sorry. I was listening, but not hard enough to get the dates right I guess. But I know you'll blow everyone else on the panel out of the water with your sheriff-ing smarts. And I do remember that after the conference you and one of your friends are going to Madison on Saturday to see your college roommate and have a bro-fest at all your old haunts. While you're away, I'll keep the home fires burning. When you get back, I'll have your slippers ready, a beer in the fridge, and your favorite meal in the oven. I read somewhere that's what men expect."

"Not this man. I expect that you'll keep investigating, and if the trail gets hot, you'll scarcely realize that I'm gone. And if my favorite meal is in the oven when I get back, I'll know your mother was here."

"Oh, that's cold!"

"But you know what? I don't love you because you defer to me, or put aside your own work for me, or cook for me, or wait by the fire for me. I love you because I know where I stand with you. You're there for me when it really counts. I can trust you, and rely on you, and—"

"Okay, you're making me sound like a Maytag washing machine. On the eve of your departure to the big city, where who knows what temptations and dangers you might face, especially on the bro-part of your trip, can you really not think of something a little more romantic to say? Miguel will not approve if I tell him."

"My romance words are not for Miguel's ears, thank you."

"Point taken. But I would like you to center a little more on my surface charms. You know, like you're crazy in love with me because I'm witty, smart, cute, and I know how to make s'mores."

"All of the above and more. Please stay out of trouble, and by trouble I mean danger. This is a murder investigation, remember. Remember this, too," he said, and leaned in to kiss me.

When we drew apart I said, "You know I can't stay tonight. Sam's on new medication and I don't want to leave him alone. However, I could be persuaded to stay a while longer."

"Is this persuasive enough?" He kissed me again, longer this time.

"Why, yes. Yes it is."

52

Thursday morning a heavy rain was falling as I woke up. I glanced at my weather app and saw that the temperature was a chilly forty-five degrees, and we were in for off-and-on showers all day. It looked like early fall was giving us a preview of late autumn. I would have liked to snuggle back down in the covers, but I had a coffee date with Miguel. Fortunately, it was just across the street at the Wide Awake and Woke coffee shop.

I made a quick call to Ross to tell him about the necklace but had to leave a voice mail. He must be making an early start to the day, too. Then I dashed across the street to Woke.

Himmel's newest coffee place has an entirely different vibe than the Elite Café. The building had seen a variety of uses after the drug store it originally housed closed. But from fitness gym through storefront church, none had lasted more than a year or so before Miller bought it. His renovation had made use of the good bones of the structure. The brick walls were exposed, and the battered oak floors were brought back to life. The bar behind which the baristas prepare amazing coffee and tea drinks is a reclaimed piece of wood that once served as the counter for the drug store's soda fountain. All the booths and tables are sleek and minimalist in style. The overall effect is that you've wandered into a trendy urban café. The

Elite will always have my heart, but I'm fond of the ambiance and the convenience of Woke.

"*Chica!* I have hardly seen you. What is going on? Are you making progress? Also, did you hear that Stella at the library is with Owen Fike now?"

Miguel had begun talking as soon as he came through the door and saw me sitting at a booth in the back with his mocha latte waiting for him.

"Good morning to you, too, Miguel. You sound like you're about three espressos in already. Why are you so wired?"

"I'm just happy to see you!"

"Miguel, it's only been two days, not two weeks since we talked. But I'm happy to see you, too."

"Did Connor find out anything yet?" he asked, sliding in across from me.

"He did. And it's making Fourey look worse. Also, there's a new motive now for Fourey. Though to balance that out, he came up with a pretty strong alibi when I talked to him yesterday."

"Tell me everything. And yes, I understand it's not for publication yet."

I updated him on what Connor had learned, my conversation with Fourey, his newly revealed alibi, and the new motive courtesy of the appraiser's letter.

"Fourey stole the necklace from his mother?"

"It looks like it. Ross is running that lead down. But I'm more interested in where he was when Miller was killed. Fourey is awfully cocky about his alibi and what the security footage will show."

"But the video could be altered. You can change the date and time-stamps. Or it could be edited to cut out Fourey or Georgia leaving or coming back in the early morning."

"It's possible, yes. But one of them would need to have technology skills and I doubt either of them do."

"They could pay someone to do it for them."

"True. But the more people involved, the more vulnerable they become either to blackmail or to someone turning them in."

He was quiet as he sipped on his macchiato, his eyebrows drawn together in an uncharacteristic frown. Then he smiled.

"What if they didn't go through the front gate? There is a road that runs behind the property, maybe there is a back way to get to it? Couldn't one of them park a car on the road, and then leave from the back of the property without going near the security camera?"

I thought about the layout of Maple Hill Farm for a minute. Miguel was right about the road.

"Maybe. Are you thinking that Georgia came to Fourey's the night before to provide an alibi in case they needed it, so she'd be recorded on the security camera? Then the next morning, Fourey slipped out the back way so he wouldn't be?"

"It could work," he said.

"Hold on a second." I pulled out my phone and called the number for the Caldwell home.

"Caldwell residence," a familiar voice said.

"Hi, Mrs. Obuchowski. This is Leah Nash."

"Leah, hello. If you're wanting to talk to Mrs. Caldwell, I'm afraid that's not possible. She's not having a good day at all."

"I'm sorry to hear that, but it's you I wanted to talk to. Is there a back entrance onto the property?"

"You mean from Ditmer Street? There's not a real entrance, not one that a car could drive through. But there's a gate. It hasn't been used in years, though. Mr. Caldwell had it put in when the boys were young. They kept tearing their clothes climbing over the stone wall as a shortcut to the river."

"Thanks, Mrs. Obuchowski. I'll talk to you later."

I hung up before she could ask anything else. I leaned over and ruffled Miguel's perfect hair.

"The hair! Why is it always the hair?" he asked, as he restored his look with a few expert pats at his head.

"I can't resist. It's like doing raspberries on a baby's belly. It's my gesture of love, Miguel. Yes, there is a back way into the Caldwells'. A gate that opens onto Ditmer Street. A car can't drive through it, but Fourey could have parked on Ditmer. Then he could've just walked from his place, opened the gate, hopped in his car and driven to the county park. I need to take a look at it, though."

"No, let me do it. I don't want to just be the listener. I want to be a doer, too."

"Hey, you are a doer. I don't know anyone who is more than you. And you have a job, a real, actual, work-twelve-hours-a-day job. I don't want to take advantage of you, and I know that I do sometimes."

"It's not taking advantage to ask me to help. That's what friends are for. I can always say no."

"You never do."

"That's because I always want to. I can go out to the Caldwells today. I have to take some photos near there anyway, after I interview Eddie Garcia's father. I want to do it." He spoke firmly and sincerely, and I was really touched.

"Okay. Thank you, I appreciate it."

Sometimes I wonder how a not-that-nice person like me can have such great friends.

"Why are you interviewing Eddie's father?"

"We're doing a feature story on the cold case investigation. I wish I didn't get that assignment. It will be so sad. Then I need to talk to Coop about it and also the prosecutor."

"Did you know that Coop's gone until Sunday? He's at a conference in Milwaukee and then he's going to Madison to meet up with his college roommate and some other friends."

"I didn't, but that's okay. The story doesn't run until next week. It's a feature, so we'll put it up on the web and into print on the same day. I can catch Coop later. But now, I should go, or I'll be late for the interview."

I looked at my watch.

"I should, too. I want to see Patty this morning. I haven't talked to her since the memorial service. But, geez, Miguel, we didn't even get to regular happenings! I could use a little time talking about things that aren't murder. Like what about Stella and Owen Fike? I kind of assumed that he was gay, but no? Why don't you come over tonight?"

"You are always wrong about that. Owen is not gay. But I can't come over tonight. I'm doing an interview for my podcast and then I'm going to a concert with some friends."

"What about tomorrow? You have the day off, right?"

"Yes, but I'm going shopping with Courtnee in Madison. You could come with us. When we're done, we can go to Lombardino's."

He said the last in a wheedling tone, knowing my weakness for the Italian restaurant. But with Courtnee as part of the package, even that wasn't incentive enough.

"Oh, I would love to, but I think I'm busy then."

"When?"

"When are you going shopping?"

"We're leaving for Madison at ten."

"Oh, shoot that's when I'm busy."

"Fine. I know you aren't, but I have one thing I cannot let you refuse to do any longer."

"What's that?"

"Our training. We have not gone running since Miller died. You have only started for one day. I will not let you back out of the library run."

"Miguel, I really, really don't like running."

"You promised."

"That was under duress. You and my mother ganged up on me."

"You said yes."

"All right, all right. I'll start training again with you on Monday. For real. Just give me a few days to work up to it again."

53

It was raining hard when I dashed across the street. I ran up the front stairs to grab a jacket from my place and then down the back stairs to the parking lot. As I was about to push through the back door, I heard someone call my name.

"Leah? Hey, Leah!"

I turned. A middle-aged blonde woman with lots of hair and a wide smile advanced on me. It took a second for me to recognize her.

"Leah! It's me, Jan. Jan Hudson. You know, from the vet clinic. I was just talking to your mom."

"Oh, Jan. Yes, sure. Hi. Nice to see you. I'm sorry but I'm just on my way out."

I wondered why she'd been talking to my mother, but not enough to stop for a chat. Jan had other ideas.

"Did you get a chance to ask Miguel about getting me on his podcast? You know, to talk about my vampire novel?"

"I'm sorry. I've been kind of busy with—"

"That's all right, hon. I know about Miller Caldwell dying and all. I mean who in town doesn't? I didn't know it was murder, though, 'til I got back yesterday. I've been at my sister's in Glenwood City. We always have a big family to-do Labor Day weekend. It's loads of fun. Unless my cousin

Doris comes. And you don't even want to know some of the things she's done. Three years ago, she shows up with her new boyfriend Wayne, who she knows very well my sister Veva was engaged to and—"

"Jan, I don't mean to be rude, but I really do need to go."

"Oh, hey, that's all right. I didn't come to see you. Wait that sounds kind of rude. I didn't mean it like that," she said, laughing. "I heard you guys were looking for an office cleaner. I just interviewed with your mom. Like I was telling her, this place would be a piece of cake to clean after the kind of stuff I've had to clean up at the clinic! I'm not sorry to see the back of that place."

"You quit your job there?"

"No, Dr. Fuller fired me."

"What happened?"

"He said I was unprofessional, if you can imagine that."

Actually, though I liked Jan, I could imagine that.

"Why did he say that?"

"Because I found a button."

"A button?"

"Yes! See, a week ago Wednesday, I'm cleaning Dr. Fuller's office, doing the great job I always do. And I find this button under his desk. I pick it up, and right away I see it's handmade. I do a lot of crafting myself. I always have a booth at Founders' Day. Maybe you've seen it?"

I shook my head.

"Well, anyway I know this button isn't something you can just walk into a store and replace. Somebody's gonna be looking for this one. I slip it into my smock pocket to check with the Doc, because obviously it was from someone he saw for a consult in his office. Only I forget about it until I'm doing laundry yesterday and check my pockets and there it is. So when I go into work, I show it to Dr. Fuller. I ask if he remembers who was in his office for a consultation last Wednesday, because I found it in the afternoon when I cleaned. He got snotty with me."

"I'm sorry to hear that," I said, edging closer to the door.

"First he asks what was I doing cleaning in his office on a Wednesday, when I know he doesn't come in on Wednesdays. I say nobody ever told me that, and I clean every office every day I work. Then he says I must not clean very well, because nobody was in his office for a consult on Wednesday, and the button was probably there for weeks. Well, you can imagine how I felt!"

"I can and I don't blame you. But—"

She had me by the arm then, so I couldn't leave. I felt like I was the wedding guest, and she was the Ancient Mariner.

"I said Dr. Fuller, I get right down on my hands and knees every single day I clean to make sure I reach every nook and cranny. I am a professional. No way was that button there for weeks. And it wasn't there on Tuesday afternoon when I cleaned. I found it on Wednesday, so it had to get there during the day on Wednesday. I resent you implying that I do anything less than a thorough job. Then he says, I don't see how you can with the amount of talking you do."

"Well, I can see why that would upset you. But I really—"

She rolled on as though I hadn't spoken.

"You can say a lot of things about me, but you can't say I don't take my job seriously. I told him off good. And then he fired me. What do you think of that?"

"I think you did what you felt you had to do, Jan. I'm sorry you lost your job."

"Oh, I'll land on my feet. I always do. Your mom said she was interviewing a few more people. You could probably put in a word for me, right?

"I'm sure that with your experience—"

I realized then that I had lost her attention. She was staring over my shoulder. I turned and saw Miguel walking in. Jan let out a small squeal.

"Miguel! It's you! I can't believe it! I've been wanting to meet you. I listen to your podcast all the time."

She scooted around me and right up to Miguel. I had no idea why he had suddenly appeared when he was supposed to be interviewing Benny Garcia, but I took my opportunity without question.

"I'll let Jan introduce herself, Miguel. It was good to see you, Jan. I'll talk to you later, Miguel."

54

Patty was sorting through files in Miller's office when I walked in. She turned when I tapped on the door and then came straight toward me with her arms out—not typical at all for her.

As she stepped into the hug I offered she said, "Leah, I miss him so much!"

"I know, Patty. Me, too."

She nodded against my shoulder, sniffling back tears for a few seconds, then pulled away and dabbed at her eyes.

"I'm trying to get things sorted out and keep everything going for Gabe. He's got so much to do until he hires another attorney. But every time I pick up a file, I remember the last time Miller and I worked on it. What he said, how he joked with me about this case, how he figured out a solution on that one. I just want to walk in here and have him look up from his desk and smile when I start scolding him for scheduling his own appointments."

She stopped and took off her glasses and patted her eyes with a tissue again, then took a drink of water from a bottle on Miller's desk.

"Oh, I'm sorry. Would you like something, coffee, or water?"

"No, that's okay. I just dropped by to see how you are."

"Oh, I'm all right," she said, then gave a shaky laugh. "Not that I sound like it, I know. It comes and goes. You know, Leah, I keep thinking if only I'd

realized that Monday was the last day that I'd ever see him. I would've trea-
sured every moment. Why don't we realize that every ordinary day, filled
with work to do, and people we love, and a sense of purpose, isn't ordinary
at all. It's an extraordinary gift."

"I don't have an answer for that, Patty. But I understand what you mean.
I saw Miller late that afternoon. I ran in to pick up a folder I'd left behind
that morning. I was actually annoyed with myself for forgetting it. But now
I feel lucky that I did, and lucky that Miller was still here meeting with a
client. I had the chance to talk to him one last time."

"Miller was with a client? There wasn't anyone on the schedule, or I
wouldn't have left early. I suppose it was a walk-in. He was always too available. I spent half my time reorganizing things because he always over-
booked himself. But I wish I was doing that today," she said.

Then she tapped her index finger on her lips for a second, obviously
thinking.

"I wonder . . . was it a man or woman with him?"

"A woman."

"What did she look like?"

"I don't know, um, brown hair, kind of gray, shoulder length. Glasses.
Thin. Fifty-ish, maybe."

"That sounds like Amelia Barr. I've been trying to reach her. I have
some papers that need her signature to close out her grandmother's estate.
I've left a voice message twice, but she's not returning my calls. I suppose
she might have already gone home to Pennsylvania. Maybe she doesn't
even know that Miller is dead. I didn't think of that. I could mail the papers
to her there. But maybe she hasn't left, and then the papers would be there,
and she'd be here. Maybe I should drive them over to her grandmother's
house after work and see if she's still staying there. Yes, I should probably
do that. Oh, but I've got a meeting at five thirty this afternoon and . . ." Her
voice trailed off.

Patty's dithering was uncharacteristic. She's normally a decisive, get-
things-done person. It underscored the level of her emotional distress.

"Patty, why don't you give the papers to me? I'd like to talk to this
Amelia Barr anyway. Maybe Miller took a call while she was here, and she

heard something she doesn't realize is important. Or he said something to her. I don't want to miss anything that might help."

I knew it was highly unlikely that Amelia Barr would know anything. But it was worth asking if she was still around.

"Oh, would you, Leah?"

"Sure, I will. Just give me Grandma Barr's address. If Amelia's not there, I'll bring the folder back tomorrow."

"Thank you so much! But her grandmother's name isn't Barr. That's Amelia's married name, though she's divorced now. Her grandmother was Denise Rowley. Amelia's father was her son. Now, where is that file?"

The Rowley house was a small, slate blue bungalow with a large front porch and an attached garage. The curtains in the front window were drawn, which at nine thirty in the morning could either mean no one was home, or Amelia Barr was sleeping. I knocked on the front door, and when there was no answer, I walked around the house and found a back door to try. Again, no answer. I peered through a side window in the garage. A car was parked inside. That seemed to indicate Amelia was still in residence. Though it could have belonged to her late grandmother. I pulled out my phone.

"Patty, hi. I'm at Mrs. Rowley's house. No one is answering the door, and the house has kind of a deserted feeling. But there's a car in the garage. Do you know what kind Amelia drives?"

"Yes. But the name went out of my head as soon as you asked! It's white, kind of boxy looking. My neighbor's son has one. Let me think. Oh, I know! It's called a Kia Soul."

"That's what's in the garage. So that means Amelia is still around. Maybe she went for a walk. Oh, someone's coming out of the house next door. I'm going to run over and ask if she knows anything. Bye."

I hurried over to the neighboring driveway. But I waited until the woman, who by then was deep in the depths of her SUV, finished buckling her toddler in.

As she backed out of the back seat and moved to shut the door, I said, "Hi, I wonder—"

She jumped. Then she laughed when she turned and saw me standing behind her.

"Oh! I'm sorry. I didn't realize you were there. Tristan always puts up a little bit of a fight when I try to get him in his car seat. Can I help you?"

She had a friendly smile. Her light brown hair was pulled back in a loose ponytail and she looked like she was around my age.

"Yes, thanks. My name is Leah Nash. I'm trying to deliver some paperwork for Amelia Barr from her attorney's office. No one answered the door. It's possible that she's gone back to Pennsylvania already. Do you know if she's still around?"

"Hi, Leah. I'm Kelsey Miles. No, I don't know if she's still in town. Cindy from across the street and I were talking about her yesterday. We realized we haven't seen her for maybe a week or ten days. We figured she must've left for home. It's not like we're friends she'd need to say goodbye to or anything. Just a wave hi in the driveway kind of thing. But you think she's still here?"

"I'm not sure. It was dead quiet when I knocked on the door. Her car is in the garage, though. But if you haven't seen her in more than a week, that's a little odd. I think I'll ask the police to do a welfare check just to be sure everything is okay."

"Oh, wow! Well, I hope it is. She seems like a nice lady. I'm sorry, but if I don't leave now, we'll be late for Tristan's pediatrician appointment."

"Oh, sure. I don't want to keep you. Thanks."

I got back in my car. The fact that the neighbors hadn't seen Amelia in days, and that her car was still in the garage gave me a bad feeling. Amelia could be ill. Or worse.

When I walked through the door to the reception area at the Himmel Police Department, Owen Fike was standing at the counter talking to the department secretary. He held a coffee in one hand and was using the other to gesture as he told a story.

Owen's all right, but he's very by-the-book, and we'd had a few run-ins when he was with the sheriff's office. He's not a big fan of journalists. I think part of the reason he left the sheriff's office was that he thought Coop was giving me special treatment. I wish.

"Owen, hi. I'm glad I ran into you. Have you got a minute?"

I could tell he wanted to say no, but it was hard to pretend he was too busy when he was just gabbing with Melanie.

"What's it about?"

"It won't take long, but I've got something I think you'll want to check out."

I knew that would get his attention. Not because he viewed me as a source of good tips, but because he'd want to know what I was up to. I felt pretty good that this time, I could say with an entirely clear conscience that I was just passing along helpful information.

As I sat down in one of the two visitor chairs, he made a beeline for the power seat behind his desk. There was no way Owen would ever pull up a seat beside me and just chat.

"What's on your mind?"

I explained my mission for Patty and added that I had actually seen Amelia the day before Miller died, when I came in as she was leaving Miller's office.

"Funny how you always seem to be in the middle of police business, Leah."

"Funny how you're always looking for a way to put me on the wrong side of things, Owen. I happened to see her because I had business with Miller—we were business partners, remember? And I was at her house today because I was doing Patty a favor. I'm not trying to put myself 'in the middle of police business.'"

"I wasn't accusing you of anything. I was just making an observation. No need to get emotional."

I bit my tongue. This was not the time to engage in a discussion of the gaslighting tactic he had used by calling me 'emotional,' when I was stating facts he found inconvenient. I turned the conversation back to what I'd seen at the Rowley house.

"The thing is, I looked in the garage and her car—Amelia Barr's car, I mean—is still there. I'm a little concerned because the woman who lives next door told me that she hasn't seen Amelia for a week or so. And Patty called Amelia a couple of times in the last week and left voice mail, but Amelia hasn't called her back. Maybe it's nothing. I just think it should be checked out."

"Actually, we're already on it, Leah."

"You are? Did someone else call it in?"

"Yes, just a little while ago, as a matter of fact. A neighbor of Amelia Barr's in Pennsylvania. She's taking care of her cat. Amelia told her she'd be back Tuesday. But she wasn't, and she didn't call. The neighbor called her yesterday, got no answer, left a voice mail. Amelia hasn't responded. She tried the nursing home where Amelia works as an aide. They have a no call/no show policy. When Amelia didn't come to work on Wednesday, she was fired."

"None of that sounds good."

"We're checking it out. I sent Darmody over to the house. It could be nothing. The neighbor said she inherited some money. Maybe she met a guy who's helping her spend it. That happens."

I thought that Owen was being pretty cavalier about Amelia's disappearance. On the other hand, he might have been glossing over it because he didn't want the paper poking around just yet. I didn't argue with him. If Dale Darmody was checking on things at the house, I knew I'd be able to get in and look around myself.

"Okay, I won't worry about it then. Thanks, Owen.

55

I hurried back to the Rowley house, hoping Darmody would still be there. I knew technically—even nontechnically for that matter—that it wasn't my business. But now I was curious and also concerned. I saw Darmody coming around the corner of the house from the back as I pulled into the driveway.

"Hey, Darmody! Wait a second."

Dale Darmody could have, and probably should have, retired at least five years ago, but he loves being a cop. He's a pretty bad one, to be honest. He got hired when the requirements were quite a bit looser than they are now. I don't think he'd stand a chance of getting on the force today. But he's willing to take the jobs no one else likes doing: night shift, barking dog calls, loud party calls, park patrol, so that comes in handy for his sergeant. He wouldn't be my first choice to call on in an emergency situation, but I can't help liking the guy. And his propensity for talking when he shouldn't is very useful to me.

"Leah, hey, how are you?"

He pulled a handkerchief out of his pocket and blew his nose as I answered.

"I was just with Owen. I stopped by to see Amelia and she didn't answer the door. Her neighbors haven't seen her in a week or so either. I asked

Owen if HPD could do a wellness check and he said you were already here. So should we go in?"

I tried to imply that Owen had basically sent me over to help out with the situation.

"I can't get an answer either. I tried the front and back door and they're locked. She's still not answering her phone either. I don't really wanna break down the door, but . . ."

He rubbed the back of his neck with his hand as he spoke, trying to work out his options.

"Did you look under the mat for a key?"

"I did but there isn't one."

I was somewhat surprised at this evidence of proactive thinking on Darmody's part.

"Did you try for an unlocked window?"

"Nah. I mean even if I found one, I'd have a pretty hard time getting through. Too many visits to Bob's Donuts, I guess," he said, laughing as he patted his prominent belly. "Don't tell Angela I said that."

Angela is Darmody's wife and she's as energetic as he is laid back. She's also on an unflagging but to date completely ineffective crusade to manage his diet.

"I think I could squeeze in if we found one. Let's go around to the back. No need to put on a show for the neighbors."

The first two windows we tried were either locked or painted shut, but the third one opened when Darmody put his full weight into it. I clambered through and landed in the kitchen. I unlocked the door and let Darmody in, and then we both began calling for Amelia.

"Hello? Amelia?"

"Hello, is anyone home?"

There was no answer.

"I guess we better look around," Darmody said.

"Yeah," I said, opening the old-fashioned white refrigerator that held an outdated container of cream, a carton of eggs, and some butter. An inspection of the cupboards revealed a can of coffee, a loaf of bread tinged green with mold, and a jar of peanut butter.

Besides the refrigerator, the kitchen included a small gas stove and a yellow dinette set with vinyl and metal chairs. On the counter was a coffee maker with a clean mug sitting on it, as though waiting for the next morning's brew. In the far wall was a door I presumed led to the attached garage.

"This looks like my mom's kitchen. Everything shipshape," Darmody said.

"I don't think it's a good sign that there's an empty mug ready for Amelia's morning coffee. Why didn't she use it? Come on, let's check out the rest of the place."

We both continued to call out as we moved through the rooms in the silent house. I don't think Darmody had any higher expectations than I did that we'd find Amelia.

The living room was clean and orderly—no magazines, no half-folded afghan on the worn couch, no shoes, or slippers sitting next to it. The medicine cabinet in the bathroom held only toothpaste, a tooth brush and deodorant. A faded towel was neatly folded over the rack on the shower door. There was a small collection of toiletries on a shelf.

The house had two bedrooms. The first featured a double bed with a handmade quilt. On the pillow was a neatly folded nightgown.

"She laid her nightie out, all ready for bed. Angela does that, too. Looks like the room is just waiting for her to come back, doesn't it?"

"Yeah, it does."

When we opened the door to the second bedroom a musty smell greeted us. Boxes were open and half unpacked on the bed, and a stack of them stood untouched against one wall. I noticed a pile of photos in frames in the middle of the bed and I went over to look at them.

The first one I picked up was a picture of a little girl of three or four. Judging by her clothes and hair, it probably dated from the 1970s.

"I'll bet this is Amelia," I said as I put it aside and picked up another. This picture was of a man and a woman seated in front of a Christmas tree. The child in front of them was older than in the first picture, but it was clearly the same girl. She wore a ruffled holiday dress and presented a gap-toothed smile to the camera. The next one I looked at had been taken in the backyard of this house. A tall, angular woman with iron gray hair stiffly sprayed into a bouffant style looked sternly into the camera. Next to her was the same little girl, Amelia, I was sure, with her Grandmother Rowley.

The photo had been taken when Amelia was a little older, maybe eleven or twelve—on the edge of that gangly adolescent stage. She held a framed award noting that she had read two thousand pages for the Summer Reading Program.

I turned to show it to Darmody, but he had moved on to another room. As I put it back on the bed, I noticed another box marked "Mia's Things." I reached for it just as Darmody shouted for me.

"Leah! C'mere! Quick!"

I ran toward the direction of his shout, my heart pounding with nervous dread at what he might have discovered.

Darmody stood beside the open passenger door of the white Kia Soul, holding a patchwork purse aloft.

"Lookee—it's Amelia's purse. It was on the passenger seat. See, here's her wallet," he said, pulling out a faux leather billfold and opening it. "Here's her driver's license," he added. He moved to hand it to me to look at.

I shook my head.

"No, probably the fewer people handling her things the better. Something is very off here, Darmody, don't you think? The house looks like she just stepped out to run an errand—the food in the fridge, coffeemaker ready to go, nightgown laid out on her pillow. But nobody's seen her for days, she's not answering her phone, and the food in her cupboard is moldy."

"Yeah, right, right," he said. As he shoved the wallet back in the purse I noticed something gray on his fingers.

"What's all over your hand?"

He held it out, looked in surprise at his smudged fingers, then began to wipe them on his pants.

"It musta come off the car floor. I dropped the purse and—"

He was bending over to look at the mat on the passenger side as he spoke. "Yeah, there's like dirt, or ashes, or something there," he said, pointing to the car mat. I could see a small pile of something that did indeed look like ashes.

"That's weird."

"Yeah. Why would she just drop her cigarette ashes on the floor? Angela would kill me if I did that. Well, first she'd kill me if I smoked a cigarette, and then she'd kill me again if I dropped the ashes on the car mat."

I stooped down and reached around him. I pinched a bit off the small pile and stood back up. I rubbed my fingers together.

"It's not dirt. I don't think it's cigarette ashes either. It feels kind of sandy."

"What is it then?"

"I have no idea. But I think you better call in and get someone out here to go over the house and the car."

He had started to call when I added, "Hey, Darmody, there's no need to tell Owen I was here and get him all upset, right? "

His eyes widened as he mentally calculated the potential fall-out from letting me into the house now that it had moved from a wellness check to a missing person's case.

"Yeah, roger that. Thanks, Leah."

"No, worries. I'll catch you later."

56

My mind raced as I got back in my car. Amelia Barr had been Miller's last appointment. Now Miller was dead, and she was missing. Was there a connection, or just a coincidence? I called Patty.

"Hi, me again, Patty. Amelia Barr not only isn't at her grandmother's house, she definitely isn't back in Pennsylvania either. It looks like she's missing."

"Missing? What on earth?"

I explained.

"Patty, do you know if Amelia has a Himmel connection, besides her grandmother I mean?"

"I don't believe so. She said that she and her mother lived here until they moved to Pennsylvania when she was twelve. That was forty years ago, and she had never come back. She was quite surprised that her grandmother left her the house. Apparently there was some bad feeling when her parents divorced and her grandmother sided with her son, Amelia's father."

"Well, I'll get the file back to you, and I guess you can just hang on to it, because no one knows where she is at this point. Oh, also, keep that to yourself, for now, will you? The police will be issuing some kind of statement later today, I'm sure. But I'd rather Owen Fike didn't know I got this involved, at least not yet."

"I've been a legal secretary for thirty-seven years, Leah. I think I know how and when to keep a thing confidential!"

I was pleased to hear a bit of the usual caustic spark return to Patty's voice, even if it was aimed at me.

"You absolutely do, Patty. Sorry, I lost my head. Talk to you later."

So, Amelia was fifty-two. Miller had been fifty-two also. They'd both lived in Himmel. They must have been in school together, or they were until Amelia had moved to Pennsylvania. I needed to know more about Amelia Barr, the Himmel Years. Normally, I go to my mother for the backstory on people in town, but we hadn't lived in Himmel in the 1980s. I wasn't even born yet.

As I waited at a stoplight, it hit me. Claudia Fillhart, the librarian. Amelia had been holding a summer reading award. Miss Fillhart had started the program while she was in college and it's still going strong. She had probably known Amelia. I made a call as the light changed.

"Himmel Public Library, this is Pam."

"Hi Pam, this is Leah Nash. Is Miss Fillhart in?"

"No, she's working one o'clock until nine today, Leah. Can I give her a message?"

"That's okay, Pam. I'll swing by her house and see if she's home."

"Oh, I think she will be. She's helping Tim with some of his research."

"Thanks."

When I rang the doorbell at the home of Claudia Fillhart and her husband Tim Mullen (Miss Fillhart had kept her own name when she married, a practice I support), she was the one who answered. I noticed that her short, light brown hair seemed a bit grayer. But her dimpled smile and lively green eyes were the same.

"Leah, how nice to see you! It's been quite a while. Come in. I'm just making tea for us. Would you like a cup?"

"Hi, Miss Fillhart. Yes, thank you. That would be great."

"Are you ever going to call me Claudia instead of Miss Fillhart?

"I try to remember, Claudia," I said emphasizing her name, "but old habits die hard."

As we entered the living room, Claudia's husband Tim rolled in from the opposite end of the house in his wheelchair.

"I thought that was you, Leah. How are you?"

"Good, Tim. How's the Himmel history coming?"

Tim is a political science professor who retired a few years ago because of health issues. The Himmel Historical Society had immediately snagged him to work on a history of the town. He has kind brown eyes, brown hair that's beginning to recede a bit, and a British accent that I never tire of hearing. He and Claudia met when she spent a summer in England. Claudia always says she had no intention of ever marrying, but he followed her home, so she had to take him in. It's obvious to everyone that they adore each other.

"Really well. I'm up to the 1980s. How is your writing coming? I heard you're trying your hand at fiction for your next book."

"I am, or I'm supposed to be anyway. I've got a draft done that needs major revising, but I put that aside to try and find out who killed Miller Caldwell."

"But aren't the police investigating his death?"

"Oh, Tim, you know Leah well enough to know she couldn't sit on the sidelines on something like this." Claudia had called out from the kitchen, where she'd gone to make our tea. "Am I correct, Leah?"

"You are. In fact, it's why I'm here. I'm hoping you can help me with something."

She reentered the living room then with two mugs of tea and handed one to Tim and one to me. As she went to fetch her own, she asked over her shoulder, "You think *I* can help? How?"

"I'm hoping you remember a girl named Amelia Barr. She was in one of your summer reading programs years ago. A lot of years ago. Like forty years."

When she came back carrying her own tea, she sat down across from me in a chair next to Tim.

"Oh, you're taxing my memory, Leah. That was a very long time ago. I ran the summer reading program when I was home from college. But the name Amelia Barr doesn't ring a bell."

"Amelia is fifty-two now, so probably it would have been 1981 or '82? I saw a photo of her holding up an award from the library—that's what brought me to you. She looked about eleven or twelve."

She shook her head. "I'm sorry, I'm just not recalling that name."

"I may be able to help," Tim said. "I've been going through the bound volumes of the *Himmel Times* that Claudia brought home for me. I just finished the summer of 1982, and there's a photo of the summer readers in it. I noticed it particularly because Claudia was in it."

We followed Tim down the hall to his office. A bound volume of the *Times* lay open on his desk. He wheeled up to it and began leafing through the pages.

"Oh, here it is."

He pointed to a photo that spanned three columns on an inside page. "Look at Claudia there. She looks exactly the same, doesn't she?"

Tim pointed to a slim young woman with a wide smile standing behind several rows of kids.

"Oh, Tim, I do *not*. I was nineteen then. I'm fifty-nine now," she said, shaking her head.

She was right, she didn't look "exactly the same." But I liked that in Tim's eyes, she did.

"My goodness, that was my very first summer reading group. All of those children have children of their own now—or grandchildren!"

I peered over her shoulder.

"Is that Miller Caldwell?" I asked, pointing to a tall boy with a longish, feathered hair style.

"No, that's his brother Fourey. Miller is the one behind him."

I saw my mistake immediately. Fourey's early John Stamos look was not one that the buttoned-down Miller would have sported.

Claudia began identifying other kids in the photo. I recognized some of the names—though it was hard to connect those young faces with the adults they had grown into.

"That's Crystal Bailey—she wasn't Georgia yet. Billy Davis, Joy Kendrick, Marty Angstrom, Tom Fuller, Mary Beth Delaney—she was a

Martin then. Davina Markham, Jeff Ralston. Oh, look, there's Eddie, poor little boy."

Her finger pointed to a small boy with round glasses, a short haircut, heavy on the bangs, and a shy smile.

"Eddie Garcia was in that group? He looks younger than the rest of them."

"He was, by a few years. But he was an advanced reader. Still, it was a mistake to put him in with the older kids. He tried so hard to be accepted, but at that age a few years can make a big difference. He got teased a bit by most of the boys, Billy, Marty, Tom, Jeff, but never Miller. Fourey was the worst though. He wouldn't stop until Eddie was crying. Fourey had a bit of Eddie Haskell about him in those days—bullying the younger kids, but sweet as pie to the adults."

"Eddie Haskell?" Tim asked.

"A character in an old sitcom who sucked up to all the parents but behind the scenes got all the other kids in trouble."

Claudia gave me a surprised look.

"I was a *TV Land* kid growing up," I said by way of explanation. "I know a lot about sitcoms before my time. But you said Fourey and Mia gave Eddie a hard time. Which one is Mia?"

She indicated a slender girl in the second row. Her dark hair was long and straight, and her eyes stared defiantly into the camera. She was the only one in the photo not smiling.

"Claudia, that's her! That's Amelia Barr! She was in a reading group with Fourey, and Miller, *and* Georgia?"

"No, Leah, that's Mia Rowley, she—"

I smacked the side of my head in frustration at my own stupidity.

"Amelia Barr used to be Amelia Rowley when she was a kid. Well, actually I guess she went by Mia then. I was just at her grandmother's house— Amelia is here to settle her grandmother's estate. I saw some photos of her as a kid. She's the same girl who's in this picture."

"I only knew her as Mia. And I only knew her for that summer. She and her mother moved away not long after this photo was taken," Claudia said.

"She doesn't look very happy," I said.

"I don't think she was. Her parents had divorced—her father married someone else and left town. I don't remember the whole story, but I think her mother had tried to commit suicide, and Mia's aunt came and took them both to live with her out of state somewhere. That was right around the time that Eddie went missing."

"Well, she's been back in Himmel for a while, staying in her grandmother's house. But no one has seen her for a week or more."

"You mean she's missing?" Tim asked.

"It's not official yet, but all signs point that way."

"Oh, I hope nothing's happened to her. I always felt sorry for Mia. She had a difficult life for such a young girl. I had hopes that she and Crystal—Georgia that is—might become friends that summer. Georgia didn't have it easy at home either," Claudia said.

"But they didn't?" I asked.

"No. Georgia wasn't interested. Now looking back on it, I think they both had a crush on Fourey, so that was probably not a good pairing. But why are you looking for her, Leah?"

The photo combined with Claudia's comments had set a number of ideas caroming around my brain. I needed to sit down alone and sort them out.

"When this morning started out, Amelia was nowhere on my radar. But I learned that she was Miller's last appointment the day before he was killed. He was handling her grandmother's estate. Now, I've just found out that she, Miller, and Eddie were all in the summer reading group in August 1982. And of the three of them, two are dead and one is missing. That seems suggestive."

"Suggestive of what, exactly?"

"Of course, you'd ask the hard question, Tim. I don't know. Nothing is clear at the moment, but I have some thinking to do. I'd better get going," I said, standing.

"You're seriously going to leave us hanging, Leah?"

"I seriously am, Claudia. Mostly because I'm kind of hanging myself, until I pull together what I've got. Right now, everything's a jumble."

"Well, I'm sure you'll figure it out."

"I hope so. Thanks for the information. I'll see you later."

57

It had started raining again, and the wind picked up as I reached home. I made a dash for the door. I didn't check in the newsroom, or pop into my mother's office when I got inside. I headed right upstairs to think. As I opened my apartment door, Sam came running over to me and rubbed his head against my leg. I reached down and petted him.

"Hey, you. It's kind of nice to have someone greet me at the door. I'm glad you're feeling better. I've got some serious thinking to do, or I'd play with you a little. But if you want to go sit on the window seat, I'll meet you there."

I'm not saying he understood me. But I'm not lying when I say that he did saunter over to the window seat. I gathered up my reporter's notebook that contained all the notes I'd taken either during or after each interview; my trusty yellow legal pad on which I would try to pull together what I knew, and a lidded cup and straw combo that I'd filled with ice and Diet Coke to get my brain going.

Once I had my pillows just right behind me, I sat down with everything in easy reach. Sam snuggled up to my stocking feet and kept them warm.

As the carbonated burn of my first sip went down my throat, I began flipping through my notes. I jotted down, trying not to overthink it, anything that struck me.

- Fourey had a history of lying and cheating
- Fourey was not a wealthy businessman; he was a con artist
- Fourey and Georgia had been lovers off and on for years
- Fourey's luck had run out in Florida, and he narrowly escaped going to jail
- Georgia had lost a ton on a bad Bitcoin investment
- Georgia had threatened to reveal information Miller wouldn't want known
- Fourey knew what that information was
- Miller's last appointment the day before he was killed was Amelia Barr
- Amelia Barr was known as Mia Rowley when she was a kid
- Miller had been part of a summer reading group Mia belonged to in 1982
- So were Fourey, Georgia, and several other people I knew: MaryBeth Delaney, Tom Fuller, Davina Markham, Marty Angstrom, as well as others I didn't know. Also Eddie Garcia.
- Eddie wanted Fourey to like him. Fourey and the other boys teased/bullied him
- Fourey started the story about a man in a van following Eddie
- Miller had been killed, Amelia had gone missing, and Eddie's remains had been found all within the last two weeks
- Miller was killed the morning after he met with Amelia
- Sometime after her meeting with Miller, Amelia disappeared
- An heirloom necklace owned by Eleanor Caldwell was actually a fake
- Miller had kept a random baseball card in his desk
- Only a few people had access to the necklace, and only one had the motive and the means to convert it to cash: Fourey
- Georgia and Fourey both knew Miller was gay before he and Georgia married
- Georgia was Fourey's alibi for Miller's murder, and he was hers
- Eddie collected baseball cards

I read the list out loud in the hope that doing so would make it all come magically together into a cohesive theory of everything. It did not. I tossed my legal pad on the floor in frustration. The movement earned me a dirty look from Sam, who had been sleeping. He jumped down and went to the bedroom as someone knocked on the stairway door that opens into my office. Miguel stood on the landing when I opened it.

"Hey, come on in. I didn't expect you back so early."

"It's almost four o'clock, not so early. You look tired. Did I wake you up?"

"No, I've been thinking hard, and getting nowhere. I didn't realize what time it was. Want some coffee? Soda? Water?"

"Yes, coffee. I think you should have some, too. Sit down, I'll make it."

"You know what? You make your coffee, but I think a Jameson on the rocks is what I need right now," I said.

When we were seated across from each other at the kitchen island, our beverages of choice in front of us, I noticed that Miguel's hair was quite damp. And there were flecks of mud on his pants, and a large blotch on the sleeve of his jacket.

"Oh-oh. Was there an incident at the Caldwells? Your outfit from this morning, and your cute, cute hair look a little worse for wear."

"It started raining while I was crossing the field from Ditmer Road to the Caldwells' fence. And then the sky, it just let go! But I completed my mission. The gate is there. So now we know he could leave with no camera to record him. And all this," he said sweeping his arm in a wide gesture that took in the damage to his hair and ensemble, "I did for you!"

"Thank you for coming through for me. Your bravery will not be forgotten."

"You know I will always come through for you."

As he spoke both our phones pinged with the notification of an update to the *Times* website. We both clicked through to it. A press release from the Himmel Police Department had just been posted. It asked the public for information on a missing person, Amelia Barr. It included a physical description, that she was from Pennsylvania, that she had been in town to settle her grandmother's estate, and that she had last been seen leaving the Caldwell & Hoffman law offices. It also included a bad photograph that looked like a driver's license mugshot. But it was definitely the woman I'd seen at Miller's office.

"Well, good to know Owen is taking this seriously," I said.

"Who is she? Do you know what's going on?"

"Yes. You're not the only one whose been busy today."

I took him through my day, starting with Patty and ending with Claudia and Tim.

"I've been going over all my notes, and making lists, and staring into space all afternoon and I feel like I'm not getting anywhere. But you're here now, Miguel. You're my murder muse. Help me think."

This time I was the one who got up and began walking and talking as I told a story, though I didn't have Miguel's full-body flair and flourishes.

"All right, stay with me here because I fully admit this isn't even a half-baked theory. It's more at the batter stage right now. First, let me recap some highlights in order. So, in the summer of 1982, Miller, Fourey, Georgia, Amelia Barr (Mia Rowley then), and Eddie are all in the same library reading group, along with a bunch of other kids. But Eddie doesn't fit in. He's younger than the others, kind of nerdy, maybe a little needy. He tries too hard to make the older kids like him. Instead, they tease him or ignore him. Fourey in particular, along with Amelia, gives him a hard time.

"On the Saturday before school starts, Eddie persuades his dad that he can stay on his own for a few hours as long as he doesn't leave the house. But when his dad gets home, Eddie isn't there and neither is his bike. When Eddie doesn't return, his father raises the alarm. The police get involved, and several kids come forward. They say Eddie rode past the park that afternoon, and they noticed a white van pull out from a parking space and drive off slowly in the same direction Eddie was headed. Weeks go by, the van and driver aren't found, and neither is Eddie. Eventually, people move on, the kids grow up, Eddie's disappearance becomes a cold case, and the story fades away."

I paused to sip my Jameson, and then turned on the fireplace. The gathering darkness and rain outside seemed to call for both comforts.

"So, we come to the present day. A few weeks ago, Amelia Barr comes back to Himmel because her grandmother died and left her a small inheritance. Miller is her grandmother's attorney, so she and Miller reconnect. Amelia stays at her grandmother's house. She's pleasant to the neighbors but keeps to herself."

"Was Amelia one of the other kids who told the police about the van?"

"No. She and her mother moved to Pennsylvania to live with her aunt the day after Eddie went missing. I doubt she was even questioned, but I'll check with Coop."

"Okay, but then I don't understand. Do you think Amelia is connected to Eddie missing in the past, or to Miller's murder in the now?"

"I think 'the now' is linked to what happened back then. I think Miller may have been murdered because of what Fourey and Amelia did to Eddie."

58

I hadn't realized that's what I was actually thinking until I said it out loud. That's the power of having an on-call muse.

"We know that Amelia and Fourey were friends. Fourey bullied Eddie. And after Eddie disappeared, Fourey is the kid who first said he saw a van following Eddie. Now we don't know if there ever was a stranger in a van. But we know there was a Fourey."

"You think Fourey killed Eddie?"

Miguel's voice had started out strong but ended in a squeak of astonishment that would have made me laugh if the conversation wasn't so serious.

"You're getting ahead of me. The day Eddie disappeared was the last Saturday before school started. It was also the day before Amelia was going to move away. I think Fourey and Amelia hang out together for the last time. They go cruising around on their bikes looking for something to do. They run into Eddie on his bike. Fourey, or maybe both of them together, decide it will be fun to play a trick on Eddie. They invite him to ride with them, and they go to a burned-out house in the woods. It's the kind of place kids love to explore and keep secret."

"You're talking about the place where Eddie's body was found?"

"Yes. Maybe the plan is just to leave Eddie there to find his own way home. Maybe they decide to play a game of dare instead, and that's how

Eddie wound up in the well. Maybe it's not intentional. In fact, it probably wasn't. They were just kids. But something goes wrong, and Eddie dies."

"So if it was an accident, why wouldn't they just tell the police?"

"Kids don't always think straight when they're in trouble. And Fourey's first instinct is always to lie. Amelia follows Fourey's lead. They decide to cover up whatever happened. They toss Eddie's bike into the well with him and go back to town. When Eddie is reported missing, Fourey comes up with the story about the van and convinces a few susceptible kids that they saw it, too."

"What about Amelia?"

"She leaves town the next day with her mother and her aunt. She's not around after that. She probably didn't even get questioned."

"Okay, but why do you think Amelia was with Fourey? He could have taken Eddie to the woods on his own."

"Two different sets of fingerprints were found on Eddie's bike and on his inhaler. Neither matches Eddie's prints. That means two people were there. If one of them is Fourey, it's logical that Amelia is the other one. And also, there's the baseball card."

"What baseball card?"

"When I was at Charlotte's yesterday, she was going through a box of things from Miller's office desk. It tipped over and a bunch of stuff fell out. One of the things was a baseball card, an old one. I assumed it was a childhood souvenir of Miller's. But I never heard Miller talk about baseball, or collecting cards, or going to Brewers' games, or anything like that. But Eddie collected baseball cards. His dad told Coop that he had one signed by his favorite player. He said it was his lucky card, and he carried it with him."

"You are making me work for this, *chica*. What does that matter?"

"The player on Eddie's card was Robin Yount. I didn't pay attention when I picked up the card at Charlotte's. But now I'm willing to bet it was Robin Yount. In fact, I'm going to call Patty right now and see if she remembers.

"Patty, hi. I'm sorry to bother you again, but I have a quick question. Do you have a minute?"

"Just about that, I'm looking for a file for Gabe."

"There was a baseball card in the box of Miller's things you sent over to Charlotte. Do you remember who the player on it was?"

"Robin Yount," she said without hesitation. "He was my father's favorite player. Why?"

I ignored her question in favor of my own. "Did Miller have the card in his desk for a long time?"

"No. He had the desk refinished about a month ago. When it came back, he asked me to put everything back in it. The card wasn't there then, I'm sure."

"Did it seem odd to you that Miller had an old baseball card in his desk? I mean he wasn't a big baseball fan, or a collector, at least as far as I know."

"No, he wasn't. But Miller did keep odds and ends in his main desk drawer. I noticed it when I packed it up for Charlotte, but I didn't think about it. I'm sorry, Leah, but I really have to find that file."

"Oh, sure. Thanks, Patty. I'll talk to you soon."

"But wait a sec. Why are you asking?"

"I'm just thinking, Patty. If my thoughts ever amount to anything, I'll let you know. Talk to you later."

"What? What did Patty say? What are you thinking?"

"Okay, this is more imagining than thinking, but go with me for now. I think the Robin Yount card from Miller's desk belonged to Eddie. And that Amelia gave it to Miller shortly before, maybe even just the day before, he was killed."

"How would Amelia have it to give to him?"

"Maybe Eddie lost it that last day and she found it. Or maybe he gave it to her, trying to impress her."

"Okay, but why would she still have it all this long time later. And why would she give it to Miller?"

"I think she kept it all this time as a penance, an ongoing reminder of the terrible thing she'd done. Fourey and Amelia are different. After they cover up Eddie's death, Fourey goes on without missing a beat. Amelia can't. I think she told Miller about that day, and she asked him to give the card to Eddie's father, because she couldn't face him."

"She told Miller about Eddie?"

"I think guilt about Eddie haunted Amelia all her life. She has no family, no friends. The only person who even realizes and vaguely cares that she's missing is a next-door neighbor who barely knows her. Amelia can't forget what she did. She knows the pain she caused Eddie's parents, the lie she took part in, and it eats away at her. The memory doesn't fade with time for her. It's always there. When she has to come back to Himmel to settle her grandmother's estate, it gets even worse."

"Yes, because everything she doesn't want to remember is everywhere," Miguel said.

"Exactly. She's face-to-face with Miller, a direct link to Fourey—and to that summer, and what happened to Eddie. It's overwhelming for her. She has to tell someone what she did, and she tells Miller. He says that he will go to the police with her if she wants to confess. She does, and she wants Eddie's dad to have his baseball card back. That's why it's in Miller's desk. He's going to deliver it for her."

"Would Amelia go to prison now if she told the police?"

"I doubt it. If Eddie's death was an accident, and I think it was, back then Amelia and Fourey might have been charged with reckless homicide, but they would have gone through the juvenile system. The statute of limitations on that is fifteen years, so that ran out long ago. I don't know of any other charge that could be brought at this late date."

"What about Fourey, do you think she told Miller he was involved, too?"

"I don't know. But even if she tried to shield his identity, it wouldn't have been hard for Miller to figure out who it was. Especially because Miller is fresh off finding out about his mother's necklace. Right then, he's seeing Fourey as he is, very clearly. He could connect the dots."

"So, then what happens after that?"

"I have some ideas. I know that Miller asked Charlotte to meet him for dinner, but she couldn't go. I think he may have wanted to tell her about the necklace, and also that Fourey was going to be implicated in Eddie's disappearance. He wouldn't want her blindsided by either thing. When Charlotte said she couldn't make it, I think Miller decided to call Fourey and have it out with him that night. What he knew had to be weighing on him tremendously."

"Do you think he would turn Fourey in?"

"Absolutely, if Fourey didn't agree to turn himself in. Now, think about this, Miguel. Miller calls Fourey to meet with him. Fourey is completely unprepared for what Miller hits him with that night. He thinks he got away clean with stealing the necklace. And he has no idea Amelia is even in town, let alone that she told Miller what the two of them did to Eddie. He's stunned when Miller confronts him with both things. So stunned he's unable to come up with a story to spin. To buy himself time, he gives Miller what he wants. He confesses and promises to go the police with Miller and Amelia the next day. But he has no intention of following through. Even if he won't go to prison for his part in Eddie's death, he will for the necklace theft. And an investigation of that could turn up even more dirt that puts him in still more legal jeopardy. Fourey has been a liar, a cheat, a hypocrite, and a thief all his life. It's not such a big step to murder. He doesn't have long to act though."

I could tell Miguel was following my line of thinking by the way he could barely wait for me to finish.

"Your turn," I said.

"Fourey knows Miller's running schedule and his route. He will wait for him in the tunnel and kill him there. It's risky because the park is a public place. But he has no choice. He takes Miller's watch to make it look like a robbery. But what does he do about Amelia? Is she dead, too?"

"I think she must be. Fourey had to act fast there, too. He leaves Miller that night, and he goes to Amelia's. She's not that surprised to see him, because she's asked Miller to invite Fourey to come forward with her. Fourey makes up some reason for her to go with him in his car, and then . . ." My imagination faltered at that point. Miguel's was still going strong.

"He takes her to the abandoned gravel pit outside of town. He kills her, and he weights her body down, and he throws her in! He thinks she will never be found. No one will look very hard for her. She has no family."

"It's got to be something like that. It's grim, but it fits, Miguel. Then Fourey, after he's killed two people, thinks everything is fine. He gets questioned about his brother's death, but he's not a serious suspect because there's Noah. And after Noah, the random robbery idea comes into play, and there's Dennis Warby, too. And I'm out there floundering around and Fourey thinks his usual luck will hold."

"What about when Eddie's remains are found? That would make Fourey worried."

"Maybe a little, but I don't think that concerned him as much as the story about Amelia's disappearance in the *Times* is going to. The attention the story brings to her might stir up memories that could lead to a link to him and then back to what they did to Eddie."

"Do you think Fourey will run?"

"That would look suspicious when his mother is so ill, and he's told everyone he's here to be with her to the end. But he might have to if Ross moves fast on the necklace theft. If they get him for that, there will be plenty of time to build out murder charges against him."

"Are you going to tell Charlie what your theory is?"

"I'll run it by Ross, the great buzz-killer, and see what holes he can poke in it. And Coop, too. If it makes sense to them, then things could move pretty fast. Thanks, Miguel. I always think better with you."

59

"So, that's what I've got. What do you think of our theory of everything?"

As soon as Miguel left, I had called Ross to give him the rundown on what we'd come up with.

"It's not the worst theory I ever heard, Nash."

"Please, you know that kind of over-the-top praise embarrasses me. What don't you like about it?"

"It's plausible, mostly, but you're makin' a lot of leaps. Especially with the Eddie, Fourey, and Amelia part."

"I know, but until you beat a confession out of Fourey with a rubber hose, it's pretty hard to know what really went on among the three of them forty years ago. One of them is dead, one is missing, probably dead, and the third one is a congenital liar."

"Are you gonna talk to Owen, let him know what you got on his missing persons case?"

"Owen doesn't appreciate my help the way you do. Wait a minute, maybe he does—which is not at all. I think you should be the one to fill him in. His investigation into Amelia's disappearance ties in with your investigation of Miller's murder. He'll listen better if it's coming from you. It'll be more official. Owen likes things to be official."

"You got that right."

"Did you talk to Fourey after you got my message about the necklace this morning?"

"I don't want to talk to him about the necklace until I verify things myself. I talked to Charlotte, and I got the letter, and I'm gonna talk to the appraiser tomorrow morning. I couldn't reach him today. When I see Fourey, I want my ducks in a row. I'm waitin' on some call backs from some Florida sources, too. I haven't been sittin' on my hands, you know."

"I'm sorry. I'm just a little worried that Fourey might start getting nervous now that Amelia's disappearance is out there. Do you think he might bolt? I wish you could get

a blood sample and fingerprints from him. The blood would prove he was at Miller's murder scene, and the fingerprints would put him right in the middle of Eddie's case."

"We don't have enough to get a warrant from a judge for either blood or prints yet."

"But fingerprints to tie Fourey to Eddie's case, couldn't you get those without a warrant? I mean lift them off something he touched, like a coffee cup or a bottle of water from a restaurant?"

"You been watchin' cop shows again, haven't you? Just hold your horses. This is a real complicated deal here. We gotta do things right so we don't blow it. Okay? I do know somethin' about how a police investigation works."

"I know you do. I just don't want Fourey to get away. But okay, I'll back off a little. What about DJ then? How did your interview with him go?"

"He's one scared kid. I couldn't get him to move off the story he told you. I'm more worried he's gonna take off than I am that Fourey will. Allie's gonna be really upset if he does. I feel sorry for DJ. The sooner we can get the goods on Fourey, the better."

"So you do think I'm right?"

"Let's say I don't think you aren't."

I had been hearing the background sounds of people talking, chairs scraping, and other noises that said Ross wasn't home since our conversation began. Suddenly, there was a loud crash.

"Where are you, Ross? Are you okay?

"Yeah, yeah. I'm at McDonald's with Jennifer's kids. Somebody just dropped a tray of food and soda all over the place. Oh-oh. I gotta go."

"Where? Why?"

"The somebody was Ethan. Now he's cryin'. I really gotta hang up. I'll call ya tomorrow. We can grab a beer and do more sharin' then."

And then he was gone. But he'd really listened to me this time. He'd even seemed a little impressed.

I started to call Coop, just as a call from him came in.

"Hey, you. How are things in the big city?"

"Good. They'd be better if you were here."

"What a nice boyfriend thing to say! From the chatter and clinking glasses in the background, I take it the conference has adjourned to the bar. How did your panel go?"

"That's tomorrow. Today was great though. I picked up some things I'm going to try in the office. What about you? Anything new?"

"You could say that. How much time do you have?"

"Enough. Tell me."

I launched into everything I'd already shared with Ross.

"That's really solid work, Leah. Especially the Amelia link. Have you—"

"Yes. I talked with Ross before I called you."

"Good. But what I was going to ask is if you'd talked to Owen."

"No, I'm leaving that to Ross. I don't want Owen to ask how I got in the house to see the photos that made me connect Amelia with Fourey and Eddie."

"You deserve to get the credit for what you found. It's a big help to our investigation."

"Not at Darmody's expense. Though to clarify when you say 'our' investigation, am I included in the 'our'?"

"Technically no, but practically speaking, yes. You're after the same thing we are, even if you aren't part of the sheriff's office."

"Just think if I was. If you hired me as a police consultant, I could get right in there and help you and Ross full-time. Or maybe even lead the investigation. Like that television show where the writer teams up with a police detective and they go around solving murders. Mostly the writer does because he's got the imagination to see the big picture and take risks."

"Uh-huh. But think about this. If you were an official consultant hired by the office, you couldn't say that I'm not the boss of you, because I would be. Wait a second. Let me think about it a little more."

"I withdraw my suggestion."

"I thought you might. So, what have you got on for tomorrow?"

"I'm not sure yet. I'm really beat right now. All that thinking I did today took a lot out of me. I'll figure it out in the morning after I get some sleep. I'd better rest up. Ross and I are going out for a beer tomorrow and do some more 'sharin'.' So, you and your bros won't be the only ones having a wild Friday night. Ross and I will be taking this town by storm."

"I'd like to be there to see that. In fact, I'd like to be there to see you. I miss you."

"I miss you, too. Knock 'em dead on your panel tomorrow. Call when it's done. I know you'll do great."

60

I skipped dinner and instead made myself a big bowl of popcorn after I hung up with Coop. Then I watched two of my favorite old movies. *A Stolen Life* is a Bette Davis over-the-top melodrama I can't resist. When *The Thin Man* came on right after, I stayed for the witty dialogue and the way Myrna Loy plays Nora Charles. But I found myself yawning hugely through the last fifteen minutes of it. As the credits rolled, I turned off the television.

"I'm going to bed, Sam. Are you coming?"

To my surprise, he followed closely behind me and claimed a spot on the bed while I brushed my teeth. When I climbed in, he nestled next to me. I reached out and petted him and quickly fell into a deep sleep from which I didn't move until the phone rang at five thirty in the morning. I reached for it sleepily. Miguel.

"Are you okay? What's going on?" I asked, shaking the sleep off.

"I'm fine. I'm at a one-car accident on Pinkley Road. The car smashed into a tree. It's really bad. They used the Jaws of Life to cut the driver out, but he was already dead. It's Fourey Caldwell!"

"Fourey!? But he's my prime suspect!"

It wasn't the most compassionate response to another human being's death, but it was the first thing that came out.

"Do you think Fourey did it on purpose? You said the news about Amelia could shake him up. Maybe he thought he didn't have a way out?"

"I think Fourey would be more likely to run than to kill himself, Miguel. But if he was running, Pinkley Road would be a weird getaway route. It just leads to a bunch of other dirt and gravel roads until you cross the state line into Minnesota. I don't see Fourey heading to a hunting shack in Bemidji to hide out. But I also can't imagine what he was doing on Pinkley Road at all. There's nothing out there."

"Grady's Tavern is across the county line," Miguel pointed out.

"That's true, but that's not a Fourey kind of place at all."

Grady's is a hole-in-the-wall bar that attracts serious drinkers not interested in food or ambiance.

"Though having said that, it's a good place to go if you don't want to run into anyone you know. Who's at the scene from the sheriff's office?"

"One of the new deputies, Cam Stetzler, was here when I got here. Charlie showed up about ten minutes ago, but I haven't talked to him yet."

"Well, don't let on how much you know about everything, it would just make him unhappy."

"I would never. I know how Nash & Santos Investigations works. All in confidence, and confidence in all. And all means me and you."

"Good man, Miguel."

"But with Fourey dead, how will we ever know if he killed Miller or Amelia or covered up Eddie's death?"

"Don't sound so discouraged. With Fourey dead, police can get both blood and fingerprint samples to link him to Miller and Eddie. That will tell a lot. Oh, I've got a call coming in from Ross. I'll talk to you later."

"Ross! What the what? Fourey's dead? I just talked to Miguel."

"They don't come any deader, Nash. It was a real bad accident. I saw Miguel talkin' on the phone, figured it was to you."

"He didn't have any details. Do you?"

"Not many. Some guy goin' to work at the bakery in Hailwell drove by, saw the car smashed into a tree, and called it in at four thirty a.m. He didn't see it happen. He didn't hear anything either. A crash like this woulda made a lotta noise. It could've happened ten minutes before he called, or two hours. We have to wait for what the medical examiner says. It's too dark still to see much, and the State Patrol will handle the reconstruction anyway. Fourey could've missed the curve, or tried to dodge a deer, or maybe he was drunk."

"But at least now you can get the blood sample and fingerprints from Fourey during the autopsy, right? We might know for sure later today or tomorrow if he really was involved in Eddie and Miller's deaths."

"Hold on there. Yes, we can get the prints and the blood. But I told you, the crime lab is backed up. It could be more like weeks than days before we get any results."

"But Fourey is the lead suspect in two deaths and one missing person!"

"He's *your* lead suspect. And I'm not sayin' you're wrong. But right now, this is a car crash and it's not gonna get priority unless I can draw a pretty heavy line to connect the dots we been talkin' about."

"But the lab results are the pen we need to draw that line!"

"Take it easy. Timmins can call in a favor or two if he likes the case we're buildin'. But I gotta get some things in order—like checkin' out for myself the gate at the back of the Caldwells' property, see if I can hustle along some answers from Florida on the necklace, get the appraiser for it in for a formal interview, verify Fourey's connection to Amelia, talk to—"

"Steve Northam can verify the back gate; the appraiser interview is a formality if you have the letter and the backstory on the necklace from Charlotte. If you pressure Georgia she may know about—"

"Hey, I got this, okay? I know what I need to do. Here's my idea on what you need to do. Spend a few days workin' on your real job, writin' books. You came up with some good stuff on Fourey and Amelia. Thank you. Now let me work with it. Officially."

I was so surprised by the 'thank you' that I didn't know what to say. Ross took advantage of my uncharacteristic loss of words.

"I'll see you later. We'll have that beer, but it might not be tonight. Depends on how the day goes."

I felt frustrated at not being part of things, but Ross was right. At the moment there wasn't a role for me to play. I did need to call Charlotte, though. But I should wait until at least seven.

I fed Sam—he did seem to be enjoying the new dry cat food I'd found for him—and took a shower. When I heard my phone ring, I jumped out to get it, in case it was Coop. It wasn't.

"Leah, have you heard about Fourey?"

"Hi, Charlotte. Yes. It's quite a shock, isn't it?"

"Detective Ross called me. I can hardly believe it! Dad is murdered, which is unbelievable in itself. Then it looks like Fourey might have done it, which is even more unthinkable. And now Fourey is dead? How will we ever know the truth now?"

"Hey, we're still going to find out who killed Miller. We've got some new leads and we might get some physical evidence that will go a long way toward linking Fourey to Miller's death."

"What leads, what evidence? I want this nightmare to be over. Last night, Gran slipped into a coma. She's not going to wake up. You know your life is pretty messed up when the best news in it is that your grandmother is about to die. But at least this way, she'll never have to know about Fourey."

Charlotte sounded even worse than she had Wednesday night. I felt like I had to give her some assurance that made her feel like the investigation was moving ahead.

"Charlotte, I'm going to tell you something, but you can't tell anyone else yet. Not Sebastian and definitely not your mother. Did you see the story about the missing woman, Amelia Barr?"

"Yes, but what—"

"There may be a link between her, Fourey, and your dad's murder. And if I'm right, a whole lot of questions are going to be answered, and in a pretty short time."

"You think she killed Dad?"

"No. I think Fourey may have killed *her* because of something she told your dad. Listen, I can't really give you more than that until I know for sure. But things are coming together, even though it might not look like it at the moment. Trust me, Charlotte."

"I do trust you, Leah. I'm just so tired, and worried, and worn down. I feel like I'm five years old and I want my dad," she said, her voice shaking.

"Mother called a few minutes ago. I'm sure it was about Fourey, but I didn't pick up. I don't have it in me to deal with her self-centered hysteria right now. In fact, I should call Sebastian before she gets hold of him without any warning. He doesn't need that. Please, call me as soon as you can tell me more. Or even if you can't tell me more, just call me, okay?"

"I will, Charlotte. But remember, don't talk to your mother, or Sebastian or anyone else about Fourey or Amelia Barr—except Detective Ross, if he asks you, of course. It could really cause problems if you do."

"I understand. Goodbye."

I'd known it ever since Miller died, but it really hit me after we hung up. Charlotte was carrying the whole weight of the Caldwell family on her slender shoulders. She had to cope with her father's murder, her uncle's possible involvement, a dying grandmother, an emotionally fragile younger brother, a mother who was impossibly demanding, and everything going on with Miller's businesses. I'd been trying to help, but I'd just added another thing for her to worry about—Amelia Barr and the possibility that Fourey had killed her, too.

"Nice going, Leah," I said out loud.

Sam meowed in what sounded like agreement.

"Thanks, Sam. Like I don't feel bad enough already?"

61

I called Coop before I settled into doing what Ross had suggested. Working on the long-neglected revision of my manuscript. But my call went directly to voice mail. He had probably turned it off to get ready for his panel discussion. I followed his lead and put my phone in airplane mode as I headed to my office to start working. When I'm really serious about writing, I usually do it sitting at my desk as opposed to on my window seat, which is more a thinking and reading place for me. I pulled up Clinton's marked-up version of my manuscript, determined to get it right this time. I thought a few of the notes were overly picky, and a couple I strongly disagreed with. But looking at it objectively, as I tried to do, I had to concede most were spot on.

I soon got lost in making Jo Burke seem more real to readers. And for the first time, the low-key thrum of grief that had been with me since Miller died receded. It was replaced, for a time, by following Jo around the Upper Peninsula as she chased a killer of Native American women—and, in one scene, was chased herself by an angry mama bear.

I got so involved that I didn't stop for lunch. I didn't stop at all until I heard a tap on my back door and my mother calling to me.

"Leah? I brought you something to eat. I texted earlier and then called to find out what you knew about Fourey Caldwell's accident. That was a shock! But when you didn't answer I knew you must be working hard. But you have to eat something. It's actually a little early for dinner. I guess it's more of a late-late lunch."

"Mom! That smells so good! It's Tater Tot Hotdish, isn't it? Thank you. Come on, let's go to the kitchen so we can eat this. I didn't realize that I was even hungry, but now I feel like I'm starving."

"I probably have less on Fourey's death than you do," I said, getting out plates and forks. "Miguel called early this morning to say Fourey had been killed in a car crash. I talked to Ross, too, but he didn't have much to add. What's the word on the street?"

"That Fourey was drinking at Grady's Tavern last night and drove off drunk and smashed into a tree. But I don't think that can be true. What would Fourey Caldwell be doing at Grady's Tavern?"

"It doesn't sound like him, does it? I know the sheriff's office is on it, but my inside source is out of town. I called Coop, but—oh!"

"What?"

"I just realized I probably didn't hear back from him because I had my phone in airplane mode. I forgot all about it. Just a sec."

I checked my phone. Coop had called me back after his panel, and then he'd texted me just a little while ago. There was a text from Ross, too, saying he'd have to take a rain check on our beer. And one from Miguel.

"I should call Coop back. Do you mind?"

"Don't be silly. I'll dish up the food and get our drinks."

Coop picked up on the first ring.

"Hi, I'm sorry I missed your call and text. I had my phone off and I got so busy working I forgot to turn it back on. How did the panel go?"

"Great! But I'm glad it's over. I know about Fourey. Charlie's got too much to cover. I'm not going to go to Madison tomorrow. I need to get back."

"I'm sorry. I know you were really looking forward to your Boys Weekend."

"We'll do it another time. But I have to stick around here tonight. I've got a dinner set up with one of the speakers. I want to talk to him about doing some training for us. But I'll head out early tomorrow morning. I should be back by seven or seven thirty. I'll come by then if you'll be home."

"Where else would I be at seven o'clock on a Saturday morning?"

"With you, I never know."

"Isn't that what keeps you around?"

"That and a few other things. Hey, I've got a call coming in. I'll see you in the morning."

"I'll make a fresh batch of Cheerios."

"Can't wait."

"Coop's not going to Madison?"

"No. He wants to get back because of Fourey."

"Ah. Yes, let's get back to Fourey," she said as we sat down to the hotdish. "As we were saying, Grady's Tavern seems like an odd place for Fourey to be. On the other hand, there's nothing else out that way."

"All good observations, Mom. Hopefully, Ross is busy finding out."

"Which means you know something, but you don't want to tell me. Well, what do you know about this Amelia Barr missing person case? The press release said she was last seen leaving Miller's office around five p.m. The day before he died. The next day Miller is murdered, and this Amelia disappears. That's pretty interesting, isn't it?"

I felt in that moment as Coop must sometimes feel with me.

"It is. But you know what's pretty great? This hotdish. So, so, good!"

I took a large bite and busied myself with chewing.

"Okay, fine. Go all top secret on me. But I guess that means some kind of positive progress is happening. Speaking of positive progress, I hear you and Coop are house hunting! That's exciting."

"What? No, we're not. Well, Coop is, but I'm not involved. Where did you hear that?"

"I saw Sally Denman at the gym today. She said she showed the old Ashford house to Coop. It's way too big for one person. It's even pretty big for two. She assumed, and I did, too, that you were both considering it."

"She assumed wrong," I said.

It came out a little sharper than I'd intended.

"Well, it's a nice house. Needs work, but it's got good bones. The third floor would make a great workspace for an office or whatever."

"So, do you and Paul have plans for the weekend?" I asked, making it clear that I was done talking about Coop, houses, and me.

My mother knows when to retreat and live to fight another day. She asked how my revision was coming, and we spent the rest of the dinner talking about that. After she left, I sat on the window seat with Sam and watched the sun go down and the street lights come on. I was happy with the work I'd done, and I'd enjoyed the retreat into Jo Burke's world, but I knew I couldn't do that again the next day.

"I'm not sure what I'm going to do, Sam. But it's not working on the manuscript again. Maybe I'll try for a coffee instead of a beer with Ross tomorrow. I'd really like to hear what he's finding out."

62

I'd gone to bed at eight thirty. That early morning wake-up from Miguel, followed by a full day of brain work had taken a lot out of me. At ten, I woke up abruptly to the sound of gagging. I sat up and flipped on the light.

"Sam? Sam, where are you?"

I jumped out of bed and ran in the direction of the sound, which was the living room. I found him in the corner of the window seat. He was huddled behind the curtain, a puddle of vomit next to him. His meow sounded like he was crying.

"Oh my god, Sam, what's the matter?"

He kept making coughing, choking noises and then he threw up again.

I grabbed my phone and found the emergency number for the vet clinic. I was surprised but glad when Tom picked up instead of a call service. Even though I had soured a little on him as a person after finding out about his relationship with Charlotte, he was still a good veterinarian.

"I'll meet you at the clinic, Leah. I don't think this should wait until morning, but there's no need to panic."

"I'll be right there."

No need to panic. Easy for him to say. He wasn't listening to Sam's yowls of pain.

I threw on a hoodie and a pair of jeans. My tennis shoes! Where the hell did I leave my shoes? I didn't have time to look. I grabbed the first pair my hands reached in the closet, slammed my feet in, and didn't bother to tie the laces. Sam felt so miserable, he didn't even fight the carrier.

"I'm sorry to drag you into the office so late," I said as Tom opened the clinic door for me.

"No, that's fine. I'm glad I was the vet on call tonight. Sam's a favorite of mine. Now tell me again what the symptoms are and when they started."

I explained as we walked down the hall.

"What kind of plants do you have in the house?"

"I don't have any! Well, there is a spider plant in my office—Oh, Tom. Tell me I didn't poison Sam."

"No, no. That's perfectly safe for cats. Sam hasn't been outdoors, or around other cats? Could he have eaten any uncooked eggs? Raisins?"

"No, I live in a third-floor apartment. Sam never goes out. And we don't know any other cats. I don't have eggs or raisins in the house. What's wrong with him, Tom? He was fine when we went to bed."

"Take it easy. You go wait in my office. I'll take him to an examining room, and we'll figure out what's going on."

"I want to go with him."

"It'll be easier to do the exam without you there, Leah. Really, just go in, have a seat and I'll be back as soon as I can."

I couldn't sit still after Tom left. I started pacing. That's when I realized for the first time that I was wearing a pair of clunky boots better suited to a hike at Devil's Lake than a worried circling of Tom's wooden office floor.

"Well? What's wrong with him?" I asked as the door opened and Tom came in.

"Don't look so worried, Leah."

I felt my anxiety lift a little.

"Sam has a blocked urethra. It's fairly common in male cats, especially those who've been neutered. The symptoms can be frightening, but with treatment he'll be fine. Has he been eating a lot of dry food?"

"I picked up some for him to try, he seems to like it. Was that bad?"

"Well, there is a link between dry food and blockage of the urethra."

I felt a stab of guilt. "I caused this?"

"Not necessarily. But it would be a good idea to move him more into a wet food diet. We've got a brand we recommend. I'll give you that information when we discharge him after treatment."

"What's the treatment?"

"Tonight, I'll sedate him, place the IV catheter, remove the blockage, reverse the sedation, then make sure he wakes up okay. After that, we'll want him to stay a day or two to make sure things are back on track."

"But he's going to be okay, right?"

"Yes, he'll be fine. The procedure is going to take a little while and he'll be really dozy after that. Why don't you go home, and get some sleep? You look done in."

"No. I want to stay. I'm not tired."

The involuntary yawn that escaped on the last word made the lie obvious.

"Leah, I had dinner with Charlotte this evening. I know how hard you've been working. But from what she said, it sounds like you're closing in on the answer. You'll prove Fourey killed Miller—now that shocked the hell out of me when Charlotte told me. But—"

"You had dinner with Charlotte? But I thought—"

"She said that she'd told you about us. You look like you don't approve."

"It's none of my business, Tom."

That doesn't usually stop me, but he was about to operate on Sam. I didn't want to say anything to upset him.

"I don't blame you. I behaved very badly. To my wife and to Charlotte. I'm in love with her. So, I did what I should have done at the start. I told my wife the truth. I've moved out of the house, and we're getting divorced."

"I see."

"I wasn't going to contact Charlotte until the divorce was final. But she called me this afternoon. She was beside herself. I had to go to her. We had a long talk, and we're back together. She thinks the world of you, Leah. I hope you won't think too badly of us."

Actually, I did think a little badly of him, though not of Charlotte. She had no one else. She was distraught, and she turned to the person she loved. But I did wish that Charlotte hadn't been quite so free with the information I'd asked her not to share. I also thought Tom had moved pretty quickly to take advantage of Charlotte's vulnerable state. But he had my cat, and I wanted him treated, now.

"If Charlotte's happy, then I'm happy for her. She's got a lot to contend with. But I really don't want to go home until I know that Sam is all right."

"Okay. I understand. It'll be a while, though. Feel free to stretch out on the couch. I'll wake you when the procedure is finished."

"Thank you."

63

I took Tom's suggestion and lay down. I immediately fell asleep, and into a very unsettling dream.

I'm sitting in Miller's office, and he's there, too, sitting behind his desk. Sam is perched on his shoulder. A surge of relief and elation courses through me.

"Miller! You're alive! I'm so happy you're alive!"

He smiles at me quizzically.

"Of course, I'm alive. Would you open the mail for me? I'm expecting a baseball card."

He hands me a letter opener. I insert it into an envelope that appears without explanation in my hand. Sam jumps on me, and the letter opener slips, cutting my hand. Blood begins gushing out.

"Oh, let me take a look at that."

Tom Fuller is standing in front of me with a Band-Aid. "Cat bites can be nasty," he says.

"Sam didn't bite me. It was an accident."

Suddenly, as is the way with dreams, the scene shifts. I'm in the Purrrfect Kitty Boutique. Davina Markham is there, wearing an enormous diamond pendant in the shape of a cat. I can't stop staring at it.

"It's beautiful isn't it? My Sabrina. And there were enough ashes left over to

keep in this little urn," she says, holding it out for me to examine. "You could get one for Sam."

"Sam isn't dead!" I say.

"Oh, but he will be someday. They all die. Here, look at this urn. It's really nice, isn't it?"

She reaches out to hand it to me, and I brush it away. The urn falls and breaks, and Sabrina's ashes scatter on the floor. Davina begins to cry, and I bend down to brush them up. They're grainy and stick to my fingers.

A horn honks and I'm suddenly outside as Charlotte drives up in a small white car. I open the door to get in, but Tom is in the passenger seat.

"What are you doing here?"

"I'm going running with Miller," he says. "Charlotte is dropping me off at the park."

My eyes widen when I see blood running down his arm.

"What happened to you?"

"Fourey stabbed me," he says.

Then he reaches over and pulls me into the car and starts shaking me.

"No! Stop! Stop it!" I cry.

"Leah, wake up. I just came back to tell you the procedure is finished. You must have had a nightmare. You were shouting when I came in. Are you okay?"

Tom was peering down at me, his brows drawn together in concern.

I sat up, dazed the way you are when you're pulled abruptly from a vivid dream.

"Yes. Yes, I'm fine. Yeah, I'm fine. Is Sam all right?"

"He came through it like a trooper. I unblocked the urethra and reversed the sedation. He's pretty sleepy still. I've got some things to take care of. I'll come and get you in about twenty minutes. You can see him, then go home and rest easy."

"Thanks, Tom," I said. I squeezed my eyes open and shut a few times to bring myself back to full alertness.

"Here," Tom said, handing me a paper cup of water he'd filled from the cooler in the corner.

"I'd offer you coffee, but I don't want you to be wired when you get home and can finally sleep. I'll be back."

"Right. Thank you again."

He left, closing the door behind him. I got up and wandered around the room, still unsettled by my weird dream. His bookshelf was filled mostly with medical references. Though an impressive tennis trophy on a marble base proclaimed him the winner of the Men's Singles tennis competition at the country club.

The wall behind his desk was filled with framed credentials. His college diploma, his veterinary diploma, half a dozen certificates of completion for required continuing education credits, even one for completion of crematory certification training—not something I'd care to go through. Beneath that was a laminated article from the *Himmel Times*, from five years ago, noting that Tom had received the "People's Choice Award" as Best Veterinarian in Grantland County. Well, at least that affirmed that Sam was in good hands. It was also clear that Tom liked awards of all kinds.

Another huge yawn escaped me. I pulled out my phone to look at the time and noticed that I had a voice mail. It must have come in when I was running around the apartment like a crazy person. I opened it and pushed play to listen. What I heard took my breath away.

"Nash, I'm at Grady's Tavern. I just got done talkin' to this waitress, Rosalie. She didn't know Fourey by name, but she picked him out of a batch of photos I showed her. Said he was in a real intense conversation with another guy. You'll never guess who Fourey's drinkin' buddy was. And for my money, if he was with Fourey, he's mixed up in Miller's murder somehow. It was that veterinarian, Tom Fuller."

64

Ross's message flooded my brain with so many thoughts at once that I had trouble sorting them out.

- The photo of the reading group. Tom Fuller was there.
- Tom was one of the boys who picked on Eddie Garcia.
- Tom ran with Miller sometimes, on the same route where Miller was killed.
- Amelia went missing after she left Miller's office the day before he died.
- Tom canceled on Charlotte the night before Miller died.
- Charlotte saw a small, white car with an out-of-state license plate in the parking lot at the vet clinic when she checked up on Tom, also the night before Miller died.
- Amelia had a small, white car with a Pennsylvania license.
- There was a little pile of ashes in the car. They were gritty to the touch.
- The cremains that had spilled from Davina's plastic bag when I met her in the parking lot—they'd felt gritty and sticky when I picked them up for her.
- Amelia had to be dead but where was her body?

- My eyes went to the Crematory Training Class award hanging on Tom's wall.

Holy shit! I had to get out of there.

I hurried to the door, but it opened before I reached it. Tom stood on the other side.

How long had he been there? Had he heard Ross's message?

"Sorry I startled you. I didn't want to interrupt. It sounded like you were talking on the phone."

"No, no. I was just listening to a voice mail from my mother."

Shit! Why did I say that? Why didn't I just say I was talking out loud to myself?

"Is everything all right? It's pretty late for a phone call." Something in his tone of voice and the way he had stepped in closer to me sent alarm bells ringing in my head.

"Uh, yes. Sure, she's fine. She's a night owl. She just wanted to know if I still have her cake pan at my house. I should call her back, or she'll fret about it and wind up calling me again at three a.m."

I reached for my phone, intending to hit 911, but Tom was too quick. He grabbed it from my hand.

"Let's listen to your mother's message again. Replay it for me."

I had no choice. I unlocked the phone as he held it and we listened to Ross's voice mail.

"I think we should sit down on the sofa and have a little talk, Leah."

He slipped my phone into the cargo pocket of his scrubs and shoved me over to the sofa.

"Why did you lie to me, Leah? And why does your friend Detective Ross think I'm connected to Miller's murder?"

My mind raced for a way to turn things around. I settled on throwing Ross under the bus.

"I'm sorry, Tom. You just saved Sam's life. I didn't want to explain that Ross has this dumbass idea, and have you think I give it any credence. He's an idiot who couldn't detect his way out of a roundabout. It's obvious Fourey killed his own brother and probably Amelia Barr, too. But Ross can't stand it that I figured it out while he's in over his head. It was stupid of me to lie."

"Charlotte told me you had Fourey as Miller's killer, but she didn't give me any details. I'll forgive you for telling a little white lie if you give me an insider's look at your theory. I'm a big true crime fan."

"Um, well, since you just saved Sam's life, I guess I owe you one. How about tomorrow, though? I want to see Sam and then I really need to get home and go to bed. I'm whipped," I said, finishing with a huge fake yawn.

"Sam's still pretty sleepy. You'll feel better if he's a little more awake when you see him. We've got time for you to tell me how you figured things out. I promise not to share it with anyone else, okay?"

If I kept resisting, he'd get more suspicious and that wouldn't be a good thing.

"Okay, sure."

It was easy enough to tell him the truth, I just had to be careful not to slip and say anything that revealed I knew I was mostly right about the way things went down, but way wrong about who had committed the crimes. He seemed satisfied when I finished.

"That's quite a story. I've known Fourey for forty years. He's always been a self-serving guy. But I can't believe that he and Mia killed Eddie on purpose, even though Eddie was a pain. It must have been an accident," he said.

"I agree. But Miller's death wasn't. Now Fourey gets away without facing the consequences again."

"I'd say dying is a pretty big consequence," Tom said.

I was breathing an internal sigh of relief. He'd visibly relaxed as I had talked him through my theory, though I was careful not to give away all the details that had led me to it. I made a final push to ensure that he believed I had no inkling about him. That I was all Fourey, all the way.

"I think he got the easy way out. Like he always did. His real punishment would have been spending the rest of his life in prison, knowing he was never going to escape that misery. And now he won't even be held accountable for Amelia."

"But there's no proof that she's even dead, right?"

"Oh, she's dead all right. I just hope someday her body will turn up like

Eddie's did. And maybe it will. A body's a hard thing to get rid of. There's only so many ways you can do that—bury it in the back yard, dump it in the woods, throw it in a gravel pit, burn it up in—"

I stopped suddenly, realizing I'd said the one thing I wanted to avoid. I couldn't help it; my eyes went to the cremation certificate on the wall as if a magnet drew them.

Tom followed my gaze. His own eye hardened.

"In a cremation unit in a veterinarian's office? Leah, if you don't already know the truth, you're damn close. Too close for me to let you go."

65

"What? Tom, I don't understand."

But I did. I hadn't fooled him at all. He'd just been playing with me, letting me rattle on to find out exactly how much I knew. Before he killed me, too.

"Yes. You do. Maybe not all of it but enough to make you dangerous."

I've noticed on occasion that being on the verge of death can really crystalize your thinking. Now that all pretense was gone, I wanted to get as much from Tom as I could. Before I escaped. If I escaped. It was obvious that Tom was very pleased with himself. I tried to get him to talk more by stroking his ego.

"You fed Fourey the van story, didn't you? You wanted to throw off the investigation into Eddie's death, but you didn't want to risk putting yourself out there. Clever. Why did you pick Fourey to tell the story?"

"He loved attention. Giving a tip to the police would give him that. And he lied all the time anyway, so I knew that wouldn't bother him."

"Didn't he want to know why you didn't go to the cops yourself?"

"Sure. I told him I saw Eddie and the van following him when I snuck out my window that afternoon. I couldn't tell the police though because I was grounded. I said my dad would beat me senseless if he found out I'd left the house. Fourey knew my dad. He believed me. Besides, he and I covered for each other sometimes. His dad was almost as bad as mine. He owed me one. Fourey was a great storyteller. He spun the van story so well, some of the other kids picked up on it and that sold it to the cops. So, it was all good."

"You ruined the Garcias' lives. Eddie's mother died never knowing what happened to her son."

"That was sad, yes. But it was the Garcias' tragedy. It didn't have to be mine. Chrissie—that is, Mia—and I were just two kids playing a joke, having some fun. But the cops wouldn't see it that way. We'd been in some trouble that summer. Nobody would've listened to us that it was an accident. Why should we wreck our lives over something that could have happened to anyone?"

"To anyone who forced a scared little boy with asthma to climb down into a well, and then left him there. Was I right about Amelia? Did she tell you she was going to the police to confess?"

"You're basically right about everything if you replace Fourey with me. But nothing beyond Eddie would've happened if Mia hadn't come back to town. When she called me that Tuesday after she met with Miller, she said she had something important to talk to me about. I knew it had to be about Eddie. We had nothing else in common. I had her come to the clinic after it closed that night."

"She tried to convince you to come forward with her?"

"Mia had nothing to lose—no family, no money, a nothing job, a nothing life. But I had everything to lose—my reputation, my practice, Charlotte. And for what? An accident that was over and done with forty years ago? What was I supposed to do? Let her ruin my life because she didn't have one?"

"I know what you did to Miller. Did you steal his watch to make it look like a robbery?"

"I did. I thought the police would focus on a homeless person or a kid on drugs as the suspect. But now that I know about Fourey's legal and financial troubles, he's an even better fit. And if, someday, a hiker finds the watch lying in the woods where I tossed it, no one will even connect it with Miller. For planning things out on the fly, I think I did quite well."

"What about Amelia? You killed her right here, didn't you? Then you cremated her body and drove her car to her grandmother's house with the ashes sitting on the floor of the passenger seat."

"Very good. How did you figure that out?"

"The bag holding them leaked. There was a small pile of ashes on the floor of her car. I didn't figure out what they were until tonight."

"I'll have to be more careful with yours."

I almost passed out from the wave of terror that swept over me at his words.

I didn't want him to know how scared I was. I tried to sound matter-of-fact.

"How do you think you'll get away with that? I'm not a stranger in town that no one knows or cares about. People will be looking for me."

"No one knows you're here. And when I'm done there won't be any evidence that you were."

"My phone can be tracked here."

"If it is, I'll say you brought Sam in, but I couldn't find anything wrong with him. You left with him. I have no idea where you went after that. But you did seem worried about something. In fact, I asked you if anything was wrong. And you said it was silly, but you felt like a car had been following you here. I went out to the parking lot with you, but it was all clear. You felt better and drove off. But maybe there really was someone following you. Oh, and I think the security camera tape from tonight will be corrupted, for some inexplicable reason."

"What are you going to do with Sam?"

"He'll go with you, of course. You're bonded now, it would be cruel to separate you now."

"You think you've got everything covered. But you don't. The police have a blood sample from the murder scene. Miller fought back. That's where you got the "cat scratch" you showed me at Miller's memorial. That blood is going to hang you, Tom. That and the fingerprints they recovered from Eddie's bike."

His eyes registered fear for a second, and I felt a thrill of satisfaction. But he recovered quickly.

"It won't do them any good. I've never been arrested. They won't have my blood or my fingerprints to compare with the sample and the prints they have. So, no match, no problem for me. There's no reason for them to suspect me anyway."

I almost blurted out that Charlotte had seen Amelia's car in the parking lot but stopped myself when I realized that would put her in danger, too. God I hoped I wouldn't die. With what I knew and what Ross and Coop could prove, Tom would go to prison for life.

"I figured it out. Coop and Ross will, too."

"I don't think so. They already have Fourey, thanks to you, and he ticks all the boxes. And he's dead, so no further investigation.

"Fourey figured it out, too, didn't he? After the story on Amelia ran, he put things together. He tried to blackmail you, and you killed him."

"He was more subtle than that. He asked me for a loan. But I knew where he was coming from. And I knew he'd keep coming back. He didn't get the chance to, though, because he drank too much, drove too fast, and killed himself."

"That accident was awfully convenient, Tom."

"I've always been lucky," he said. "It will be hard to prove it wasn't an accident, and even harder to prove I was involved. We're done now, Leah. It's almost twelve thirty and it takes four hours for the cremation unit to complete its work. I need to get you down there."

I could see we'd come to the end of the line. I had to make a move. I elbowed Tom in the ribs and launched myself off the couch. I lunged toward the door, but he grabbed me midway there. I tried to twist away. He lifted me up and slammed me to the floor. It knocked the wind out of me and as I lay there gasping he punched me hard in the side of my head. I was out.

———

When I came to, my head was throbbing and I had no idea how long I'd been unconscious. Tom was gone. I got to my feet slowly and got my bearings. Then I ran to the door. I grabbed the handle. It barely moved when I turned it. It was locked. I could hear footsteps coming down the hall. Tom.

Without conscious thought, my reptilian brain in full control, I grabbed the tennis trophy off the shelf. I stepped back so I'd be hidden when the door opened. Adrenaline coursed through me and set my heart thumping as I lifted the trophy above my head, prepared to strike.

Keys jangled outside the door. The knob turned and then the door opened wide. Tom stepped in. He paused for a second when he saw I wasn't lying on the floor. I used the moment to bring the trophy down on his skull. But his reflexes were good. He turned and it grazed his head instead of smashing down on it. He lost his balance and staggered. He grabbed the corner of the desk with his left hand. As he fell, I saw the syringe in his right. I took off running and cursed myself for wearing such heavy boots instead of tennis shoes.

When I reached the intersection of two hallways, I hesitated. Was the way out to the right, or the left? Tom's feet thudded behind me. I chose left. Yes! I could see the reception area and the front door just yards in front of me. Suddenly, my head jerked backward.

Tom had grabbed the hood of my sweatshirt and yanked me back toward him. As he pulled me closer, he wrapped his arm around me at the neck. The syringe was still in his hand. His breath was in my ear.

"There's no way out, Leah. Stop fighting. You won't feel a thing."

I lifted my foot in its beautiful, heavy, thick-soled hiking boot. I smashed it down on top of Tom's trainer-clad foot as hard as I could. He cried out in pain and his grip loosened. I twisted around and thrust the heel of my hand up to smash the underside of his nose. Blood gushed out and over my hand and arm. Tom lifted both hands to his face, howling in pain.

I grabbed my phone out of the cargo pocket on his pants and hit the emergency 911 button.

"Now who's got no way out, Tom?"

I was waiting outside when the first cop car arrived a few minutes later.

"He's inside."

Through the glass doors I could see that Tom had managed to get to his feet. He was lumbering away down the hall when the cops reached him.

More sirens screamed and cop cars continued to arrive, as did three vehicles I knew very well.

"*Chica*, what is happening?" That was Miguel.

"Nash, what the hell?" That was Ross.

"Leah, are you all right?" That was Coop. And his were the arms I fell into.

66

Hours later, after a brief visit to the ER, a long interview with Owen Fike, and a short, hot shower, I was seated on my sofa between Coop and my mother. Miguel was cross-legged on the rug in front of us, and Ross sat in the rocking chair. I had just finished giving them the overview of what had happened.

"What I would like to know is why am I always the last to find out? How is it that everybody else was able to rush to your aid, but I didn't even know you needed help?"

"Because you're not on my emergency contact list, Mom."

"Well, I should be. I'm your mother."

"Miguel set up my emergency contact list for me the last time I switched phones."

"Oh, no, no. I will not take the heat from Carol for you. You told me not to add her to the list."

"Nice, Miguel. Don't think I won't remember this. Mom, I told him not to put you on the list because—"

"Because when Nash gets in trouble she doesn't need her mother, Carol," Ross said. "She needs the cops, maybe the fire department, maybe a Navy Seal team, and someone to write up what the hell happened."

"You're not helping," I said. "Mom, if I'm in need of some emergency advice, or baked goods, or literary quotations, you're my first call. But if I'm in danger, I don't want to put you there, too. Coop called you, right? You were there holding my hand and yelling at me in the ER, weren't you? Why aren't you rejoicing that Tom didn't turn me into a pile of cremains like he did Amelia?" As soon as that last bit came out, I wished it hadn't.

"Oh, my God, that's what happened to her? Leah, why can't you ever think? You don't have to almost get killed to be an investigative journalist. Jane Mayer does it, Bob Woodward does it, and they don't wind up wrestling with murderers."

"To be fair, Mom, they don't usually investigate murders."

"Stop it! That's not the point. You could be dead right now! And we might never have found you!"

Her anger came through clearly, but I also heard a slight tremor at the end that told me she was on the edge of tears. My mother is not a crier.

"Mom, I'm sorry. I really am. But we've had this conversation before. I didn't go to the clinic to confront Tom. I went because Sam was sick. I never —almost never—put myself in danger on purpose. You're the one who raised me to follow my instincts, to be independent, to do hard things even when I'm scared. Don't be mad at me for being like you. Be glad I can fight for myself—and that I have friends who are there when I need them."

I turned and looked around at all of them.

"I want to get serious for a minute. It was pretty great to see you all come rushing up to the clinic door tonight. You mean the world to me."

Miguel, always in favor of sentimental moments, jumped up from the floor, stretched his arms around Coop, me, and my mother in a group hug. He then bounced over and hugged Ross, who looked uncomfortable yet gratified.

"All right, let's not have any waterworks here," Ross said.

"You know Ross, it's really your fault I was in danger at all."

"Hey, why am I getting dragged into it?"

"Because it was your voice mail about Tom and Fourey that reshuffled my thinking, and the answer came out Tom. If you hadn't left a message and just waited to tell me about Fourey and Tom in the morning, everything would have still clicked in, but when I was a safe distance away from Tom and his cremation unit."

"Stop talking about cremation," my mother said. "Coop, will you be able to find Amelia's ashes at her grandmother's, to prove that's what happened to her?"

"It's possible to determine that ashes come from a human source, but I don't know of any reliable test that can link them to a specific person, Carol. But HPD has the evidence from Amelia's car—the pile of ashes that Darmody and Leah found. That supports the story, even if Tom tries to recant."

"And there's Charlotte. She saw Amelia's car in the parking lot at Tom's clinic the night Amelia was killed," I said, though I couldn't hold back the huge yawn that escaped as I finished the sentence.

"All right, I think this wrap party is over," my mother said. "Let's go and let Leah get some sleep."

Coop spent the night—or the little that remained of it—with me, periodically checking to make sure I was really sleeping and not unconscious from a concussion. I didn't wake up fully until ten a.m. When I did, I sat straight up in bed and reached for my phone, which wasn't there.

"Coop!" I yelled as I got out of bed in a kind of slow-motion scramble to accommodate the battering my body had taken the night before. "Coop—"

"What is it? What's wrong?" he asked, dashing into the room.

"Where's my phone? I have to check on Sam. He's alone at the clinic. Who's taking care of him? Tom's in jail and—"

"I put your phone in the kitchen so no calls would wake you. Sam is fine. I already called the clinic. I talked to Dr. Molby, the other vet. He's handling what he can, and there's a retired veterinarian in the area willing to fill in while they figure things out."

"Can Sam come home today?"

"He's doing well, but his catheter needs to stay in for at least another day, and they'd like to keep him there to monitor him. You can stop by and visit him today."

"Oh, good. Thanks for checking on him for me. I need to talk to Charlotte. I'll go by the clinic before I do that. She knows about Tom by now, right?"

"Charlie stopped by to see her first thing. I imagine Owen talked to her, too."

"Did Ross say how she's doing?"

"Not great."

"That was a dumb question for me to ask, wasn't it? Her dad's dead, her uncle's dead, and her boyfriend is the killer."

"Add her grandmother to the list. Mrs. Caldwell passed away early this morning. Charlotte's been hit with a lot in just a couple of weeks."

"At least Fourey isn't much of a loss, and she was prepared for her grandmother's death, but holy cow, the news about Tom is devastating. That leaves Sebastian as the only close family she has to count on. Charlotte has always taken care of him. I hope he's got it in him to do the same for her."

"A crisis brings out the best and the worst in people, Leah. Sebastian may step up just fine, once he knows he's needed. He loves his sister, and they're just about all that's left of the family—if you don't count Georgia. And I'm pretty sure you don't."

"I hope so. But speaking of stepping up, I forgot to ask. How did you get from Milwaukee to Himmel so fast when you got the emergency notification from my phone?"

"I wasn't in Milwaukee. I got back to my room after dinner with Greg—that's the guy I want to do some training for the office—around ten thirty. I wasn't that tired, and I missed you. So, I decided to drive home early. I was pulling into town when I got the message."

"You know what? You're getting really good at this boyfriend game."

"It's not a game to me, Leah. Sometimes it's a pleasure. Sometimes it's a pain. But it's never a game. This is the real thing for me."

"That was a nice thing to say."

I leaned over and kissed him.

"But," I said, "What do you mean sometimes it's a pain?"

67

When Charlotte opened the door, she was dry-eyed, but the signs of tears were still there. I hugged her as soon as I stepped inside.

"Charlotte, I'm so sorry. About Tom, about your grandmother, about everything."

"Thank you. To be honest, grandmother's passing is a blessing. She didn't have to find out about Fourey. She didn't want a funeral, so just Sebastian, me, and Mrs. Obuchowski are going to her cremation ceremony tomorrow. Her ashes will be buried in her plot next to Grandfather."

"I'm glad you and Sebastian have each other."

"Me, too. He's been wonderful. Leah, I feel like such a fool about Tom. A guilty fool. I called him, you know, and he came over last evening. I was feeling so lonely, so overwhelmed. And Tom was so loving and kind. We had the best talk. Ha!"

She shook her head. "He said everything I'd been wanting to hear. That he loved me, that he'd talked to his wife, she understood, she'd been unhappy, too. He had already filed for divorce. They were going to tell their kids next weekend. We didn't have to hide anymore. Leah, I was so happy! But that was all a lie, wasn't it?"

She didn't wait for me to answer.

"When I think of him holding me, comforting me, talking about a future! It makes me feel physically ill. He killed my father, and Detective Ross said that he almost killed you! How could I have ever been in love with a monster like that? I can't stop thinking about his family, either. His wife and kids must be in shock. I thought about reaching out to her to tell her how sorry I am for getting involved with Tom when I knew that he was married. Then I realized that would probably make things even harder for her. I can't try to ease my conscience by hurting his family even more. And maybe Tom never talked to her, and she doesn't know that he was ever with me. I hope so. But I can't stop thinking that I loved a man who killed my father—not to mention Amelia and Eddie Garcia, too."

Apparently she wasn't aware of Tom's involvement with Fourey's 'accident' yet. And without knowing how the investigation into it was going to come out, there was no way I was going to lay that on her at this point.

"Tom is a twisted man. He fooled a lot of people for a lot of years. You're not alone."

"That's not much comfort right now. Nothing is, really. I'm going back to Chicago with Baz. I have to get away from here."

"Oh, sure, of course."

I worked hard to tamp down the selfish thought that had popped into my head—namely that Charlotte might pack it all in. Sell her dad's businesses, including his share of the *Times*, and go somewhere without all the bad memories Himmel now held for her.

But Charlotte read the self-centered concern on my face.

"Don't look so worried. I'm not leaving for good. I just need to get my bearings. I won't let Dad's legacy—or the *Himmel Times*—die. It's just that right now, I don't feel like seeing or talking to anyone."

"Right, of course," I said, standing.

"No, oh, no! I didn't mean you, Leah. In fact, I need your advice. I would have called you if you hadn't come over."

"What about?"

She handed me a letter.

"Read this, please."

I finished and looked up at her.

"This is the 'truth' Georgia threatened your father with, isn't it? Fourey is Sebastian's biological father."

She nodded. "I think so. The letter came to Dad's house yesterday, but I didn't read it until this morning. Mother must have told him he wasn't Baz's 'real' father. Dad wouldn't have taken it on faith. He had DNA tests done to see if she was telling the truth. It looks like for once, she was. But it wouldn't have changed the way he felt about Baz, I'm certain of that."

"I'm sure you're right but then why did Georgia think Miller would pay to keep the truth from coming out?"

"Mother knew that finding out Fourey was his father could be a crushing blow to Sebastian. And clearly, she didn't care. But she knew Dad would. I assume she thought he'd give her the money, rather than let her spring the news on Baz. I told you before what a struggle it was for him to reconcile with the choice Dad made to keep his sexuality a secret. He felt so deceived, so confused. Mother was counting on Dad protecting Baz from more emotional baggage for him to carry. She was perfectly happy to use Baz as a pawn."

"I'm a little shocked by how coldly manipulative that is, but—no offense —knowing your mother, I'm not that surprised."

"No offense taken. I came to terms with who Mother is a long time ago. Sebastian still hasn't. He always thinks people are better than they are. It's one of the reasons I love him so much. But it's also one of the reasons he feels betrayal so strongly."

"So, the leverage that your mother thought she had was your Dad's loving heart. But Fourey warned her to drop the whole thing after Miller died, because if she came out with the truth, it could backfire. Sebastian could turn against your mother, and against Fourey as well, and that would cut them off from any hope of getting money out of you two."

"Pretty horrible, isn't it? Is it wrong to despise your own mother?"

"It's not worth doing that kind of damage to your own peace of mind, Charlotte. Georgia is what she is. She's the product of the way her mother raised her—or didn't. Luckily, you're the product of the way Miller raised you. You don't have to love her. You don't have to despise her. You just need to see her clearly enough to protect yourself. I think you're already there."

I felt quite proud of myself for rising to the occasion with the kind of advice I felt Father Lindstrom would have given—though I wasn't sure that if it were me, I would take it.

"If you mean I don't have any illusions about Mother, you're right. But Baz still does. That's why I'm not sure what to do about this information. I'm afraid if I tell him now, he's going to feel like he's lost both his parents. Dad's gone, Fourey's gone, Grandmother is gone. Does it matter now?"

"I think you know the answer, Charlotte. Your mother is still here. If and when she decides this information is to her advantage, she'll tell Sebastian. And I doubt it will be with the same level of love and support you will. And I think it's what Miller would want, too, given how he felt about secrets."

"It's not what I hoped you'd say, Leah. But I know you're right. I'm sure Dad would have told Baz and me, as soon as he had confirmation that Mother wasn't lying. To be honest, I don't know how to tell Baz. I'm not sure I can help him through finding out. But he deserves the truth. I'll tell him once we're back in Chicago."

"Do you think it's safe to wait that long? You never know what Georgia is going to do."

"Oh, she's not here. Thank God. I booked her a week in a luxurious spa in Arizona. I didn't want to take the chance that she'd get to Baz before I decided what to do. I told her she needed it to recover from all this trauma. She was very happy. She's probably on her way to the airport right now. I just hope I can find the right words when I talk to Baz."

"Don't worry about the words. Just tell him the truth—that Miller loved him, and you do, too. You can't fix it for him. But you can be there for him while he goes through whatever he needs to in order to come to terms with it."

"Thank you, Leah. For everything. Oh, I almost forgot. I'm so, so, sorry, but I haven't found anyone to take Sam yet. I don't want to take advantage of you any longer. I called the boarding service Dad used when he traveled. They'll take care of him until I come back. They're going to try to find a permanent home for him, too."

"Actually, if it's all right with you, I'd like to keep Sam with me permanently. We're kind of used to each other. And he's a good listener."

"All right? It's perfect. I think Dad would be very happy with that."

When I stopped to see Sam, the mood at the clinic was about as confused, uncertain, and depressed as you'd expect it to be, if you'd just found out that your boss was a murderer. The waiting room was full, though. The news didn't seem to be scaring away clients. In fact, some of them were probably there because of the news.

Despite the catheter and an IV line attached to him, Sam looked a lot healthier than he had the night before. The vet tech told me that he'd be pretty mellow from the pain medication, and he did seem very relaxed, greeting me with a small meow and a slight lift of his tail.

"Hey, there, Sam. We had quite a night didn't we? They tell me I can probably take you home tomorrow. But you're going to have to go on a special diet, so this doesn't happen again. Also, when I say home, I mean home as in my place. If that's okay with you?"

He nudged my hand so that I'd rub his head, and I took that for a yes.

68

A text pinged on my phone as I walked into the *Times* office after leaving Sam. Clinton.

"In the hospital passing a kidney stone. Remind me never to have a baby. Thrilled you're back at work. Have absolute faith in you. Talk when I get out."

That explained why he hadn't responded to my voice mail. He'd been in too much pain to care. And how surprisingly synchronous of the universe to give both Sam and Clinton similar medical problems at the same time. By the time Clinton felt better and wanted a progress report, I should actually have a good one to give him.

I'd intended to stop and visit a bit in the newsroom. But when I looked in,

Troy was working the phone. Maggie was, too. Miguel was typing away madly on his computer and only gave me a wave when I caught his eye. They were all trying to beat the television and online news crews from around the state who were now, too, chasing the sprawling story that had begun forty years earlier.

I left them to it without going in. I felt a little sad that it wasn't my job anymore, and they obviously didn't need me. But I also felt a lot tired and equally glad that they didn't.

Back in my apartment, I sat down on the couch for a minute and closed my eyes. When I woke up it was four o'clock.

I picked up my phone to see what we had on the website. There was a straight news story, which I only skimmed because I already knew the details. But there was also a feature on Amelia Barr. And someone had gotten hold of a photo that was much nicer than the driver's license shot that had run with the missing person's press release from HPD.

Amelia was smiling in this picture. It was taken outdoors. She wore a blue denim jacket with red buttons, over a white shirt. She held a little flag in one hand, and a sparkler in the other. It must have been taken at a Fourth of July celebration. At least she'd had some happy moments in her sad, lonely life.

My phone rang before I finished reading the story. I didn't recognize the number.

"Leah? Hi. It's Jan. My button is her button!"

"Hi, Jan. I don't really know what that means."

"Amelia Barr in the story. The missing woman. The jacket she's wearing. It has the same buttons as the one I found in Tom's office. I opened it up big, so I could see and it's exactly the same. Red, with a white starburst on it. It's hers. It has to be. Do you want to do a story on me?"

"Not just yet, but I think you should take the button with you and go the Himmel Police Department. Talk to Owen Fike. Tell him everything you know about it. You might have an important piece of evidence in your hand."

"Oh! This is so exciting! I can help that asshat Tom Fuller get what he deserves. I'm sorry, Leah. I can't talk to you anymore. I have to go."

I smiled as I hung up, imagining Owen Fike interviewing Jan Hudson. And then I yawned. And then I fell asleep again.

I had just awakened from my second nap of the day when I heard the door open, and Coop come in. "Hey, are you okay? Why's it so dark in here?" he asked as he flicked on the lamp.

"Because I've been sleeping more than I've been awake today. What time is it?"

"Seven o'clock. Did you get my text?

"I probably slept through it. What did you say?"

"That I'd be here about seven, that I'd bring over dinner tonight, and that I love you."

"That was a nice text. So, what have you been doing while I've been napping?"

"Meeting with Owen, Charlie, and Cliff Timmins. Figuring out where our cases overlap, looking at the evidence we've got so far, and what we need to get. Tom's hired a big deal criminal lawyer from Milwaukee. We need to make sure we do everything right on this one."

"You will."

"We've got a good start. Charlotte told Owen about the car with the Pennsylvania plates in Tom's parking lot, and as you already know that's a match for Amelia's car. Thanks to Tom bleeding all over your sweatshirt after you popped him in the nose, we've got plenty of blood to compare with the blood sample from Miller's murder site. And now we have both Tom's and Amelia's fingerprints to compare to the ones from Eddie's inhaler and bike."

"How did you get Amelia's?"

"She got fingerprinted the same time Eddie did. The prints were in a box at her grandmother's house marked "Mia's Things.""

"Coop, what about Eddie's baseball card? Can it go back to Eddie's father?"

"I talked to Kristin about it. She'll be doing the real work on the cases. Cliff will just show up to strut his stuff in court. She said because we can't prove that Amelia had the baseball card or that she gave it to Miller, even though we're sure she did, it won't be admissible at trial. So yes, I think we can return it to Eddie's dad."

"Oh, that's good! I have some news, too."

I told him about Jan and the button.

"That's direct proof that Amelia wasn't just in the parking lot at the clinic, she was inside Tom's office."

"That's what I thought, too. I think Jan is really going to enjoy her time in the spotlight. She might even get her wish and wind up on Miguel's podcast."

Early the next morning I rode my bike to the cemetery to see Miller. Even though he'd been cremated, his ashes had been buried in a grave site. Charlotte had said that she and Baz wanted an anchor for their memories. I understood. I don't need to visit the cemetery to think about my two sisters, Annie and Lacey. Still, I like to go there sometimes to talk to them. But that day it was Miller I had come to visit. I had quite a lot to say to him.

I told him about the investigation, how amazingly well Charlotte was handling everything, how sure I was that Sebastian and she would be there for each other, how we were going to go ahead with the plans we'd made for the *Times*, how much I wished he could be there with us.

"I don't know what happens after we die—how the eternity thing works, or even if there is eternity. But at the same time, I can't believe that the soul of a person can just vanish into nothingness. I know you still exist in some form, like Annie and Lacey and my dad. That being the case, I hope your mother has joined you. Personally, I wouldn't want Fourey in the same 'other world' with me, but that's not my call.

"I miss you like hell, Miller, and Sam does, too. We're both having trouble adjusting to life without you in it. But we've decided to stick together. He's my tangible link to you, and I'm his. I think we're going to do all right. Maybe I'll bring him with me to see you one day."

Then, before I left, I said out loud the words that I had never said to him when he was alive. I want to believe that he heard me.

"I love you, Miller."

DANGEROUS GAMES: Leah Nash #11

When a good man with a troubled past perishes in a fire, only Leah Nash can unravel the tangled mystery behind his death.

In the quiet town of Himmel, the sudden blaze that engulfs the local library is only the beginning. Among the smoldering ashes, a lifeless body is found —it's Luke Granger, a hardworking young man striving to escape his family's criminal past. His tragic death shocks the community, and although she is initially hesitant, intrepid journalist Leah can't help but investigate.

As Leah delves into the case, she untangles a twisted web of lies, deceit, and dark secrets that threaten to destroy the reputations of the town's most affluent citizens. Luke's death is just the tip of the iceberg in a chilling tale of greed, love, and thwarted ambition. As she races against time to uncover the truth, Leah finds herself caught in a perilous game where one wrong move could be her last.

Can Leah expose the hidden truth before it's too late, or will she become the next victim in a dangerous game of cat and mouse?

Get your copy today at
severnriverbooks.com/series/leah-nash-mysteries

ACKNOWLEDGMENTS

Writing is a largely solitary pursuit, but I never feel like I'm going it alone. I'm grateful for family and friends who listen to me think out loud—or whine out loud—when I'm stuck. I'm appreciative of honest beta readers willing to tell me things I don't want to hear—like I need to cut a favorite scene because it doesn't serve the story. And I'm happy to have readers who engage with Leah and her world in their comments, reviews, and in the emails I receive. Thank you, one and all.

I have a specific acknowledgment to make for this book to my daughter, Sara Hunter Sell. She provided me with an idea that sparked the plot development for *Dangerous Choices*, and then read selected segments to make sure that what happened in the book could actually play out in a "real life" setting, which was invaluable. Finally, as always, I want to single out my husband, Gary Rayburn. He reads every draft, makes me laugh every day, manages the chai latte supply line, and cheers me on to the finish. He keeps up the laundry, too.

ABOUT THE AUTHOR

Susan Hunter is a charter member of Introverts International (which meets the 12th of Never at an undisclosed location). She has worked as a reporter and managing editor, during which time she received a first place UPI award for investigative reporting and a Michigan Press Association first place award for enterprise/feature reporting.

Susan has also taught composition at the college level, written advertising copy, newsletters, press releases, speeches, web copy, academic papers and memos. Lots and lots of memos. She lives in rural Michigan with her husband Gary, who is a man of action, not words.

During certain times of the day, she can also be found wandering the mean streets of small-town Himmel, Wisconsin, looking for clues, stopping for a meal at the Elite Cafe, dropping off a story lead at the *Himmel Times Weekly*, or meeting friends for a drink at McClain's Bar and Grill.

Sign up for Susan Hunter's reader list at
severnriverbooks.com/authors/susan-hunter

Printed in the United States
by Baker & Taylor Publisher Services